FLOWERS FOR MEI-LING

FLOWERS FOR MEI-LING

by Lorraine Lachs

Carroll & Graf Publishers, Inc.
New York

Copyright © 1997 by Lorraine Lachs

First Carroll & Graf edition 1997

Carroll & Graf Publishers, Inc.
260 Fifth Avenue
New York, NY 10001

Lachs, Lorraine.
    Flowers for Mei-ling / by Lorraine Lachs. — 1st Carroll & Graf ed.
      p.   cm.
    ISBN 0-7867-0414-4 (cloth)
    I. Title.
  PS3562.A2452F58   1997
  813'.54—dc21   97-4277
                                                                   CIP

Manufactured in the United States of America

For Sherman and Aileen

Acknowledgements

I am indebted to those authors who have written about their experiences in China during the Cultural Revolution, especially Jung Chang, author of *Wild Swans: Three Daughters of China*, and Heng Liang, author, with his wife Judith Shapiro, of *Son of the Revolution*. I am also indebted to many journalists and scholars whose works guided me through the difficult terrain of modern Chinese history and the British reign in Hong Kong, especially John K. Fairbank, Harrison Salisbury, Orville Schell and Frank Welsh. I have benefited from accounts of radical politics in the United States during the period of the Vietnam War and the Civil Rights movement, especially Todd Gitlin's *The Sixties*.

It was my privilege to teach a number of Chinese students who came to the United States as young adults. A few generously shared their experiences in China with me.

Kent Carroll, my publisher, edited the manuscript and made suggestions that significantly improved it. Beyond that, I am grateful for his faith in my first novel. Adam Dunn shepherded the manuscript through the publication process. Johanna Tani was the copy editor. Howard Norman and Spencer Smith read portions of earlier versions and offered useful criticism. Dr. Fred Lyon, Ob/Gyn, patiently answered questions about medical matters. My agent, Barbara Braun, represented my work with energy and enthusiasm. My daughter, Aileen Lachs, and my sister, Florence Ross, gave unflagging encouragement during the long years of writing.

Sherman Lachs, my husband, deserves a paragraph to himself. His sensitive reading and insightful criticism of successive versions of the manuscript have been invaluable. I thank him.

FLOWERS
FOR
MEI-LING

Part One

~

1979

Montreal, Canada

⁓

THE SMELL OF death he once knew about only from books had seeped into his food, his clothing, the tobacco he stuffed into his pipe. Even now he noticed how it lurked in the upholstery and carpets when he came in from outdoors. Jack Ramsden's wife had been ill for more than a year before she died. Faithful always, he had nursed her dutifully, but he couldn't help feeling set free when she finally exhaled the last of the foulsmelling breaths that had haunted his dreams for months.

For a long time after she died, Jack hated to shave in the morning. Washing and lathering his face forced him to look in the mirror: the loose-fleshed turkey neck, the three brown moles bordering his thinning hairline, the gray patches in the hollows of his cheeks, the bloodshot eyes that didn't clear till after breakfast. Though awake with first light, he would put off shaving as long as he could.

From his bedroom window high above the city, he would look out at the solid brick and stone houses, the spreading green of Mount Royal Park, the distant spires and rooftops emerging from the gray, smoggy sky. Montreal. He would turn away from the window and force himself to shave, dress, and eat. He had to be at his desk by nine o'clock.

*   *   *

Lately, while looking in the mirror as he scraped at his cheeks and chin through the white lather, he would try to encourage himself, speak silently to his freshened image: *You're not really old, only fifty-seven. You're a healthy, reasonably prosperous middle-aged man with many years ahead of you.*

His wife's death had left him depleted, empty of resolve, unable to muster enthusiasm about anything, not even the warm brioche and coffee he had always looked forward to before beginning his banking day. Sometimes he thought back to when Celia had resembled the young Wendy Hiller in films, pert and charming, saucy, back to when they had been college sweethearts. After a few such reveries, he sadly concluded that the term itself—*college sweethearts*—was now probably obsolete. Like fidelity in marriage, the Anglican Church, the British Empire: ceremonial relics of the days of his youth. When he caught sight of himself in a mirror, he appeared slumped over. He had to force himself to straighten his shoulders.

This was 1979; in keeping with the times, he had perfected his French. What had once been a mere cultural decoration had become a commercial necessity. Sometimes, when he turned a corner and ran into an aging couple of the old stock in their stout shoes and woolens, their hair gray and plain, so unlike the coiffured and shiny French, they seemed to him fading illustrations from a forgotten novel. He, of course, was well tailored and smart. His work demanded an aura of confidence and control, but at times he wondered how long it would be till he too was obsolete. When he confessed to his priest a lack of enthusiasm about the daily round of his life (he said nothing to his grown sons, who were busy with their own lives and families), that good man told him quite rightly: "These feelings are natural when one is grieving. They'll pass and you'll feel yourself again."

Guilty of his freedom, bewildered by an ambiguous moral failure he couldn't put into words, Ramsden sank into himself. At first, when the weather was pleasant, he took long, solitary evening walks. Occasional Sundays he spent time with one or the other of his two married sons. More than that made him feel an intruder. At times he thought he should call one of the women his colleagues wanted him to meet, but somehow he never got around to dialing the telephone numbers that had been pressed into his hands. What would he say?

Instead, when Montreal was gripped by winter chill and wind, when the once-green expanse of Mount Royal Park glowed bluish-white and the sky grew dark early, Jack Ramsden went to a movie downtown two or three evenings a week. After finishing work, he'd stop for a light meal at a bistro near his office. Occasionally, he'd linger a while at Barney's Pub on his way home. Once, an attractive youngish woman spoke to him at the bar. But when he realized she was a prostitute, that their encounter would be a commercial transaction, he lost interest. He had enough of those at the bank.

One evening in March, the breeze turned mild. After an early dinner, Ramsden decided to take a long walk before returning home. Aimless, wandering for an hour, finding himself in a neighborhood he would not have chosen, he saw a movie marquee lit up in the distance. Like an imprinted duckling, he headed toward it. The title of the film was unfamiliar, but the glassed-in posters of openmouthed pink nudes with breasts the size of cantaloupes made clear enough what sort of film he would see if he decided to enter. He smiled. He thought to himself: *not exactly my usual fare.* Warily, checking first to make certain the faces in the street were unfamiliar, he pushed his money under the glass window and passed into the darkness. He thought of himself as a traveler exploring the netherworld and was amused, slightly titillated.

Once inside, Ramsden's eyes adjusted soon enough. The audience seemed to be composed entirely of men alone. He noticed that each sat discreetly apart from the others so as to ensure a privacy of sorts. Imitating their etiquette, he chose a solitary seat, and when the film began lost himself in the anatomical pyrotechnics. He had seen all the parts before, but never arranged and rearranged in quite the same way. It was as if he were being given an education in a foreign language that used the English alphabet.

Ramsden left the theater feeling . . . how did he feel? . . . cheered, more robust, certain that if he looked in the mirror at that moment his skin would have turned rosy. It was still early and mild. Why go directly home to his empty rooms? He set out to the florist. Perhaps he'd arrange to have a good-sized pot of yellow tulips sent to his flat to cheer the place up. It was, after all, almost spring.

Before he could locate the florist, Ramsden stopped for some chocolate. A magazine on a rack near the candy shelf caught his eye. An almond-eyed Asian beauty smiled out at him from the cover: hair shining like obsidian, luminous rose-tipped breasts, wisps of dark pubic hair barely concealed by shapely, lotus-folded legs that rested on a pink satin cushion. For the second time that evening, he exchanged money for an illicit pleasure. He forgot the chocolate. The tulips, he decided, would wait.

At home, before taking up the magazine—he thought one didn't actually read such things—Ramsden showered, critically appraised his modest potbelly, dusted himself with lightly scented powder he discovered in the vanity, a relic of Celia's. He poured himself a large glass of chilled vodka with lemon. Settling into the sofa rather than his bed with its nearby stack of books on interest rates and banking for the twenty-first century, he began to look.

Page after page of luscious heart-shaped buttocks, cushiony thighs, winking vaginas. Delightful breasts, some pointing proudly, others falling forward as if waiting for a mouth to suck the tight nipples. Yards and yards of silky hair, thick and curly, straight and shiny, a devil's rainbow of gold, red, auburn, brown, and black. While he masturbated, Ramsden remembered, as if from some great distance, the warm delights and guilty pleasures of boyhood. Soon he slept soundly, not even switching off the lamp. The magazine was open on the floor when he woke. He picked it up and riffled the pages. In the light of morning their charm was considerably diminished. But he had slept well, better than at any time since Celia's death.

While shaving, he suddenly thought of Boisvert. The loan he had arranged the week before for Boisvert's company, the long luncheon and drinks afterward, the smutty jokes that were Boisvert's stock-in-trade, the stories about his deal-making travels to Europe and Asia, the allusions to fleshly pleasures easily come by after business was done for the day. He had met Boisvert's wife at a cocktail party. She was a plump but not unattractive redhead, perched on tall heels and encased in a tight brown leather suit that gave her the look of a wet seal. A friendly seal. She had been cordial, was kind, sent a note of condolence in fractured English after Celia died. What her note lacked in grammar, it made up for in thoughtfulness. Ramsden's acquaintance with her had seemed unimportant to Boisvert during his boozy recitation of foreign exploits. Indeed, his parting words to Ramsden had been "Let me know if you want something really nice in London or Amsterdam or Hong Kong. All work and no play makes Jack's life dull." Unlike his wife, Boisvert spoke perfect English, his accent barely perceptible.

When Ramsden arrived at his office the morning after his tame if uncharacteristic debauch, he found a message from Boisvert on his desk asking if he was free for lunch at noon, a few minor matters to be settled. Telepathy? he wondered, and made the appointment. As usual, Boisvert was all business at first, all boozy camaraderie at last. Ramsden returned from their lunch to his desk at the bank in possession of a card Boisvert had pressed into his palm with a handshake and wink. He looked at it:

Pleasure in Amsterdam
Luxurious Accommodations
Quality Personnel
Confidential Service
Day, Night, Week
Call 24 Hours

Printed at the bottom right-hand corner was the telephone number complete with international code.

That afternoon he arranged with Charley Mayhew for a week off at the beginning of April. That night he called. A female voice answered in English, businesslike, professional.

"Pleasure in Amsterdam. May I help you?"

"I'm going to be in Amsterdam at the beginning of April, April third."

Before he could explain further, she broke in. "Do you wish to arrange for a day, night, or week?"

Ramsden hesitated. What if he didn't like her? He supposed he could cut out early so long as he paid . . . perhaps ask for another girl.

"A week," he heard himself say.

"European, Asian, African?"

Again he hesitated. The Dutch were nothing if not efficient. Remembering the magazine cover, he answered, "Asian."

"Credit card, cash, or traveler's checks?"

Good Lord, he thought, did people put such things on credit

cards, cards that were handled by his bank, where records were kept?

"Traveler's checks."

"Very good, Mr. . . . ?"

She wanted his name, his respectable name. Well, the fat was in the fire. It was apparently done all the time. Boisvert did it, and he had a wife to worry about.

"Ramsden, Jackson Ramsden."

She gave him the name of a hotel in Amsterdam, one of the best, she assured him, assured him also of the exceptional quality of their personnel, told him the fee in Dutch guilders and American dollars, allowed time for him to recover his breath or perhaps back out when the amount had sunk in. When he didn't, she said, "Your reservation is confirmed, Mr. Ramsden. Mei-ling will arrive promptly at six o'clock for your pleasure and will remain with you for the entire week. Enjoy your stay in Amsterdam."

He heard himself thank her as she clicked off. Six o'clock! He wondered when he and Mei-ling were expected to have dinner, before or after his pleasure. Would she speak English? What would they say? Perhaps this had been a mistake.

Amsterdam

ONLY A FEW hours after departing Mirabel International Airport, where a gray layer of snow still clung to the wide, flat, almost empty landscape, Ramsden was cheered by the neat green fields surrounding Amsterdam. Bustling Schipol Airport was reassuring: the politeness, the accented but grammatically correct English, the rapid handling of documents and baggage. The Dutch knew how to do things.

On the way to having some currency exchanged, caught in a busily moving crowd that was surprisingly varied in color and costume, he was stopped short by the sight of two grim-faced men in thick bulletproof vests sporting heavy weapons of a kind he had seen before only in films. Those were artful fakes; these were undeniably real. Most people hurried past, ignoring the gunmen as if they were pillars holding up the ceiling. Only a few paused for more than a glance. Even the passengers at the El-Al counter seemed more agitated about their baggage and children than about the presence of armed men poised alertly for an attack. The sight reminded him of the days when exploding bombs were a not-uncommon occurrence in Montreal. Well, he thought, no place was safe anymore, not even the airport in sane, civilized Holland.

Ramsden felt perspiration on his neck and a flush in his face. For all the world like a woman in menopause, he thought. Fretting, he wondered how on earth he, a banker, a respectable widower, had impelled himself into so tawdry a situation. He was, after all, about to pay for sex with a stranger. Well, he thought, for what it was costing him, he could at least be reasonably sure he would return home without an infection. He remembered the woman on the telephone throwing in, almost as an aside, "You can be sure that all our employees are full of healthy high spirits." At the time all he heard, and that with a tinge of embarrassment, was "high spirits"; now he felt naive, not recognizing the code word, the kind of thing used in banking all the time.

A KLM hotel shuttle deposited him. A liveried doorman arranged for his bags while another uniformed man escorted him to his room. They both spoke English. In Holland he expected miniatures, but his room was large, thickly carpeted, and richly furnished in shades of plum and teal. His eyes circled the room: a cushioned floral love seat flanked by two velvet lounge chairs, a television and stereo cabinet, a rosewood table-desk, a wide rosewood chest topped by an equally wide mirror. Through the looking glass he caught sight of the bed nestled into an alcove: an expanse of quilted teal velvet that dropped to the plum-colored carpet.

Ramsden looked at his watch. Four o'clock! Two hours to Mei-ling, whoever she was. Probably imported from Hong Kong, he thought. Then again, who could know where she was from; the Chinese spread out like the tide. He unpacked, took a shower, then dressed in brown slacks and a cream silk shirt that he would later remember was Celia's last gift to him.

He sank into the love seat, sipped a vodka and lemon from the well-stocked bar, and closed his eyes, wondering if Mei-ling would look like the girl on the cover. He dozed off, then caught himself. He didn't want to miss the knock at the door. When it came, he felt a sudden shyness, but he pushed himself forward. What greeted his eyes at the door *was* a miniature, one that reached barely to his shoulder on high heels. Ramsden wondered if she could possibly be much more than twenty. He didn't know what to say. In a voice too deep for her size, the Chinese doll spoke. "I'm Mei-ling. You are expecting me, Mr. Ramsden?"

Mei-ling's heart-shaped, high-cheekboned face was pretty

rather than sultry; her shoulder-length dark hair was thick and stylishly cut but not shining black silk as he had hoped; her mouth smiled, but her eyes, more round than almond-shaped, as in his reverie, suggesting a touch of the European, did not. They looked into the room as if surveying a field of operations. Although she was attractive, even chic, in a slate-blue silk dress topped by a fluffy white mohair jacket, a chain of gold circles dangling from her ears, he was slightly disappointed.

He hadn't known what to expect . . . was relieved she didn't have the look of a tart . . . told himself the reality never matches the fantasy . . . told himself to pick up her soft leather suitcase and follow her into the room, where she was holding a white box tied with blue ribbons that she proceeded to set down on the table-desk. He heard himself say, "Let me take your coat."

She said, "Thank you," and handed him the fluffy mohair.

When he turned away from the closet a moment later, his breath caught. A miniature, but a perfect one. Stripped of coat and parcel, she stood in front of him . . . surprisingly full-breasted for one so small . . . tiny waist . . . curved hips . . . slender ankles . . . not a child at all. She turned around to reach into the purse she had put on the table, giving him a rear view. His breath stopped a second time. Turning back again, moving slowly as if she were a statue on a rotating stand, she handed him an envelope. "From Pleasure in Amsterdam," she said.

It was a formal bill professionally typed on heavy white paper. *Payment required in advance* was printed in English at the bottom of the page and a return envelope was included. The efficient Dutch! He wondered if they had invoices printed in French and German as well . . . in Japanese perhaps. He felt foolish sitting in a lounge chair signing traveler's checks, but it was obviously what he was expected to do.

Just as he slipped the signed checks into the envelope, Mei-ling's hand reached his mouth. She fed him a cold shrimp in a piquant sauce, took the envelope with her other hand, and put the saucy finger into his mouth to be licked off. In seconds he was wildly tumescent. Giddily, he remembered his curiosity about when they would eat. Ah, the efficient Dutch took care of everything.

One shrimp at a time, she fed them both. Every so often she surprised him with a sweetly spicy dumpling.

"Tasty?"

"Very."

"You like the sauce?"

"Delicious."

As if he were the child, she coaxed him to eat, touching his mouth lightly with her fingers so he could lick the sauce.

"You like champagne?"

He didn't especially, but felt as if he were in a play or film and ought to. He would do anything she asked, reasonable or not, be the man he had never before been. "Yes, I'd love some."

She reached into the white box and brought forth two silver goblets, popped open a nicely chilled bottle, filled the glasses, gave him one, and took one herself. She raised hers in a toast. "To your pleasure."

He nodded and smiled, then drank. She slipped onto his lap and settled there, dinner apparently ended. Dessert would be of a different order, he thought, as he leaned his head back and Mei-ling began to fiddle with the buttons on his shirt.

While they played, he remembered the movies of his boyhood, the hero carrying the beauty to the bedroom, the door closing, the fade-in to morning with no image in between. Now he would fill in the picture. He rose with Mei-ling in his arms, light as a child, and set her on her feet. He was trembling but managed to reach the zipper that ran from her neck to her derriere. The blue silk slipped to her feet. She stood there for him to admire: her rounded breasts barely covered by the blue lace and satin of her bra, a matching bikini with attached garters that held up dark stockings. The ivory skin of her upper thighs held his eyes. Like porcelain! She turned and walked to the table. He gazed at the curve of her back and buttocks, the shape of her legs, and said a spontaneous prayer of thanks to God, whom he had not thought of as just or loving in a long time.

Mei-ling produced a large satin sheet, also from the magical white box, and opened it with a flourish. "Do you wish the carpet or the bed?"

He didn't know what to say. He and Celia always had sex in bed; it was all he knew. He realized with guilty delight that a whole week lay ahead. Whatever brought him pleasure was before him. He had only to choose. He decided to stay with what he knew.

"The bed."

Ramsden watched as Mei-ling, still in her charming undergarments and high-heeled shoes, walked to the bed, neatly folded the velvet coverlet and draped it on a nearby rack, then spread the satin sheet and fluffed the pillows. She stepped out of her shoes, stripped off her stockings, dropped her panties, and popped the snap between her breasts that fastened her bra. Naked, she climbed to the foot of the bed and, facing him, fixed her legs in the lotus position. Not exactly the girl on the cover, he thought, but she would certainly do.

She beckoned him with her hand. As if walking through heather, he made his way and stood facing her: lifting and caressing her breasts with his hands, he gave himself up to her. The condom she seemed to produce by sleight-of-hand was silky and rolled on smoothly. It seemed to him that she was the director and he the novice actor in their play. But early in the morning, when he felt her breathing beside him, he took his turn as director and felt afterward that he had proven himself. Later, while shaving, he preened as he looked in the mirror. The three brown moles seemed less noticeable.

After they showered together, after Mei-ling slipped on a silk kimono splashed with flowers, after room service wheeled in a sumptuous breakfast on a tulip-bedecked cart, he thought of Celia. They had always enjoyed weekend and holiday breakfasts together. If they were at home, she would bake tasty muffins, fry omelets, brew dark coffee. On vacation they'd take breakfast among palm trees and flowers that bloomed scarlet and yellow and purple in the tropical sun. When they were young, he had been aroused to passion by Celia, loved her with frightening intensity. Of course, he craved her less often later on, thought about other women occasionally, understandably, he assumed. But, he wondered, had he ever so completely delighted in sex as he had with Mei-ling the night before? He didn't think so, but how could he be sure? Memory was like Mei-ling, he thought; they both turned astonishing tricks.

Mei-ling poured their coffee. "Sugar?"

"One spoon, please." He felt oddly formal with her.

"Cream?"

"A little."

While he watched, she stirred their cups, sliced the ham, buttered the warm rolls. Then she picked up some scrambled egg on her fork, and reaching across the table, began to feed him. After a single mouthful he decided to feed himself. Too much of a good thing, he thought, cloying, but he didn't want to hurt her feelings by telling her to stop. He realized that she was simply doing her job. He said, "Why don't we help ourselves?" She understood, heaped some ham and eggs on her plate, and concentrated on the food.

They were both hungry. He enjoyed watching her. In spite of her graceful hands and delicate gestures, she ate with gusto. For someone so small, she took in so much—two rolls as well as generous amounts of ham, eggs, and fruit. He was amused. Well, he thought, she certainly gets plenty of exercise; it will be some years before she has to worry about putting on weight. Immediately he was irritated by his crudeness. As if to make up for an insult, he heard himself say, "The sun is shining, and I have never been in Amsterdam before. Will you be my guide?"

"If that will give you pleasure."

He wished she didn't sound as if she were fulfilling the terms of a contract, however much that might be the case. He said, "I would enjoy it very much."

"What would you like to do?"

"I've always wanted to see the canals."

"We can ride in a boat. The canals are lined by many interesting seventeenth- and eighteenth-century buildings. It's the best way to see the architecture."

Architecture! So she knew something beside her own trade. Not that he was concerned about being bored. Still, he hated stupidity and was satisfied that he would not have to tolerate it. Ramsden's curiosity was piqued. "How long have you been in Holland?"

"For some years."

"Where are you from originally?"

"I was born in China and grew up there and in Hong Kong before coming to Amsterdam."

She was hardly grown up now, he thought. "You speak English so well."

"I went to an English school in Hong Kong."

"A wandering life for such a young woman. How many years have you been in Holland?"

"Don't you think some mystery between a man and a woman is desirable?"

He wondered what he could say to that, thought of the previous night. "I suppose it is."

"We should dress now so that we have enough time. My office must have mentioned that my free time is from four to six every day."

He couldn't exactly recall that, but he certainly had no objection. He would look forward to her return after a drink and a nap in privacy.

Seated together in the glassed-in canal boat, Ramsden and Mei-ling glided through the waters. "Look," she said, "there are six different styles of roof in this group, all dating from the seventeenth century." She leaned across him and pointed. The pressure of her breasts on his chest and the craning of his neck to see the roofs brought on a momentary vertigo. But he recovered quickly. He was enchanted by the city: the narrow stone houses that were being built while John Milton was writing *Paradise Lost*, when Montreal was still a wilderness outpost of French imperial dreams; the tall, glass-walled rectangles built only yesterday; the houseboats moored in the canals, some with potted plants on their decks; bicyclers of all ages pedaling past the water craft; strolling mixed-race families—children, parents, grandparents—in shades from palest blond to darkest dark, legacies of empire. Harbingers, he wondered, of the world to come? To be sure, he had seen some of that in Montreal, but here, in the old-world heart of northern Europe, it was as if generations and geography had been broken into bits and pieces, then rearranged in an arresting new mosaic, the mortar not yet dry.

"Look, that church is very old . . . see the detail . . . medieval, but inside it's very plain . . . Protestant. If you like, we can go inside later in the week."

"By all means."

Ramsden heard himself sound stuffy . . . "by all means." Couldn't he think of something more charming to say, something younger? Did the other passengers, he wondered, see him as a randy old man with a girl, a joke? She could be his youngest daughter if he had daughters. There was even a slightly European cast to her face. But, he thought, Mei-ling sounded so much older than she appeared, looked so unlike what she was. He would have liked to pretend they were a couple on vacation, but instantly Celia popped into his mind. The canal ride was just the sort of thing they would have enjoyed together in the past. Celia's presence in the present troubled him. It was as if she were standing in judgment. Hoping to banish her ghost, he took Mei-ling's hand, stroked her skin, pressed his lips lightly into her hair, breathed in her perfume.

By the time he returned alone to the hotel, Ramsden was tired. He was looking forward to a hot bath and a drink. He soaked in the tub and sipped his vodka. After toweling himself dry, he lay down for a nap on the soft velvet coverlet, clothed only in his boxer shorts and covered by the satin sheet Mei-ling had draped over the bedside rack. The pleasant scent of bath oil still clung to his skin. Mei-ling would return by six. They would have time to play before they went out to dinner at the Indonesian ristafel she assured him was the best in Amsterdam. He pictured her smiling from across the table. "I will wear red tonight," she had promised. He closed his eyes.

A troubling thought kept him awake. He couldn't remember being told about her being away two hours every afternoon. Could she be earning an extra something on his time? If so, he didn't like it . . . not that she hadn't had dozens before him. There was no reason for jealousy; theirs was purely a commercial transaction. He had no objection to her being away for several hours. It gave him some privacy. But she was costing him a great deal and he didn't want to share her. In spite of himself, Ramsden was roiled. But he mellowed after a second vodka, decided she was probably shopping (and why not if the results were so pleasing). Besides, he thought, she probably didn't get a fair cut of the outrageous fee he was paying.

He was sleeping soundly when Mei-ling lay down beside him. He stirred but didn't rise, just lay there on his belly half asleep. She caressed his back and buttocks and thighs with her fingertips, then with her breasts. She stripped off his shorts. Just as he thought he was about to burst into fragments of bliss, she turned him over, rose up, and sank into him. She was, Ramsden reflected later, an artist in her way, like a dancer with perfect timing, a singer with perfect pitch.

The restaurant was fragrant with unfamiliar spice and crowded with prosperous-looking Dutchmen and tourists. Seated at a table for two, Mei-ling urged him to let her order for them both. "They have some wonderful specialties you'll enjoy," she said. The thought crossed his mind that she might get a cut for bringing clients here, but then he felt foolish. It was obvious that the packed and lively restaurant didn't need the trade she could provide. He wondered what Mei-ling did with her money. Did she squander it on luxuries, or save some for when she would need it? When would that be? He couldn't help feeling a bit protective toward her. How long could an intelligent young woman do this sort of thing? What came afterward? No point in his worrying about that, he thought. It was hardly his business.

After the Indonesian waiter took their order, Ramsden looked at Mei-ling sitting opposite him in a red jacquard silk dress, smiling slightly. Professionally? he wondered. Her dangling, emerald-tipped earrings tinkled like wind chimes when she moved. Were the emeralds genuine or quality fakes? Beautiful jewels in any case, but no lovelier than she at that moment.

"You are very beautiful tonight."

"And you are very kind." She smiled more broadly. "Did Amsterdam give you pleasure?"

"More than I could imagine."

"Good. Did you find your way back to the hotel easily?"

"Yes. I walked so I could see more of the city."

He was reminded of her time off. "Those lovely earrings that you're wearing, did you buy them this afternoon?"

"No. I have owned these for a long time. They were given to me by a client."

He couldn't tell if she was trying to deflect his curiosity or suggest that expensive gifts were in order. He certainly had no intention of shelling out for costly jewelry, no matter how well she did her job. An expensive dinner was one thing, a pleasure for them both, but jewelry, when he would never see her again, was quite another. Best to forget the afternoon hours, go on to a different subject.

But his determination not to be gulled or compromised got the better of him. "You didn't go shopping? I thought women found shopping irresistible."

"No. I don't enjoy shopping very much."

"What did you do, then?"

She smiled again. "The Chinese believe that mystery between a man and a woman is desirable."

He wondered if she had been coached or encouraged by her

employers to assume the role of the mysterious Asian, if they thought it enhanced her charms. Still, he would not be put off. "But I want to know."

"But why? Aren't you pleased with me?"

"Very. That's why I want to know more about you."

The waiter returned with a rectangular brazier on which he set several small platters of skewered meats and shellfish and vegetables, each accompanied by a savory sauce. As the waiter busied himself arranging the food, Ramsden found himself thinking of how much Celia would have enjoyed such a feast, how she had jokingly encouraged him to try new things when Montreal began filling up with newcomers from every dot on the globe and exotic restaurants were opening all over. Well, he thought, he was trying new things now.

"I spend two hours with my daughter . . . in the afternoon when she arrives home from school."

Ramsden wondered if he'd heard right, if perhaps a woman at the next table were speaking. When he didn't say anything, Mei-ling said, "You wanted to know more about me. Now you know more. Are you disappointed?"

"No," he lied. "Not disappointed. Surprised. You don't look old enough to have a child in school. I wasn't expecting you to have a child."

"What were you expecting?"

"I don't know. I was just curious about you."

"I can tell you are disappointed. You see, mystery *is* desirable." She speared a prawn. "Now we must eat before everything turns cold."

"My wife would enjoy this kind of food."

"You should bring her with you next time you're here."

Ramsden didn't understand. Was she joking? Then he realized she knew nothing of Celia, that he had spoken as if she were still living. "I'm afraid that would not be possible. She died last year."

"Oh, I'm so sorry. I didn't intend . . . "

"It's quite all right. You had no way of knowing."

"It's just that most of my clients have wives. I expect it. They come for a change, recreation, the kind of sex they can't get at home. They go back to their wives and forget about me."

He wanted to tell her he would never forget her. Instead, he said quite truthfully, though quite irrelevantly, "Your English is perfect."

"As I told you, I did go to an English school."

"How old are you?"

"Twenty-nine. Do you like satay?"

"Satay?"

"The skewered meat in the peanut sauce."

He ate some. "It's wonderful." He paused. "Like you."

"Thank you."

"You look so much younger."

"So I'm told. Perhaps because I'm not very tall."

On their fourth night together, Ramsden asked Mei-ling to spread the satin sheet on the plush carpet of his room. In the soft radiating light of the lamp, they lay naked on their sides, his eyes lingering on every curve and shadow of her beauty. He felt a shudder of delight as he stretched and reached for her. At that precise moment, an excruciating pain seized his right leg from toe to knee. He cried out. Mei-ling rose quickly and helped him to his feet. He leaned on her tiny frame for support as he hobbled around the room. Gradually, the pain slackened.

"Are you feeling better now?" she asked.

"Much, thank you. Seems to have been a cramp, but it's gone now. I'm sorry if I frightened you. Terribly embarrassing, never happened before."

She helped him into his robe and put hers on as well. "Would you like something to drink?"

"No. I'm fine now."

He looked at the satin sheet on the floor and felt like a fool, a randy old man who should have known better. Mei-ling fluffed the pillows on the bed, then went to the bathroom. Tactful, he thought, giving him time to compose himself.

When Mei-ling returned, she said casually, "Don't look so serious. Things like that happen all the time." She laughed. "At least it wasn't a heart attack."

He couldn't manage to laugh along with her. She had likely experienced worse than his leg cramp in her career. How, he wondered, could such a lovely and intelligent young woman do what she did?

When they settled into the bed, he did not feel desire. He wanted to lie quietly. He would have liked to have Celia next to him, Celia before she smelled of death, reading a book, the two of them drowsing off to sleep together.

But when morning came, Celia was forgotten. Refreshed from a good sleep, he felt Mei-ling next to him. She was, he reflected, skillful enough at her work for him to feel a gentle affection for her. He wondered if he was behaving strangely, enjoying their visits to museums and churches and antique shops. She seemed to know so much and was such charming company. He looked forward to their day.

By eleven they were inside Rembrandt's house. So old, he thought, and almost holy in its way, a shrine. Etchings, drawings, scenes from the Bible. Rembrandt in likenesses of himself, a rumpled man in his fifties, reduced in circumstances, living among Jews, illuminating souls. Though he and Celia had always been interested in painting, Ramsden had not expected to be so moved. Mei-ling knew the place well. Had she been here with other "clients" before him? Or by herself?

On their fifth day together, before parting after a long lunch, Ramsden said aloud what he had been thinking a moment before. "Why don't you bring your daughter to Keukenhof Gardens with us tomorrow? Little girls love flowers."

"With us? You are not serious."

"You can tell her I'm a traveler you are showing around Amsterdam. You won't be lying. It's quite true."

"I have never mixed my family with my business."

"Of course not. But Keukenhof has nothing to do with business. How can a flower garden and a day away from school harm her?"

"I have never had a client make such a request. I can't see the sense. Why do you want to bother with a child?"

Ramsden didn't know, but he answered, he supposed truthfully, "Because she's your child. And it's no bother at all. When my boys were young, we'd take them everywhere. Sometimes I miss having a child around . . . but if you're uncomfortable . . . "

"I'll decide before I return. If she comes with us, we'll have to get her early in the morning."

Ramsden hoped his invitation hadn't been rash. Still, he was curious about the child, curious about Mei-ling's life. And they would have the night together.

⌒

The next morning at Keukenhof, a casual observer might see three people holding hands: a petite attractive Asian woman, probably Chinese but perhaps some mixture; a beautiful little girl, certainly Eurasian; an older man, Caucasian, perhaps the child's grandfather. A more deliberate observer, however, might see, mistakenly, an almost old man married to a very young woman with whom he has fathered a lovely child. But the three-some is not an object of scrutiny. They walk unremarked and unremarkable in the showplace garden of this small, rich country. The path turns, a new and splendid vista opens up: long ribbons of color catch the sun of the northern sky. Ramsden thinks: *a tidy paradise.*

Together the three make their way through acres of dazzling blooms—daffodils, hyacinths, tulips—that fan out in spectacular formal plantings: a vast mosaic in vivid shades of red and purple and yellow and orange and pink and white held together by a mortar of green turf. They walk and chat beneath the graceful branching of pink and white ornamental trees . . . early blooming . . . softening and highlighting the passionate colors and neat out-lines of the flower beds. The little girl skips ahead while the man and woman stop at a bed of red-and-yellow-striped tulips.

She says, "These are an old variety. Do you remember them in the painting by Bosschaert in the seventeenth century wing of the Rijksmuseum? You admired it there."

The older man looks at the young woman before answering, as if trying to choose his words carefully, but he cannot seem to find them. Everything is out of balance. He had not expected her to be as intelligent as she was beautiful. Finally, he gives up and responds to her question.

"The painting was magnificent. It hardly seems possible, but the tulips are even more beautiful here. The variety seems to have lasted hundreds of years in a pure state."

"The growers see to it. They know where their money comes from. Holland's first tulips were imported from Turkey. They made people rich." She smiles. "Until the bubble burst."

"Is there anything you don't know?" he asks, amused and delighted by her. She laughs aloud for the first time since they met.

When the child skips away again, the man takes the woman's hand and kisses it. She withdraws her hand and nods in the direction of the child. He says, "I'm sorry. I don't want you to be uncomfortable."

They walk on and are soon confronted by an anomaly . . . an English garden, or what is labeled as one on a small wooden plaque planted near the path. Perhaps because it is still early spring, the garden is drab and uninteresting, lacking the brilliance and shapeliness of the other plantings. Ramsden says to himself: *Why do they bother, they can't do this sort of thing, they should stick to what they know.* Mei-ling says to him: "I don't understand why they try this kind of garden. The English do it better."

Struck by their confluence of thought, he asks, "Where did you learn about English gardens?"

"Books. I like to read about gardens and houses . . . the photographs and illustrations especially. I visited England and toured some of the gardens there."

"Did you! My wife and I did that years ago. When were you in England?"

She pauses. "A while back . . . for a week . . . a Saudi businessman. He worked during the day."

They both study the garden in silence. Mei-ling finally looks around for the child, who is kneeling in front of a bed of brilliant red tulips, carefully stroking the petals. She calls out, "Juliana, we're not allowed to touch the flowers."

In the late afternoon Mei-ling takes Juliana home while Ramsden returns to the hotel. She has told him that her mother lives with them and cares for Juliana in her absence. Ramsden is pleased to learn this sound and respectable aspect of Mei-ling's otherwise dubious maternity. He approves. It does not cross his mind that she may be married or may once have been or that Juliana's father is anywhere in evidence, but he does ponder Juliana's paternity. Is she the result of her mother's livelihood? An early love? He is pleased that the child was well-behaved, cheerful, delighted by the flowers. When it was time to leave, she reached up to kiss his cheek and said, "Good-bye, uncle."

Was this a Dutch custom, he wondered, or Chinese perhaps,

or was Juliana, Mei-ling's reticence to the contrary, a charm on her mother's professional bracelet? Well, he thought, it was of small concern to him now. Tomorrow he would return home. It had worked out well, beyond his expectations. Who could have imagined Mei-ling's delights in exchange for mere traveler's checks?

Alone in the hotel room, Ramsden sipped his vodka and lemon, then lay down. Between rest and sleep, he conjured a vision of Mei-ling—lotus-folded legs, bud-tipped breasts, jewels in her ears—then slept secure in the knowledge that when he woke, the aphrodisiac scent of her skin would be only the first of the pleasures to follow. Ah, he thought as he slipped from consciousness into sleep, money *could* buy happiness. For a time, at any rate.

Settled into a wide, comfortable seat in the first-class cabin to which he had treated himself, his conscience niggling because he had always traveled coach with Celia, Jack Ramsden began to have regrets. Here, now, flying through clouds, Celia returned. She was reasserting her place in his life. She reminded him that he had paid for sex with a prostitute. In his defense, he recalled that Mei-ling was not a prostitute in any ordinary sense, more like a lover. She had made him happy. Didn't Celia want him to be happy? He had never been unfaithful while she lived. It was too soon to think of another wife. He might not want to marry again.

There was no denying it hadn't been the commercial transaction he had expected. He'd been pleased to the point of extravagant foolhardiness, insisting upon a gift, a too-expensive antique jewel they had seen in a shop window, an enameled gold pendant in the shape of a tulip. When she wore it hanging from its gold chain, it rested just above the separation of her breasts. Nude, on their final night together, she had modeled it for him. He had insisted the jewel was an Easter present, but now he wondered who beside himself the glossy red petals would charm.

What would Celia have thought if she knew he had taken Mei-ling's hand just before they parted and pressed into it a folded piece of paper to which he had clipped the considerable remainder of his signed traveler's checks. He had said, "If you are ever going to be in Montreal, I will be your guide, though not so perfect a one as yourself."

She had smiled up at him but did not speak. Was he mistaken, possibly deceiving himself when he saw a slight moistening of her eyes? Perhaps, but he embraced her small, velvety form, ran his hands for the last time down the curve of her back and over the two smooth cushions below it, finally lifted her up so that he could sink his face in her breasts and memorize her warmth and her scent. Only after seeing her to a waiting taxi did he board the KLM shuttle to the airport.

Now, in the air over the Atlantic, passing in and out of diaphanous clouds, Ramsden wondered if he had not been a bit of a fool. Why had he given her all that extra money? He would never see her again, however much he might enjoy the pleasure. It was best to put it all behind him. She surely would . . . and go on to her next "client." Wasn't that the word she used? Well, he had had an adventure. Soon it would recede into the past. After the flight attendant removed his lunch tray, Ramsden settled into a comfortable sleep.

He woke as the plane was descending through the clouds into the dismal plain surrounding Mirabel Airport. The patches of gray snow still clung to the fields. In Montreal, the remains of winter were everywhere. He had been away, after all, for only a week.

But the next morning he was hungry for breakfast. He relished his brioche and coffee for the first time since Celia's death. His "vacation" had done the trick. When he arrived at his office, his secretary presented him with a week of messages. In among them was a call from Boisvert asking him to lunch. Ramsden knew what he wanted. He also knew Boisvert wouldn't get it. He decided to invent a tall, long-waisted, buxom blonde with a wide mouth and large teeth. That would satisfy Boisvert nicely.

Part Two

1968

China, West of Nanjing, Open Country

~

A BRISK WIND raises great clouds of dust that swirl up and around, turning morning into dusk. A long, slow convoy of flat-bed trucks mounted with wooden side rails stretches into the distance like a fat snake uncoiling itself. Mei-ling watches it pass. Hair unkempt and dirty, trousers torn at one knee, a soiled red scarf trailing from her jacket pocket, she stands fixed in place: stunned, silent, alone in the hectic crowd. Her clothing is splattered with dark, shiny clots of blood that cling to her like clusters of beetles. Her mouth opens as if she is about to scream but no sound comes out . . . only a putrid smell.

The dry, endless plain, barren but for a few outcroppings of rock and dry wild grass, normally empty to the horizon except for a railroad track that cuts through the desolation, is swarming with traffic and people. The long train that brought them is empty, motionless on its track. Like the dust that stings their eyes, the departed passengers fly in all directions. Most are very young, in their teens and early twenties. Like Mei-ling, they wear the bright red scarves and armbands of the Red Guard. Poised for adventure, they move briskly, push ahead, jump into the trucks, shout, smile. Bright with virtue, they are eager to be on their way to small villages scattered in the remote countryside, ready to "learn from the peasants" as Mao has instructed, a crusade of children vaulting into history, seizing their place in the great Cultural Revolution.

A few have begun to sing.

> The golden sun rises in the East;
> its radiance spreads.
> The East wind sweeps over the land;
> flowers bloom;
> red flags wave like a vast ocean.

Mei-ling hears the song as a dull echo, a distant chorus in some unfamiliar opera. She is staring at the spot in the dusty road where minutes before a body lay splayed like a carelessly tossed rag doll. She had watched wide-eyed and breathless as it flew into the air when the truck struck it, saw it quickly dragged away out of the line of traffic as if it were a roadblock. Already, road dust mixes with the blood that gushed from the body like a plume. The dark certainty takes hold that only she among so many in the vastness of this place is still thinking of him. The others, too many to count their number, are playing their parts in another drama. Mei-ling does not even know his name, only that he tried to help her. That he tried and failed.

Slowly she awakens to the pain in her groin and thighs, the ache in the small of her back, the sickening stickiness of her clothing, the putrid smell of her breath, the certainty that innocence is gone forever. Suddenly, a young man's voice is in her ear, harsh and demanding: "Hurry, hurry, no lagging behind." She cannot move. A firm hand takes hold of her shoulder and pushes her forward. "Move. The trucks are leaving. Do you want to be left behind?"

Yes, she thinks. But she is mute and does not move of her own will.

He pushes and shouts again. "Move! Quickly!" The noise fills her ears. She turns to look at him. The voice and hand pushing against her shoulder belong to a young man only a few years older than she, no more than twenty. He wears a uniform, dull green, a cadre of some kind, a leader. He is ugly in her sight: too broad in the chest, too hard in the chin, too harsh in the eye. His cheeks are spotted with eruptions and tiny scars. His earlobes are fat as birds' eggs. His red scarf flies up like a flag in the heavy wind. The force of her rage gathers itself. She brings her mouth to his ear as if to share a secret. When she is close enough, she fastens her teeth to the lobe and bites down hard.

"Aaah!" he screams. He reaches his hand to his ear, then brings it down and looks at it. Thin streaks of blood stain his fingers. She watches as a moment of mingled pain and bewilderment crosses his face. Then the bloody hand is raised again and closes into a fist that blinds her with the force of its blow. She sinks to the ground, her breath coming in short gasps like the breeze from a paper fan.

She does not know if she has lost consciousness. A distant voice, a woman's voice, says, "Over here. In this one." Hands grasp her ankles and wrists, lift her high and toss her onto a hard surface. She bounces slightly, like a sack of grain, then sinks.

Something is rumbling beneath her. At first she thinks it is an earthquake. Perhaps they will all die. She is strangely indifferent. The rumble continues. No, she decides, not an earthquake, only the motion of a truck on a bumpy road. She does not open her eyes, does not want to know where they are going. She hears the same woman's voice: "Do you know why she did it?"

Then the voice of the ugly man: "No. I was trying to help her."

"Do you think she is crazy?"

"I don't know, but she won't be any good here. She'll only get in the way of our tasks. We'll have to send her back. She's useless."

Mei-ling forces herself to lie motionless, as if she were unconscious. The flicker of her eyelid frightens her. She tells herself: *I will be sent home.* A joyless relief passes through her.

Then the questions begin, circling over and over like the wheels of the truck. Mother, where has her mother been sent? The sorrows thick as storm clouds, why have they gathered so suddenly? Father, is he in prison? Worse? The sight of him spread on all fours in the filth, barking like a dog, scarcely human any longer . . . can it have been a dream? Can such things be possible? Surely Mao would not permit them to happen. The men in the rail car, the beasts who laughed as they held her . . . who were they? Could such undesirable elements have found their way into the Red Guard? What is happening in China?

Mei-ling is stiff but forces herself to lie still, eyes tightly shut.

She struggles against the pain inside her groin that pinches like a crab's claw. Will it ever stop? Where, she wonders, can I bathe myself clean? She is so dirty, so terribly soiled. Her eyelid flickers and twitches again, then stops. She must be still, mute, crazy, or the ugly man will decide to keep her here.

Bandung, Indonesia

⁓

Verhoeven SINCERELY ENJOYED being rich. He could not imagine any other reason for living, not even women. They were delightful to be sure, but like everything else worth having, they had to be paid for. Even as a struggling widow's boy in damp, cramped Holland, he understood that basic truth. Now, with the political situation in Indonesia at a critical stage, he would have to plan the transfer of his assets carefully. The bribes alone would come to a considerable sum.

While he sat at the café table nursing his schnapps, waiting for Coelho, who was late as usual, Verhoeven was feeling uncharacteristically nostalgic, as if he had already left Bandung and the past thirty years behind him. It was not for nothing, he thought, that his favorite city in all of Indonesia was so often described as a second Paris. No matter how busy, he had managed to savor its many pleasures: the pungent spiciness of the food; the piquant charm of the women; parks and gardens patterned like Persian carpets in tropical colors; the bruised but grand colonial buildings; the handsome university rising like some equatorial Versailles. It was beautiful.

Perhaps most of all, he had taken pleasure in the cafés, so charming, insouciant, delightful. The Dutch, he thought, should be given credit for all they'd accomplished, bringing civilization to what was little better than a jungle; instead, little yellow and brown men constantly denounced them as imperialists, as if the word hadn't long since lost its meaning. Who was it who had created the wealth everyone else was scrambling for, including the hypocrites who prattled endlessly about land reform and socialism? If it weren't for the Dutch, Sukarno and Suharto and all the rest would be scratching in the dirt and wiping their behinds with banana leaves instead of living like royalty.

Verhoeven glanced at the headlines of the English-, Dutch-, and German-language newspapers spread out on the table before him. He preferred them to the local liars. One might at least learn something approximating truth. But the news they offered him was not encouraging. Anarchy was looming everywhere; Indonesia was the rule rather than the exception. And anarchy was bad for business. Any kind of business. He smoothed his hair. Except explosives or guns, of course.

The Americans in Vietnam were one thing—the United States was a great power—behaving foolishly but no more foolishly than great powers before them. And there were the usual small wars. But why suddenly all the assassinations, student uprisings, political turmoil around every corner? Why so many places at once? It would take an astrologer of great gifts to determine which crossing of stars made 1968 the year of the wild.

Reminded suddenly of the insult of the wedding, he took a generous swallow from his glass and felt himself flush. It had been years since Verhoeven thought of Holland as his home. Certainly he had no desire to return there, but when he saw the headlines and read the news story, he found himself choking back an anger so furious it had turned to bile. He had never been fond of Princess Beatrix, who reminded him of a round, waxy Edam cheese, and was much less fond of the titled German fortune hunter she was marrying, but that was all beside the point. When those radical Provo hooligans smoke-bombed the wedding procession, it was an attack on the nation. Did they want to topple the House of Orange that had reigned through centuries, that had created so much wealth? What would they put in its place? A Dutch Stalin who would clap rogues like themselves in irons before they were dry behind the ears and send everyone else to the poorhouse?

Verhoeven drank again, this time to calm himself before resuming his survey of the news. He wished Coelho weren't always late. But what could one expect of a Portuguese who had been born in Indonesia? He had taken on their habits. Although he now turned away from the newspapers, Verhoeven couldn't dam the flood of images from around the globe that crowded his brain, that were in some mysterious way linked to his having to pack up and leave. Young Czechs climbing aboard Soviet tanks to rid themselves of an invasion was one thing, futile yet understandable, but millions of fanatical Chinese only a few years out of diapers waving Mao's Little Red Book and worshipping his portrait as if he were the second coming, how to explain that? Rumors buzzing from Hong Kong said they were destroying everything, burning and killing. Even older Communists weren't safe from the rampage.

Had young people all over the world gone mad? In Paris there were wild demonstrations, even too wild for the Communists. They were led by a smiling, chubby-cheeked youth with red hair. Daniel Cohn-Bendit, according to the caption in the newspaper, nicknamed Danny the Red by his followers who carried him on their shoulders in some parody of a hero. Cohn-Bendit. A Jew, of course, Verhoeven said to himself, or at least half a Jew. Hardly a surprise. The photograph had looked as if Danny the Red and all the rest were having a fine time laughing and chanting and disrupting everything. Someone else would have to clean up the mess.

Well, one expected eruptions in Paris from time to time—that was the French for you—and the Irish would be at war with the English to eternity, the Israelis and the Arabs would always be at each other's throats, the Hindus and the Moslems would leave India bleeding, but up to now one could count on North America to remain both sane and prosperous. Instead, even in the United States, endless stupid political passions were plunging the nation toward anarchy. A parade of college students, most of whom hadn't done a day's work in their lives, had gotten rid of the president. Verhoeven recalled astonishing photographs of blacks with guns stalking university campuses without anyone trying to stop them. Incredible! The Americans would rue the day they let their blacks get out of line. And even in a backwater like Montreal, the Quebecois had been going at the English Canadians with plastic explosives. Nasty stuff, that. Well, Verhoeven sighed, the demons were let loose and would have to spend themselves into exhaustion. Then it would be business as usual.

Verhoeven had been doing business in Indonesia for a very long time. Except in rare moments, he thought of it as his home, spoke the local languages as well as he spoke his own. Despite his tall, substantial frame, his thick blond hair, and bright blue eyes, he felt as if he belonged here on the lip of the equator among the smaller, darker-skinned people of the archipelago: the Javanese, Malays, Chinese, the scattering of striving Indian and Arab traders. And the other Europeans: Portuguese, English, a remnant of the Dutch. And the rarer Eurasians, always so provocative, especially the women with their silken skins and mysterious eyes. It had been a lifetime since he'd left the cold and damp of northern Europe.

Dirk Verhoeven had been lucky. He arrived in 1937 and settled at Palembang, deep in the Sumatran jungle, where Royal Dutch Shell took him on immediately for their oil-field operations. Although he hadn't known it at the time, Palembang meant "gold out of the ground." Black gold it turned out to be, and all the world was greedy for it. He had borne up well under the debilitating heat, the mosquitoes, the moldy damp, and the fetid vegetation, much as an athlete bears up under a grueling training regimen while he prepares for his day of glory. Intelligent, shrewd, hardworking, deferential to his superiors, unsentimental about the sweating Asians who labored in the oil fields, he had intended to be rich while still a young man. The world seemed all before him.

But the war changed everything. The Japanese invaded and conquered. Interned in a wretched prison camp with other Europeans, he endured the beatings, smothering heat, insects, malaria, and semistarvation. But he was young then and eager to survive. He had no illusions about the goodness of human nature, was not offended by corruption and cruelty. Verhoeven adjusted quickly to his captivity and even prospered after a fashion. Like his venturesome Dutch ancestors, he discovered in himself a knack for trade. His business was in anything that brought a return: cigarettes, quinine, sex, food, and—on those rare occasions when they came on the market—gold and jade. He mastered the fine art of bribery. A few of the guards and aspiring native traders from nearby villages became his unofficial business partners. Under the noses of the Japanese, he plied his trade and kept his belly full enough.

As much as possible, he kept to himself. Even as a boy, he had never been one for friendship, had been uncomfortable with the obligation it implied. Perhaps that was why it had been so easy for him to leave home. Coelho, for whom Verhoeven was now impatiently waiting, was his closest friend, his only one if he bothered to think about it. They had done profitable business together, shared on occasion in more fleshly pursuits, but as for mutual affection . . . well, that was something he didn't think about. He didn't quite know what it was.

By the time the British marched through the prison camp gates in 1945 to liberate them, Verhoeven had been in the Far East for almost ten years. Still, it came as a shock to see that most of the British troops were dark-skinned East Indians. It was the first intimation he had that the days of the Europeans in Asia were numbered, that soon Asia might belong to the Asians. Yet at that moment, still young, happy to be free, eager to get on with his life, he saw only opportunity ahead and decided to remain where he was. There was nothing to return to in Holland after the war except cold and hunger and rubble in the streets. In Indonesia he managed to buy and sell at a profit—not always legally, of course, but what did that matter—be useful to someone in power, take his percentage. Eventually Sukarno knew him by name and called upon him when he needed the confidential service of a closemouthed European who understood the special needs of men in power.

Ever since Sukarno had been forced to yield the presidency to Suharto, Verhoeven felt his situation to be precarious. But it was only during the last few weeks that he had reluctantly come to the conclusion that significant changes in how and where he did business would have to be made. His influence with Sukarno—now virtually a prisoner in his own palace—was less than useless. It was dangerous.

If Verhoeven were a man of feeling, he might have been bitter. Here he was, almost past his middle years, intimations of mortality crowding in on him, and he was being forced out. All because Sukarno had gotten too close to the Communists, had not paid attention to business, was too busy fucking his beauty queens to notice that he was going to be overthrown. Verhoeven understood that Sukarno, like most men who were subject to flattery, who needed to feel loved more than they needed to be respected, was easily deceived about matters of loyalty. He had not felt the ground shifting beneath his feet. That was the mistake Verhoeven was determined never to make.

He had acknowledged, well before the present crisis, that the European imprint in Bandung was fading year by year. Mold crept like lichen up the sides of buildings. Planned and built by energetic and ambitious colonials like himself, the city would soon become a cemetery, its markers eroded by the elements till they could no longer be read. All of Indonesia would. Even after the Dutch had been forced to leave, the country might have been salvaged if the local Chinese, who knew how to make money and run the show, hadn't been almost finished off in 1965, slaughtered by the tens of thousands in a frenzy of jealous hatred, blood running through the streets like a flooding river, smeared like paint on the walls of buildings. Verhoeven had seen it himself. He shuddered at the memory. The butchers claimed the dead were all Communists, but he knew better. Some certainly were, but most were simply the envied Chinese, rich and capable. It was their power and wealth that fired the rabble who drew the blood.

Now the rabble were worse off than before. Without the Chinese to keep things going, the country was near chaos, the economy a disaster. Even an old hand like Coelho, whose family had come from Portugal hundreds of years before, was leaving. So many of the Chinese he had done business with were dead or had fled, shops shut down, schools closed. But they were too numerous to destroy entirely. Many were waiting and working quietly, patiently, silently, hidden behind closed doors. Others had escaped, found connections abroad, like his friend Kung in Hong Kong, who was already prospering. They were, Verhoeven thought, like some of the European Jews who had managed to survive the slaughter. They would rise again.

At times he fancied himself like them—the Chinese and the Jews—adaptable and clever, a sturdy transplant taking root and thriving in an alien climate. But such fancies were short-lived. Though he was happy enough to do business with them, he was at a loss to understand either the Chinese or the Jews. They shared the same oddly contradictory qualities: an uncanny ability to make money that he found entirely admirable, and a sentimental attachment to communist ideas that was incomprehensible. Politics was their undoing. Verhoeven could never understand why people with such talent for business would involve themselves in anything as unprofitable and stupid as communism. How could they imagine a perfect society when mankind was inherently corrupt? One had to begin with that assumption. As for himself, he knew with certainty that it was always a mistake to mix sentiment with business.

But, he thought, one should never underestimate the Chinese. Now, only three years after the massacre, they were surfacing again all over Indonesia, encouraged by Suharto and his supporters, who needed their financial resources. All the while, his own patron, Sukarno, for whom he had done countless favors, for whom he had made lucrative deals, for whom he had found the most beautiful girls, was powerless for the first time in twenty years.

Fortunately, Verhoeven had put something aside. More than something. He believed in enjoying wealth, not squandering it. Now he must find a way to hold on to it.

When Verhoeven looked up from his thoughts, Coelho, the busy little Portuguese, was striding toward him, smiling broadly, his teeth gleaming white against nut-brown skin. He's always smiling, Verhoeven thought, for no reason at all except an effusion of high spirits. He would never understand the Portuguese either. Coelho stuck out his hand.

"Sorry I missed you yesterday. Did you get my message?"

"Only that you'd be here today instead. Did business hold you up, or our friends in the government?"

Coelho's "business" was smuggling rubber from Sumatra to Singapore without paying the export tax to the government. Verhoeven often made the arrangements. Quite naturally, officials at the docks expected their fair share for averting their eyes.

"Neither," Coelho said, "but both are getting more difficult every day. Nothing works right. One of the rubber managers told me that the plantations are going to ruin . . . less export today than in the 1930s. It's just as well I'm getting out. Nobody here knows how to *do* anything anymore, and nobody cares."

"That's independence for you. Got rid of their 'foreign masters.' Fat lot of good it did them. Our friend Sukarno thought a smile and a slogan would solve everything."

"*Your* friend," Coelho corrected him. He had the Catholic's distaste for flaunting sexual license, though what one did in private was another matter entirely. Men were men. But Sukarno had gone too far.

"*My* friend, then. Such a pity. All that talent gone to waste. He might have been great if he paid more attention to business and less to women. The people still seem to love him."

"So they do. One of theirs, but he should have taken some lessons in finance from his Chinese friends. He wouldn't have gotten out the printing presses whenever he needed some money for one of his palaces or useless projects. You heard about the paper mill in Kalimantan?"

Verhoeven laughed. "The one they couldn't get logs to once it was finished . . . a fortune down the drain?"

The two men had had conversations like this many times before. It was a form of relaxation, a confirmation of their superior judgment. Each knew full well that if Sukarno had been less subject to flattery, less corrupt, more able, more like Prime Minister Lee in nearby Singapore, neither of them would have turned a profit.

A waiter came over with a plate of peanuts in palm sugar, golden coconut cookies, and a pot of tea for Coelho. The men, no strangers here, sat back and relaxed. Coelho said, "You can't imagine what it took to get here from Jakarta. Some parts of the road are complete rubble, but it's worth the trip just to be in Bandung again. Jakarta is like a sewer . . . worse every day. The palace still looks like a dream, but everything else is a nightmare. The hospitals can't keep up."

"I've heard they have plague now. I want to get out of here before I see my first black tongue."

"Didn't Malthus say that plague was one way to deal with population that was growing too fast? There isn't room to move in Jakarta."

"I hear that Suharto is going to encourage birth control."

Coelho frowned and changed the subject. He had a large family. "Nothing will help if they can't do something with the economy."

"I hear he wants to bring in foreign investment again. They should have stuck with the Dutch . . . didn't know when they were well off. When I first came to Sumatra, Royal Dutch was pumping out eighty-five percent of the oil. They knew how to do things right. Left to go their own way, these people can't drill a hole in the ground."

Coelho thought to himself that no people in the world were quite as smug as northern European Protestants, especially the Dutch. But, he was forced to admit, they knew how to make money and keep the natives in line. His own people had been trading here for generations, all the way back to the original settlement. He had heard more than one story about the "benefits" of Dutch rule. They were greedy brutes, worse than the English, didn't pretend they were after anything but money, no hypocrisy about education and civilization . . . white man's burden and all that . . . treated the natives and Chinese laborers like soulless animals whose only purpose in life was to extract riches from the ground for the Dutch back home to grow fat on. They thought Portuguese like himself beneath them. Indians and Arabs they considered little better than servants, no matter how clever or rich. The Dutch, he thought, had gotten what they deserved when they were kicked out. But there was no denying they knew how to do things right. All the while he said these things to himself, Coelho smiled at Verhoeven, his teeth shining through bites of cookies and sips of tea.

Verhoeven finally got to the business of the day. He asked, "Have you made up your mind yet?"

"It's settled. Macao."

"Why?"

"Cousins. The place is still full of Portuguese, and half of them are connected to my family. They can help me get started if I'm willing to invest enough."

Cousins, thought Verhoeven, his lips tightening to a narrow line. He had no family left so far as he knew, and he didn't care. Let others have their cousins: the Portuguese, the Indians, the Chinese could always make a connection. But, to his way of thinking, if cousins helped you, you were expected to help them. He preferred to be without encumbrances. Coelho in Macao would be a useful contact.

"What about you?" Coelho said. "Have you decided?"

"Singapore appeals to me, but isn't quite right for my"—he smiled—"talent."

Coelho understood. Prime Minister Lee was not the sort of man to cut you in on a lucrative deal because you paraded a voluptuous eighteen-year-old under his nose. More likely, you'd be slapped into prison for attempted bribery and you wouldn't be able to pay your way out.

"Sometimes," Verhoeven said, "I wonder about going back to Holland. They say Amsterdam is not as dreary and provincial as when I was young. It's taken on an international flavor. The long-haired wastrels have settled in." He looked away. "Lots of poppy trade."

Coelho didn't think Verhoeven dealt in that sort of thing, didn't approve, but he felt obliged to respond. "Could you set yourself up?"

Verhoeven frowned. "It wasn't a serious thought. I hate the climate, couldn't wait to leave."

"Where, then?"

"Hong Kong would give me some room to maneuver."

"Who can help you?"

"Kung. Do you remember him? The gold shipments?"

Coelho, who had profited handsomely because Verhoeven had needed his help, was impressed.

"So Kung escaped the massacre. Lucky for him. I should have known. Clever men like Kung don't get mixed up in politics. They always land on their feet. You will too, and it will do you good to make a change, do us all good. When is it to be?"

"Within the month. But it's complicated, getting the money out. What about you?"

"I'm counting on next week. My wife and children are there already, staying with relatives." A broad smile. "Before long you'll be visiting me in Macao, old man. We can spend some time at the gaming tables."

Verhoeven liked the idea of the casinos. He said, "I'll look forward to that for the future, my friend, but tonight let's give ourselves a farewell party."

"What did you have in mind?"

"Folk dancing. After all, we're leaving here."

Coelho laughed, was incredulous. Folk dancing wasn't the sort of entertainment Verhoeven usually proposed.

Verhoeven explained. "Kutuktilu. I hear it's going on tonight if you know where to look."

"Why not?" Coelho said. He was excited. He loved to see the prostitutes dance.

Later that night, linked arm in arm in the pungent darkness, the two men set out together to bid farewell to Bandung, to Indonesia. After an exchange of rupiahs, they gained entrance to the dance. Some of the young women were as beautiful as flowers, country girls plucked from their villages, dark-eyed, sensuous, graceful. Their dancing grew more lewd and lascivious as the evening wore on. The jewels in their ears and navels glistened. After a while, for a price, the men who were watching began to join them. Coelho held back for a bit, content to watch. But not Verhoeven. The tall Dutchman joined in without hesitation. He moved easily to the rhythms of the ancient dance.

Hong Kong

⌒

THE TWO WOMEN walking toward Verhoeven from the harbor seem to him an odd couple. The older one—striding forward, her face set toward some fixed purpose—is a middle-aged European wearing shabby, mismatched Chinese clothing. She is holding fast to the hand of a petite, pretty but distracted Chinese girl of about sixteen or seventeen. She is pulling her forward as one might tug at a reluctant pet. They are making their way through the crowds of noisy, gesticulating Chinese. Stalls, stands, and enclosed shops line the street. Customers jostle one another as they pick their way between mounds of colorful vegetables and gleaming wet fish, bolts of bright cloth, long strings of dried chili and fungi, new and used crockery, plastic and rope-soled shoes, cheap jewelry, incense burners, sticky sweets buzzing with flies, small mats and rugs, and assorted crude plumbing supplies. But none of this seems to be of interest to the woman who, despite her threadbare Chinese clothing, does not, indeed cannot, blend into the crowd. A Caucasian female is a rarity in this section of Hong Kong.

The woman looks too poor for the girl to be her servant. Her toes poke through worn, dusty cotton slippers. Untidy gray hair streaked with hints of gingery reddish-brown flares from her head and hangs to her shoulders. It frames a pale face that despite its lines and tense expression retains a suggestion of youthful beauty. She lists slightly to one side as she walks, as if she has suffered some injury or was born with a minor deformity. Verhoeven wonders what she and the Chinese girl she drags behind her are doing in a part of Hong Kong few Europeans bother with.

Before his path can cross theirs, he is surprised to see them turn into Kung's shop, just where he was headed himself. Curious about what business the odd pair might have with Kung, he deliberately lingers in the street a few minutes before entering so that they will be busy with the transaction that brought them. When he enters, Kung is behind the counter, his glasses perched low on his nose, his expression impassive. The European woman, however, is agitated, almost stammering.

"Surely you can do better than that, Mr. Kung. This has been in my husband's family for generations. I am certain it is very valuable."

She holds a jade pendant close to her chest as if Kung were about to snatch it away. Verhoeven's practiced eye can tell it is a fine piece, an antique worth a great deal. And the woman speaks Cantonese like a native, far better than anything he can manage.

Kung is adamant. "I am sorry, Mrs. Wang, but jade no longer has the value it once had. It would be different if you had gold or diamonds to offer. That's the best I can do for the jade."

Verhoeven knows Kung is lying, is banking on the woman's ignorance of the market. While it is true that there is plenty of cheap, inferior jade around, a finely crafted antique stone like hers is a different matter entirely.

Kung called her Mrs. Wang. So, Verhoeven thinks, she is married to a Chinese. That explains why she speaks so well. Perhaps the girl she has in tow is a relative by marriage. She could conceivably be a daughter, though they don't look anything alike.

The woman is silent, trying to decide what to do. Kung nods to Verhoeven, acknowledging his presence, then speaks to the woman again. "Nobody will give you more, but think about it for a week if you want to. It's not important to me."

Verhoeven can see what Kung has seen: the woman, plainly desperate for money, is unlikely to wait the week. While he isn't a man to take pity on anyone, he is intrigued by the woman and the girl, wonders if they might be of some use to him. He guesses that she is English, though nothing like the pampered English-women one usually sees in other parts of Hong Kong. She has lost her looks, but the girl, beneath the dirt and dishevelment, is quite the tiny beauty. Cleaned up and properly dressed, she would be . . . attractive . . . exceptionally attractive. Much against his usual practice, he decides to interfere. He deliberately speaks in English, knowing Kung will understand and assuming Mrs. Wang will.

"Now, now, Kung, you ought to take a second look. This isn't any ordinary jade."

The woman turns toward him, a look of relief on her face. He thinks she might shed tears at any moment, but Kung, be-hind her, is plainly annoyed at the meddlesome intrusion into his business affairs. However, it takes only a slight nod from Verhoeven for him to understand that the Dutchman has his reasons for interfering and will make up any loss he incurs by giving the woman something closer to what the jade piece is actually worth. He waits a bit longer before speaking in order to make her feel his generosity when it comes.

"Mr. Verhoeven is more familiar than I am with a piece of this kind, Mrs. Wang. Let him look at it."

She hands over the lovely green pendant—a smooth, almost translucent oval carved at its center with the image of a tree. Verhoeven studies the jewel and hands it to Kung.

"The lady is quite right, Kung. It's a fine old piece."

When, after pretending to consider the matter and weigh the possibilities, Kung gives the woman a figure only twenty percent higher than his original offer—far less than it is actually worth—she gratefully accepts. Like a child remembering her manners, she offers a quiet "Thank you" as he hands over the money. The girl, meanwhile, has waited impassively, as if she were not involved in anything that takes place here. The woman, taking hold of her hand again, starts for the door. Verhoeven speaks, this time directly to her. "Mrs. Wang, I'll be only a moment with Kung here, and it's time for lunch. I was going to a res-taurant at the harbor. Will you and the young lady join me?"

Mrs. Wang is hesitant, wary, but Verhoeven notices the first flicker of animation in the girl's face. Her eyes focus on him. Before the woman can decide whether or not to accept, the girl answers for them, in English, in the flat tone of a sleepwalker or some mental patients.

"I want to eat in a restaurant."

He looks at Mrs. Wang and smiles. "That settles it, then. I'll be only a moment with Mr. Kung."

He wants to speak with Kung privately, and is pleased when Mrs. Wang takes the girl's hand and says, "We will wait outside until you are ready." She might indeed be the kind of person who could be useful.

After the door closes behind them, Verhoeven winks at Kung and says, "Don't worry, old man, here is your twenty percent." Having calculated the difference in his head, he counts out an amount exactly equal to what his interference has cost Kung and says, "I'll see you tomorrow instead. Don't want to keep the ladies waiting."

⌒‿

Although the restaurant is a simple place by the docks, Verhoeven is embarrassed at being seen in public in the company of such a meanly dressed pair. There are holes in their shoes and the threadbare clothing that hangs from their bones is none too clean. They give off a musty smell that is only partly masked by the rich aroma of the food being cooked and eaten all around them. But he isn't sorry that he has asked them here. He trusts his instinct that these two will somehow be of use, that they are linked to his new life in Hong Kong. He has never gone wrong trusting his instincts.

Once they are seated, rather than ask them what they want to eat, he says simply, in English, with a neutral inflection that masks his distaste for their shabbiness, "You will want to freshen up before eating. I'll order for us when the waiter comes."

The girl understands. Her face clouds over, as if she is fearful the promised meal will be snatched from her. But like people conditioned to obeying orders—and though Verhoeven has not spoken harshly—they both rise in unison and go to find the washroom.

Verhoeven chooses what they will eat and gives the order to the waiter. The harbor that he looks out on from the restaurant window is filled with vessels—some tied fast to pilings, some at anchor, others plowing the waters—merchant ships, rotting junks, sleek white pleasure craft, floating restaurants, cruise ships, wide-hulled fishing boats laden with piles of shiny fish still leaping about on deck.

While he watches, Verhoeven speculates about the women. From the clothing they wear and their general condition, he suspects they might have come from the mainland. Although most of China has been sealed off, the border with Hong Kong is like a clogged strainer. A trickle always manages to pass through. The word is out that Mao's Cultural Revolution has gotten grotesquely out of hand, children acting like vandals, big shots like Liu Shaoqui in prison, thousands, perhaps hundreds of thousands, killed. Even longtime Communists were desperate to escape. Just a lucky few did.

How, he wonders, has an Englishwoman gotten herself mixed up in such a mess, if indeed she was mixed up in it? Possibly from a missionary family or a Communist herself married to one of the Reds. He'd heard of more than one woman who ruined her life that way. Fools who think they can make paradise on earth. They should know better, he thinks, but that type never does. They're always certain that the world needs saving and that they're the ones to save it. They marry trouble if they aren't born to it.

The women are taking their time, but Verhoeven is not bored. The flags of the merchant ships make a pretty picture in the harbor: the British tricolor, of course, but also the American colors, the blues and whites and yellows of Scandinavia, even the red banner of the Soviet Union complete with hammer and sickle, the stripes and bars and crescents and stars, symbols of the world's traders. Some he can't recognize, but they are all of them busy plying their trade, legitimate and illegitimate . . . it doesn't matter . . . they are hungry for money. That, he thinks, is what really matters, what keeps the round old world spinning on its axis. He prides himself on being not only a realist and pragmatist, but something of a philosopher as well.

When the women return to the table, Verhoeven, his ears cushioned by the clatter of the restaurant and the noises of the harbor, does not hear them. Rather, he feels the vibration of their steps on the old wooden floor and turns as they reach him. He rises and bows slightly. Their changed appearance surprises and pleases him. Much fresher-looking. Mrs. Wang has combed her hair back from her face, no longer the wild Medusa. From somewhere inside her shapeless garment, she has conjured a pur-ple-flowered scarf that is draped loosely over the flesh of her neck, softening the planes of her taut face. Verhoeven wonders about her age, but it is a matter of detached curiosity. For him-self, he chooses only young girls.

He notices that the tiny girl, though still without expression, has combed her hair and arranged her clothing neatly. Her breasts are more generous than those of most Chinese girls of her age and stature, but she is thin under her loose garments. Her newly clean skin, pale ivory and smooth as a flower petal, would bloom in a dressing of silk. He gestures with his hand.

"Please sit down, ladies."

They seat themselves, the girl looking at her plate, the woman glancing around awkwardly, trying to smile at Verhoeven for politeness's sake and because they are going to be well fed. When the waiter arrives with crisply fried crab dumplings, the fragrance of sea and spice rises from the platter as he sets it before them.

Verhoeven says, "How nice," and gestures for them to begin. He can see that the woman is trying to restrain herself, though she seems famished, but the girl devours the dumplings, each in a single bite, rapidly, voraciously, like a hibernating animal who must store food in season against the time when none will be available. He has not seen that kind of hunger since the intern-ment camp during the war.

Verhoeven gestures again. "Mrs. Wang, please help yourself."

She places a few of the crisp, aromatic dumplings on her plate, but begins to eat them only after Verhoeven has done the same. They eat silently, the women devouring, Verhoeven watchful, wondering what he will do with them.

When only a single dumpling is left untouched on the platter, the waiter arrives with brimming dishes of prawns and green onions in a rich garlic sauce, a whole fish in brown sauce stud-ded with vegetables, and a large bowl of glutinous rice. As he attempts to remove the almost empty dumpling platter, the girl reaches for the lone remaining dumpling before it can be spirited away. Then she reaches for the prawns without ceremony and begins to pop them into her mouth. After Mrs. Wang helps her-self to some of the food, Verhoeven says, "It has been a while since I saw jade of the quality you sold Mr. Kung. Do you have any more for sale?"

"That was my last piece."

"Forgive my boldness, Mrs. Wang, but you mentioned that the jade was from your husband's family. Is he in Hong Kong with you?"

"My husband is dead. He died last year."

Verhoeven does not need to hear more to confirm his intuition about the woman and the girl. These two, he thinks, have escaped over the border, probably bribed their way through with jewelry or other valuables, are down to nothing. Should he do something for them?

"I'm sorry for your misfortune." He turns to the girl, still busily absorbed in her food. "And this pretty young lady?"

Mrs. Wang seems to smile and sigh at the same time. "Mei-ling is my daughter." She hesitates, but as if compelled to explain, says, "She grew up in China and looks like her father's family, but she speaks English well. I taught her from the time she was small." She strokes the eating girl's shoulder. "The past year has been difficult for her . . . for both of us, I'm afraid."

"Have you been in Hong Kong long?"

She draws back. "Are you with the government?"

Verhoeven laughs. "Quite the contrary. I have nothing to do with police or immigration. Perhaps I can help you if you need to arrange for work."

At this the woman brightens. She sips some tea. "I will need to work. Mei-ling must finish school. Her father had high hopes for her. So do I."

He smiles at the girl, who looks up at last from her food. She is remarkably pretty. He might, he thinks, find a way to see to her education. He turns again to Mrs. Wang. "Hong Kong has some fine schools. Shall I help you look into them?"

"You are too kind. First, I must find work and some permanent place to live."

"Then we may be able to help each other."

She laughs, a light English laugh. "I doubt that. I'm not in a position to help you in any way at all."

"You may be wrong there, Mrs. Wang. My business requires me to be away a good deal. I need a reliable person who speaks both English and Cantonese to look after my office and deal with people on my behalf when I'm absent." Verhoeven quite believes himself as he says this, though he'd had no such notion until after he'd met them. He likes the idea and improvises further. "There are a few rooms in the back of the office that you and the young lady can stay in until you find a permanent place to live."

Verhoeven watches Mrs. Wang's face flush. She says, "I think you must be our savior, Mr. . . ." She has forgotten his name.

"Verhoeven."

A single day after meeting Verhoeven, a scant two days after crossing from Kowloon to Hong Kong with only the clothes on their backs and a small, scantily filled canvas bag slung over her shoulder, Emma Wang and her daughter begin making a home for themselves in two small rooms behind the almost-bare space that Verhoeven calls his office—nothing more than a telephone, desk, chair, lamp, and file cabinet—on the second floor of an old but respectable commercial building.

Emma's stomach is full, stuffed as it had been at Christmas when she was a child. The tall, blond Dutchman with his accented English and poor Cantonese seems to have descended from the heavens—Father Christmas in the guise of a European businessman. How odd it is for her to think well of a businessman, a sort of capitalist.

Although she is certain that being happy is no longer a possibility for her, Emma's relief mimics happiness. It rushes through her bloodstream like a narcotic: dulling her perception, quieting her pain, giving her rest. She looks at Mei-ling and tells herself: *We are safe.*

"A small miracle," she says to Mei-ling, having forgotten that she doesn't believe in miracles any more than she believes in happiness. Their quarters seem nothing short of luxurious: one room for sleeping, one room for everything else. Each room has a large double window facing the street. Thin paper blinds are rolled halfway and fastened by cords. The lavatory with running water is nearby in the hall.

The rooms are sparsely but sufficiently furnished: a bed wide enough for two, a bureau, a bedside table and lamp in one room; a small wicker table with two chairs, a wicker sofa with floral cushions, a cabinet containing a few pieces of crockery and cookware, a teakettle on a two-burner hot plate and a sink with running water in the other room. The lightbulb on the ceiling is covered by a white paper shade in the shape of a lantern. There are no pictures or photographs or carpets or plants; it's as if nobody ever stays here, not even Verhoeven. The rooms seem to be waiting for them.

Emma hears herself breathe and sigh, the sound like air escaping from a balloon. She squeezes Mei-ling's shoulder. "We've found sanctuary at last, my girl."

"Do you think so, Mother?" Mei-ling's voice is steady and even, quite normal.

Emma sits down on the bed to rest and watches while Mei-ling goes from one room to the other and back again, touching every object, inspecting every shelf and drawer, as if testing their reality. Although she has not been able to identify exactly what is "wrong" with Mei-ling, Emma perceives in such lively curiosity a sign of reviving health. A spark of hope flickers inside her, close to her bruised heart.

If Emma feels a slight unease, a fear of being compromised in some unforeseen way by their new circumstance, she puts it aside. Mr. Verhoeven had made their arrangement clear when he showed them the office and their living space.

He had said, "You see, Mrs. Wang, my business does not permit me to spend much time here. I'm often down at the docks or traveling. That's why someone like yourself can be of help to me, speaking English and Cantonese as well as you do, and so obviously intelligent and reliable."

When he'd said that, Emma thought him entirely sincere. If she had not been sealed into China for the past twenty years, she might have detected in his cream-colored suit and velvet words a touch of deviousness. But in her current circumstance, she feels only the deepest gratitude. She and Mei-ling are alive and in Hong Kong. Safe. Sheltered. The jade tree pendant had been the only piece remaining of the five she had sewn into the thick welting of her vest. Without Verhoeven, what would have become of them in Hong Kong?

Not at all sure of what his business actually was—something to do with trade—Emma had been eager to please when he expressed confidence in her. "Thank you, Mr. Verhoeven. I appreciate your trust. I speak Mandarin as well, if it's necessary. I also speak some French and German."

"Very good. Your languages will be most helpful. They come from all over the world to do business in Hong Kong. The future is right here under our feet. But now you must get yourselves settled. I'm afraid your salary will be modest at first, but your living quarters won't cost you anything at all."

"You are too generous, Mr. Verhoeven. I'll try not to disappoint you." She felt somehow humble before him, a vassal paying homage to a noble.

Emma remembers his smile when he said, "I'm certain you won't." He looked toward Mei-ling then, saying, "And we'll have to find a proper school for this young lady."

"Mei-ling was always an excellent student."

"No doubt . . . and will be again."

Emma remembers that he pointed his finger toward the door then and said, "Well, I must go for a bit. Don't bother about the office for now. Get yourselves settled. I'll be back before long with a few things you'll need here."

After the door closed behind him, Emma had turned on the water faucet and filled the teapot. Boiled water in her own rooms! Such luxury! She must not grow accustomed to it.

Emma sips her water and waits while Mei-ling searches the all but empty nooks and crannies before drinking the cup Emma poured for her. Then she goes into the bedroom and lies down on the bed. It seems vast and soft, cloudlike.

⌒‿

True to his word, Verhoeven returns to their rooms about an hour later with a few small packages. Emma flushes when she sees a neat package of tea. He is, she thinks, so thoughtful.

Verhoeven insists that he drop them off at a shop where they can purchase suitable clothing. Before leaving them, he says, "Many of my clients are European and some American. They fly in and out of Hong Kong to do business. You may meet some of them. Generally, they don't come to the office, but if they do, or if you deliver a package to their hotel, they will be more comfortable if you are wearing western clothing of some quality. Appearances give them confidence." He gives her a knowing look. "They mistrust the East, but they like the prices."

He laughs when he says this, as if he is sharing an amusing tidbit of gossip. After a pause, when she doesn't respond because she can't think of what to say, he adds, "And the easy way with business."

"I understand," she says, sensing a reply is expected. But she doesn't understand at all. She is confused. After so many years spent in a world apart, a world in which "capitalist roaders" belong in prison, a world in which the whole point of existence had been to thrust money to the bottom rung of human needs, she feels herself adrift in an unfathomable sea. She has no more idea about how business is conducted than she has about the latest fashions or films or cars or how people go about their private lives. That there is such a thing as private life. That it has little or nothing to do with politics or principles, that it has everything to do with sex and money.

Verhoeven presses upon Emma a substantial sum, saying, "Get some nice things for yourself and the girl."

When she protests, saying, "But I have money enough from Mr. Kung, from the jade," he will have none of it.

"No, my dear Mrs. Wang, that is yours and you are buying the clothing to be suitably dressed for my business."

"But Mei-ling . . ."

"Allow me the pleasure."

"I simply can't."

"Very well, if you prefer, we can take a bit each week from your salary for her clothing."

They leave it at that, a businesslike arrangement.

When she and Mei-ling push open the glass door and walk into the shop, Emma is instantly aware that their appearance sullies the polished atmosphere. The counters and clothing racks are laden with treasures—gardens of gleaming jewelry, trees hung with shimmering silks and brocades, clouds of lustrous cotton— a pirate's fantasy. It is, she thinks, as if she and Mei-ling are two sacks of trash that have been tossed on a Persian carpet. They spoil the entire design, not simply the spot on which they stand. The staff of the shop seems determined to ignore their existence, hoping they will leave.

Emma waits while Mei-ling steps forward to finger the sensuous fabrics on a rack of scarves, gaze raptly at a glass case filled with pearls. Emma doesn't know if the pearls are genuine or faux, but it is plain to her that after the somber shades and rough materials of China, Mei-ling is being swept by a burst of sensual pleasure, a lascivious desire for what she sees. Emma is shaken. What had happened in the countryside to change Mei-ling from a studious girl to this stranger who rarely speaks but whose eyes and hands reach hungrily for baubles and silks?

Finally, a young Chinese woman dressed in a green silk suit and a white blouse, so carefully painted and coiffured she seems lacquered, approaches her on the highest-heeled shoes Emma has ever seen.

"Is there someone you wish to see?"

"No," Emma says, not without a touch of resentment at the condescension in the woman's voice. "Not someone, something. My daughter and I need new clothing." She hesitates, looks down a moment, up again directly at the saleswoman, and adds, "As you can see."

The saleswoman glances toward Mei-ling, who is caressing a red silk scarf. Emma summons up an unfamiliar English hauteur, adds, "I can assure you that I will have no difficulty paying for anything we may choose to purchase here. Of course, if you wish, we can go elsewhere."

"Oh, no, madam. I'll be pleased to help you. Shall we begin with you or the young lady?"

The young saleswoman soon enters into the spirit of their quest. She suggests the proper undergarments and shoes as well as clothing. She mentions a hairdresser they might find to their liking. At this, Emma smiles politely. She is now better disposed toward the young woman who, she decides, is a member of the working class despite her pampered appearance.

Emma catches a glimpse of Mei-ling admiring herself in the gilt mirror, obviously pleased at the sight of fresh beauty, herself in pink-and-white-striped cotton held at the waist by a shiny white belt. Her delicate feet are shod now in white sandals. How beautiful she is, Emma thinks. She is not surprised to hear Mei-ling say, "Mother, let's wear these now. I don't want those old things."

Hearing this, the saleswoman points to their old clothing and asks Emma what she assumes is a rhetorical question. "Shall I dispose of these?"

Emma flushes red. In a barely controlled voice, she says, "No, put them in a separate bag." Then she thinks: How could she have known? In a softer tone she says, "I'll take them with me."

Although the young woman clearly wishes she could lift the

old things with a stick rather than soil her hands on them, and is bewildered that anyone would wish to keep them, Emma has decided the issue. The old is packed separately from the new but is not left behind.

As the saleswoman busies herself with wrapping the various parcels, Emma and Mei-ling appraise their new selves in the floor-length mirrors. Emma sees that Mei-ling is smiling a rare smile. For a moment she is pleased. But, Emma notices, the smile seems strange, forced, like a mask, as if Mei-ling were imitating the saleswoman.

Emma, who, without ever thinking about it, prizes integrity in even the simplest gestures, wonders if Mei-ling's newfound delight in herself does not come with too high a price. Still, it is the first smile she has seen on Mei-ling's lips since that terrible day of the family's separation and humiliation, their descent into despair. Long afterward, even now, Mei-ling will say nothing about what had happened, only that she had been learning from the peasants, as Mao wished. Indeed, for months she rarely spoke at all, just fixed a dull gaze at nothing in particular. Emma thinks, this smile, even if copied, is a reason to hope.

Emma is not pleased when she takes in her own image. She coughs nervously. In navy shantung with white linen piping at the neck and sleeves, she is entirely English again. It is as if a vital part of herself has disappeared, as if a leg has been amputated. Who precisely is the expensively dressed woman whose reflected image is so like and unlike her own? She seems a stranger to herself. Has she left the real Emma Wang, her best self, behind in China? Had the epidemic of terror brought on by the Cultural Revolution deprived her of some essence she might never recover?

Emma studies her appearance carefully in the flat surface of the mirror: the lines in her face, the wide gray patches in her hair, the large blue veins in her hands. She tells herself: I am old . . . a hundred years older than I was a year ago. And she asks herself again why everything she cared about and worked for and gave her life for had gone so impossibly wrong? If Mei-ling didn't need her, would life be worth bothering about?

Summoning her courage, Emma raises her neck and shoulders and forces a smile in the mirror. Perhaps, she thinks, that is what we must do: pretend happiness till it becomes real. She and Mei-ling will have to learn to smile again if they are to go on. It would take practice. For now, there is work from Mr. Verhoeven to earn their way. Emma takes her daughter's hand and says, "Let's go home."

Burdened with parcels, they leave the shop, Emma listing to one side as she walks, as if she had been born with one leg shorter than the other. She wonders why Mei-ling never asks about it. When they are outside, Emma is struck, as she had been upon entering Hong Kong from the mainland, by how much of everything there is; even the poor seem rich compared to the mainland. Handsome automobiles make their way steadily through the streets among the darting, fragile rickshaws; new buildings rise into the sky like mountains of glass and steel; shop after shop is filled with an abundance her eyes cannot measure; countless restaurants send waves of fragrance through the air. The outdoor stalls are filled with mounds of vegetables and fresh fish, as if there is no end to the food in the world. Are the hungry invisible here?

Emma is undone by the abundance. In what she sees before her, there seems no evidence at all of what her husband, when they were still young, once described as—she could hear his voice—"mind, spirit, and matter held fast to one another, links in the golden chain of civilization." Hong Kong, she thinks, is all matter, a vast shrine to indulgence. Everyone worships the golden calf. But, at the same moment, she wonders: what was it she had fled from? Surely not some higher order of civilization. It had been hell!

⌒⌒

It does not take Emma and Mei-ling long to settle themselves after arriving "home" from their shopping expedition. Their possessions are few, the rooms spare. Verhoeven had made clear to Emma that her work would not begin until the following week, that she should ignore the telephone if it rang, that he would speak to some people he knew who might suggest a school for Mei-ling.

Emma watches as the silent girl spreads her new clothing on the bed in the modest room they are to share. Mei-ling strokes the layers of fabric. As her fingers graze the surfaces and delve into the crevices of the soft cloth, the pallor that so troubles her mother seems to leave her.

Emma promptly hangs her new clothes in the closet, hardly looking at them, speaking all the while to Mei-ling about the turn in their fortunes. "I never believed in luck before, but I think we've had some, don't you?"

"Yes."

"Mr. Verhoeven seems an intelligent man, and kind."

"Yes."

To each question or comment, Mei-ling responds, but she is clearly uninterested in anything but the new clothing. Despite her qualms, Emma is pleased to see Mei-ling taking pleasure in anything. The vivacious girl she remembers, who had always been so inquisitive, so precocious, so skilled with words, had retreated into a cocoon of silence. Emma dares hope now that her daughter will emerge as her former self, albeit older and wiser, speak openly about where she had been and what terrible things had happened there. For surely there were terrible things. There is no escaping that. Emma comforts herself: Mei-ling is young; youth is resilient; she needs only time to restore her spirits.

Emma removes her old clothing from the remaining parcel but she does not hang it in the closet. Instead, she takes the small knife she always carries with her and begins to split the seams of the padded vest she had fashioned when forced to flee. The welting around the armholes is frayed, but it does not matter. The jade pendant she had sold to Kung was the last jewel she had fixed in place there before her flight. She takes pride now that in the terror and fierceness of the moment she had understood so well that the Wang family jade would be their means of survival. She remembers her mother-in-law in the first year of her marriage showing her the jewels, encouraging her to touch the smooth polished translucent surfaces. The older woman had spoken like an oracle. "These are not simple adornments, they are the treasure of the Wang family. Care for them well when they are yours. They will care for you." So they had. But now that the Wang jade was gone, scattered among strangers, what would assure Mei-ling's future?

Emma draws from between the split seams of her vest a thin packet of folded papers. While she straightens and arranges them, Mei-ling begins to hang her clothing in the closet and place her new silk underthings in the bureau. It strikes Emma that Mei-ling seems not in the least curious about the papers, as if removing them from the lining of an old vest were the most ordinary thing in the world. After Mei-ling finishes gathering up the empty boxes and wrappings, she announces, "I'm hungry."

Emma places the folded papers in the bottom bureau drawer. Then they wash and go to find a restaurant so that Mei-ling's hunger will be satisfied.

Later that night, after Emma has fallen asleep, Mei-ling removes the thin sheaf of rumpled papers from the drawer in which they are resting. Quietly, so as not to awaken her mother, she opens the door to Verhoeven's office and sits down at the wooden desk. The hum of the night is punctuated by an occasional nearby shout or passing vehicle in the street, but Mei-ling does not notice the noise. The corners of the room recede into darkness; a dim radiance from the green-shaded lamp illuminates the long-traveled pages. She straightens them as best she can on the flat surface of the desk.

Mei-ling begins to read. She is surprised that the document, undated and untitled, is in English, her mother's native tongue. How quickly the letters shape themselves into words, the words into sentences, the sentences into paragraphs. How fortunate she learned them at her mother's knee so long ago.

Emma Wang's Journal

I write in darkness. It clings to me, surrounds me, a shroud. I cannot sleep. We are all exhausted. The others are asleep or seem to be. Loud rough breathing, snoring, choking and coughing of those who are ill—too many— the sounds mask the noise of my pencil as it scratches the surface of the paper. What compels me to write, to write in English? Beautiful English. Mother tongue, voice of Shakespeare, Milton, sweet reason, strawberries and fresh cream, roses. Am I mad to put myself in danger only to scribble on a page? What will happen if this is found? Beatings? Prison? Why do I think that death can come at any moment? It is less likely here among the peasants than in the madness of the city. The peasants do not welcome us as the banners proclaim. I did not expect them to. We intrude on their lives, nuisances, more mouths to feed. But they are not cruel, not monsters like so many of the others. Even my own comrades. Children can be forgiven, but can they? Our dear friend Chen, his hands cut off—that is the rumor—his surgeon's hands cut off for being a capitalist roader, in league with Liu against Mao. Nonsense! Madness! Perhaps Chen will commit suicide like some of the others. It is too horrible. I cannot bear it. To think that he returned from America to help China when he could have had an honorable life abroad—and wealth. But what is wealth or honor compared to transforming the world— *paving the way for a state of future bliss more permanent and more pure.* Milton, *The Second Defence of the People of England.* I remember it yet from my school days: *Those only are great things which tend to render life more happy, which increase the innocent enjoyments and comforts of existence, or which pave the way to a state of future bliss more permanent and more pure.*

It was in my school days that I first felt the brilliance of Milton's light. Where was he when he wrote those lines? Was he already blind, writing in the dark as I do, seeing more clearly in darkness, mourning the betrayal of his revolution as I mourn mine? Is the dream of a more perfect world never more than an illusion to tease us into hope and suffering?

Too exhausted to write. Not tired. Exhausted! My fingers cannot hold the weight of my pencil. I write, I prove I am alive. I must try to sleep.

The road to hell is paved with good intentions. Das Kapital. Karl Marx, prophet and aphorist. When Marx said that, he could not have envisioned loyal Professor Ma dragged from his classroom, his arms twisted back till they were sprung from their sockets though he had no crime to confess, or Comrade Hong beaten bloody by a mob because he was a landlord's son, or Red Guards waving Mao's Little Red Book like mindless robots while setting fire to the university library, or intellectuals cast into squalor and suffering to learn from peasants who had no desire to teach and resented more mouths to feed. Jeering then at liberal reformers, did Marx foresee the future better even than *he* knew?

The peasants stare at me as if I were a ghost, a spectral manifestation from another world. So do many others. I think that nobody here except for a few from universities has ever seen a foreigner before. How odd I must look to them with my blue eyes and gingery hair. It turns gray now quickly. I wonder what I look like. There are no mirrors. Just as well.

The smell is awful. In a few hours my lessons begin again. We toil and we criticize ourselves. We are building a dike. It seems that because the trees have been cut down, the earth cannot hold the water. The cause is known, but no one speaks of it. Even the most deluded of Mao's notions is holy now—the Great Leap Forward—household furnaces for the making of steel—fueled by the wood of felled trees whose roots held the good soil of China in its place. We are taught to learn from Mao and from the peasants. But what? So much we learn leads to catastrophe.

We build the dike to stem the tide that washes away the land that has no roots to hold it. They have been cut off . . . pulled out. Madness! We gain relief from our labor only for self-criticism. A heavier labor. Today Comrade Yuen said, "I understand the wisdom of Chairman Mao more every day now that I am learning from the peasants." Does he believe this? I say such things too when I am pressed, but I know it is a lie to save my life. My job is to haul stones. I bruised my ankle badly when I fell with one of my loads. It festers, but I dare not complain. Except here as I write. I must try to sleep.

The shelter we are living in—more accurate to say herded together in—is quite beyond belief, not high enough to stand, worse than the poorest peasant's house, a cowshed judging from the smell and low roof. But sickness has a rotting smell too . . . and human gases and endless filth. I itch and I scratch. I fear lice. There are over thirty of us in this poor excuse for a building. We sleep on straw or on the hard earth. Rodents scamper about. People cry out in their nightmares. Two suicides so far. Both comrades like myself. One smashed his head against stones by plunging into the deep ravine, one drowned herself at night in a watering trough. How do I find the strength to live?

Where is Mei-ling? What has happened to Wang? I fear the worst. I heard a rumor that Deng's son was thrown from a window and is paralyzed.

My back seems permanently bent. It is impossible to stand up straight because the roof of the shed presses down on us. Small as I am, even I must stoop. We lie together almost as close as nested spoons, yet the damp and cold invade my bones. They ache. My ankle does not heal. It has turned blue. In waking dreams I walk through an English garden, inhale the scent of roses in June. I see the flowers clearly in the dark. Red and pink and yellow and white. Curling petals smoother than a baby's skin. I touch them. I think more kindly now of England. Was imperial England more cruel than this? I cannot answer that. I think of liberal England. Law and justice—punishments mild and temperate as the climate—a green and pleasant land. I exaggerate. I forget the dark, satanic mills, the gray skin, and rotting teeth of the workers. But then, I never saw a mill, just went to the university, where I met Wang. Then to China together.

I think of great-aunt Sybil whom I never knew—married to a Canadian—went off together as Christian missionaries to China. "They wasted their lives," my mother said, "swallowed up by the hordes of China." Mother thought Sybil quite dotty—but kinder to her than to me when I cast my lot with Wang. I broke my parents' hearts, their only child, a deserter. Why do I concern myself with that now when they are dead, when Wang may well be dead? Was my destiny somehow linked with Sybil? I'm surely not a Christian now, nor a missionary either, though I may be wrong there. I confess. I had nothing but contempt for missionaries when I was young. Imperialist tools! Did I really think that? About people who clearly intended to *do good* a world away from the comforts of home. And often did so. Set up schools, hospitals, lived meager and difficult lives in the service of what to them was a great ideal. Many

Chinese loved them, were grateful for what they brought. How will we be judged years from now, Wang and I, the Communists? Is all this horror a temporary deviation from the main road? I do believe so. But how can one tell in a single lifetime? History unfolds so slowly. An individual life is so short. Does any of this matter? I must try to sleep.

The pain in my ankle is nearly unbearable. But I have learned to bear more than I thought possible. The swelling has not gone down. The color deepens to reddish-purple. It is difficult for me to work. I cannot sleep.

All I look forward to now is night and darkness, when I can rest. If the pain lessens, I sleep. Some of the time I write until the crack of dawn. I think again of John Milton—blind—writing *Paradise Lost* in darkness "to justify the ways of God to men." I set myself no such lofty task. The gods I knew are dead or reign in hell. Writing keeps me still among the living. I am not sure it is worth the trouble. But Mei-ling will need me. What has happened to her?

Slowly the dike appears—stones piled high—a kind of Roman wall. Will travelers come to this place to marvel at our works a thousand years from now, to praise our labors? Or will they find only a mysterious pile of rubble? Are we slaves by some other name? This most ancient of civilizations—the Chinese. Have they, by some hideous turn of history, become the barbarians they fear? I pray not. They will right themselves. I must have courage. This cannot last forever.

What has befallen my dear husband? Has he been beaten? Is he in prison? Is he alive? Where is Mei-ling? Is she safe? Does she read Mao's Little Red Book as if it were the Bible? Does she set fire to books? Not possible. A rank odor clings to me as if my body has begun to decay.

Long is the way/And hard, that out of hell leads up to light. Why does John Milton build a nest in my brain? I think of England all the time now, though I will never return. The die was cast long ago. Today, for the first time, I have been treated with kindness. I have been given light work and sent to live in the house of a peasant family until my ankle heals. The family is very curious about me. But they are kind and smile with brown, toothless smiles and share their meager food with me. The children stare at me as if I were a giraffe from distant Africa, so strange do I appear to them.

We sleep in a common room on matted straw—grand-parents, parents, children, and now me—but the air is not so foul and there is less noise than in the cowshed. I am able to stand up straight when my legs will hold me. We eat rice and vegetables out of common bowls. I am probably a burden to them. They are amazed that I speak their language. Perhaps they think I am a witch.

A barefoot doctor came to me this morning as I was mending slippers. There are few trained physicians here, none that I know of. My barefoot lass—she actually wears slippers—is a sweet young thing only a little older than Mei-ling. She applied a poultice to my ankle with much confidence and cheerful chatter. When I flinched at the touch of her hand on the swelling, her eyes filled with tears. I don't know why, but her tears made me feel better. After she finished, she offered a further prescription. "You will heal yourself if you study the thoughts of Chairman Mao."

When I told her I would, she smiled broadly. You would think I had given her a gift. She seems to have memorized a good deal of the Little Red Book. She told me she carries it with her always, convinced apparently that Mao's thoughts can heal the sick. I would prefer an orange or a bowl of strawberries. I think I might give a toe for a bowl of strawberries in fresh cream.

I am in danger of becoming spoiled. I write by light of day now. The Li family has made me their pet. I have been given only sedentary work—blessed relief—weaving reeds into hats, mending baskets, repairing slippers. My fingers are still nimble and I work quickly. I feel useful, as if I'm earning my living. My ankle is less swollen now but still painful when I walk. It has stopped throbbing so much. I think it has finally begun to heal.

A member of the revolutionary committee comes every day to see that I'm not malingering. He works with me on my reeducation—a waste of time I suspect—". . . if you rely on the teaching of Chairman Mao, you will always be victorious." I have become a skeptic. I tell the committee I am learning from the peasants as Chairman Mao urged, that I understand the errors of bourgeois revisionism, the counterrevolutionary treachery of Khrushchev and Liu, the need for constant vigilance against wrong thoughts. They tell me that I am progressing with my reeducation but that I have a long road to travel. There is certainly some truth to what they say.

I think of when I first arrived here, utterly exhausted, terrified. The painful jump to the ground from the truck. I thought I had torn something inside myself. It was raining lightly, just drizzling. When I rose from the ground to which I had fallen, I saw in the distance what seemed an enormous landscape painting: terraced rice paddies, undulating bands of green enveloped in silver mist, jagged hills jutting up through low clouds, small huts dotted here and there, tiny human figures at their work. The peasants wore wide, round-brimmed hats woven of reeds that sheltered their faces from the rain. Their rain capes, also woven of reeds, opened and closed like accordions as they moved. The peasants worked in rows, bending into the paddies like grass in the wind, as much a feature of the landscape as the fields and the mountains and the clouds drifting above them.

I was too tired then to think, but now I spend hours wondering about the peasants and their work, about families like the Li clan. For centuries it has been like this—a chain of ancestors and descendants—all absorbed into an endless cycle of sunrises and seasons, planting and harvesting, famine and plenty (perhaps never plenty), birth and death (always too much of both). Literally billions of souls over time working endlessly at the mercy of nature and whatever warlord or landlord was thrust upon them.

I have known all this in some abstract way, but only now do I understand the burden of endless labor as a way of life. Is Mao correct as well as cruel, a teacher? We intellectuals did not understand the people of China nearly so well as we understood our ideas and our desires, our "noble" purpose. But what precisely is it we are to learn here? The glorious lives of peasants who live scarcely better than the beasts of the field? Surely there is precious little glory in their lives, unless one thinks of grim submission as glorious. The reality is not at all like the landscape painting a newly arrived outsider sees. Oh, no. In the Li household, each day brings its own share of suffering and deprivation. The little children are a delight, but they will soon lose their bloom. Everyone seems to be scratching a scab or lancing a boil or nursing an abscessed tooth or spewing up great gobs of phlegm. And still they work because that is what they must do. Their lives know little or nothing of innocent enjoyments or comforts of existence. *What is there to learn from what I see here except to change it?* Only then will our revolution have some meaning and be worthy of our sacrifice—and theirs.

The Li family would be ever so happy with a few simple comforts—a sewing machine, a bit of new cloth, a radio, holiday sweets, fresh fruit, picture books for the children. Instead of bringing me to the countryside to build a dike—a few machines could do it better than hundreds of us carrying our stones—we should be bringing simple machinery and medical care and sanitation, *the good and the goods that civilization does provide.* Suffering exists to be alleviated, not imitated. I feel like a counterrevolutionary when I say these things. Have I failed the revolution, or has it failed me? Am I too impatient? Is that what we are to learn here—patience? Then I have not learned my lesson well.

Once again I write in darkness. I have been returned to the cowshed. The revolutionary committee said I was well enough to join the others at the dike. Tomorrow I take up the yoke and the buckets. The stones will seem heavier now that I have been away. I still do not walk properly. The pain in my ankle smarts and throbs.

Oh dark, dark, dark, amid the blaze of noon,

Irrecoverably dark, total eclipse
Without all hope of day!

Blind Milton again—*Samson Agonistes*—amazing that I remember. England was so long ago. Darkness, blacker than before. Wang is dead—stoned to death. By children not yet born when our revolution was victorious? Mao's children are convinced they are the future. Perhaps they are. Was he murdered by the twentieth century? I am certain of nothing. Only that Wang *is* dead. The news was brought to me by a source I know to be truthful soon after I returned to the work brigade. My husband's death is a fact I cannot change. Did he think I had deserted him? No! His faith in me was absolute—and mine in him. That cannot be taken from us.

Is civilization finished in China, the rough beast come slouching along the Great Wall, terrifying and devouring? Have I helped open the gate, been complicit in the madness without intention? Paved the road to hell? Is Wang's death my punishment? I must escape from here and find Mei-ling. But how? I am still quite lame.

The revolutionary committee was wrong about the state of my health. My bad leg gave out completely after many days of hauling endless buckets of stone. I finally went tumbling down the hill like Jack and Jill, leaving a trail of stones behind me. Comrade Chu, the head of our work unit, was angry, thought I might be malingering. He came running toward me. "Get up, get up," he shouted as if I were a recalcitrant horse. He even raised a stick. I thought he would strike me. I don't know why, but I laughed when I saw that, not a real laugh, more like hysteria. Perhaps that's what held him in check. He didn't strike me—just took me by the shoulders roughly and tried to make me stand on my feet. May as well have tried to stand a mermaid on her feet. My legs wouldn't hold me, and I was screaming in pain. They put me in some sort of makeshift sling and carried me all the way back to the Li family. It seemed to take forever. I must have fainted. I woke up in the Li house with the children staring at me as if I were a ghost returned from the dead.

I don't know what will happen now. If it weren't for

Mei-ling, I wouldn't care. Except for her, what do I have to live for?

Daylight. Here I am as before, mending sandals. I have not been shot (as others have) for malingering or causing trouble or being an incorrigible. Perhaps because nobody wants to take responsibility for killing a foreigner, though I can't imagine the British embassy caring the least bit about my fate. No matter. As far as I can tell from the rumors that are plentiful, all of China seems to be sealed off from the outside. I think more about the outside now that Wang is dead.

I have been transferred to a hospital—or what passes for a hospital in this part of the world. It is actually a clinic that was first established by missionaries years ago. Aunt Sybil reaches from the grave to rescue me! There were Christians here in the past, but there is no trace of religion now. Just as well. Bloodshed more likely than mercy to follow in the wake of absolute belief. *That* is the lesson I have learned here.

I have been unable to stand. Even my good leg is weak and a bit swollen, though not discolored like the other. A few days after I returned to the Li family, the pain grew intolerable. Then, without notice, a truck came to fetch me. I was surprised to see it loaded with rare livestock—piglets, several crates of chickens, a few ducks. Apparently someone somewhere will be eating well in this hungry province. The Li family gathered to watch. They looked longingly at the cargo while the truck driver and a member of the revolutionary committee trundled me into the cab. The family scarcely noticed. I didn't blame them. Hunger takes precedence over sentiment. Was it only a year ago that Wang and Mei-ling and I sat at table together sharing a delicious meal of pork and vegetables? Did only we Communists have pork? I fear so but can honestly say I do not know.

The driver took me to the clinic before delivering his cargo, so I am uncertain about the destination of the ducks and chickens, but I am more certain of their fate than of my own.

The doctor—a real one this time, not an untrained child in slippers—came to see me and the other patients today. I think he traveled some distance. He was old, with a lined face, probably well over sixty. He seemed very tired. He lingered at my bedside longer than that of the others, probably because he was surprised to find an Englishwoman in his care, one who spoke Chinese at that. This seemed to please him. He examined my leg carefully and asked me about the steady pain. He was unhappy about the swelling and the discoloration that was creeping up the leg, especially the dark red outline of my veins. Finally, keeping his voice low, as if he were afraid, he spoke to me in English: "What are you doing here?" It was my turn to be surprised that he spoke my mother tongue.

I kept my voice low as well. "Learning from the peasants."

He frowned and looked away a moment, as if he thought his face might betray him. "What are you doing in China? There are no foreigners here anymore."

I whispered back. "My husband was Chinese."

As best I can remember, he said, "Was? Are you a widow?"

I said, "Yes."

He said, "How unfortunate. You are still young."

I responded, unwisely, incautiously, "Revolutionary justice." Something in the tone of his inquiry had told me not to fear. I could see from the expression on his face that we understood each other. Speaking in a low voice, I told him about Mei-ling and the poisonous cloud that had enveloped us. As we spoke, a woman entered the room with a mop and a pail of water. Dr. Kung became formal. He passed on to another patient.

Later, well after the woman left, he returned. He said, "You will need further treatment for your leg. It is not available here. I have arranged for you to return with me to the main hospital. You will get the care you need there. Meanwhile, these pills will help with the pain."

I could hardly breathe, so suddenly was I filled with hope again. I took the pills with some water and slept.

* * *

I am now in a genuine hospital. My benefactor looks after me. I have been given a respite, a blessing, a kind hand. In addition to the precious medicine that he hopes will cure the infection that has overtaken my leg, Dr. Kung has given me more paper and two pencils and a copy of Chairman Mao's Little Red Book. He did this in front of the others, saying, "This will aid your recovery. You can chart your progress through your mastery of Chairman Mao's thoughts." Not entirely certain of his meaning—an ironic subterfuge? a remnant faith? an odd combination of the two?—I nevertheless thanked him profusely. But I reserved my own faith for the medicine he prescribed.

Our ride to the hospital from the clinic had been long and painful but gave me pleasure despite the difficulties Dr. Kung and I endured. We began our journey in the morning. The doctor himself helped me into the front seat of an ancient automobile. The backseat was filled with boxes of supplies, a package of food, and containers of precious fuel. As we rode over the rutted and muddy roads, sometimes bouncing about like marionettes, we spoke about ourselves freely, as if we had been acquainted all our lives.

As a child, Dr. Kung had attended a missionary school. He learned some English there and had considered converting to Christianity when he was a young man. But he decided against it, partly, he said, because he was surrounded by suffering and could not bring himself to believe that a just and loving God permitted such horrors to exist. He said, "I chose agnosticism as my creed, hard work as my calling." He had taken his medical training in America, in New York City, which he still remembered fondly. He said it was as "cosmopolitan as Shanghai and much cleaner." The Japanese invaded while he was abroad, so he stayed there for years. Like so many others, he returned to help build the new China after the Communists took over. He said, "I saw quickly enough, or thought that I did, that the Communists held the best hope for China's future. They were idealistic and wanted to introduce land reform and honest government. They had been brave against the Japanese and willing to suffer for their beliefs—like the early Christians I had read about as a child. I thought they might be the answer to China's misery." He became silent for a few moments before speaking again. "They were the answer for a while and then they weren't. Perhaps they will be again. I don't understand what happened. I stay alive and do what I can to cure people of the diseases that afflict them. I try to think less and do more. Life will go on when I die."

As we drove, I told him about Wang and myself, how we met as students in England, how we had come to China full of enthusiasm, utterly convinced that a new and better world was at hand—within our lifetimes.

Only now, when writing, do I realize that during the many hours the old doctor and I shared our thoughts I was without pain. We had risen above the earth. It was as if our two souls were chatting on some distant cloud. Did the pills for my pain contain opium? If so, I must have more.

Every few hours we stopped to relieve ourselves and add fuel to the old car. I thought I had lost all modesty in the cowshed, but further humiliation was in store for me. Once reality intruded, I could not walk without pain despite the medication or put any weight on my bad leg. I was embarrassed when I needed Dr. Kung's assistance to urinate. He held me from behind under my shoulders. He said, "Just remind yourself that I am a doctor and that blood and urine are my vocation. Try to relax. I'll close my eyes and you can tell me when you have finished."

Soon most of the day was behind us. Before it grew dark, he said we would have to spend the night in a small village en route and sleep at the home of a peasant family. He had been to the village before but never with anyone else, certainly not with a European woman. He was perplexed as to how to deal with the problem, and I felt guilty for adding to his burdens. Finally, I suggested that we pull to the side of the road, unload the backseat, and sleep in the car. He readily agreed that might be best under the circumstances. If anyone stopped to investigate, he would explain that when darkness came we were forced to pull over. In truth, the headlights were completely useless.

After we ate some cold rice and vegetables and drank from a thermos of refreshing tea that Dr. Kung unexpectedly produced, we sat for a while and watched the hills and sky, speaking occasionally as darkness slowly closed us in.

Dr. Kung told me that his wife was dead, that his had been an arranged marriage but a happy one, that his parents had chosen well. He had only daughters, two of them, and regretted not having a son. Both of his daughters—a teacher and a doctor like himself—were in Shanghai as far as he knew, but he had not heard from them since the beginning of the Cultural Revolution. He was worried but could not leave the work to which he had been assigned in order to search for them. His elder daughter, the doctor, was a woman about my age. She had never married, but his younger daughter had two children, also girls. "Very bright, the greatest joy," he said, "but girls." He expected me to understand his disappointment. I had lived in China long enough to be able to do so. I wondered what the future held for Mei-ling.

When we were weariness itself, he helped me into the backseat and covered me with a thin blanket he took from one of the supply boxes. A strange and wonderful thing happened as he spread the blanket over my body. The touch of his fingers, impersonal, a doctor's touch, quickened something in me. I, who had not menstruated for many months, felt almost like a woman again. I grasped his old hand and held it. I could hear our breathing. He knelt beside me on the floor of the car and ran his tender hand along my spine. He rested his head on my breast. We stayed there like that for a while. Then he raised his head and said, "We must sleep." He left me, took a second blanket, and eased himself into the front seat. We slept. It was cold when we woke. After we ate a little, we drove here to the hospital.

Dr. Kung is treating me with scarce antibiotics. I think I am being given preferential treatment. This will be dangerous for him if anyone complains. I hope my presence does not add to his sorrows. I can tell that he is deeply concerned because the infection may have penetrated the bone. Reddish-purple lines run from my foot to the calf of my bad leg. Is this a sign of blood poisoning? I am afraid to ask. The edema in both legs is still troublesome. He comes to see me twice a day although he is very busy. His manner is kind—as it is to the others—but he lingers longer at my bedside than is wise.

I walked today. The swelling has gone down, but I can't put my full weight on my right leg yet. Dr. Kung was pleased. He thinks the antibiotics are working.

The other patients who share my ward are very ill. Some have parasitic diseases, others bacterial infections that I fear will reach me. Dr. Kung says that the antibiotics will protect me. The woman in the bed next to mine died yesterday. I think she had cancer but it is hard to say with any certainty. She was in terrible pain. They provided a narcotic, but it didn't seem to help. It is cruel of me, but I was relieved when she finally died. Strange what can lift one's spirits.

There are shortages of basic medical supplies. All but the most simple surgery is impossible—especially since the surgeons seem to have disappeared. I fear they are learning from the peasants while their patients suffer and die. Dr. Kung does what he can. Today he brought me a gift—a dangerous gift but a most welcome and amazing one—a worn old copy of *A Tale of Two Cities*. The binding was cracking and a few pages were loose. Dear Dickens is my companion now. Lord only knows where Dr. Kung found him. Most of the foreign books and many of the Chinese classics have been banned or burned—counterrevolutionary. He took the precaution of a paper wrapping and suggested with a grave nod that I leave it in plain sight but with the Little Red Book resting on top of it. I recall his words when he handed it to me: "You have probably read this before, but it may seem quite different now. It's about revolution and sacrifice."

I have read my Dickens twice. It was like meeting a friend of one's youth in middle age. Everything between you has changed. I suppose Dr. Kung wanted me to understand that what is happening in China now happened before in France, that revolutions are not tea parties, that they devour their own, that human progress is slow and bloody and does not proceed in a direct line, that cruelty and virtue surface in unexpected places, that the best and worst of times are often one and the same but appear quite different to those directly involved and the generations that succeed them. I suppose Dr. Kung wants me to find some comfort in the notion that long past our time on earth, some good will have come from our suffering. But for me, and I think for China as well, these are the very worst of times.

Today I walked unaided fairly well. But I am not quite straight. Dr. Kung says that while the injury to my bone was not severe, the infection was. He is afraid that I may limp permanently because proper treatment was delayed for so long. Strange that such a prospect bothers me not at all. Perhaps, when this is all over, I will be able to forecast the weather with my leg.

My recovery goes quickly now—too quickly. Time and good treatment have almost completed their work. I fear that I will be forced to return to my work brigade soon unless they have forgotten about me. Dr. Kung tells me that disorder roams the country like a pack of wild dogs. Anarchy rules in the land of Confucius. No one knows what will happen next.

After Dr. Kung inquired about how I was feeling today, he asked me to walk outside with him, wanted to know if I felt pain, was I exercising my leg as he had instructed? He seemed both pleased and sad at my progress. He spoke to me quietly, and his words strengthened my new resolve. "You are almost well. I won't be able to keep you here much longer."

I decided to take him into my confidence, although I knew it meant endangering him further. I told him that I don't want to return to the work brigade.

He looked sorrowful and perplexed. He said, "But where will you go? There is no safe place for party people and intellectuals. Or anyone else. The tiger is loose."

I hesitated before my own audacity and what it might mean for the future—mine and Mei-ling's. Although we spoke in English, my voice was a whisper. I told him Hong Kong, that I want to leave China.

His face betrayed nothing. He did not speak, just stood there, thinking. When he did speak, it was in a grave voice. "What about your daughter?"

How like Dr. Kung to know in what direction my own thoughts were running. I replied that I must find her, that I would sooner die than leave her behind.

At that moment I could no longer avoid the most troubling thought: Perhaps Mei-ling was caught in the Red Guard madness, would be unwilling to leave despite all that had befallen her father and me. Or she would be afraid to leave? China was the place of her birth, not mine.

As if he read my thoughts, Dr. Kung said, "The voyage you wish to make will be through treacherous waters. What will you do if she refuses to board the vessel you provide for her?"

I said I would stay no matter what the consequences.

"Yes," he said, pleased, as if I had passed a test, though I did not know one was being given. He said, "Family is everything. Nothing, not even Chairman Mao, can change that."

I wonder. I do think he will help me if he can. I am quite certain of it.

This morning Dr. Kung said he wanted me to walk for longer periods of time each day. He decided to accompany me to see my progress. I limped along beside him, not without some pain but generally feeling quite well. As soon as we were by ourselves, he presented a plan. He said, "Soon I will be taking the car on another trip to the clinics for which I am responsible. I intend to take you with me."

He will say that he is returning me to my brigade because I am well enough to resume work. Instead of taking me all the way, we'll detour to a rail line that will take me to Nanjing. Dr. Kung says that the entire country is in unimaginable chaos that grows worse every day. He doubts that anyone will interfere with me since I speak the language and have legitimate identification papers. Although my appearance may arouse curiosity, with luck I should be able to reach my destination. Everyone is frightened and wants to avoid trouble. He says that if I am questioned, I must simply say that I suffered an injury in my work brigade and could no longer be useful, that I was told to return home and report to the local revolutionary committee. My leg and difficulty walking will be evidence enough.

On our return, just before we reached the hospital building, he said, "I can give you enough money to see you safely on your way, but if you hope to reach the border and beyond, bribes may be necessary—large ones, for the risk is very great. Otherwise, there is little chance that you will succeed. Perhaps you should reconsider."

I felt I must tell him about the jade in my possession. He was pleased that I was not without resources. When I asked him to take one piece for all he had done for me, he said, "But I have no need of jade. I'm almost at the end of my life."

Today, after giving me a cursory examination, Dr. Kung wrote some instructions for me. He also wrote a note on the bottom of the page: *Kung, Road of the Sea*. When I looked up, not really understanding, he said, "My nephew. I have never met him, but I've been told he trades in precious jewels. You may have need of his services once you reach Hong Kong."

When I told him that there were no words sufficient to thank him for all he had done for me, he said, "I have done nothing. It is you to whom thanks are owed. Being able to speak with you has lifted a heavy stone from my heart."

I must make a confession. I have stolen a needle and spool of thread as well as a tiny pair of scissors that will fit nicely into my pocket. Instead of remorse, I feel happiness. My contraband will help me prepare for the journey. Strange that such simple items are so difficult to obtain in China twenty years after the revolution.

I was eager to tell Dr. Kung about my preparations when he came to my bedside this morning, but the cleaning woman appeared with her bucket. I think she is a spy. When she entered, Dr. Kung finished with me quickly and passed on to the next bed.

For most of the patients, there is little he can do. With every passing hour, two of the women in my room sink deeper, nearer each moment to death. Death wheezes and chokes and smells like rancid fish all around me. As my own health returns, I feel myself withdraw from the dying. Has my heart grown hard?

Despite my fear of what lies ahead, I am eager to leave. Yet parting with Dr. Kung will be sorrowful. In him civilization still exists.

Only one week remains now. I spend my time walking and reading. I grow strong. Having twice read *A Tale of Two Cities*, I have returned to the Little Red Book. Having it before me for hours wins me the approval of the woman with the bucket. She smiles and nods when she sees me reading and copying from it, which I pretend to do when I am recording my own thoughts. Today she has genuine reason to approve of me because I preoccupy myself with Mao's thoughts and write them in my journal. Chairman Mao has such boundless faith in the masses and so little in their leaders. I quote from the Little Red Book.

> (1941) "The masses are the real heroes, while we ourselves are often childish and ignorant."
> (1945) "The people, and the people alone, are the motive force in the making of world history."
> (1955) "The masses have boundless creative power."

If these statements were an inspiration to me once, why do they depress me now? Is all that we think and feel ultimately subjective, contingent, conditional? Am I repelled now because my husband was murdered and Chen's hands cut off? Would I still believe if it were not for these horrors?

Aren't the masses capable of boundless evil when given the opportunity? Does Mao think this madness we are enduring now is actually creative? I fear so.

> (1957) "A dangerous tendency has shown itself of late among many of our personnel—an unwillingness to share the joys and hardships of the masses, a concern for personal fame and gain."

What joys of the masses—unrelenting poverty and toil? Romantic nonsense! Have not the senior cadre of the party shared more hardships than even the early Christians? And we who are younger, who have dedicated our lives to the revolution, do we deserve torture and death and banishment because we do not till the soil? We who welcomed hardships as if they were gifts? Did dear Wang deserve death because he worked day and night with his mind and heart instead of his back and hands? Surely there is evil here. Fewer hardships—an easier and pleasanter life for the masses—that is what we in the party have struggled and suffered for.

Is Mao's despotism (Dare I say that here?) the wave of the future? Is a humane socialist society one in a long line of fanciful illusions destined to be smothered by history? Or will our goal be reached at a distance too great to be traversed in a single lifetime? Perhaps so. The thought alone is a comfort.

I have experienced happiness. Its taste is bittersweet. Dr. Kung and I have journeyed together. This is the second day, our last. Soon we must part. He is beside me, steering our battered vehicle over the rutted roads. I hope that I will be able to understand what I have written on this bumpy journey. We stop to add fuel occasionally, but despite its years, the car, so like its driver, is sturdy and dependable, finely put together. We ride steadily toward our destination.

The anticipation of separation has made every moment of our time together a shared treasure. How quickly we have become dear to each other. How sorrowful will be our parting. I am certain that Wang would understand.

One is not often struck by the beauty and tensile strength of the old. Dr. Kung is beautiful, like a soapstone carving of a sage. The lines that mark his years seem an adornment. His face is long and narrow. His forehead is high beneath the receding line of his white hair, but his eyebrows remain thick and black above the dark eyes that seem to speak even when he is silent. His graceful hands and tapered fingers are steady and strong.

While we drove yesterday, he told me more of himself.

"I was born," he said, "not long after the century in the time of the Manchu dynasty, and I have flown on the wings of Sun Yat-sen and Mao through sunlight and clouds, always thinking things would be better. Often, a strong wind carried me where I did not choose to go. Yet always, even in the darkest days, my hopes would rise because I was convinced that the people of China would be delivered from their suffering. Now, in old age, I feel differently. I am bound closer to the earth, quite satisfied to help my patients as best I can and leave the future to others.''

Was he telling me that despite the crushing of our hopes, the loss of youthful illusion, an individual life still held meaning? My life as well as his own?

The roads were quite empty. Occasionally trucks and buses crammed with goods or people would pass and leave us choking in their dust. But the sky was clear and the dust soon settled. Twice we saw signs that the Red Guards had been at work—a smashed temple, its roof collapsed, shards of pottery and broken statuary strewn about, and an empty school, its windows broken, the charred remains of what had been the library standing like testimony to some vanished civilization. In its center was a pile of ash and half-burnt paper. These seemed the only surviving artifacts.

Occasionally, we rode through a busy town. Children trailed after the car as if we were a traveling theater, but nobody seemed to take note of me. If Dr. Kung stopped to pick up or drop off supplies, I stayed behind, face down on my arms, resting, my head carefully covered by my red-starred cap. He always returned quickly.

When we were hungry, we stopped by the side of the road, and though our food consisted only of the cold rice and vegetables we carried with us, it was like an old-fashioned English picnic. The day flew by as quickly as the countryside, quite green in spots, almost summery, but rocky and brown and dusty elsewhere. By the time darkness descended, we were tired. As before, we chose to avoid sleeping where our appearance together might pique curiosity. We found a niche by the side of the road. I had been prepared to unload the backseat and make my bed there, but before I could begin, Dr. Kung said, "The car will be cramped and uncomfortable. The breeze is light and from the south. Let us sleep together under the stars in the open air. We can unroll two of the pallets and cover them with blankets. We shall be warm and comfortable.''

He said this as if it were the most natural suggestion in the world. When one is young or even middle-aged, it is difficult to imagine the physical nature and desires of the old. Yet I, a generation apart, could not help but smile at my companion and set to work helping him arrange our bed upon the ground—first the pallets that were filled with a thin layer of cloth scraps, then a covering of quilted heavy cotton, and finally blankets that seemed to have been stitched together from remnants of hospital stock that still smelled of disinfectant. But the air around us was fresh and sweet.

We lay together in our clothing, close and secure in each other's warmth. The world was elsewhere. I was content to be beside him, settling myself into sleep as his hand stroked my hair and his breath warmed my neck. But in our night's repose under the stars, we found ourselves, like our first parents still in Paradise, sharing an innocent and blissful love before drifting off to sleep. Am I foolish thinking of ourselves like this? A romantic still?

We awakened early, stiff and a little cold in the morning chill, surely no longer in Eden, earthbound, entirely aware that before sunset we should have parted forever. We prepared to thrust ourselves once more into the labyrinth of a China we no longer understood.

Night has fallen. Once again I write in darkness. I am waiting for a train that will return me to my home. I pray that Mei-ling will be waiting for me. Whatever else waits there is a mystery, but it cannot be worse than what has gone before.

We reached the railroad terminal in the afternoon and were surrounded by tumult and noise. Dr. Kung carried my small bag and escorted me to the ticket office, where we shook hands and parted without words.

I did not attract much attention, just a brief, startled look from the ticket seller after I had pressed my way forward through a jostling crowd of people intent on their own purposes. He told me I would have to wait till morning, since the only train for my destination left earlier in the day. I bought my ticket and prepared to wait the long night.

The station is very dirty. Bits of paper and gobs of mucus and saliva dot the floors. Piles of dust grow in corners and crevices like mushrooms in a damp cave. The din assaults my ears. Here I write, a foreign woman in a red-starred cap, seeking a nest for the night. My legs are beginning to send a message of dull pain to my brain. No more of that.

"The East Is Red" is blaring from loudspeakers.

> The East is red
> There the sun rises
> China has brought forth
> Mao Tse-tung
> He works for the people
> He will free the nation
>
> Chairman Mao
> Loves his people
> He will lead us
> To build a new China
> He leads us on

The words seem like the voice of a disembodied spirit mocking me. Yet only a few years before, the same words seemed to have emanated from behind a burning bush. How can we know the lasting effects on the world to come of what we have done or believed? We who live in our small spot of time can only do our best with the tasks at hand and hope some good will come of it.

I must try to sleep now. Perhaps by tomorrow at this time, I will have found Mei-ling. She will have been waiting for my return. She will not have suffered as I have. She will not be a Red Guard. She will have made peace with Wang's death. She will be willing to leave for HK with me. I know that I hope for too much. It is my nature.

Here the journal ends. Mei-ling arranges the papers as she found them and turns off the lamp. She returns Emma's journal to its place in the bureau drawer and crawls into the bed beside her sleeping mother.

Mei-ling, on her way to class before the others, is walking past
the small room that serves as the teachers' lounge at Miss Richardson's School for Girls. The door is slightly ajar. The even,
clipped tones of Miss Sheriff's voice are clear. "Our Miss Wang
is not the friendly sort, but she does seem to have a good mind
and her English is splendid. Quite the scholar, don't you think?"

Then Miss Fowler, in her low, resonant voice: "Well, the Chinese day students have it all over our girls that way . . ." then
barely audible, conspiratorial, ". . . don't know about the birds
and the bees till their parents marry them off . . ." then a laugh,
". . . no distractions from their studies."

Mei-ling has never heard that particular expression before—
"the birds and the bees"—but she has no trouble understanding
what it means. And she is disappointed in Miss Fowler, who
teaches Shakespeare and Milton and rhetoric, who has graying
hair tied back in a neat bun, who doesn't play favorites, who
has given her essays the highest grades. Miss Sheriff and Miss
Fowler know very well that her mother is English even if her
own features and coloring are Chinese. Their praise is somehow
insulting. And they are ignorant; they know nothing about her
and understand less. Once more she reminds herself that it is a
mistake to expect much from anyone, anyone at all.

Although Mei-ling is only a year older than most of her classmates, and so small in stature that on first impression she seems
younger, their girlishness and innocence displease her. But it is
no more or less than she expected from the smug daughters of
English businessmen and officials. And the few Chinese girls in
her class—daughters of well-to-do merchants, Christians—seem
a hundred years younger than she and are of equally little interest. What can she possibly tell any of them about herself if
they exchange confidences? She speaks as little as possible. Her
schoolwork—a private, absorbing, orderly world—serves as an
anchorage while she waits . . . for something. Although there is
little else she can count on except her mother's burdensome anxiety, she is confident that Latin and Shakespeare will not disappear or disappoint.

Several weeks after she has begun attending classes, Mei-ling
is surprised to see Verhoeven sitting at the wheel of his cream-

colored Mercedes when she walks through the school gate at the end of the day. They had never crossed paths once she and her mother were settled into the flat he had miraculously provided for them. Her mother said he came to the office a few times a week to give her instructions and work for an hour or two, but that most of the time he attends to business elsewhere. Now he is directly across the street. Is he waiting for her?

Verhoeven raises his arm and waves her over. He says, "I'm going to the office for a little while. Would you like me to drive you home?"

He smiles charmingly when he says this, his even white teeth lined up like mah-jongg tiles, an unexpected dimple in one cheek. He pats the caramel-colored leather seat beside him. "Hop in," he says, just like one of the actors in a marvelous American film all the girls had seen as a special treat at school the previous week.

It had been wonderful, boys and girls her own age singing and dancing and riding in cars, but there was too much she didn't understand. The other girls laughed when the young people were in trouble, when what had happened to them wasn't humorous.

"Thank you, Mr. Verhoeven. That would be very nice." She opens the passenger door and slips into the seat. She knows what he will say next.

"How do you like school? Is it difficult for you?"

"I like it very much. It's not too difficult. We're reading Shakespeare."

She says this because it is true and because she thinks it is what he wants to hear. It is important to please him. Pleasing him means a roof over their heads and good food to eat.

"I'm not surprised . . . an intelligent young lady like you." He reaches over and pats her hand when he says this. His hand is cool and smooth. He smells of lotion, a lemon scent. Then he puts both hands on the wheel and heads into traffic.

Mei-ling sits up straight in her seat and looks around as they drive. So many Chinese, so few Europeans. She watches curious eyes, the eyes of strangers, turn toward them as they ease their way through the crowd in the Mercedes. It is, she thinks, pleasant to be driven about in an elegant automobile by a finely dressed man who is quite presentably handsome for someone so old.

When they arrive, Mei-ling goes into her room while Verhoeven busies himself with Emma in the front office. After he leaves, when she and her mother are having tea, Emma says, "Did your classes go well today?"

"As well as usual."

"Anything interesting, anything special?"

Mei-ling doesn't know quite what to say. Her mother is always eager to the point of desperation for some accomplishment, some . . . she doesn't know what.

"My essay about *Julius Caesar* was well received. Miss Fowler read a portion of it aloud."

Mei-ling watches as her mother's face grows pink with pleasure.

"Of course," Emma says. "Shakespeare is in your blood."

Has her mother ever before spoken with so much open pride about anything English? Mei-ling doesn't think so. About China they have not been speaking at all. She prefers that. It is another life. A terrible life.

She and Emma speak little. Mei-ling, oppressed by Emma's eager questioning, tries to avoid conversation. At their shared meals, they usually chew their way through silence. But this day, having enjoyed the ride in Verhoeven's Mercedes, Mei-ling thaws a bit toward her mother. While they are drinking their tea, she ventures conversation about a subject she has never given any thought to before: "How was your day, Mother?"

Emma, surprised, pauses for a moment before answering. "Actually, it was quite boring. Most of my days are quite boring and useless. Mr. Verhoeven's business seems to consist of only a few transactions . . . shipments to or from abroad, deliveries of small packages to offices or hotels, an occasional telephone message, picking up envelopes at the post. I don't really know what's in the packages, because everything's listed as general merchandise, could be anything from hair ribbons to heroin for all I know."

"Heroin!"

"No, of course not. And not hair ribbons either. It was just a way of saying that it's all trade and nothing to do with me. And the work, such as it is, hardly keeps me busy at all. He could get along quite well without me, but he insists he needs someone he can count on." She pauses. "And what else is there for me? This place is quite comfortable; it gives us a roof over our heads."

"Mr. Verhoeven drove me home after school today."

"Yes, he mentioned having some business in the area."

"His Mercedes has leather seats. I love the smell of leather. The seats were soft and comfortable."

"Mr. Verhoeven does seem to fancy quality. But I don't think we should continue to accept his largesse indefinitely."

"Largesse? What do you mean?"

Emma reaches for a definition that will clarify, but can't think of a satisfactory one. Finally, she says, "I'm uncomfortable receiving so much from a person who doesn't really know us and has no reason to be so generous. I suppose it's unforgivable of me to say so when he's been so kind . . . rescued us really . . . but I find Mr. Verhoeven quite mysterious at times."

"I like him."

"Naturally. He is a very charming man, and he seems to be genuinely interested in your welfare. He always inquires about Miss Richardson's . . . whether it's as good as its reputation and if you're happy there." She pauses. "I'm being unfair to him . . . and ungrateful. He probably misses having a daughter of his own."

Mei-ling plays with a rice cracker. "What will I do when I finish school?"

"The question is, what will *we* do? Once you finish school, we'll have to look to our future . . . whatever it may be. We can't depend forever on Mr. Verhoeven. I'll have to find some useful work to occupy myself. Perhaps we'll remain in Hong Kong. But it seems so lacking in culture. Of course, there's nothing left for me in England but sad memories. I was an only child, but I've told you that already. I suppose we can consider Canada. They still need people. I'd find work. You can go to university." Emma smiles, as if their prospects are already bright. "You may meet a dashing young man and decide to marry."

Mei-ling feels as if a glass of cold water has been poured on her head. It was a mistake to indulge her mother in conversation. She speaks forcefully: "I will never marry. Don't ever suggest such a thing."

She rises, turns her back on Emma, and heads for her room. But before she can leave, Emma says, "I hope you will feel differently later on. I won't be here forever. You'll need a family. Whatever happens, I want our lives . . . yours and mine . . . to be of more value than Mr. Verhoeven's business, certainly more than a Mercedes or expensive clothing."

"You make too much of everything . . . you say 'our lives' as if they were important."

"They *are* important! How could you think otherwise?"

Emma pauses a moment, then crosses further into territory they have both avoided. "But, of course you could . . . after all that's happened."

Emma takes a sip of tea, pauses to gather her thoughts. "I know that your father and I were naive in our expectations. There are times when I think we were fools who wasted our lives. Yet I don't really believe that. So much was improved after the revolution, so many lives changed for the better. China was still a feudal society. After the war, the entire country was in ruins. Naturally, we in the Party made some mistakes. There's so much I can't explain about the horrors that came later . . . why the Party went off in such a wrong direction . . . all that brutality . . . your father's death. But I've had time these few months to think: what happened to us and to China is only a small part of a great work in progress that we may not live to see completed, a heavenly city right here on earth that will be more beautiful than anyone can imagine. We're the architects who've drawn up an early imperfect sketch, but we're essential to the great work that finally emerges. China and the entire world *will* eventually be a place of comfort and happiness because of people like us and the sacrifices we've made. No possessions, no ordinary comfort, can compare to the touch of immortality that gives us."

Mei-ling listens with a mixture of pity and irritation. She can't help thinking her mother is naive as a child . . . if not stupid, blindly stupid. Wasn't it the family jade that had saved them and their devotion to communist ideals that had failed them? Wasn't it the Red Guards who were cruel to them and a kind businessman who helped them? What is all this talk of a heavenly city in some unknown future? Words that mean nothing. The Mercedes offers pleasure and comfort. It is there to be enjoyed, to go places. It is real.

Mei-ling is certain that Emma's understanding of the world is flawed, her own realistic. She is eighteen. She concludes yet again that she has only herself to rely on if she is to have any future, that it is she who will have to care for them both. With help in the beginning from Mr. Verhoeven, who has a knowledge of life that her mother lacks, who has made clear that he thinks well of her.

⁓

The following week Verhoeven is watching for her again. When he waves, she automatically gets in beside him. He takes a different route this time, less direct, one that passes some of the newer shops that the English and wealthy Chinese patronize. Mei-ling recognizes the one at which she and Emma had purchased their clothing. She loved the new clothing at once, but her mother had grumbled about the cost, about all the people who had nothing decent to wear. She had closed her ears.

Verhoeven drives slowly, as if he has nothing better to do, no other place to go. Yet she arrives home at almost the same time as usual, not late at all. They climb the stairs together.

Verhoeven opens the office door and faces Emma, who is sitting at the bare desk, pencil in hand, as if it is an instrument for thought. He greets her: "Good afternoon, Mrs. Wang. My business near Mei-ling's school allowed me the pleasure of bringing her home to you again. She tells me she will begin *Paradise Lost* next week. Becoming quite the English schoolgirl, isn't she?"

"Yes. I'm very proud of her, and I'm most grateful to you for making all this possible, but we can't allow you to do so much longer."

As Mei-ling goes to her room without speaking to her mother, she hears Verhoeven say, "Nonsense. It's only a loan."

⁓

The cream-colored Mercedes appears across the street from her school quite regularly after that, as often as twice a week. Mei-ling emerges from behind the gate, Verhoeven waves and smiles, she walks over, he pats the seat, she gets in beside him. Their route is sometimes circuitous but never lengthy enough to cause concern at home. Mei-ling is pleased that he does not ply her with questions, that the long, silent spaces between speech are not uncomfortable, that when they arrive at their destination he will say to Emma: "Mei-ling seems to be doing quite well at school."

When their arrival together begins to seem routine, Emma asks him not to trouble himself. Then he says, "It's no trouble. I was on my way past Miss Richardson's anyway. Shall we go over these papers?" They turn to business while Mei-ling goes off silently to her studies.

When alone, she tries to forget her mother, Verhoeven, her uncertain future, and her unspeakable past. She loses herself in the sad fate and extravagant poetry of Hamlet and Ophelia and Gertrude and Lear and Cordelia, the epic woes and golden words of Satan and the archangels and Adam and Eve. Or she explores the reign of Queen Victoria and her exotic prime minister, Disraeli, who wrote novels and married for money, who belonged to the English church but was really a Jew. It is right there in his name for anyone to see, but Miss Sheriff, who teaches history, never mentions it.

In China, before the Cultural Revolution, she had overheard Zhang's father speak to her father about Marx being a Jewish genius, perhaps of the rank of Confucius. But it was the only time she had heard such a thing about Karl Marx . . . the great philosopher of communism. She had been surprised that Zhang's father did not mention that Mao was greater than either.

The Mercedes is air-conditioned. One mercilessly hot, humid afternoon, when the sweat soaks through her white school shirt, forming moons under her arms and embarrassing dots of dampness at her nipples, she is pleased to find the car waiting. The rush of frigid air when she opens the door is refreshing, like a cool bath. She leans her damp back against the comforting leather of the seat.

"I thought you might need something cold to drink," he says, handing her a paper cup of lightly sweetened iced tea.

She sips from the cup and looks in his direction with just the trace of a smile on her lips. "You think of everything, Mr. Verhoeven."

He slips the car into gear and pulls into the stream of traffic while she drinks the tea. She reaches into the almost empty cup for a chunk of ice and presses it on the back of her neck till it is too small to hold and then slips the remaining fragment inside the front of her blouse. The hum of the motor and the cool air inside the car make her sleepy. Her eyes are already closing when she hears Verhoeven's voice.

"Open the glove compartment."

"The what?"

"The glove compartment . . . in front of you. Press the button." She looks straight ahead at the dashboard and sees the round fitting with a keyhole in the center that seems to be the button he means. She pushes it and the small compartment flies open.

"There's a package inside. Take it out and open it."

She reaches in and feels a soft, thin layer of paper. She pulls the package out: white tissue fastened with pink satin ribbon tied in a large bow that looks like a flower. She loosens the ribbon carefully, determined to save it. From the folds of paper she draws out a feather-light blue silk scarf printed in the design of a graceful tree branch covered with tiny flowers. Mei-ling rewards Verhoeven with a full, open smile. "Plum blossoms. How did you know?"

"Oh, a little bird told me that *Mei* meant plum blossom. And you, young lady, are quite as lovely as the flower. Your parents named you well."

She drapes the wisp of silk on her arm and holds it up, not ignoring his remark so much as absorbing it. She thinks: He is so pleasant and generous. But when she speaks, she says what she thinks appropriate, what he will be expecting: "You've given me so much already. I'm not worthy of such fine silk."

"Oh, but you are. Indeed you are."

She rests the silk on her lap. Verhoeven reaches over and rests his hand on hers for only a moment. He says, "Perhaps we'll drive a bit longer today . . . just to stay cool."

"That would be very nice. It's so comfortable in here. A car like this must cost a great deal . . . as much as some houses."

He laughs. "More than some. Everything fine and beautiful is expensive. That's the nature of things."

Verhoeven's ideas are so different from everything she has been taught. There must be more, she thinks, to the nature of things than what he says . . . or what her mother says. Flowers.

Plum blossoms. They are part of the nature of things and have nothing to do with money or politics.

"Perhaps you're partly mistaken, Mr. Verhoeven. Many fine things are costly, but flowers are beautiful and they can grow anywhere."

"They may teach you that at school, my girl, but it's not precisely true. Wild flowers are pretty enough, but they rarely thrive where people can enjoy them, and no wild rose can compare to its cultivated cousins. Flowers must be cared for and given the right conditions if they're to be worth anything. I spring from a nation of flower growers. I can assure you, they expect cold, hard cash for the beauty they produce."

Mei-ling thinks that she understands the point Verhoeven is making: In the end, everything is a matter of buying and selling and trading. She senses too, though not quite so clearly, that there will be a price to pay for the ride on the soft leather seat in the cool air of the Mercedes and the lovely silk scarf and her pretty clothes . . . because that is the way the world works. What Verhoeven says makes more sense than what her mother thinks.

While they ride, she folds the scarf neatly and wraps it again in the white tissue paper. She reaches back to her case of schoolbooks and places it inside. As she does so, her shoulder grazes Verhoeven's upper arm. When she turns back, she sees his fingers tight on the wheel and a rise of color in the flesh of his face. When they come to a stop at the solid old building that is their destination, she expects him to come up with her, but he says, "I've forgotten some papers and it's quite late in the day, so please tell your mother that I'll return tomorrow afternoon instead."

Mei-ling thinks he hasn't forgotten anything, that he wants an excuse to see her again the next day. She reaches into the backseat for her book bag and the scarf. She decides not to mention Verhoeven's gift to Emma. There is no rush to wear it. Having it is enough.

Before she can open the car door herself, Verhoeven reaches across her to the handle and pushes it open. A wall of heat rushes in. Verhoeven's long arm draws back across her torso, heavy and forceful as the heat. She steps out, a schoolgirl in a blue and white uniform. As she climbs the stairs, she decides that her life is going to be different, better, and that Verhoeven will help make it so. She feels nothing for him except curiosity, but it is not less than she feels for any man. And she does not fear him as her mother seems to.

When she walks through the iron gate the following day, Mei-ling expects Verhoeven to be waiting for her. She wonders what gift he will have. The Mercedes is there, closed against the heat. He waves as usual. As she gets in, she sees a bouquet of fresh yellow flowers resting on the backseat. She reaches for them almost as soon as she is seated. Before she can bring them forward, Verhoeven says, "I thought your mother might enjoy those."

Mei-ling drops them on the seat and turns around to look at him. He has a small smile on his face, as if he has played a trick on her. She says, "I think she will. She once told me that her parents had a flower garden when she was a small girl in England. I can't imagine my mother ever being a small girl, can you?" Why, she wonders, is she chattering on about her mother, and what is she saying about her? Let Verhoeven give her flowers if he wants to.

"I have not given the matter of your mother's childhood much thought. Did school go well today?"

"Yes, but it was very hot. I can't wait to change my clothes." Why did she say that about changing her clothes? What is the matter with her today?

For the first time, there is static in the silence between them as they drive, but the mood is pleasant enough when they go into the office together. A rotary fan stirs up a light artificial breeze.

"What lovely, lovely flowers," Emma says as Verhoeven offers them to her. "But you really shouldn't have. You've done so much for us already."

"Nonsense. The flower vendors were out in force today. I thought they would cheer up the office. It's quite drab, and you're here by yourself so much."

"How very thoughtful . . . and they will cheer the place up."

"I know you must be bored from time to time . . . being here alone . . . and I intend to see to it that you get out more often.

Business is picking up now. There will be more for you to do, perhaps even a few short trips to Macao. To that fellow Coelho you've spoken to a few times."

"Oh, yes, Mr. Coelho."

"Would that be all right? It would be a great help to me."

Mei-ling is already on her way to her room, her book bag under her arm, when she hears Emma say, "Naturally, if you need my help, that's what I'm here for. And I would welcome a change in the routine."

After that there are occasional gifts for both of them. Flowers and English books for Emma and small treasures for Mei-ling: a pink brocade change purse in the shape of a fish with tiny pearls for eyes, sandalwood soap, a carved ivory comb, an embroidered handkerchief.

Although they are still quite thin, both Mei-ling and Emma have begun to fill out, lose their pallor. They have plenty to eat and nice clothes to wear. They shop and walk together. Though they are sometimes tormented by demons while they sleep, the demons evaporate by day. Mei-ling notices that Emma's limp is less pronounced. They can sometimes speak to each other about ordinary things.

At school, Shakespeare gives way to Milton, Milton gives way to Pope, Pope gives way to Wordsworth. Wordsworth, Mei-ling thinks, is lovely to read if you don't think too much about what he is saying. At times his images remind her of the Chinese poets . . . the flowers and trees and lakes and clouds behaving like people. But at other times there is nothing at all Chinese about Wordsworth's poems. He can be quite childish. She reads again in her poetry book.

> I wandered lonely as a cloud
> That floats on high o'er vales and hills,
> When all at once I saw a crowd,
> A host, of golden daffodils;
> Beside the lake, beneath the trees,
> Fluttering and dancing in the breeze.
>
> Continuous as the stars that shine
> And twinkle on the milky way,
> They stretched in never-ending line
> Along the margin of a bay:

> Ten thousand saw I at a glance,
> Tossing their heads in sprightly dance.

No, she thinks, daffodils don't grow wild by the thousands; individual bulbs had to be planted before they could multiply. Mr. Verhoeven said the bulbs cost money, lots of it. And daffodils certainly don't dance or toss their heads. Wordsworth's daffodils are nothing like those Verhoeven had told her about. They aren't real . . . they are more beautiful than reality . . . that is the point.

Wordsworth, she thinks, is in his way like Emma, wanting to create a world in his imagination that is different and much better than the one that actually exists. His poems are so pretty and satisfying . . . no cruelty, no suffering . . . only a comfortable sadness. She thinks that is why he is called a "romantic" poet.

The word—"romantic"—is confusing. It has nothing to do with men and women and what they do to one another. It certainly has nothing to do with what flesh-and-blood people think of as making love. The girls at Miss Richardson's don't know what they are saying with their foolish talk about feeling "romantic" toward some silly boy in white flannels they saw at the cricket field.

A few of the students at Miss Richardson's are already buzzing about the prospects of engagement and marriage. With graduation looming, others are talking of a return to England with their parents. A few who are more intellectually inclined think they might continue their studies at a university. At lunch one day the conversation turned unexpectedly political.

Elizabeth Imbrie, whose father was in shipping or maritime insurance or something else to do with sea trade—Mei-ling wasn't sure—said, "My father thinks that the Communists are going to move into Hong Kong before 1997, when the British lease is up. He says that the smart money should start making plans now about what to do and where to go."

When she heard this, Mei-ling felt a chill, as if she were about to break out in the flu. Weren't they safe here? She was surprised to hear a girl who rarely spoke at meals, a Chinese day student like herself, the daughter of a prominent clothing manufacturer, say, "My father is setting up a branch of his business in Singapore, just to be safe. He says he's also going to look into Canada. He wants our family to be secure no matter what happens."

Canada. Mei-ling remembers her mother considering Canada as a place they might live one day. She wonders what that strange, distant country would be like. She read somewhere that it is very cold.

⌒

Mei-ling is delighted by the fine chain in a black velvet box. It was waiting for her in the glove compartment of the Mercedes. She is delighted but confused. She doesn't know what it is for—too small for her neck, too large for her wrist—and is embarrassed to ask. Verhoeven soon clears up the mystery.

"Ankle bracelets are the latest fashion in Europe and America. All the young girls love them."

He hands her a copy of *Elle* open to a page of long-legged girls in bikinis frolicking at the beach, each one sporting a chain on one ankle. She looks at the photograph intently. They all seem to be without a care in the world, rising into the air like waves, beautiful, with their hair flying and eyes laughing and smiles as wide as the horizon. She wants to be just like them. Is it possible to erase the past?

The ankle bracelet Verhoeven has just given her is different from his other gifts; it is gold. He has never presented her with jewelry before. She is quite confident that Mr. Verhoeven has something special in mind, that the chain links them together.

Verhoeven parks the car, and they climb the stairs. Mei-ling expects Emma to be waiting for them as usual. But she isn't there. During the past few months, Emma has been away for several hours at a time on business matters for Mr. Verhoeven. But if she is going to be away, she has always told Mei-ling in advance. Mei-ling turns to Verhoeven and says, "Mother must have stepped out a moment."

"No, she won't be back till tomorrow. Didn't she leave you a note? She said she would."

Mei-ling sees a white sheet of paper held fast by the edge of the lamp base. She picks it up and reads it.

Dear Mei-ling,

A matter has come up that requires me to be away overnight in Macao—a matter of some importance to Mr. Verhoeven and his associate, Mr. Coelho. Mr. Verhoeven knows where to reach me if you should need me for any reason. I will return tomorrow.

Forgive me for not letting you know in advance. All this came up after you had already left for school. I look forward to seeing you tomorrow.

Affectionately,
Mother

Mei-ling puts the note down. "Why didn't you tell me she wouldn't be here?"

"I had quite forgotten. And you were busy with your ankle bracelet. Besides, what does it matter? You aren't afraid to be alone, are you, at your age?"

Mei-ling realizes that for the first time since they left the mainland together, she will be separated from her mother overnight. But, she thinks, Verhoeven is right: What does it matter? She says, "No. I'm fine."

"Good. Now make us some tea while I go over a few papers."

He taps her behind as if to shoo her out of the office, playfully, familiarly, as if it is his right. Suddenly, everything is different between them. The gold ankle chain is the first piece of precious jewelry he has given her. Perhaps it will not be the last. And, of course, as he has made clear, he will expect something of value in return. She knows what it is.

After she puts the kettle up to boil on the hot plate, Mei-ling scrubs herself with a damp cotton washcloth and changes from her formal school uniform and tight stockings to a loose white cotton shift that she ties at the waist with a red and white sash. She leaves her legs bare and slips her feet into a pair of thongs with thick cork soles. Then she opens a package of sweet biscuits and lays the table for tea.

She feels nothing—not hope, not fear, not anger—nothing perhaps except a dull curiosity. What can Mr. Verhoeven expect of her that would be more terrible than what had already happened? He will not be as cruel and brutal as the men on the train had been. It is clear that he wants to be kind to her. He is kind. And generous. She turns the heat down when the water comes to a boil . . . and waits.

When Verhoeven comes in from the office, Mei-ling faces him directly but says nothing. She watches him look down at her small, unstockinged feet, the shiny nails, her delicate toes nestled against one another, the curved line of her instep, the shapely indentation of her ankle—all of which she has never seen the same way before. His voice is husky when he says, "Where is your new ankle bracelet? You must let me put it on for you."

She turns off the heat under the simmering kettle and goes into the bedroom. When she returns with the gold chain in her hand, Verhoeven is sitting on the floral sofa. He pats the seat beside him but doesn't smile as in the Mercedes. He takes the chain from her and, although his hand is trembling slightly, he leans over and fastens it to her ankle. Then he runs his cool hand slowly and smoothly up her leg while she leans back and closes her eyes.

Chicago

DAVID LEVY'S THROAT is still sore from the gas. He is lying in bed in the dark, near naked, alone in the hot, quiet night. The sirens have stopped screaming. But he cannot sleep. He is too charged up, agitated. Where, he wonders, has Pete disappeared to?

When he closes his eyes, images come crowding in. Frames from a surrealist movie: the army of chanting and singing war protesters overflowing the park; police fencing them in like barbed wire; foul-mouthed crazies (who are they?) and pumped-up Yipees (friends? allies? weirdo freaks?) hamming it up for the cameras; gas-masked National Guardsmen piling out of their trucks like aliens invading from outer space; a sudden choking mist; the crowd stampeding like a herd of prairie buffalo. Levy opens his eyes and the pictures go away, but the stinging doesn't. He takes a drink of ice water from the table beside the bed, closes his eyes again, and tries to calm down.

A vision of Carrie appears before him in a flowered Mexican blouse and jeans, her neat round bottom embroidered in red with *End the War,* her hair a thick wheat-colored braid that reaches almost to her waist, her thin, gentile face serious and serene. An erection rises. He helps it along. He comes and is happy, relieved. He dips his fingers in the milky juice. But after he wipes the stuff off, he is depressed. Once again it is not the real thing. Carrie is in Boston, he is in Chicago, and he is still a virgin. He is twenty-one. Why can't he be more aggressive? None of the girls holds back anymore, so why doesn't he do it with someone else? It doesn't have to be with the girl he loves. Nobody believes in that anymore. Nobody? How about him? It's embarrassing. Should he see a shrink?

Levy's mind wanders to his feet. They still feel as if he has been walking on ground glass. He remembers sinking down on the sidewalk and leaning against the front of a men's haberdashery store, wiping his sweating face and streaming eyes with a handkerchief, gasping for breath in the suffocating air, concentrating on breathing. His throat and eyes burn. He coughs and is afraid he will vomit, but the sour taste of bile reaches the back of his mouth and stops there. The crowd is scattering in panic around him. He asks himself: Can this really be happening here in Chicago at the 1968 national convention of the Democratic Party? With the whole world watching on television? He is certain that people are going to be killed! He should move on, but he doesn't stand up. He doesn't think he can.

It is, Levy thinks, like being in a movie, but real, not reel: the police pushing their horses against clusters of choking demonstrators, backing them into plate-glass windows that crack under the pressure and shower them with shards of glass. Blood dripping like greasepaint down frightened, bewildered faces. The crowd dashing past his outstretched feet, his eyes at the level of their knees, a dog's view of the world. He sees the high leather boot beside him at the same moment the billy club smashes into the soles of his soft summer sneakers. The blow flashes from his toes to his skull in an instant. He cries out. A voice snarls, "Outa here, fucking wise-ass scum. No loitering in the streets." The law!

He is scrambling to his feet, stumbling along, immersing himself in a gathering of pilgrims—a mass baptism in pools of tear gas and blood. A cop is yelling, "Get the nigger-lovers."

Only minutes earlier they had been in Grant Park across from the Hilton. The crowd was so thick, you couldn't see the grass, and the cameras were telling the world they were there and Lyndon Johnson wasn't. It was great. "Hell no, we won't go." "Out of Vietnam now." He remembers a few guys near him—definitely not "clean for Gene" types—yelling "Kill the pigs," "Off the cops." He was worried the cameras would pick it up, they'd hurt the cause. Then someone was lowering an American flag, and he was watching it happen. A couple of other guys were raising a red flag, homemade, not Vietnamese or Chinese or Soviet, just red. Were they deliberately enraging the police, waving a red cape in front of the bull? Could they be undercover cops planted there to provoke the crowd into something stupid, to give the cops an excuse for whatever happened? His father told him about things like that. Provocateurs. Was he getting paranoid? Suddenly, the police—shielded and armed, massed in ranks like a Vandal horde out of the Dark Ages—were sweeping over the crowd, swinging their clubs.

The demonstrators were trying to hold their ground, chanting for the cameras: "The whole world is watching, the whole world is watching." The cops were forcing them closer and closer together till it was hard to stand or breathe. He remembers hearing the boom and hiss of the tear gas canisters being released, not knowing what it was till the air filled with the gas and the crowd surged crazily forward to escape. He was looking around for Pete, who had traveled with him from Cambridge, who always towered above any crowd, but Pete wasn't there.

Lying in bed now, safe, he imagines himself fighting back instead of running: raising barricades, hurling stones, tumbling cops to the ground by scattering marbles under their horses' hoofs. Someone—he didn't remember who it was—once told him it could be done. But his political fantasies are as brief and unsatisfying as his sexual ones. This isn't a game of cops and marbles. It's real . . . they lost.

What, he wonders, is the antiwar movement going to do now? Even before tonight, some of the crazier radicals on campus were making noises about arming themselves, waging guerrilla war, as if they were Vietnamese peasants or Che Guevara in Bolivia. A few had armed themselves with berets that they tucked into their bureau drawers along with their joints and the odd available manual on explosives or people's revolution. Levy smiles to himself as he imagines a stoned regiment in berets and Dunham hiking boots practicing guerrilla war at Walden Pond when they aren't busy studying for exams. Just what, he wonders, do they think they're going to blow up, and why? "Loony," he says aloud to himself, "plain loony." They make him nervous. But, he thinks, who could blame them for going off the deep end when the war is blazing away with no sign of ending? Even Pete, who is generally sane, has been making direct action noises lately. But what kind of action? What would they accomplish? Lots of noisy politics got rid of LBJ, not guns.

Although he is uneasy about what may have happened to Pete, David is grateful for his time alone, time he needs to arrange his thoughts, fit the events of the night into a pattern that makes sense. Should he go back to Harvard after a night like this? Only a year till graduation. Should he drop out? Put his body on the line? What line? Nothing violent, but resist violence actively— like Thoreau, like Gandhi, like Martin Luther King. If only people would behave decently, Levy thinks, do right, live up to their highest ideals (actually to his, but he is too young to understand the distinction).

Lying there, hot and restless, Levy's mind wanders further back in time.

1965. He is in his first year at Harvard, feeling as if he has landed in a spaceship, has been beamed up from the Union Park Co-ops in the Bronx to this sacred place. A faulty control, a mistake. He and Pete are rooming together, getting acquainted, getting along though born on different planets. Pete puts a copy of *The New York Times* on his bed with an article circled in red. A man named Norman Morrison has just made the supreme sacrifice. There is no photograph, but the grisly details of his story are picture enough. Levy wonders if anyone but he still remembers the horrible image it conjured up: a ball of fire; the charred and blackened body on the Pentagon steps: a young man nobody seemed to know dousing himself with liquid, setting himself ablaze, dying in flames to protest the Vietnam War. A martyr. He turned out to be a Quaker, opposed to violence. It was hard to fathom.

Morrison *did* something important to protest the killing, Levy thinks, something that caught people's attention, made them come to grips with the evil the U.S. was doing in Vietnam. But he is not ready to go up in flames anymore now than he was then, when he first read Morrison's story. Life is the point, he tells himself, not death. Isn't it? He begins to wonder (not for the first time) if he lacks physical courage, if he is afraid of suffering for his convictions.

1964. He is still living with his parents, leaving his house every morning with a brown paper bag in which his mother has packed a tasty, nourishing lunch—chicken or tuna or egg salad on bakery rye, an apple or a banana, and a cupcake or chocolate-covered doughnut. It is toward the end of his senior year at the Bronx High School of Science: he has just turned eighteen; he is captain of the track team; he has been accepted at Harvard; his parents expect him to walk on water any day now. He would like to save the world, especially oppressed blacks. But when he hears about the voter registration drive in Mississippi, about the call for volunteers, he holds back. Fat-bellied southern sheriffs, snarling attack dogs, rednecks with beer cans and rifles and light, steely eyes, all loom up in his mind like furies. He sees his mother (who has done her own share of demonstrating years before) weeping herself to sleep every night while he is away. This last convenient image persuades him. He will join something useful when he gets to Harvard. He isn't sure of exactly what it will be.

Then the terrible headlines. Philadelphia, Mississippi. Andrew Goodman and Michael Schwerner—New York Jews from left-wing families, guys just like himself—murdered and dumped in a ditch with James Chaney, a local black they were working with, trying to register voters. It could have been him. But it wasn't! While they were being buried, he was getting ready for college. And he was *glad* he was alive! But he knew in his gut that he owed someone something.

Tonight, in sleepless, hot Chicago, David Levy wonders if it isn't time to pay off.

〜

Just as the first tug of sleepiness begins to settle him down, Levy hears the door open and slam shut. Pete has arrived. David is relieved and wide awake again. He has often noted that even in ordinary things—entering a room or jogging or folding himself into the seat of a car—Pete makes a vivid impression. Not surprising, since he is six feet six inches tall, broad-shouldered, long-armed as a basketball center, and a nonstop talker. He is talking now.

"Dave, am I glad you're here. I've been looking all over the place. The whole town's been gassed. It's a fucking police state. A goddamn fascist takeover in Chicago."

"I know. It's been fucking wild. My throat's like sandpaper from the gas and my feet got clubbed. It still feels like I'm walking on broken glass." He turns on the light switch. "What about you? Any damage?"

Peter ignores the question. He scans the room as if searching for hidden danger. "Everything's going to be different after tonight." He asks David, "Where've you been?"

"The street mostly. The gas was awful, but I got back a while ago. I couldn't find you. I was starting to worry." He looks up at Peter in the soft light. "I hope you feel better than you look, 'cause you look like you ran into a truck."

Peter's right eye is swollen shut and his nose is considerably larger than it was a few hours earlier. A bloody gash runs from his cheekbone to his jaw. He says, "Actually, the long arm of the law reached down from his horse with considerable force to achieve this effect. It hurts like hell."

At this particular moment Peter Parsons looks nothing like the eldest son of a family descended from Dutch and English gentry, a Harvard legacy for generations back. But, bruised and bloody as he is, he remains self-assured. He lopes into the kitchen and pours a tall glass of orange juice. He drinks it down, smiles, and sighs. "Much better. Anything stronger around?"

"Some beer in the fridge."

The blood on Peter's face is bright and still runny. David reaches up and touches two fingers to the puffed eye and slit cheek and shudders a little. He says, "Right now you're uglier than Godzilla. We better get you cleaned up."

The odd couple—Levy, compact and wiry, unruly red hair framing his intense dark-eyed face like a ragged halo; Parsons, almost a head taller, dark blond hair falling into neat waves that accent the fine bones under his bruised skin, one clear blue eye wide open, not missing anything—squeeze themselves into the tiny bathroom. The bright light emphasizes the billy-club damage. Peter sits on the lid of the toilet, talking, while David makes do with a washcloth and some peroxide he finds in the medicine cabinet. Peter winces as David dabs the disinfectant, but his mind is elsewhere.

"Did you hear about what's happening at the convention . . . Dan Rather and Mike Wallace getting slugged by Daley's security people? The shit has definitely been hitting the fan. Almost everything is on television. The country is going to be with us, Dave. It wouldn't shock me to have my dear old Republican dad go along with us just this once. There's nothing he hates more than an Irish pol like Daley. Thinks they were the beginning of the end for the country."

He giggles, still giddy with fear and exhilaration, as if he had ingested laughing gas instead of tear gas. He gives David a light, playful punch in the belly.

"Cut it out. I'm almost done. Try to keep still, including the mouth. And I wouldn't count too hard on your dad. He's going to be real pissed when he sees you looking like someone who went a few rounds with Rocky Marciano. Does he know you're in Chicago?"

"Hell no! He'd be having fits and blaming my mother because she voted for Roosevelt before I was born. He never forgave her for it. He trots the story out every four years." Peter's voice is buoyant, but he winces as David lifts a small ball of clotted blood from his cheek.

"If he gives you a hard time, you can always blame Harvard and the radical professors. It's the best excuse for everything from a nervous breakdown to the clap. And he won't want you to quit or be expelled."

"He'd kill me if I quit . . . but maybe I ought to . . . do something real for once. Hell. What's the point of going back to the books after all this? A Harvard degree is just a door-opener if you think about it."

"Door-opener? First time I heard it called that." Levy pauses, realizes that things will work out for Parsons no matter what, as they do for most people who are rich and well connected. He says, "Hey, don't listen to me. Do what feels right."

"I can always go back later if I want to. Now it's the war that counts. If we're serious, we should be taking on the government, stop the whole fucking machine from working till they stop the killing."

"Yeah, but how?" David rinses the cloth in fresh water. The water turns pink. "Hey, I don't like the way this looks. It starts bleeding again as soon as I clear up where it's clotted. I probably should get you to a doctor. You might need a few stitches."

"No doctor. Just give me the cloth to hold against my cheek. Let's turn on the TV. It's late, but they may be replaying what's been happening."

The tube fills with light as they sit facing it. An offscreen voice is saying, ". . . this tumultuous night and the events that led up to it." Scenes of battle appear on the screen: a montage of G.I.'s poking bayonets into thatched huts, helicopters evacuating wounded soldiers, bombs dropping loads that explode in fireballs seconds later, American top brass confidently assuring the country of "the light at the end of the tunnel," children stripped naked by explosions running like rabbits down cratered streets, young Americans burning their draft cards in front of the Pentagon, an aging, solemn Lyndon Johnson announcing to the American people that ". . . there is division in the American house now . . . I shall not seek, and will not accept, the nomination of my party for another term as your president."

David shouts and applauds as if this were fresh news. "Way to go, Lyndon."

Peter says, "We'll just get another bastard instead. Humphrey's not exactly my idea of progress. Face it. The system is rotten. You can't trust the guys in power. Anyone over thirty has a stake in keeping the lid on. That's the way history works. Everywhere, not just here. Look at what happened in France. Even the Communists were against the students, sided with De Gaulle when it was showdown time."

"But we got rid of Johnson, people like us, and I'm barely old enough to vote. Think of what'll happen when eighteen-year-olds vote. It's coming soon."

Before Peter can reply, their eyes are drawn again to the screen, where a reporter is interviewing a handsome young black man named Robert Moses, the coordinator of the voter registration drive in Mississippi for the past several years, a legendary figure among activists on campus. Moses is a Harvard graduate David and Peter have heard about, but this is the first time they actually see and hear him. He is earnestly voicing a plea for "principle in politics."

David can hardly contain his enthusiasm. He bounces in his seat. "Moses ought to run for president someday." He laughs. "When he's old enough."

Peter shrugs. "You are a dreamer, Levy, if you think the 'democratic process' is the answer to all our troubles. Have an election, sign a few bills, wave a wand, and racism disappears. Moses is a great guy, the greatest, but he'll be lucky if he doesn't end up with a bullet in his back from some cracker sheriff. They don't care that he went to Harvard. In fact, it might make pulling the trigger more fun."

Before they can carry the conversation further, the amiable plastic face of Hubert H. Humphrey appears on the screen.

Peter scowls and gets up. "I can't stand this guy's bullshit."

He stalks off to the kitchen, where he rinses the cloth that he has been holding to his cheek. He reaches into the refrigerator for more orange juice and takes the container and two glasses back to the living room with him. On the screen is old footage of Martin Luther King, Jr., speaking at the Lincoln Memorial.

"Hard to believe he's dead," Levy says.

"Maybe he's lucky." Peter sees David blanch and explains. "He was good for his time, but times are changing fast. He was starting to be irrelevant."

"Just because some loudmouths . . ."

Levy is agitated, but as the camera pans from the massive stone replica of Abraham Lincoln to the serried ranks of upturned faces—black and white—being carried skyward by the burnished cadences, the majestic vision, both he and Peter grow silent.

I have a dream that one day on the red hills of Georgia the sons of former slaves and the sons of former slaveowners will be able to sit down together. . . .

The image disappears, to be replaced by President Lyndon Johnson signing the Voting Rights Act in 1965.

Levy says, "At least he did one decent thing."

"Doesn't mean a fucking thing."

"No?"

"No. The cops are still racist pigs. And they have the guns."

"But now the law is on our side even if the cops aren't. Everything can't happen overnight."

"Window dressing. Wait till . . ."

Their attention is drawn to a drama onscreen, an incident the announcer says took place earlier that evening. The handsome, urbane governor of Connecticut, Abraham Ribicoff, political ally and friend of the martyred John Kennedy (the same Irish lad who in life was Mayor Daley's darling boy), stands on the podium and in a trembling voice rails about the police using

Gestapo tactics against the young people on the streets of Chicago, whereupon the chunky, pugnacious mayor of the city rises
from the audience and shouts something that is unintelligible to
the viewer but which clearly shocks those nearby.

"Could you make out what he said?" asks Peter.

"No, but it must have been a mouthful."

The mayor is enraged, out of control. They don't need his
literal remarks to catch their spirit. Having experienced the Chicago police at first hand, they are amazed that Ribicoff, a mere
liberal, a Democratic Party insider, should have risen to their
defense.

Peter says, "Hot damn! Will wonders never cease? I could
vote for that man if I thought voting made any sense at this
point."

David nods his smiling agreement, but the smile is tangential
to his private thought: Ribicoff's a Jew . . . he's got an early
warning system . . . it's not politics . . . it's gut . . . he's scared of
what happened tonight. (When, within a few days, David learns
what many within hearing distance say the mayor shouted at
Ribicoff—"Fuck you, you Jew son of a bitch, you lousy motherfucker, go home."—he is stunned and frightened himself, finds
it hard to believe. This is America!) At the moment, however,
David feels a touch of pride in the ancient tie between himself
and the popular governor. Shame too, because he views religious
and ethnic bonds as irrelevant to the brotherhood of the young
and the good that will soon reshape the world in its own image.
It is happening already, he thinks, in France, Czechoslovakia,
Cuba, and in China, where the Red Guards—kids younger than
he is—are waging the Cultural Revolution without dropping a
single bomb, a revolution welling up from the people not coming
from the top down. David recalls a phrase of Mao's he heard
or read somewhere: "the boundless creative power of the
masses." He loves the sound of it. It does not strike him as
incompatible with democracy. Quite the contrary. It is masses
of young people, his generation, who will sweep away the past
and its evils. About that at least, he and Peter completely agree.

The tear gassing and clubbing he has suffered earlier takes on
a brighter meaning. Despite everything, he is glad to be in Chicago. He is part of history. Someday he will tell his children
about it. He laughs to himself. It is the first time he has ever
thought about having children of his own. When he looks up,

he sees Peter scowling again. This time it is Richard M. Nixon's face that fills the screen.

⌒

David and Peter are sitting side by side. It is late afternoon. The bus is humming its way through Indiana, but they are still re-hashing Chicago. Pete says, "The country is going to be different after this."

"Do you think Chicago was a turning point?"

Peter scarcely pauses before answering. "I think the Fascists showed their true colors. It's pretty clear now that all the weap-ons are in their hands. Songs and peaceful protests and even passive resistance just won't do it for us. Not that I'm sure yet exactly what will. But we'll have to fight back with more than slogans."

"You don't mean guns or anything like that?"

"What else can you suggest when the other side has them and uses them?"

David's throat constricts. He waits before speaking. "I can't imagine myself shooting at anyone."

"Not to defend yourself? Not even when blacks who defend themselves are being gunned down while the cops look the other way or do the shooting? Look at what's happened to the Black Panthers."

"Yeah, but the Panthers' guns didn't help them. Look, it was bad at the convention, really bad, but the cops didn't shoot. Nobody was killed."

"We're white. But it will come to that if we get in their way, and we'd better be prepared. It's live bombs and bullets in Viet-nam, and Americans are using them. The My Lai massacre? Napalm? If we don't end that, who will? If the cops try to stop us from demonstrating and protesting, should we just lie down in front of them and think of Gandhi? Don't forget, the army was out there last night too."

"It was the National Guard."

"When did you become such a stickler for accuracy? You know what I mean. It was the government."

"Hey, Pete, I hated what they were doing as much as you did, but what sense does it make for me to pick up a gun here if I'm morally opposed to killing people anywhere?"

"If we're serious about changing things, we have to prepare ourselves for any eventuality."

"But who am I supposed to shoot? What am I supposed to blow up? Lyndon Johnson? We got rid of him by nonviolence. Besides, we've had enough assassinations to last awhile."

"I'm not talking about assassination. I'm talking about defending ourselves."

"You're talking about getting ourselves killed for acting like damn fools. We'll be mowed down if we arm ourselves . . . and we won't gain or prove anything. What's going on in your head?"

"It's clear as can be, Dave, it's right here in the land of the greedy and the home of the needy, where the real struggle is going to happen. And after Chicago, I'm pretty sure guns are going to happen too . . . whether we like it or not. We'd better prepare ourselves."

David is silent a moment. Then he says, "I just can't see college boys packing pistols. That's not the way things happen in this country, not now anyhow."

"The draft is what's happening now in this country, and I'm not going into the army. What are you going to do when Uncle Sam wants you?"

David remembers the sticker he saw plastered to an army recruiting station in Times Square last year. It said SEE CANADA NOW. He says, "I've been wondering about Canada or maybe even Sweden, if I can pick up the language. But it would kill my folks if I left." He pauses and laughs. "Hell, it would also kill them if I went to Vietnam. And it might just kill me too."

"I think we should stay and fight it out here even if it means winding up in the slammer. There's worse places. Anyway, I'm sure as hell not going to Vietnam to kill innocent peasants so that the world can be safe from communism."

"Yeah, but I'd rather be in Canada than in jail."

⌒

At dawn, having slept on and off through the night, David Levy and Peter Parsons are silent as the bus winds its way toward Cambridge through the undulating countryside of upstate New York. Traffic has not yet begun to build. As they head east into the lambent sunrise that ascends from deep pink to peach to lavender to blue, they are gathered into the green beauty of the late summer landscape: the shapely vineyards with grapes dangling like jewels from well-tended vines; spreading fields of tall corn festooned with tassels of silk; hillsides of apple orchards, each tree studded with ripening fruit. Here and there a farmhouse, a barn, a steeple, a small town in the distance. No weeds in the fields, no parasites on the trees, no peeling paint on the houses, no children crying. Distance lends enchantment.

It is, David thinks, like a scene from "America the Beautiful," the song he had sung as a child in school. The window next to them is open to the cool morning air. In the refreshing mist, the smell of tear gas that had clung to them since Chicago vanishes. As he looks out at the hills and fields, a surge of powerful feeling he can't explain surprises him.

Peter, speaking softly, breaks the silence. "Don't you wish it could always be like this . . . for everyone?"

David feels no need to answer. Pete knows the answer. That's why they're here together. They ride in silence for a bit, college boys, the weight of the world on their shoulders, a vision of future possibility before their eyes. Then David turns away from the landscape toward Peter. "It's possible to love a country and hate what it's doing. There's no contradiction that I can see. I sometimes feel that way about my mother or father."

Peter thinks a moment and says, "Nah, a country is only an abstraction. Your mother isn't. It's a myth—loving your country—and the government uses it to get everyone worked up to go to war. Nationalism is a dead idea . . . like religion. Borders are going to disappear. In a hundred years we'll be thinking it was some kind of superstition."

David thinks that Peter is probably right. Yet he cannot deny the moment, the feeling, the pride in belonging here. It is all so defiantly beautiful, as if it were a poem or a dream. It will be very hard to leave when the time comes.

Montreal

An explosion that reverberates like thunder sends a shudder through forty-two floors of the Commonwealth Bank's flagship building in central Montreal—all the way to the top floor, where Jackson Ramsden's right hand grips the telephone hard. His photo of Celia and the boys tilts facedown and crashes into the black onyx ashtray on his polished mahogany desk. He hears the glass break at the same moment Claude Boisvert shouts into the telephone: "Hello, hello. *Mon Dieu,* what happened? Are you all right?"

Ramsden's voice is controlled but cannot suppress a faint tremor. "I think so."

Suddenly, he would like to slam the phone into its cradle. It is extremely distasteful to be speaking to one of the French, even a client as rational and potentially valuable as Boisvert. If it weren't for the bank, he would have nothing to do with any of them.

At the other end of the line, Boisvert says what they are both thinking: "I hope it's not some of those crazy fools from the Front de la Liberation de Québec."

Ramsden doesn't want to discuss the fine points of Quebec politics with Claude Boisvert; he is convinced that by one means or another the French in Quebec, all of them, want to take over the entire province, won't rest till they rip Canada apart and bring the economy to its knees. Deliberately changing the subject, he says, "They're doing construction in the street. Perhaps it was an accident at the site. I suppose we'll know soon enough if anyone was hurt." He mops his brow with his handkerchief.

"Do you still want to meet for lunch today? We can postpone it." Incongruously, Boisvert chuckles loudly enough to be heard.

Ramsden wonders: nervousness? perverse satisfaction because the English are vulnerable? What goes on in their minds?

When Ramsden doesn't answer immediately, Boisvert attempts a weak joke. "Not too long, of course. We need the money."

"I wouldn't hear of postponing, Claude. Shall we meet at one, Chez Claire?"

"*Oui*. Very good."

Ramsden rests the phone in its cradle and wipes his sweating upper lip with a handkerchief. Then he decides to telephone Celia. Ramsden picks up the shattered picture frame on his desk and loosens the broken shards of glass. He tosses them into the wastebasket and stands the photo of his family in its customary position. He looks at Celia, himself, the boys. Now that the glass has been shattered, the glossy photograph is exposed to the elements. They are vulnerable. What will happen to them, he wonders, if the FLQ succeeds? Will they have to leave Montreal, move to Toronto or Ottawa? What about the bank itself? It oppresses him to think how many families and businesses have already packed up and relocated, some as far away as Vancouver . . . as if a tornado had carried them off.

Ramsden dials his home. He knows that Celia will answer on the third ring. She always answers on the third ring unless she is in the shower. It is Wednesday. Veal on Wednesday. Chicken on Friday, beef or lamb chops most other days. On a Tuesday or a Thursday they go to the theater or a concert, to a "foreign" restaurant by themselves or with friends on Saturday, to visit her parents with the boys twice a month on Sunday, to a film when it is convenient.

Each year since the boys were old enough to be left in the care of her parents, they have taken a winter holiday in the Caribbean, either Jamaica or Barbados. They read novels, swim in the turquoise sea, play golf and tennis. Celia has kept her figure and still looks fetching in a swimsuit, though her thighs are a bit looser than they were. He's noticed that they shake like jelly when she runs along the beach.

The phone is ringing for the third time. Ramsden relaxes into a smile as he waits for her to answer.

"Good morning."

"Jack here."

She is surprised to hear from him. Not long before, they had breakfasted together as usual: warm brioche spread with apricot preserves, the Blue Mountain Jamaican coffee she brews fresh every morning. "Did you forget something, Jack? Shall I run it over on my way to the hospital?"

"No. Nothing like that. I just wanted to catch you before you heard anything on the radio and started to worry."

"What's happened? Are you all right?"

"I'm fine. Apparently the FLQ has been at it again though. It's not certain yet, but they seem to have planted some explosives in the lobby of the bank. Sounded worse than it was, I'm told."

"Was anyone hurt? Good Lord, I hope they haven't killed anyone again."

Ramsden hears a tremor in her voice, seeks to reassure her. "Mostly damage to the lobby. All that expensive marble."

"It's frightening. They seem to target financial centers."

Jack, recalling the old bank-robber joke, is surprised to hear himself laugh. He says, "That's where the money is, Celia. I suppose they consider banks symbolic. Try not to worry. Soon they'll find another target for their lunacy."

"Well, I wish they'd stop their infernal bombs and give us some peace."

"So do I, but it's important that they interfere with our lives as little as possible. I've got to get back to work now."

"Take care of yourself, Jack. I'll see you tonight. Veal for dinner."

He smiles. As if he doesn't know! But he doesn't go back to work. He can't concentrate on the documents in front of him, allows his thoughts to ramble, makes a decision to vacation in Barbados this year because it is safe. He has read about tourists in Jamaica being killed by bandits with machetes and robbed at gunpoint in their hotel rooms. Well, he thinks, the barbarians are at the gate everywhere these days, civilization going down the drain fast. Why, he wonders, are so many people bent on destroying orderly government when they need it if their lives are going to be decent? It's irrational!

~

Boisvert has spent the morning brooding over the explosion. The moment his words to Ramsden about the FLQ were out of his mouth, he regretted them, felt like a traitor. But why? He meant what he said. The FLQ had the entire province in turmoil since they began with their damned explosives. Five years of madness. He doesn't like the English any more than they do, but one has to do business with them. Still, he should not have spoken to Ramsden as he did. What would the children say if they heard him?

At times Boisvert thinks it would serve the English right if all of Quebec were French-speaking in ten years. If Simone has any-thing to say, he thinks, everything will be French and the English can learn or leave. It would be what they deserved, the way they'd kept the best jobs and the money for themselves all these years. And so smug and self-righteous about it.

But Boisvert is uneasy thinking about Simone, the most intel-ligent of his children: her radical ideas, her posters on the walls, her boyfriends who are forever in need of shaves and haircuts, who don't know the first thing about putting bread on the table, who never seem to think of marriage, who might wind up in prison and take his daughter with them. He shudders at the thought. What good is a Jeanne d'Arc for a daughter? He wants grandchildren. He has earned them.

Boisvert reaches for one of his antacid tablets, wonders how he'll be able to enjoy lunch with the sour juices erupting in his stomach. The restaurant has a fine chef. And Ramsden will be paying. Boisvert hates the idea of not being able to enjoy a good free meal and hopes the tablets will do the trick. He has worked hard for his money, and now the hotheads in the FLQ were going crazy, threatening to ruin everything with their separatist lunacy. And who were they? Not hardworking men like himself who had mastered English and business management on their

own, who had been able to cut themselves a generous wedge of
the pie without making a lot of noise about it. No, they were
the young, the educated, the privileged, the ones who had never
soiled their hands with hard work, the ones who wore work-
ingmen's overalls as a costume while they sat in cafés. He spat
some sour-tasting phlegm into his handkerchief.

He is beginning to think that the French have made mistakes
in the past: listened to their priests too much and went out into
the world too little, crucifixes over their beds instead of cash in
their pockets, letting the world pass them by.

Why shouldn't more of the French—men like himself—
succeed in business instead of being content to hew the wood
and haul the water and say their prayers while the English
lived in fine homes and wore fine clothes and traveled to the
capitals of the world? If he could gain something by doing
business with the English, he would. He didn't have to like
them. Why shouldn't he see Paris and London too? And why
should he let the FLQ stop him? They were nothing but a
bunch of fanatics who wanted to bring everything down with
their bombs. What did Simone know about the real world?
She had never had to worry about earning her bread. He had
done it for her.

As for Ramsden at the bank, he seems a decent enough fellow,
though something of a prude, like so many of them. Boisvert
reaches into his desk for the loan agreement he and Ramsden
have worked out. He is pleased with it. The business will be able
to expand. He puts the papers into his briefcase, a Hermès black
leather imported from France. Expensive. The smell of good
leather pleases him. Then he gets up to wash and change clothing, prepare himself for lunch.

Boisvert washes his face in the small private bathroom next
to his office. He admires his thick dark hair and high cheekbones
and the cleft in his chin that still drives the women crazy. When
he was younger, he had worried about the slight slant of his
eyes, thought it might reveal a trace of Indian blood. But now
that he is rich and about to get richer, he thinks his eyes as
handsome as the rest of him. God (if it was He who was responsible) has blessed him. Boisvert puts on a white shirt and
red and blue foulard tie, a navy blue suit tailored in London.
He has learned a thing or two about how to do business with
the English.

Boisvert's stomach is calming down. He is looking forward to the food and wine and, of course, the money once the loan goes through. As for the FLQ, he thinks, they are small in number and influence even if they make a big noise. He absentmindedly crosses himself in the mirror.

Part Three

1973

Amsterdam

WHEN THE PLANE lands at Schipol Airport, a thin drizzle is coating the tarmac. Mei-ling is pale and spent, scarcely able to look outside. She finally turns her face toward the window and catches her first glimpse of Europe. Through the gray mist of the isolated airfield, Amsterdam's fabled charms are distant and invisible. Mei-ling sees only a vast expanse and large shadowy objects, some moving, some still. Dinosaurs. The other planes remind her of dinosaurs. The smell of vomit still chokes her nostrils; an ebb tide of nausea unsteadies her legs. She feels very weak and a little frightened.

Mei-ling watches as Emma gathers up the sealed effluent bags and several damp paper towels she had used to clean and comfort her during the long flight from Hong Kong. Emma dumps them all together into a black plastic trash bag, ties the end of the bag into a knot, and leaves the putrid waste on the floor of the plane before they make their way out.

Verhoeven had rushed out of the passenger cabin before them, saying, "I'll go ahead to see to our documents and baggage." Mei-ling knows better. He was revolted by the mess and wanted nothing to do with it. He had run from the plane to escape.

Emma has not set foot on European soil since she was a young woman more than a quarter century earlier, and that was England. Despite the low clouds and misty drizzle that obscured the city as they were flying in, she is curious to see Amsterdam, wonders if she and Mei-ling might eventually make it a home of sorts. It would be wrong to say Emma feels hopeful—far too late for that. But even as she gathered the waste and stuffed it into the plastic bag, she warmed to the thought that it would not be long before she and Mei-ling would be at the Rijksmuseum, looking at the Rembrandts and Vermeers and cloudswept Dutch landscapes together. They would visit the flower market. They would take long walks beside the canals. And soon there would be a child, her grandchild.

Can it be, she wonders, that despite Verhoeven, despite herself, despite all the losses, she is almost happy? Can a child yet unborn effect so unlikely a miracle? Is that what the Christian mythos is about? What was the Christ child if not the symbol and promise of future joy even in the midst of life's sorrows? Good heavens, she thinks, is she becoming a Christian again after so many years? No, she decides, one needn't be a Christian to hope, to discover the promise of life after death. One's own grandchild would do nicely.

The passenger compartment is almost empty when Emma takes Mei-ling's arm. Most of what remains behind consists of discarded magazines, twice crumpled bags, rumpled blankets and pillows—the detritus of a wearying flight. They walk down the aisle of the plane and through the passageway to the moving sidewalk, then into the main terminal, the last passengers to deplane from Hong Kong.

Both of them wear raincoats; brass-buckled leather bags hang from their shoulders. Verhoeven had insisted that they wear as much jewelry as possible and carry the rest on the plane in their handbags. He had assured them that he had great faith in gold and diamonds—"the only friends who are always ready to help you"—no faith at all in baggage handlers and bureaucrats—"all thieves." Though only the gold and diamonds of their earrings remain visible, Mei-ling and Emma carry a considerable weight of precious gems, gold chains, and antique ornaments underneath their raincoats as they look around and try to get their bearings.

The terminal building is bright as daylight and extremely busy, but they are able to find two seats near the KLM service counter, where Verhoeven has arranged to meet them once he takes care of the baggage. Emma rests her arm on her daughter's shoulder. "You're looking much better already," she says. A lie meant to comfort. In actual fact Mei-ling has the listless pallor of a famine victim.

Verhoeven, waiting none too patiently for the baggage to come tumbling through the chute onto the conveyor belt, is in a mood as foul as the weather. He had hated the chill and damp of Amsterdam when he was a boy, and he hates it now. Actually, the penetrating cold that runs through him is a vagary of imagination brought on by the wet weather outside; the baggage area itself is quite warm and comfortable, the air filtered and temperature controlled. He is pleased to be by himself. Mei-ling had retched her way through all the time zones from Hong Kong to Amsterdam and smelled like sour milk. He wondered if she would ever stop spewing and heaving.

She had disappointed him, was behaving like an invalid, couldn't keep a bite of food down for almost two months, lost weight when she should have been gaining, developed dark circles around her eyes that gave her the furtive look of a raccoon. He grimaces. He wonders when she will take a turn for the better. Once the morning sickness stops, she will begin to swell and waddle, the veins in her legs will pop out. More of nature's nasty tricks, he thinks, always making you pay too much.

While he waits in the midst of the shifting crowd gathered around the baggage conveyor, Verhoeven marvels again at the mysterious impulse that had possessed him so late in life. To desire a son, he who had always been indifferent to children, who above all did not want to be bound. Now, by his own choice, he would be burdened with a smelly, mewling, shitting infant he might not live to see grown. And a young wife—oh, yes, he intended his son to be legitimate—who by simply standing still could evoke the lust of even a dedicated priest. But it is too late to turn back. He has no wish to. His son will be born in Holland, in Amsterdam, the city of his own birth.

Verhoeven usually succeeds in not remembering the event that triggered his desire for an heir, but it comes back to him now. Emma had been away. He'd succeeded yet again in finding a task plausible enough to have her occupied overnight elsewhere, keeping alive the charade they all practiced. He and Mei-ling had gone to dinner at The Charles, one of the few decent European restaurants in Hong Kong. He enjoyed showing her off, being seen among the colony's Europeans with his arm at the waist of a young beauty nobody would mistake for his daughter. Their silent envy and overt disapproval deeply pleased him.

That particular night he was feeling tired. He'd drunk too much wine with dinner, was annoyed with himself because he'd spilled some brown sauce on the fly of his white trousers. When he tried to clean it with water, the stain spread in ripples like a whirlpool. He was embarrassed and they left.

After taking Mei-ling home, he had begun to make love to her: undressing her slowly in the ritual they had perfected; caressing and kissing her arms, her neck, her back, the sweet hollow at the base of her spine; sucking her nipples till they hardened into plump buds; bringing her hand to him as his erection rose; easing his finger inside her while she rolled her hips and moaned softly. But when they lay down together, everything was gone. He was completely limp, unable to function. It was the first time, the only time. To her, he'd said, "I've had too much wine. I don't feel very well." But an inner voice whispered to him: "I'm getting old. I'm going to die." He couldn't think of another time when he'd been so frightened and humiliated, not even in the internment camp during the war.

Yet here and now, in Amsterdam where he'd been born, where his son would be born, he laughs to himself at how he'd been so foolishly discouraged, alcohol and fatigue working their worst. Even the strongest stallion has a weak moment. Mei-ling's pregnancy is proof enough that he isn't an old man. He must stop thinking morbid thoughts.

After Mei-ling delivers his son, she will still be beautiful. She seems to have grown quite fond of him. And why not? He has made clear that he is going to marry her; she will be respectable, the mother of his son.

His reverie ending happily, Verhoeven becomes impatient again for the baggage. When he spots it riding toward him on the conveyer, he grabs it, finds a porter, then goes to claim the two women.

Once settled into the hotel—a generous suite for himself and Mei-ling, a comfortable room of her own for Emma—Verhoeven attends to business: funds to be transferred, connections to be established, government regulations to be studied and mastered. He thinks it isn't wise to remain at the hotel indefinitely; the cost is outrageous and even the best hotel begins to feel cramped after a few weeks. For the present, though, with Mei-ling still ill for hours each day, they will stay where they are. The food and service are excellent. When the time comes, he will find a suitable permanent flat with enough room for them and the boy when he arrives. Of course it will be a boy. It has to be.

Emma rarely speaks to him. Verhoeven would like to be rid of her and her silent contempt. It is difficult for him to judge how much Mei-ling loves her mother—the girl keeps her thoughts to herself—and he knows enough to choose his battles. Plainly, the two women will be parted only by the grave.

But Verhoeven finds a way to wound Emma soon after their arrival in Amsterdam. She had broken her usual silence while Mei-ling was taking a nap, had spoken directly to him: "I'm not familiar with Dutch law. Is there a long wait for a license to marry?"

Recognizing that she was eager for a formal ceremony to legitimate Mei-ling and the child, he had taken his time answering. "There's no point in rushing," he'd said, smiling broadly to irritate her further. "It will be months before she delivers."

From the moment he realized Emma would be rankled if he delayed, he had reason enough to do so. What did it matter to him? She hated him already. The hypocrite! The communist puritan! The failed revolutionary with her smug, superior ways. The penniless bitch he'd rescued treated him as if he had leprosy. She was no fool. She closed her eyes so that she and Mei-ling would be safe and comfortable in the home he gave them. She was happy enough when he paid Mei-ling's fees at that fancy English school. She was happy enough to accept his gifts, wear silk dresses instead of threadbare castoffs that stank of blood and sweat. She was happy enough to stay at the best hotels when

she traveled for his business. She is no better than he is. He, at
least, makes no pretense to virtue.

⌒

Mei-ling, half asleep, her eyes still closed, hears the quiet rhythm
of bicycle tires through the open window: working people are
pedaling to their shops and offices. No shouting in the street.
No crates crashing noisily on the pavement. No horns blowing.
Only the steady hum of bicycle tires. She is far from China, far
from Hong Kong.

Mei-ling opens her eyes. She sits up and waits, but the expected wave of nausea doesn't overcome her. For the first time
since she has begun to carry the child, a film of sour saliva does
not coat her mouth. Its absence is sweet. Only the taste of sleep
lingers on her tongue. She rests herself against the headboard.
A shaft of pale northern sunlight brightens the ivory-colored
wall next to her bed. Verhoeven's bed has not been slept in, the
blue and white spread unwrinkled as the windowpane. It doesn't
matter. He does as he pleases. He leaves her to herself now. And
to her mother.

Yesterday's flowers—yellow daffodils and blue hyacinths—
rest in a white bowl on a table in front of the sunny window.
They are still fresh and lovely, but later a maid will change them
for a fresher bouquet, perhaps narcissus or tulips, a service of
the hotel. One must be rich to live for several months in a first-
class hotel in such comfort and beauty. Mei-ling enjoys being
rich. It is so pleasant. About many things Mr. Verhoeven (she
still sometimes thinks of him that way) has been right. And he
is so good at the business of making money. He always has more
than enough, though he complains occasionally about the expense, says he must find something more permanent.

Cautious against the return of nausea, she swings herself
around slowly, hangs her legs over the side of the bed, and drops
her feet to the floor. No nausea. No urge to vomit. She feels
pressure on her bladder, stands up easily, and goes to the bathroom to relieve herself. The bathroom is all white: porcelain
fixtures and ceramic tile gleaming like wet seashells, towels thick
and soft as clouds. She soaps and rinses her hands, runs a quick
shower, and brushes her teeth. The aftertaste of the minty tooth-
paste is a treat. Mei-ling is surprised by a rush of hunger, the

first in many months. She tells herself: *I feel better, so much better. I hope Mother hasn't had breakfast yet.* She would like to reward Emma with a cheerful meal together.

Mei-ling takes fresh underwear and stockings from her drawer and a loose-fitting dress from her closet. Although she has not been able to eat much, and her arms and legs are very thin, her waist has begun to expand so that many of her fine clothes are too tight. Her brassiere pinches a little, her breasts full and heavy. She looks at them. They remind her of pictures she saw years ago in China in one of Emma's books with characters that seemed so strange and oddly shaped. Her mother was reading to her in English about a farm in England with spotted cows in a grassy pasture. The cows had large appendages hanging from them like sacks of rice. She had pointed and asked: "What are those big things the cows are wearing?"

Emma had laughed and said, "Those are the cows' udders. It's where they store milk for their calves."

Mei-ling lifts each surprisingly pendulous breast separately, as if she were weighing it. She smiles and speaks aloud to herself. *"Udders!"*

She sits at the edge of her bed and begins to pull on her stockings. Noticing that her feet and ankles are swollen, she is displeased. Chinese. Small feet are beautiful, swollen feet are ugly. Will this child steal her beauty? What then? But Mei-ling is distracted by a flutter. The tickle of a feather underneath her skin, below her navel. She sits calmly and waits for another flutter, another tickle under the skin. But nothing happens. Had she imagined it? A quick calculation: the end of her fourth month. Still early. A few minutes later, as she raises her arms to bring her dress over her head, the flutter comes again. Tiny fingers tickle her. The child quickening? Yes. Why does she smile?

Mei-ling is fully dressed when she dials her mother's room. She is not surprised at the response, always one anxious word: "Mei-ling?" She is the only one who calls.

"Have you eaten breakfast yet?"

"No. Do you need something?"

"Nothing. I thought we could have breakfast together. I'm hungry, *very* hungry."

"How wonderful!" Emma's voice is high and happy, like notes on a flute. "Shall I come over now?"

"Yes. I'm ready."

The hotel breakfast room has many empty tables, some round, some square, all spaced comfortably apart on the dark polished parquet. They are covered with rose-pink cloths that reach almost to the floor. At the center of each table is a cylindrical crystal vase filled with a cluster of white, bell-shaped flowers. Most of the tables are freshly set with simple white china and stainless steel utensils that have been finished to resemble pewter. Resting on each serving plate is a crisp pink napkin that has been folded into a pleated semicircle.

Mei-ling and Emma are seated at a round table near a window that looks out on landscaped grounds: grass and flowers and trimmed shrubbery artfully planted, some of it in early bloom. The waiter knows Emma and greets her in English as he presents the breakfast menu. They order rolls and cheese and a boiled egg each. And tea that comes in clever little pots shaped like half-moons, suspended from bamboo handles that remind them of Hong Kong.

Mei-ling, speaking with a mouth half full, says, "This is delicious." She smiles. "I think it will stay down."

"You look so much better. I'm quite relieved."

"You worry about me too much. After all, many pregnant women have morning sickness."

"But not all day, every day, for months on end."

Mei-ling pours some tea for herself and brings the warm cup to her mouth. "Perhaps the change of climate made it worse."

"I'm happy it's behind you." She pauses, then says, "Do you know what I'd like to do today?" Emma does not wait for an answer to her question. "Let's visit the Rijksmuseum. You seem well enough to enjoy it."

Mei-ling remembers a painting she had once seen in a book of Renaissance art at Miss Richardson's school. A plainly dressed woman with a bird on her shoulder. At the time, it hadn't seemed especially important. She'd thought some of the other paintings with richly robed women and winged angels more beautiful. She doesn't remember the artist's name. But it was one of a series they were studying: *The Annunciation*. Between sips of tea, Mei-ling says, "A bird perched on my shoulder this morning."

"But that's not possible. You haven't been outside."

"It whispered a message in my ear."

"What are you talking about? The food has made you giddy."

"I felt the baby inside me this morning. It tickled me with a feather."

They both laugh. At that moment, Mei-ling gags slightly and feels a sour taste rise in her throat, but the discomfort passes. She cautions herself: It is unwise to give way entirely to happiness. Bitterness always returns.

⌒

The urgency Verhoeven felt at first to find permanent quarters passed quickly. Mei-ling was surprisingly content at the hotel, not nearly so fragile as he'd feared. He had stashed enough cash in Swiss and Dutch banks to keep them all comfortable for a considerable time. Soon he would hear from Coelho and Kung. A shower of money would be pouring in. He was certain of it.

Verhoeven decided to explore the city before selecting a permanent residence. He rode the trams and walked the cobbled streets near the center. Everything was so much smaller than he remembered, so much older, so oddly foreign. Yet, he had to admit, impressive in its solidity. All that stone and brick after a lifetime of bamboo and rattan. The bicycles were an odd delight, the riders speedily negotiating their way through the city in polite, orderly patterns so unlike the chaos of the Asian cities he had left behind. Like a ballet on wheels. Not that he had any desire to get around on a bicycle. When the time came, he would purchase another Mercedes, perhaps a forest-green color with maroon leather seats. He had seen one that pleased him.

Sometimes, quite by chance, he turned a corner into a remembered square, or saw an old freighted barge moving slowly through a canal as it had when he was a boy, or smelled before he saw a herring vendor hawking his wares. But these scenes from childhood were of only casual interest. Once, he passed the window of a used-book store cluttered with the same maritime prints of ships under sail that had first kindled his desire for adventure in tropical seas. Impulsively, he went in and bought several—a gift for his son. He had them carefully wrapped and tied. It would be some years before the boy could appreciate them.

Verhoeven was surprised at how seedy some once-fashionable streets had become, streets where the wealthy families he used to envy had lived in the luxury he craved. They were shabby now and none too clean. More often than not, dark-skinned people, immigrants from the colonies, from Surinam and Indonesia, stood behind the counters of the local stores, wrapping parcels and taking cash, walking in and out of the houses with net bags full of vegetables, a gaggle of children clinging to their sides. No matter. He always adapted himself to circumstance, always found a way to be rich and live as he pleased. Amsterdam was the place for his son. He did not regret having come.

Walking through Vondel Park, Verhoeven spied dozens of smashed syringes under graffiti-covered benches, a few on the paths and in the grass. Hardly naive about the drug trade in Amsterdam, he was shocked to find the evidence here of all places: near the museums, not the brothels or Dam Square, where Dutch and foreign addicts congregated. In his youth, Vondel Park had been pristine, beautiful; now it had the decaying appearance of a worn-out old whore. Even the shrubs needed pruning. Verhoeven had always prided himself on his lack of sentiment about the homeland he had so blithely, so unregretfully escaped from, but now he was a little sad at the decay of what had once been beautiful and well cared for. Of course, there was no denying that millions could be made in the poppy trade, practically overnight, if one had the overseas sources. If some of these young fools wanted to spend their lives in stuporous languor, why shouldn't an enterprising businessman take advantage of the situation? Nobody was forcing them to do it. Still, the park was in deplorable condition.

With Amsterdam daily reminding him of his youth, Verhoeven was soon off to see the ladies in their windows on the Wallen. It was one of them, a plump blonde with purple-painted fingernails and herring on her breath, who was his first woman so many years ago. He remembered admiring the businesslike way she went about unfastening his clothes and then her own while he watched, the ease with which she had given him his money's worth. He did a quick calculation, thought to himself: probably dead by now or very old, no more purple fingernails or boys' flies to fiddle with. Not one to dwell at length on the past, he stopped thinking about her.

The old, narrow, winding streets near Dam Square were almost as he remembered them, but not quite. Like everything else in Amsterdam, the whores in the windows had altered in appearance since he had last seen them: bored rather than sensual, strangely unalluring in what were intended as provocative costumes and poses. He had wanted a blonde, a variation, but the only one he thought might be suitable turned out to have stumpy legs. He changed his mind. He tried to choose from among the others—quite a few Asians and various mixed bloods—something for every taste. Every taste but his apparently. There was no connection between what he saw and what he wanted. He would find a better class of girl somewhere. He let the matter drop. An opportunity would present itself.

Without precisely knowing why, Verhoeven had delayed returning to the house he'd lived in as a boy. Perhaps he was half hoping it had been demolished to make way for something new and undoubtedly better. He remembered the name of the street but wasn't certain of the number, knew he'd recognize the place once he saw it. He wanted to ride up in style to the boyhood home that had seemed more a prison: cramped rooms, endless herring and potatoes, a sternly pious widowed mother. He hired a car. The driver turned out to be a talkative fellow with a heavy accent, a Kurd from Turkey who was saving to buy a restaurant that would feature Turkish-style pizza and take Amsterdam by storm. His cousin had managed the feat in The Hague. The Kurdish future entrepreneur, resourceful as well as voluble, easily found his way, dropping Verhoeven off in front of a row of narrow four-story brick buildings that seemed less forbidding and less tall than his memory of them. His boyhood home was in the center of the row. When he looked up to the top floor, he saw the window from which he had once looked out at the world. Nobody in the busy street seemed to notice his triumphant return except a few children, who were more interested in the vehicle than in its passenger. What had he been expecting?

The house was not as shabby as he thought it would be, nor were the others surrounding it. Quite the contrary. In the mysterious chemistry of cities, the neighborhood seemed in the early stages of transformation. He was surprised to see that the two street-level flats of his own building had been broken through and converted to an art gallery and a café where the rear flat had been. He could smell the coffee. Before climbing the steep

staircase that led to his old place, where he hoped someone
would be at home and permit a quick look around, he decided
to go into the gallery.

When he entered, the effect was open and spacious: one great
room with an archway at the far end that led to something
smaller beyond, the café no doubt. Paintings and wood sculpture
were displayed against a stark backdrop of white-painted walls.
The wood floors had been scraped and varnished to a warm
honey color. A brochure on a table at the door said that the
artworks were all by Ethiopians now living in Holland. What
on earth, he wondered, had brought them here to the house
where he was born?

He didn't have long to consider the question, because a pretty
young woman with a brown velvet skin, a long neck, a high
forehead, and the narrow features of northeast Africa came
walking toward him. She was wearing an exotic dress of batik
cloth printed in brown, black, and white. Circles of heavy copper wire unevenly punctuated by bright beads hung from her
neck and ears. Well now, thought Verhoeven, a dusky beauty.
He was glad he had thought to enter.

The woman smiled sedately and spoke in pleasantly accented
Dutch: "Please feel free to look around. You'll find the brochure
helpful. I'll be here if you have any questions."

He thanked her and busied himself with the brochure that
described the artists and their work in both Dutch and English
and explained that prices were available upon request. Verhoeven made his way through the gallery that at this early hour
was empty except for the woman and himself, the various carv-
ings, and richly colored paintings—some representational but
many in intriguing patterns not unlike the woman's dress. Toward the back of the large white room, he came upon a glass
case filled with intricate beadwork—jewelry, belts, slippers, and
hair ornaments—in turquoise and umber and a deep coppery
pink. He thought of Mei-ling, who was always so fond of a new
trinket, who was beginning to look more and more like a fat,
yellow-fleshed squash. One of the beadworks might be just the
thing for her. He wanted her mood to brighten while she was
carrying his son. He didn't want the boy to be moody.

A necklace caught his eye: closely worked rows of turquoise
beads formed a large round collar that was edged with strings
of umber and pink beads dangling like the fringes of a shawl.

While he was looking at it, the woman who had greeted him—he couldn't tell if she was a clerk or the gallery owner—came up behind him so softly, he didn't realize she was standing there till she spoke. Her voice was low and musical, like a whisper over his shoulder, unexpectedly provocative. "Is there something in the case you'd like to see? It's no trouble to take a piece out. The beadwork is very fine and quite distinctive. You would have to travel to Ethiopia to see anything like it."

Verhoeven pointed. "That necklace, the round one that looks like a collar."

She stepped in front of him to open the case. He caught a pungent scent floating toward him, spicy and sweet. She lifted the necklace from inside the case and spread it across her palms. He ran his hand over the surface. She smiled up at him. "Do you like it?"

He did, and he liked her as well. He'd never slept with an African woman. Their flat noses and kinky hair and extravagant gestures didn't appeal to him. When it came to whores, some men seemed to favor them over any other kind; he'd never understood. But this slender beauty with the musical voice and long neck and stately posture was something different, a model for a statue, all curves and lines and glowing surfaces. "I'm not certain how the necklace would look on. Could I trouble you to wear it for me?"

"It's no trouble at all." She removed the necklace she was wearing and put it on the case. Then she said, "This one won't look right with the print on my dress. Just a moment." She placed the beaded collar in his hands and dashed toward the back. When she returned, she was wearing a long white caftan-like affair that set her eyes to shining. She took the beaded collar from Verhoeven's outstretched hands and fastened it around her neck.

"Very lovely," he said, "very lovely indeed. How much is it?"

When she told him, he was surprised at how low the price was. He'd been prepared to spend double, perhaps triple what she was asking. Was everything so cheap? Knowing he would take it, but feeling reckless and playful, he said, "And the lovely model?"

The woman's smile was still fixed in place; she parried in an even tone, "The model is not part of the sale, sir."

He smiled back. "Double?" He had nothing to lose by trying.

They were all whores at heart, he thought, every last one of them if the price was high enough. And why not? They might as well make the most of what they had while they had it. What was marriage if not a business arrangement? All that Christian nonsense about a sacrament. Every woman was a kept woman one way or another. And their charms never lasted very long. Best to take advantage while they could. He never blamed them.

She said, "Sir, do you want to purchase the necklace?"

Verhoeven did want it, but he also wanted to see where his little game would lead. "Triple?"

Her smile dropped and her lashes fluttered. "The necklace. Do you want it?"

"Quadruple." Silence. "It's the last offer."

She hesitated, then looked at him with steady eyes and nodded. "I like a man who appreciates fine jewelry and is willing to pay what it's worth."

Verhoeven was pleased with himself . . . and her. He had won the little game they were playing. In only a moment or two, she wrapped the necklace in tissue, tucked it into his jacket pocket, and slipped the wad of money he gave her into a fold of her long dress. She shut the front door, twisted the dead bolt, and turned the cardboard sign to CLOSED.

⌒

After his disappointing encounter with the Ethiopian early in the day, Verhoeven is in a testy mood when he returns later to the large flat he had finally settled them in a week earlier (though he has decided to stay at a hotel when it suits him). He is angry. The bitch had been ready enough to spread her legs for cash but made not the least pretense of pleasure, making it difficult for him to finish the job at all. A whore who knew her trade—one of the higher-class sort—would have been better. Finally, he had faked finishing and got out of there without bothering to go upstairs to his boyhood home. He couldn't get the Ethiopian bitch's parting smile, more like a sneer, out of his mind. The entire day had gone badly after that.

The moment he sees Emma, all thought of the disastrous morning vanishes. Something is terribly wrong. Emma, who usually ignores his coming and going, who tries to make it her business to be in her own two rooms in an adjoining flat when he is at home, greets him at the threshold with frantic eyes. Her voice trembles.

"She's been bleeding. It's my fault. I insisted we go for a walk. The doctor said she needed fresh air and exercise."

"Is it bad?"

"I don't know. It didn't start till a little while ago. We had just come in. I was making some tea."

Mei-ling is in the bedroom, lying down, calmer than her mother but looking grave. The first thing Verhoeven does is take one of the bed pillows and place it under her feet. He'd heard somewhere that is the thing to do to prevent miscarriage.

"Is that more comfortable? Are you in any pain?"

"Not really. More like a pulling feeling. Just a little blood, not gushing out or anything."

When he hears this, Verhoeven feels light-headed, as if he's drunk champagne very quickly. His son is still safe.

Mei-ling's color is good. He touches her forehead. No fever. He turns to the shaken Emma. "Have you called the doctor?"

"No. It only just happened."

"Call the doctor . . . whichever one you've been taking her to. Explain the situation. Explain that she's in bed with her legs raised and that we can't move her because she's bleeding."

When Emma leaves the room, Verhoeven places a chair next to Mei-ling's bed and sits down. He takes her hand. "Your mother's calling the doctor. Try to rest." He smiles and attempts a joke. "It's only my son kicking up a fuss inside your belly. He wants me to know how strong he is and that he wants to come out into the world."

Mei-ling understands that Verhoeven means what he is saying, that he isn't merely trying to be amusing, that he thinks of her as an incubator that must be kept running properly for the child's sake. It is as she expects. She will be well taken care of. She closes her eyes and tries not to think of the dull pulsing between her legs.

Verhoeven is surprised when he meets the doctor. She seems to him more like a fashion model than a physician: very tall and thin in a sharply tailored navy suit, wide blue eyes, thick yellow-blond hair cut in the shape of a bowl. Like a neat hat. But her manner is too brisk and businesslike to please him, so different from the women of the Orient, so . . . unfeminine. Just as well, he thinks, for a doctor.

Dr. Westerveldt sends him out of the room while she performs her examination. He and Emma wait together. Only a few minutes pass before the doctor calls them back in. Mei-ling is smiling a little and seems relaxed. The doctor says, "None of this looks serious to me. There was only a little bleeding that seems to have stopped . . . no sign of early contractions. The baby's heartbeat is strong."

She turns to Mei-ling. "Rest in bed for a few days with your legs raised, and avoid constipation so that there's no strain with bowel movements. Drink lots of water."

Ignoring Verhoeven, she reaches into her bag and brings out a small plastic container that she hands to Emma. "If the bleeding starts again, or if she feels contractions, give her two of these and call me." She pats Emma's hand. "But I doubt you'll need them. She's carrying well and should come to term nicely. These things happen sometimes."

Dr. Westerveldt excuses herself to wash her hands. Verhoeven, relieved and delighted that his son is not in imminent danger, leans over and, despite Emma's presence, plants an almost fatherly kiss on Mei-ling's brow. "See, a lot of fuss about very little. Almost made me forget what I have for you."

Before he can bring the beadwork necklace out of his pocket, the doctor comes back into the room. Emma, who'd left the moment he kissed Mei-ling, follows her back in. The doctor reaches for her medical bag and speaks to Mei-ling. "I'll see you at your next regular appointment. Keep your spirits up. Before long, you'll deliver a fine baby."

Verhoeven walks the doctor to the door. He says, "Thank you for coming."

"Not at all. By the way, I think you should refrain from intercourse until she delivers. Just to be on the safe side."

Verhoeven is momentarily taken aback, not so much by her frankness, which is to be expected, as by the reminder that some couples persist in intercourse to the last months of pregnancy, a prospect he finds disgusting. He has no difficulty acknowledging the doctor's caution. "Of course. I won't think of it. Nothing's more important than the birth of my son."

Dr. Westerveldt laughs aloud. "What makes you so certain it's going to be a boy? Why not a girl?"

He smiles at her but replies with utter seriousness: "I want a son very much, and I'm a man who gets what he wants. Not that girls aren't pleasant enough creatures, but it's only natural for a man to desire a son, isn't it?"

Verhoeven had no intention of offending the doctor, has no idea that he'd done so even when she responds with a dry "Not really."

She tries to leave, but Verhoeven, relieved and grateful because his posterity is still assured and this woman is in some way responsible, holds on to her arm. "I know I can count on you for a healthy birth." He smiles knowingly. "And it will be a boy."

The doctor takes in Verhoeven's absolute assurance and wonders what to say to his absurd remark, is increasingly annoyed that he is fathering a child by a young girl when he should be playing with grandchildren. Gets what he wants, indeed, she thinks. He is plainly ignorant of the biological dice, or chooses to be. She has seen it before, certainty about a child's sex based on nothing more than intense preference. Pity the poor child who disappoints.

Unsmiling, she says, "We'll see soon enough, won't we?" Then she leaves, closing the door behind her.

As soon as she is gone, a wave of doubt shakes Verhoeven. "The arrogant bitch," he says to himself. But he refuses to let her spoil the pleasure of his anticipation. The child is destined to be a boy. Boys, he reminds himself, dominate in his family tree. He stops there; to go further he would have to acknowledge that the tree has been stripped of almost all its branches and could be dying out.

Emma and Mei-ling are chatting and drinking tea when he returns to the bedroom, but their conversation stops as soon as he enters. Emma hands him a cup of tea in his preferred style—a little sugar but no milk—and leaves mumbling something about the kitchen.

As Verhoeven draws the necklace from his pocket, a momentary distaste for its source takes hold of him. But he is a practiced liar. "I passed the most interesting shopwindow today, and the moment I saw this I thought of how lovely you would look in it." He holds it up. "Do you like it?"

Mei-ling examines the beadwork carefully. If nothing else, Verhoeven thinks, he's taught her to judge the quality of jewelry. She says, "The beadwork is very fine . . . beautiful colors. Where is it from?"

"Somewhere in Africa. I don't know. Let me put it on for you."

She hands it back. He places the beaded collar around her neck and is surprised by a tremble in his fingers as he fastens it, a tremble that reminds him of the first time he'd fastened a jewel to her warm flesh. Although, pregnant, she no longer piques his desire, he thinks of the delights she's given him these several years, how well worth the cost. And soon she will present him with a gift beyond price.

The chaste design of the necklace gives Mei-ling's face a demure look, innocent, not unlike that of a child or a Madonna. He wonders if this episode is a sign that he should finally arrange for a wedding ceremony. They had had a fright, no doubt about that. The baby might have been born prematurely, still could be if that smug doctor doesn't know her business as well as she seems to. He decides to look into the details the very next day and set a date for the ceremony.

⌐﹏⌐

The gray-haired magistrate, whose perfunctory smile reveals a well-crafted set of false teeth, is indifferent to yet another couple standing before him. He has seen so many in his long career, and, in recent years, far too many brides with swollen bellies like this one. Most had been fair, blue-eyed Dutch girls who had gotten themselves into trouble. Not that they or anyone else seems to care anymore. Sometimes, the bridegroom was a dark-skinned foreigner, a Greek or Italian or Turk. For some reason he cannot fathom, many beautiful Dutch girls seem to favor them. And, increasingly, brides too were from the Orient or even Africa. Holland would never be the same.

This foreign bride is more beautiful and better dressed than most. Genuine gold and diamond earrings. Fine leather handbag and shoes. But quiet, unsmiling. The magistrate scans their documents, looks them up and down. Most bridegrooms aren't as far along in years as the handsome old buck in the cream-colored suit. Almost as old as he is himself. Must be rich. They're the ones who get the beautiful young girls. Show off by getting them pregnant. Well, a few words from him and they will be legally wed, the child legitimate. He will have done his bit in the service of civilization. Earned his bread.

These two in front of him are the last couple of the day, and none too thrilled with each other from the look of them. No friends or relatives except for the gray-haired woman who seems anxious. No merriment, no flowers, no smiles, no pleasantries, no jokes. Best to get it over with quickly, finish speaking the words, signing the papers.

He does. They leave. Now it is time to go home for the day. His wife will have a hot dinner waiting for him and a good bottle of beer. Let the world go to the devil if it wants to. There is nothing he can do about it.

⸺

Less than two weeks after the wedding ceremony and about six weeks before Mei-ling was due to deliver, Verhoeven began to feel a burning sensation every time he urinated. Pus oozed from his penis and stained his underwear. A smell like rotten meat seemed to follow him. He sprinkled himself and his shorts with scented powder, but it did no good. Soon, he couldn't urinate without sharp pain. "The bitch," he said to himself, "that cold black bitch must be the one who gave it to me . . . whatever *it* is."

And just as a son was to be born, a small shipment on the way from Coelho, a promise of another connection from Kung, the money beginning to flow in a steady stream. Now he can't pee without pain to the point of nausea. He had always hated doctors, prided himself on being better off without them, able to shake off any illness through sheer force of will. But he is not young anymore.

Pain and fear being hard masters—even for him—Verhoeven sought medical help. After examining him and his ugly excretions, the doctor, a brash fellow much younger than he, said, "What's an old tomcat like you getting into trouble like this for? Don't you know how to protect yourself? Where did you pick it up?"

Verhoeven felt a shiver in his bowel. "Is it very serious?"

The doctor's back was turned; he was fiddling with something in his desk drawer. Wasn't he paying attention?

"Serious enough, but not as bad as some other things I've seen. The drugs will take care of it. You'll have to take them till the infection is completely gone. Otherwise, these nasty bacteria have a way of hiding till you think they're done for and then sneaking back to attack again." He took a breath. "And we will have to know where you contracted the infection for the public health records."

The doctor was looking him in the eye now. Verhoeven said, "Only one possibility. An Ethiopian bitch who runs an art gallery." It satisfied him to say this, though he wasn't certain.

The doctor frowned and turned to look at some papers on his desk. "You are married, I see. We'll have to examine your wife, of course."

Verhoeven flinched at mention of his wife. "My wife is in the late stages of pregnancy. We haven't had sex for many months . . . haven't been in the same bed. If we had, I wouldn't have needed that bitch and wouldn't be infected."

"So it's your wife's fault, is it?" He wrote something down. "I suppose there's no point in upsetting her if you're certain there was no chance of infection."

"I'm certain."

The doctor handed Verhoeven a pad and a pen. "Please write down the name of the woman. I assume you were willing partners and that no crime of any kind was committed, but we will have to examine her and notify any other partners she had contact with."

Verhoeven took the pen and paper the doctor offered him and began to write. But what? He had no idea what her name was because at the time it was of no importance. He said, "I don't know her name, but I remember the name of the gallery and the address. It's in the building where I was born."

The doctor looked startled. "Where you were born?"

"Yes. It's never been a lucky place for me. I probably shouldn't have gone back, but something drew me there." He jotted down the information for the doctor and, as he was handing the pen back, said, "Actually, I don't believe in bad luck. This never would have happened if I hadn't been careless and the whore so greedy."

The doctor shrugged. "Not for me to say, any of this. But I must remind you to take the pills till they run out and then come to see me again."

On his way home, Verhoeven stopped at a shop to purchase new underwear. He had been throwing his stinking shorts into the trash, taking care to wrap them first in waste paper. He resolved to follow the doctor's instructions, take all his pills, put the whole messy business behind him. In the coming weeks there was money to be made and a son to be born. Nothing was to interfere with either of these.

~

Sweat spreads across Mei-ling's chest, neck, upper lip, forehead, and scalp like a rash of tiny blisters. Screaming and the effort of not screaming has reduced her voice to a whisper. She is exhausted by hours of relentless labor, so spent that at the last moment she is caught unprepared by the commonplace miracle of birth: the final burst of pain, the separation, the baby's trumpeting wail.

Nor does she expect the fierce, echoing maternity that envelops her when Dr. Westerveldt places the child in her arms and announces: "Well, Mother, you have a healthy, beautiful daughter." Nor does she anticipate the shudder of fear that overtakes her a moment later, when the doctor laughs and says, "Your husband is in for a great surprise when he hears that his son is a daughter. But he'll get over it. They always do. I've seen it before. As soon as I get cleaned up, I'll tell him and your mother."

Mei-ling holds fast to the infant girl who is resting quietly from the rigors of her journey. She knows that Verhoeven will not "get over it" as the doctor had said. And while he won't drown the infant, as some Chinese peasants did in secret when a girl baby was born, she fears he will find another way to rid himself of the child. Perhaps of her as well.

Mei-ling drifts into a mildly anesthetized sleep. For so long she has locked her demons away. Now they rise up in the blackness. Their breath hisses a stinging orange fire. She clutches the infant and holds on. Soon the fire burns itself out, the demons melting to soft pools like spent candles.

In the quiet, Mei-ling wakes and raises her head. Her bedclothes are soaked, but the baby is sleeping securely in her arms, waiting for the world to begin. In that small patch of time before the baby cries for milk, Mei-ling begins to weave a future for herself and her daughter, one that does not include Dirk Verhoeven. For the first time since she and Emma had gone to live in the two rooms behind his office in Hong

Kong, Mei-ling begins to contemplate a life without his protection. Have she and Emma not given him much in return for all he has given them? What does she owe him? Nothing! Not even a son.

Verhoeven is never cruel, she thinks, but he cares only for himself and his desires. Too many men, she decides, are selfish without thinking about what they are doing. But not all of them. Not the round-faced stranger with the brown teeth who had tried to save her. Not her dear lost father. Professor Wang's earnest, intelligent face takes shape in her mind's eye. She sees it clearly as it was when she was a child: a crown of straight black hair cut short in the English style, a high forehead and spectacled, studious eyes framed by thick brows, thin lips that would open in a wide smile when she reached to embrace him and close again quickly under the weight of his burdens. Did he open that mouth to scream when they tortured him?

Mei-ling is suddenly grateful that death has spared him the knowledge of her and Emma's bitter suffering and flight from the mainland, their years with Verhoeven in Hong Kong. He could not have understood. Warm tears, strangely soothing, fill her eyes. Her father's death cannot be undone, but she and Emma have survived. Because of Verhoeven, they have had time to gather strength. Without intending it, he has given her a future. It is sleeping in her arms.

She remembers their first intimacy, after he had presented her with the gold ankle chain. The sardonic tone of his voice moments after he slid off her. "So you're not such an innocent as I thought. No matter. The virgin state is much overrated." Then he'd chuckled softly. He never asked how it had happened. She never tried to explain. They simply went on—she pleasing him, he providing for her, Emma not seeing what she could not bear to see.

Sometimes, in those Hong Kong years, when she and Verhoeven were in bed together, Mei-ling wondered at the shuddering wildness that would seize and hold him to the end. Men were so . . . *physical*. For herself, once he had shown her what would please him, none of what they did seemed terribly important; it was pleasurable enough and he never hurt her. She'd been grateful for that. It had not taken long to notice that when she especially pleased him, when she moaned aloud, when she licked him playfully with her tongue, Verhoeven arrived the next time with a more precious gift than usual.

Then, about a year before, there had been a sudden change—not so much his growing tired of her as his growing tired. Blaming the stress of business. Blaming drink. Then a few frenzied spurts of renewed energy.

Mei-ling, whenever she thought about it, was certain he had deliberately impregnated her, careless and impetuous where he had always been careful. Unlike his normally reserved self, he had been openly enthusiastic when he learned she was expecting, presented her with diamond earrings, said, "We will go to Holland to be married. The child must be born there."

Emma's reaction to the news had been like a quick stab of a sharp knife: "For your father's sake, I'm happy you're to be a wife rather than a . . . concubine. Even though he was a party member, he was old-fashioned in some ways. The disgrace would have humiliated him. Now the Wang family honor will be preserved."

They had spoken no more about it after that. Emma had remained at her side, standing watch, never voicing disapproval. As to Verhoeven, he had busied himself with preparations for their journey and stopped physical intimacy entirely.

Dr. Westerveldt's voice breaks into her thoughts: "I'm leaving now, but the nurses will look after you. I'll speak to Mr. Verhoeven and your mother on my way out. Have you decided on a name?"

"Not for a girl. It wasn't supposed to be a girl. I'll have to think of one."

"You can always name her Juliana, after the queen. She's a Dutch subject now, like her father. He might like that . . . soften the blow, if you understand me."

"It's a pretty name."

"She's a pretty girl. It's hard to tell when they're so young, but I think she's going to look like her father." She stroked the baby's head. "Look at all that hair . . . and blue eyes too, though they can change later."

"I don't care what she looks like, so long as she's healthy. I was afraid after the bleeding."

"She's perfect."

Mei-ling bends her head toward the tiny face crowned with dark hair. "She is."

That bitch doctor of Mei-ling's was pleased, Verhoeven thinks. She seemed to be laughing at him when she said, "I have a nice surprise for you, Mr. Verhoeven. You have a beautiful daughter." He would have liked to slam his fist into her teeth. What use was a daughter? He desperately needed a son at his age. Who would carry his name now?

Verhoeven drums his fingers on the table. Why on earth had he been so quick to marry the little whore? What was the point? Now he was saddled with the two of them—three if he took the English hypocrite into account. Verhoeven lifts his glass and drains it. His doctor has warned him not to, says it's bad for his condition. Damn him too! He calls to the lone bartender for a second beer.

The bar is dark and empty at this hour, brown and dull as old shoe leather: tables, chairs, floor, even the speckled lampshades, all shrouded in murky brown. In Bandung, in Hong-Kong, light penetrated everywhere. He had been a fool to return. Possessed. So certain it would be a boy. The bartender brings the beer to his table. Verhoeven drinks it quickly, wipes the foam from his mouth. Oh, Lord! Suddenly, the pressure to pee is urgent. He stands up. But where is the men's room?

"Over there." The bartender is pointing—experienced with emergencies in his business. But when Verhoeven reaches the urinal, it is already too late. A small amount has leaked and dampened his new underwear. After he relieves himself—if you could call it that, since a dull pain was now part of the process— he checks his shorts. No stain. He sighs, humbled, grateful for small things. Then he begins to weep.

More than anything else, it is his weeping that frightens him. And rescues him. He cannot remember ever weeping before, not even as a child. He washes his hands carefully and splashes cold water on his face. Then he finds courage to look at himself in the mirror. He combs his hair deliberately, decides he is still a handsome man, only a few lines, the kind many women find attractive. He frowns. The devil with the whores. What does he care if they find him attractive or not? There are more important things to consider now.

Any day he expects to hear from Kung about a shipment they

are working on together. It should be winding its way from Afghanistan. If everything went as planned, the results would be little short of stupendous. He had already ordered a new Mercedes, dark green upholstered in maroon leather. A gift to himself for work well done. Coelho had been disappointing, hardly worth the trouble it took to stay in touch, but Kung won't let him down.

In the time it takes to walk back into the bar, cleaned and freshened, Verhoeven decides to look for a larger office. A place in one of the better neighborhoods, with an extra couple of rooms where he can entertain clients or guests in private, where he can stay by himself in comfort whenever he wishes. He will furnish the new place handsomely, perhaps hire a professional to decorate it for him.

As for Mei-ling, wife or not, what use is she to him now? He has spoiled her. That would have to change. He would make some arrangement that suited them both. It was unfortunate that he had been so quick to marry her, but he need not let her stand in the way of his other interests. Not that he didn't intend to fulfill his obligations and do what he must for the little girl she had unfortunately given birth to. He has no intention of abandoning them. He is not a beast.

⌒

One afternoon, not long after she has brought Juliana home, Mei-ling hears a knock at her door. She wonders who it might be. Emma is out, Juliana asleep in her room. She has no friends here, is stabbed for a moment by the memory of returning home with her child to the quiet flat: no joyful group of family or neighbors inspecting the baby as she remembers happening in China, no delicacies, no little gifts. Not that she or the child want for anything. It is the emptiness.

Mei-ling opens the door. A pleasant-looking stranger stands there—a woman neither young nor old, perhaps in her early fifties, brown hair neatly trimmed at shoulder length, brown eyes, a brown-and-white-checked suit with a white blouse fastened at the neck by an antique cameo, and low brown shoes polished to a warm shine.

The woman holds a package under her arm, a thin rectangle wrapped in white paper and tied with a curly yellow ribbon. She balances a large baking dish that gives off a rich aroma of apples and cinnamon in the palm of her other hand. Mei-ling assumes the stranger is at the wrong door, and hesitates. But the woman speaks up cheerfully: "I wanted to welcome the new baby. I live three doors away. Was it a boy or a girl?"

Mei-ling opens the door wider and says, "Please come in," motioning the woman over the threshold. "It was a girl." She doesn't quite know what to do about the aromatic baking dish or the package, both of which are being offered to her.

"Please," the woman says, "for you and the baby, a present."

Mei-ling takes them and places them on the rosewood lamp table. "Thank you. Won't you sit down."

She knows these are the proper words to say, but she is awkward with a stranger.

"I saw when you were pregnant and then when you came back with the baby. My name is Berthe, Berthe Roosenburgh." She extends her hand.

Mei-ling takes it. "I'm Mei-ling . . ." She is about to say Wang but corrects herself and offers instead the name that seems false. "Mei-ling Verhoeven. Please sit down. Would you like a cup of tea?"

"Please, don't bother yourself. I can't stay. And it's always so busy with a newborn. This is just for good luck, for you and the baby."

She points to the wrapped package. Mei-ling has been accustomed to receiving gifts from Verhoeven over the years. He always expected her to open them in front of him. She reaches for the package and says, "Shall I open it now?"

The woman nods cheerfully and watches as Mei-ling unwraps what turns out to be a book bound in white leather and embossed on the cover with the plump-cheeked face of a baby. Mei-ling opens it. The title page reads: *Baby's Book*. Inside are spaces for photographs, locks of hair, dates when the baby first smiled, turned over, crawled, sat up, gained a tooth, spoke a word—and, in between, large empty spaces for whatever the mother chooses to write or paste there. On the final page there is space for a first-birthday photograph.

Mei-ling is delighted with the book. And from a complete stranger! She smiles at Berthe, says, "Juliana is sleeping now, but we can take a look if you want to see her."

"Juliana. A little queen. A good name."

The women walk softly into the room where Juliana lies sleeping quietly in her crib. They look at the child and then at each other, sharing an unspoken delight in the small creature. When they return to the living room after a few moments, they remain standing, awkwardly, wondering what to say.

Berthe speaks first, almost wistfully. "You will enjoy her. She's so beautiful. Her nose and mouth are like flower buds."

"Thank you. Are your children grown?"

"I don't have children, but I enjoy other people's children just the same. Life is precious."

"I'm sorry. I just thought . . ."

"No need. Well, it's time to go. You should rest while the baby is sleeping, keep up your strength."

They walk toward the door. Mei-ling says, "Thank you for the baby book. It's lovely." She glances back into the room. "And for the cake. It looks delicious."

"It is. A good Dutch lady taught me how to make it. It's a typical Dutch cake."

Something in the way she said "Dutch cake" makes Mei-ling ask, "Aren't you Dutch yourself?"

"No. I'm here only since the war."

Mei-ling remembers from her teachers at Miss Richardson's, and from Verhoeven as well, that whenever a European spoke about "the war" they were referring to World War II, which had ended before she was born. Verhoeven had once told her about his imprisonment, had joked about having gotten his start in business in the camp, then never spoke of it again. She asks, "Where did you come from?"

"I grew up in Germany, in Berlin, in a Jewish family."

Mei-ling is not sure she wants to hear any more. But she is grateful to Berthe for the baby book and a little curious as well. She says, "Did you have to run away?"

"I wish we had sense to run when we could. My family's big mistake was to stay and hope for the best."

Mei-ling thinks of her flight from China, clinging to her mother at every step. "It's hard to leave everything and be alone in a strange place."

Berthe stands with her hand on the doorknob, seeming to weigh what Mei-ling said. "Hard, but better than what happened."

Suddenly, Mei-ling sees the face of their old neighbor, the

distinguished Dr. Chen, a noted surgeon, the stumps where his hands had been. Nothing this woman might say could be worse than that.

Berthe relaxes her grip on the knob and leans against the door as if she is resting. "After Hitler came in power, my father lost his business and I was forced from school. We sold my mother's jewelry for nothing near what it was worth, for food and protection. But it was no use. We were rounded up and sent to a concentration camp in Poland. Do you know what that is?"

Mei-ling nods.

"I am sorry. I don't know why I'm bothering you with this . . . a silly apple tart. Rest. Enjoy the baby. I should go."

"No, I want to hear. My mother once sold her jewelry to keep us alive. Won't you sit down?"

Berthe remains at the door as if she will go, but continues her story. "In the camp we starved and froze and worked like slaves. Then a few of us, young girls, were sent to the hospital. I was happy because the food was better and it was warm. Then a doctor made an operation. That's why I have no children."

Mei-ling would like to shut the spigot now, but the words are pouring out.

"After the liberation I was what they called a displaced person. Really, I was a skeleton that still breathed . . . more dead than alive. But I was luckier than the rest of my family. I don't know if they went up in smoke or were rotting in the ground. I was sent to Holland. A Dutch family took me in and fattened me up, though they had little enough themselves. They were very kind."

Here she stops and smiles, not at Mei-ling but at some long-ago memory of happiness. "Especially the son who was a nice-looking fellow with blond hair and blue eyes. He looked like a picture in a book, like a grown-up Hans Brinker. He must have been sorry for me. We were married later on even though he knew we would not have children. I learned to bake apple cake as good as his mother's."

Berthe stops, having brought her story to a seemingly happy conclusion, then opens the door wide. "I'm talking too much. Take good care of the baby. Enjoy her."

Mei-ling watches as Berthe walks down the corridor to her own flat, waves her hand, and lets herself in. How old was she, Mei-ling wonders, when those terrible things happened?

Before Mei-ling can dwell further on Berthe, Juliana awakens from her nap and begins to cry for food; Emma returns from the market. While Emma is busy emptying parcels and filling shelves, Mei-ling nurses Juliana. Then Emma puts the kettle on. Mei-ling tells her about Berthe's visit and shows her the baby book and the apple tart that has a sad story with a happy enough ending attached to it. Emma slices a piece for each of them to have with their tea. It is as good as Berthe's promise, fruity and buttery, with hints of lemon and spice and caramelized sugar that linger deliciously on the tongue.

"Well," Emma says, "I'm happy someone thought to bring my grandchild a gift. She sounds a nice woman. Perhaps we'll invite her for tea one afternoon."

"I think she'll come. We're somehow alike, you know, fated to be in Amsterdam together because we had to flee. If the Cultural Revolution had not gone insane, you and I might still be in China. Father would be alive. He would be teaching his students." Mei-ling looks at Emma intently, openly. "How could people have been so cruel? Father was such a good man?"

Emma feels a rush of gratitude toward the stranger she has yet to meet for providing the key that has finally unlocked Mei-ling's tongue. Perhaps, before long, Mei-ling will speak about the countryside, what had happened there that froze her into stillness, that changed her in ways Emma cannot understand. It would be a mistake to ask now, Emma thinks.

Berthe's story calls up other memories for Emma. "Your father was a brilliant man . . . so serious, but charming and quite merry when we were alone together. We had several Jewish friends in England, Communists like ourselves. It seems almost laughable now, but we thought we could save the world if the world would only let us. I still don't understand how it all could have gone so wrong once we were given our chance."

Even as Juliana sucks at her breast, Mei-ling reaches for her mother's hand and holds it. She says, "But we're luckier than Berthe. She lost everyone and she couldn't have children. The three of us are still together." She pauses. "Despite everything."

Tears fill Emma's eyes.

Without warning, Mei-ling begins to sob openly. Juliana, hearing her cry, or perhaps feeling the heave of her breast as she weeps, stops sucking and starts to howl. Mei-ling and Emma both decide this is funny and begin to laugh with tears running down their faces. Hearing this, the baby promptly stops howling, puckers her cheeks, purses her lips, and then opens her mouth and gurgles.

Later, both women swore that Juliana had smiled. Her first smile. Mei-ling dutifully recorded the date in the baby book.

Montreal

⌒

THE BLACK CALFSKIN belt that circled Jack Ramsden's waist was still stiff and new, a size larger than the one he had been forced to discard. He'd always been naturally slim. Now his trousers pinched and strained. He was uncomfortable, felt as if he were waddling instead of walking. He stuck his thumb behind the belt to stretch and soften the leather. He was disgusted with himself. Damned if he would go to the trouble and expense of an entire new wardrobe! No, he decided, he would have to go on a diet.

When he first began to feel uncomfortable in his suits and undershorts a few months earlier, Ramsden told himself that his increasing girth was the result of middle age. But as his paunch and discomfort grew—an embarrassing buildup of gas, small stabs of pain in his lower back, indigestion—he decided the culprit was food. Furthermore, he was certain that it wasn't solely the rich meals that accompanied the wedding festivities, both sons having married within the past six months. No, it was Celia's current passion for gourmet cooking that was wreaking havoc with his wardrobe, not to mention his health and vanity. As for Celia, somehow she hadn't put on an ounce, indeed had lost a few pounds in the two months since the second wedding. He couldn't imagine how she had managed it.

On his way home from the bank, Ramsden wondered which of Celia's "creations" awaited him. Wednesday. He used to be able to count on a grilled veal chop, baked potato, and green salad. Now he was likely to be presented with decidedly more stylish fare. He had already sampled Celia's veal Cordon Bleu bubbling with cheese, veal Prince Orloff swimming in cream, veal Marengo drowning in olive oil, and for good measure fried Wiener schnitzel topped with a fried egg. And it was all marvelous! Even the crust on the schnitzel was exactly right, crisp and not greasy. How could she expect him to restrain himself?

Was he being churlish blaming Celia for his poundage? Of course he was! He would have to find a way to get her to return to simple fare without hurting her feelings. She had wanted to please him and she had. As always. It was simply too much of a good thing.

Ramsden was just inside the door when he noticed that the fragrance of herbs and spices was not wafting through the air as he expected. Strange how habits established themselves. Had Celia been reading his mind about the rich food? They'd been married long enough. When he went into the kitchen to kiss her on the cheek as he did every evening, he saw two potatoes baking in the toaster oven and two raw veal chops waiting for the grill. Celia was slicing tomatoes and arranging them on a bed of lettuce. The wire whisk was nowhere in sight. She smiled when he kissed her, asked how his day went.

As was his custom, he poured a scotch for himself after he loosened his tie and removed his jacket, then went to the den, where he sat in his leather easy chair to read the newspaper while Celia finished the dinner preparations. He enjoyed the quiet in the house. He and Celia went out less and less, had the house to themselves now that both boys were married. Annie, the Jamaican maid Celia was so fond of, was always gone by the time he arrived. Peace. He scanned the front page.

Celia's hand tapped his shoulder. "Time for dinner."

He roused himself from his doze. The newspaper had slipped to the floor. "Oh. Already?"

She laughed lightly. "You've been sleeping quite a while."

"Won't be a minute. I'll just wash up."

He was hungry and relished the simple chop and potato, but

he noticed that Celia seemed to pick at her food, was less talkative than usual. It crossed his mind that she was moodier because of menopause. The occasional hot flash wasn't too troublesome, just uncomfortable, but she had begun to tire easily. Of course, it wasn't like her to complain.

To take her out of herself, Ramsden brought up a favorite subject, her volunteer work. "How did things go at the hospital today? You were telling me about that little girl who had the heart surgery."

She was looking at her plate when she said, "I had to cancel for today. I'm afraid . . ."

When her voice just trailed off, Jack suspected that something was wrong. Celia always finished her sentences.

"What's the matter?" He looked at her as he spoke, noticing what he hadn't seen before. She usually applied fresh face powder and lipstick before he arrived home from work, but she wasn't wearing any makeup at all. Her skin was less than pale. It had a bluish cast, as if she had become anemic. Why hadn't he noticed?

"I wasn't feeling quite right, Jack, but not really bad either. I thought it was the excitement of the weddings . . . one after the other like that . . ."

When she trailed off again, Jack felt a cramp pinch his stomach. Before he asked the question—"Are you ill?"—he knew the answer.

Her voice was subdued and she didn't look at him when she spoke. "Dr. Owen thinks I may have uterine cancer. He's done a number of tests and a complete physical. I should have all the results in a few days, but he wasn't very hopeful."

With all his heart, Jack wanted to say a comforting word, but all he could manage was to clutch his stomach and stammer— "a terrible cramp"—before rushing to the bathroom. When he came back into the room, Celia was still in her chair, the cold veal congealing on her plate.

He took her hand. "What happens now?"

"I have another appointment with Dr. Owen for Monday, but he's scheduled surgery already. He said we could cancel if it was all a false alarm."

Jack raised Celia from her chair and took her in his arms, wrapping her in himself for protection. "I'll go with you on Monday for the appointment." He kissed the back of her neck, said, "We're in this together . . . as if we were one person. You know that, don't you?" Even to himself he sounded like a cliché, but what else could he say?

Celia began to sob then and clutched him. After a minute or two she calmed down. He helped her clear the table and load the dishwasher. While they worked, he had a vision of their first apartment, Celia with her hands in a sudsy dishpan, her brown curls bouncing as she scrubbed, he with a checked linen towel drying the dishes, how much in love they were. He was already working at the bank. Then the boys came along, healthy children, bright and lively. Some small troubles along the way. Fewer than they had a right to expect. They had been lucky for a long time.

⌒

Celia and Jack Ramsden sit side by side in Dr. Owen's office facing his desk. The doctor sits opposite, composed and professional but grave. Celia has been his patient for many years. When he speaks, the news is worse than their fears.

"As I suspected, we have a uterine cancer, a sizable one."

Jack silently bristles at the "we." He means Celia. There is no "we" about it.

"We'll have to do an immediate hysterectomy. The appointment is already scheduled." He pauses only a moment. "I'm sorry to say there seems to be another problem as well. There's a suspicious tumor in the left breast, small but worrisome in combination with the uterine cancer."

Celia remains silent but Jack finds his voice. "Does that mean a mastectomy?"

"It's not unlikely."

"When?"

"During the same hospital stay."

"Good Lord. What then?"

"We'll let Celia recover some strength." He looks at her. "Then we'll begin chemotherapy."

Jack watches Celia's eyes fill with tears. She rests her trembling left hand on Dr. Owen's desk. The doctor pats it before speaking again.

"The side effects—some nausea, loss of appetite, hair loss—

are the worst part. After the treatments are completed, the hair usually grows back and the appetite returns. It's your best chance, Celia."

Jack flinches when he hears that. Only a chance. How long does she have? He reaches for Celia's right hand. He is surprised at how cold it is. Her hands are usually warm, even outdoors in winter. Will she be gone, he wonders, before winter comes?

Celia says, "Am I going to die soon, Dr. Owen? If so, I don't want to go through the chemotherapy to prolong the misery?"

"I won't lie to you. I have no way of knowing for sure. Every patient is different, and I've seen more than a few miracles. If we can get you through the next few months, you can have several good years ahead of you, perhaps more than that. The chemotherapy is difficult, but it often does the job. And if you get through the next five years, you can go on indefinitely." He smiles for the first time. "Watch your grandchildren grow up. They're bound to come along in due course. No promises, of course."

She takes a deep breath. "What shall I do between now and the surgery?"

"The nurse will give you a sheet of instructions on your way out." Dr. Owen rises from his chair and moves away from his desk, signaling for them to leave.

When Celia stands, she is suddenly woozy, grabs hold of the desk for support. Jack grabs hold of her.

Dr. Owen says, "Better wait a moment." He goes to a cabinet and pours a small amount of red liquid into a cup. He hands it to her. "Drink this. It's a mild sedative, cherry flavor, quite pleasant. You'll calm down a bit."

On their way out, the nurse hands Celia presurgery instructions and a prescription for a sedative. She says cheerily, "Two of these will give you a good night's sleep. Chase all your worries away."

Celia says, "Thank you."

Jack would like to tell the nurse to stop grinning like an ape but says nothing. He takes Celia's arm as they leave. "Are you up to something special for lunch?"

"Lord, Jack, I'm not the least bit hungry. I couldn't eat. Drop me off at home. Then you can go to work."

He is pleased with Celia's practical attitude, her wanting him to get on with things. He takes her hand and squeezes it. "That's my darling. Soon all this will be behind us."

He doesn't believe a word of it.

⌒

Celia is in surgery. She has been in there for hours. Jack has already called the boys to tell them there is some delay. To each, he had said in the heartiest voice he could muster, "Don't worry. She'll come through and be her old self before we know it. You know Mother. She's tough. I'll call you when the surgery is over."

He thinks: how useful meaningless clichés are, so much better than having to speak frightening truths.

Other people are in the waiting room with Ramsden, but he ignores them. He has had troubling dreams the last several nights. Weird, erotic nightmares. In one, he is having sex with a large-breasted woman who is warm and fleshy, like soft fruit in a hot sun. She is nothing like Celia, whose body is spare, neat, and well proportioned. The woman's face is masked by her long, thick hair. While they are locked together, sweating and grunting and heaving, her flesh begins to give off a putrid smell that forces him to turn away. He goes limp. When he turns to berate the fleshy woman for spoiling things with her nasty smell, her skin begins to darken and shrink and putrefy in front of him, as if they are in a horror movie. He feels as if he is choking and wakes up.

Damp with sweat when he woke, Jack knew it wasn't necessary to consult a psychiatrist to interpret his dream. The others that followed were variations on a theme: interrupted copulation, locked boxes that gave off revolting smells, bloody accidents, disgusting flesh. He fears his reaction to Celia's mutilated body as much as he fears her death.

Ramsden looks at the clock and wonders if Dr. Owen will ever come out of the operating room. He can't concentrate on any of the magazines stacked on the tables. Periodically, there is an announcement on the loudspeaker. Two small children are chasing each other through the waiting area, shouting as they go. They are giving him a headache. He and Celia would never have allowed their boys to disturb everyone like that. He wonders if the parents are beyond understanding that children must have limits if they aren't to become savages. He is pondering the decline of civility in urban life, when he hears his name on the speaker. "Mr. Ramsden, desk please."

When he rushes over, Dr. Owen is waiting for him, unsmiling. Ramsden asks, "How is she?"

"She took the surgery very well, but the tumor was large. As I feared, the breast was cancerous as well and there was some spread to the lymph nodes. We removed all we could, but I can't guarantee we got everything."

"When can I take her home?"

"We'll know better when we see how she does the next few days."

"Can I see her now?"

"She's still in the recovery room. You can look in on her after they take her to her own room, but she'll be heavily sedated. By tomorrow she'll need you more than she does now. You'd better get some rest yourself. Take my word, you'll be needing it."

The doctor's advice was like a presentiment. He shudders. "How long do you think she has?"

"I'd tell you if I knew, but I don't know. It *may* help if you can keep her spirits up through the chemotherapy. The desire to survive can be as potent as the treatment itself."

Ramsden notices the doctor's emphasis on *may*. He will do the best he can, but is there any hope? How much will Celia suffer? "What do we do now?"

"As soon as she's sufficiently recovered from the surgery, we begin chemotherapy. Some people take it well. Some don't. It's her best chance." Dr. Owen takes Ramsden's hand and shakes it. "Sorry I couldn't give you better news." He turns to go, but Ramsden holds on.

"Can you tell me, Doctor, do people still . . . after something like this . . . if they recover . . . you know . . . I must be insane thinking about it now . . ." He feels himself flush.

"If you're asking me about sex, Mr. Ramsden, there is no blueprint. From what I've seen of these matters, a lot depends on how things were between you and Mrs. Ramsden (Why did he avoid the familiar Celia?) before the surgery. But let's take one thing at a time, shall we?"

Ramsden flushes. "Of course. Thank you. I'm very grateful." What possessed him to say what he did? He wants to avert his eyes. Dr. Owen pats his shoulder and turns to go.

The children are still racing through the waiting area, but Ramsden is oblivious of them. He wonders what he will do with himself for the next few hours, after he calls the boys. He fishes for coins in his pocket and tries to think what he will say. No, how to say it. They are not expecting good news.

⌒

Celia is home from the hospital but goes for her chemotherapy treatments on an outpatient basis. Each morning when they wake, tufts of her hair remain behind on the pillow—patches of fur—as if she were molting. Jack tries not to notice, just sighs inwardly and goes to the bathroom to prepare his body for the day ahead. He has become preternaturally aware of the physical body: ingestion, excretion, respiration, mucus, tears, fingernails, skin, teeth, appetite—none of which can be taken for granted any longer. He studies his face in the mirror. Tired but sound. Not like Celia's.

Since chemotherapy began, Celia has eaten very little. The pounds have fallen from her like leaves in October. She is changing color. Her skin has taken on a blue pallor, her teeth and eyes a jaundiced yellow, her remaining hair the powdery gray of dust. She is tired and sleeps a good deal of the time. She is always cold. A winter tree. Jack thinks she is dying.

Jack is grateful for Annie. Faithful Annie has asked for and gotten a generous raise. It is only fair. Although Celia is no trouble, Annie's responsibilities are much greater than they have ever been. She arrives early so that he can leave for his office on schedule. She keeps the house stocked with supplies that she orders by telephone. She chats with Celia and helps to keep her spirits up, as up as possible in the circumstances. Her Jamaican accent is lively and warm, a soothing poultice. Annie leaves in the afternoon only after Celia has fallen asleep, so that she will not have to be alone too long before Jack returns home in the evening. Annie has dinner waiting for him on the stove. Sometimes, the spicy flavor of the Caribbean is a bit too strong, but he doesn't tell her for fear of hurting her feelings. He is afraid to lose her. Jack cannot remember how many years Annie has been working for them. He rarely saw her. Until Celia was taken ill, he never thought about her at all, just knew that Celia was pleased with her.

He thinks about Celia all the time, even when he is working. Before he leaves in the morning, he tries to coax her to eat something, anything. She apologizes.

"Forgive me, Jack. I can't eat a thing."

"Just a little. Dr. Owen says it's important."

"I can't." Then in a sharper tone, tears welling in her eyes: "Damn. Don't nag. Can't you see how miserable I am?"

He knows that she would eat if she could, if only to please him. It is not like her to be sharp. He recalls an article in a magazine in the doctor's office. Its main idea was that illness can change personality. He will have to live with it. So will she. For as long as she does live. He wonders if Celia might be going through all this for nothing, if she might not be better off letting the cancer take its course, better off dying sooner rather than later, terminating the suffering.

He wonders if *he* would be better off and feels a mantle of guilt descend on him. Best to take it a day at a time. Anything else is intolerable.

That night he dreams that he is on a train, watching the scenery pass by. Then a train traveling in the opposite direction obscures the view. He sees Celia in the window of the passing train. She is waving to him, smiling, then she is gone. He doesn't know what to make of seeing her, because she was supposed to be traveling with him but is traveling farther away, instead, on a different train. How will he find her? Before he can decide, he has to hurry and grab their luggage because the train has stopped. He rushes out into a splendid day full of sunshine and greenery, but the station is empty. Celia is nowhere in sight.

A pale early morning sun is filtering into the room. Celia is sleeping beside him, giving off a moldy smell. Trying not to disturb her, he slips out of bed quickly and quietly. When she wakes later, he says, "I had a hard time sleeping last night. Did I disturb you much?" Before she can answer, he says, "You might be more comfortable if I wasn't bothering you. I could sleep in the boys' room."

She thinks for a moment. "No. Please don't. I'm afraid to be alone. I know it's silly."

He doesn't mention it again.

Before he opens his eyes, Jack smells the coffee. It is Saturday. He wants to remember that. He wants to remember that on a Saturday in November 1973, the world began to turn right side up again. He wants to remember that the chemotherapy is working, that Celia is showing signs of getting well, that the week before she had begun to eat a little more than nothing, had asked Annie to cook apple sauce, had asked for an extra portion of mashed potato. Without opening his eyes or feeling for her side of the bed, he knows that Celia is awake, moving around, making breakfast. Is that Bach or Telemann he hears? Celia has always had a taste for the baroque. She must have put the tape on.

When he goes downstairs, still in his pajamas and bathrobe, quietly so that he can look in on her, Celia is cracking eggs into a bowl. She is wearing the new pink velour bathrobe the boys gave her. It lends a touch of freshness to her pale skin. The wire whisk is on the counter. It has been in the drawer for three full months. Jack is happy to see it back in use, but when Celia's hand reaches for the whisk, he feels a fresh stab of pain.

Celia's hand and wrist are skeletal, the fingers like thick wire. Her fingernails are almost blue. A pretty flowered scarf neatly tied at the base of her skull hides her nearly bald head. She has tried not to let him see her baldness, refused to talk about it when he suggested a wig might help her morale till the hair grew back. But the scarf slips off when she sleeps and sometimes in the morning light he sees a few stiff gray tufts where once, not long ago, there were beautiful brown waves. When this happens, Jack's heart twists with sorrow and pity. But just as often the twist is in his belly, and what he feels is best described as revulsion. He refuses to name it that, prays his thoughts are invisible.

He goes upstairs to dress, and when he returns in a green plaid shirt and casual trousers, Celia is ready for him. The table has been prettily set with woven blue place mats and white china plates rimmed in cobalt blue. A pot of strawberry jam, a dish of butter, and a blue-and-white Delft cream pitcher are in the center of the table on a little straw mat. They look like a still-life waiting for an artist. As if it were the most ordinary thing, Celia says, "Let's have omelets, Jack. I haven't eaten a good one in ages."

"That would be lovely." He puts his arms around her bony

shoulders. They are thin as clothes hangers beneath the soft velour of her robe. He says, "It's marvelous to see you on your feet again."

She smiles. "I think I'm going to make it, Jack. This past week I've been feeling quite a bit better."

He pours the coffee while she makes a large omelet for them to share. She sprinkles it with chives. Sitting opposite her while they eat, he notices that she has touched her cheeks with a bit of rouge and painted her dry lips a pale pink. The cosmetics don't improve her appearance much, but they are a hopeful sign. Perhaps she'll be willing to reconsider a wig until her hair grows back. If it grows back. He'll get one of the daughters-in-law to suggest it, perhaps both of them when they visit in the afternoon.

As he and Celia chat over their food, Ramsden thinks back to Dr. Owen, what he said about sex, wonders how it is going to be with them now that Celia is getting well. What does getting well mean? Her body has been plucked, cut, and eviscerated, like a chicken being shipped to market. All that remains of her beauty is memory. Will that be enough? He wonders if the hardest part of all this is only now beginning.

Celia is one of Dr. Owen's miracles. She is almost herself again. But she can never be herself again, her womanly self, not really. They pretend.

Their days are almost as they once were. They visit the children. They go to restaurants with friends, to the movies, watch television. Celia's hair has grown in quite well, so much nicer than the wig she finally consented to wear. She keeps it cut short because the "new" hair is wiry and difficult to manage. But the gray color is surprisingly flattering. He doesn't want her to dye it. She has gained weight, bought a green suede coat that highlights the hazel of her eyes. A prosthesis in her specially constructed bra fills her clothing nicely. To look at her now, Jack thinks, nobody could guess that she had been so deathly ill, so ugly. Of course, she has grown old.

Celia talks about getting out more. She doesn't want to return to the hospital as a volunteer because she doesn't want to be around sick people. He tells her to take her time before making up her mind. She says, "Every minute counts. Do you think they need volunteers at the museum? We've been members for years."

When he is at home, Celia welcomes his arm on her shoulder, his hand at her waist, a kiss on her cheek. She seems to desire nothing more. Jack is relieved. But memory troubles him: His delight in pulling Celia's nightgown over her head so that she can be completely naked in his arms, her breasts melting into him. Now he has no desire to draw her close. Which is not to say he has no desire at all. Sometimes, when he sleeps, an erection springs up. Was he dreaming of someone else? Of Celia before cancer? He can't remember. He turns and tries to sleep.

One evening, when he arrives home for dinner, a pungent smell greets him at the door—freshly baked bread. Celia is busy in the kitchen again, but she does not use much butter or cream now. She takes care to flavor the food with wine and herbs. He prefers it. After dinner they finish the bottle of Mouton Cadet he opened for their meal. Celia is being a bit coquettish, cooing over his shoulder as they settle on the sofa to watch television. He tells himself it is only the wine. But she is charming, something like her old self. It is pleasant to have her beside him.

For several weeks they have been engrossed in *The Forsyte Saga*, a marvelous series from the BBC that more than passes the time. Grand emotions sweep the screen. Soames's beautiful blond wife embraces her lover, gives way at last to her illicit passion. Celia's head leans on his shoulder, his hand drifts to her knee. She kisses his neck, his hand slides to her thigh. She is wearing the perfume he selected for her birthday. It has a lovely fruity smell. Celia reaches her arm across his chest, then down his torso to where his trousers are moving. Soon they are kissing, ignoring the screen.

He says, "Let's go upstairs."

"Ummm."

They lean against each other like movie drunks as they climb the stairs. They don't turn the light on in the bedroom. Better that way. Better not to see. They are still wearing clothing from the waist up when he is into her. It is far from the best they have ever had, but it is far better than nothing. And the border has been crossed. They are safe in another country.

A dry spell. Weeks pass in their ordinary way. Then they go to the movies, a film they both look forward to—*Klute*, with

Jane Fonda and Donald Sutherland—about a private investigator from a small town who falls in love with a call girl. All the critics recommend it. Henry Fonda's little girl playing a prostitute. What can she possibly know about it? Not that he can imagine what actual prostitution is like either. He has never been remotely tempted to pay for sex. Degrading all around. You might pick up a disease.

The theater is warm; the seats are comfortable. Jack and Celia sink into the film. Sutherland has become obsessed with Fonda. Is her passion for him real after so much faking with her customers? Is she using him? Jack is riveted by her low, warm voice, the intensity of her beauty. He thinks: a knockout, all right, just like her father but all female. The sex scenes are arousing. It's almost like the real thing. Jack feels a lively warmth in his groin. Finally, there is an unlikely happy ending to the film that neither he nor Celia expected. They leave the theater with a lift.

Before going to bed, Jack and Celia have a nightcap. The bed linens are a little chilly, but the down quilt soon takes care of that. As they drift off to sleep, Jack thinks about Fonda doing it with Sutherland, how real it was. He falls asleep but awakens later with an urgent erection. This time he reaches for Celia, runs his hand over her buttocks, under her gown. The flesh is still good there. He circles her, mounts her. She is awake now, touching him from behind, where he likes it best. She is crying out, her hips and legs pushing forward. Her mouth is moist when he kisses it. No pretending.

They don't make love often. The right drinks, the right movie—secondhand foreplay, but it works. They are happy again.

Three years later, when Celia is getting dressed for work—to Jack's surprise and dismay, she had found a job as a clerk in a bookstore—she feels a small lump in the other breast. She has surgery but refuses chemotherapy. She suffers and takes painkillers, is forced to leave her job. It takes fifteen months for her to die. Jack is relieved when it is over. Relieved, and lonely as Crusoe.

Amsterdam

CLAUDE BOISVERT IS emptying his second glass of Heineken. Only a little froth remains in the bottom. He thinks he might enjoy a third. Boisvert likes the Dutch beer as much as he likes the direct way the Dutch do business. None of the fake politeness of the English. The Dutch let you know where you stand. A little cool perhaps, but no chillier than the English. And he is in Amsterdam to make money, not friends.

His meeting at the old brewery earlier in the day had been a great success and the entire operation decidedly interesting, a bit like watching a good movie: mammoth copper brewing tanks looming up like space stations, fermentation vats bubbling like hot springs, crates of beer rolling out in platoons like tanks. Impressive!

And they didn't keep him dangling on a string. They placed a sizable order for cartons on the spot: a good price for them despite the shipping costs and a good profit for him. The best kind of deal. He smiles to himself and offers a prayer for Quebec's endless forests. Quite amazing the way the world is shrinking, he thinks, and Claude Boisvert on his way to being a rich man. He leans back in his chair and signals the waiter for another glass. He can afford to relax.

It is still early evening. The bar is pleasantly dark and only half full: a few couples, but most of the customers are men, alone or in pairs, who've stopped off for a drink on their way to another place, home perhaps. How will he spend his evening? Not much point going off to a room-service meal in his empty hotel suite, comfortable as it is. A good dinner in a restaurant would be nice, but the prospect of eating alone is not appealing.

The waiter brings a frothy glass and sets it down in front of him. When he is halfway through it, Boisvert thinks how pleasant it would be to have a woman. Not a whore—not a common cunt like the ones he saw the night before when he walked past their windows. He wants a high-class, well-dressed woman he can be seen with in a restaurant and take back to his hotel. A shame, he thinks, that he doesn't have the least idea how to find what would so please him.

After downing his third beer, Boisvert goes to the men's room. When he returns to his table, he signals the bartender for another. A new arrival is removing his coat and placing it on the back of a chair at the table next to his. The man is tall, a good-looking, sturdily built fellow with a square jaw and thick blond hair that seems to be turning white. Hard to tell in the dim light, but he's no youngster, probably a few years older than himself. No doubt about his height though; so many of the Dutch are surprisingly tall. Boisvert feels as if being in Amsterdam has caused him to shrink several inches. But, he assures himself, brushing his tongue along his upper lip to lick the foam, he is big enough where it counts.

The tall man sits down. Boisvert notices his light-colored suit, a fine creamy wool, expensively tailored but slightly out of season. He has a ring on his left pinky, a good chunk of diamond set in hammered gold. It sparkles when the man lights a cigarette. His fingernails are carefully trimmed and lacquered with clear polish, manicured. His shirt and tie have the sheen of silk. *Expensive,* Boisvert thinks. He wonders if this prosperous-looking fellow in the eye-catching clothing and jewelry could help him find a woman for the night. At least, he thinks, he has nothing to lose by getting acquainted. He leans over and speaks in English.

"Would you like to join me for a drink? Unless you're expecting someone. I'm in Amsterdam by myself . . . on business."

Verhoeven looks up, hesitates, then stands and turns his chair to Boisvert's table. "Thank you. I'm also alone at the moment."

He turns and calls out to the bartender before sitting down with Boisvert.

When a waiter brings his beer, Verhoeven lifts his glass, nods, and empties half of it in a single swallow. He says, "Now, what can I do for you?"

"Nothing at all. Just a little company."

"Nonsense. Of course you want something, or you would be offering a drink to a woman instead of me." He looks Boisvert over. "You don't look like a fairy to me."

Boisvert laughs aloud, decides he has found the right fellow. "Now that you mention it, I'd prefer a woman, but I don't know where to find one."

"Have you looked in the windows off Dam Square?"

"Not that kind of woman. Someone more high-class I can take to a hotel."

Verhoeven puts his chin in his hand and thinks. "I'd like to help you, Mr. . . . ?"

"Boisvert."

"French?"

"Quebec . . . Montreal."

"Ah, we've both traveled a long way."

"But you look Dutch yourself. Aren't you?"

"Actually, I am, but I've done business in the Far East for most of my days. I just returned quite recently."

"So, a businessman. What kind of merchandise do you deal in?"

Without hesitation, Verhoeven replies, "Spices. I import spices. And what brings you to Amsterdam?"

"Paper products." Remembering his coup of the morning, he chuckles: "Quebec can be cold for people, but it's perfect for wood. We can be very competitive when it comes to paper. I've just had a good order from the Heineken people. Put me in the mood for a woman."

"Well, good luck to you, but I'm afraid I can't help. If I knew where to find what you're looking for, I'd keep you company."

Boisvert pats Verhoeven's shoulder. "It would have been nice, but no great matter. I'm flying back to Montreal in the morning. Just as well I go to bed early."

Verhoeven stands up. "Allow me to give you my card. If you come to Amsterdam again on business, call me. And try to give me a little notice. Who can tell, I might know just the right

woman by then. At the very least, we can have a drink together."

Boisvert tucks the card into his pocket. He asks, "Why not
stay a bit for another beer?"

"I'm afraid not." Verhoeven hesitates. "Doctor's orders. But
thank you, and remember to call me when you return to Amsterdam on another trip."

Boisvert rises and extends his hand. "Good to meet you."
"Likewise."

Verhoeven takes his coat and walks out the door as two
young couples walk in. They seat themselves noisily at a table
opposite Boisvert. They are dressed American style in worn blue-
jeans and rumpled work shirts. Their hair needs cutting, Boisvert
thinks, just like Simone's friends.

Boisvert remains standing. Finally, he puts his coat on, tosses
a tip on the table, pays his bill, and walks out into a fine drizzle.
He decides on his warm hotel and room service. A good night's
sleep won't be so bad, he thinks, but a woman would have been
better.

Verhoeven has taken to investigating his penis, or, as he now
refers to it on his visits to the doctor, his "goddamn prick." He
pokes and prods it, tries to explore its ancillary sacs and ducts,
worries about its color and tenderness and flaccid habits, the
often alarming odors and textures of its secretions. Actually, he
is angry at it. He has begun thinking of it as his badly behaved
son, a part of himself but with a mind of his own. It will not
obey—no matter how well he treats it.

If Dirk Verhoeven were still the man he thought himself to
be—the man who never flinched when forced to face facts, the
man who always made the most of the worst situation—he
would have admitted to himself weeks before that he has become impotent, that his sexual failure is the result of a venereal
infection that refuses to respond to treatment, that he contracted
the infection because he was careless, that he waited too long
before seeing a doctor because he believed he was . . . well . . .
invincible. But age and pain are hard realities; the facts are
bleak. And he is not the man he once was.

Verhoeven avoids Mei-ling. He has forgiven her for not bearing a son, has decided that it was her witch of a doctor who put a curse on them, that Holland had always been an unlucky place for him. When he cannot sleep, which is often, he torments himself with memories of Mei-ling's warm, moist flesh: the taut softness of her skin, the yielding roundness of her breasts, the musky odor between her legs. What is the point of having a beautiful young wife if he isn't able to enjoy her in bed? As things stand, she and the child are nothing but a drain on his fast-shrinking pocketbook.

Such thoughts remind him that both Coelho and Kung have disappointed him as well, that the river of white gold that he expected to flow from Afghanistan through Hong Kong has dried up . . . or been diverted elsewhere. And he can do nothing about it because they need nothing from him. They have all the cards, probably found a more profitable outlet. What's past is past. Loyalty, friendship: the words do not occur to him.

It is still quite early in the evening when Verhoeven lets himself into the handsomely furnished office/living quarters he has fashioned for himself. One of those people who lives only in the present, he is unaware of having repeated the pattern he established in Hong Kong: an office in front for business, a living place behind. He had stopped off briefly at a small Indonesian restaurant for some pork satay and rice after his beer with Boisvert. But the meat was dry and the rice too sticky. Wistfully, he recalls the meals he enjoyed in Bandung. The food, the money, the women, had all come so easily to him. He curses Sukarno for his failure.

After hanging his coat in the entrance hall closet, Verhoeven catches a glimpse of himself in the full-length mirror that hangs inside the closet door. He used to enjoy seeing himself reflected in a glass, but now his belly has begun to lap over his belt and the flesh on his neck hangs in thin folds. When did it happen? He strokes the convex curve of his belly, decides to watch his eating. No sense making everything worse by turning into a fat man, old before his time.

He'll begin tomorrow. What he would like most at the moment is a good bottle of schnapps. He hears the doctor's voice: "Absolutely no alcohol, strictly forbidden with the new medication we're trying." As a consolation, he's brought some fine chocolate home, bittersweet cups filled with Curaçao liqueur. Not enough alcohol to make a difference, he thinks, just a slight kick and a bit of pleasure. One may as well enjoy what one can. If that young masochist of a doctor had his way, all enjoyment would be denied him.

Verhoeven goes from the entrance hall past the closed office door to the spacious reception room straight ahead. The room is a little like a Mondrian painting: furniture and carpet in rectangles of color—vivid blue and yellow predominating. The tables are slabs of black, the lamps columns of dull red metal with opaque white glass shades. It is a room that manages to be luxurious and comfortable while giving off a spark of excitement. It had cost him plenty for the high-class designer, but the result was worth it. Anyone he brought there could not fail to be impressed.

But where are the guests he had intended to entertain? Connections have been unexpectedly difficult. And what is the point of bringing a woman there if he can do *nothing* with her? He calls a halt to his thoughts, worries he has become sentimental and morbid because of his illness, resolves again to follow the doctor's orders.

Verhoeven presses a switch, and the music of Puccini fills the room through a splendid sound system—*Madame Butterfly,* one of his favorites. He decides that the sound equipment is worth every penny it cost him. Why make do with the second-rate? He settles into the sofa and reaches for the chocolate. He pops one into his mouth and feels the tickle of the Curaçao on his tongue, the melting of the chocolate in his mouth. He takes another. He tells himself that the right new drug will come along soon and cure him. He recalls his last checkup, when the doctor faced with yet another disappointment had said: "We're working on new drugs all the time. Try to be patient. You'll be cock of the walk before long." Well, what choice did he have? He had to be patient.

Meanwhile, he had better find a way to make money. His pile was still large—enough to last a while—but so were his expenses, what with Mei-ling and the child and living in Amsterdam, where prices fly into the stratosphere. He pops another chocolate. Where is the money going to come from? He taps his teeth together, scratches his scalp. At his age . . . after all his hard work . . . he should not have to be worrying about his pocketbook.

As Verhoeven reaches for yet another piece of the chocolate that he finds so satisfying, almost as consoling in its way as a glass of good wine (if not schnapps), he thinks about the fellow he met in the bar early in the evening. He grimaces, reminded that he has disobeyed the doctor once again. Well, he decides, one beer is not a tragedy. A French Canadian. Verhoeven had never met anyone from Quebec before. But, he decides, they're just like men everywhere, and what they want at the end of the day is a good lay.

How bold the fellow had been, asking him where he could find a high-class whore instead of something ordinary. Did the fellow think he looked like a pimp? Verhoeven grimaces. Well, who should know better than he that it's important for a strange girl to be clean and healthy. If he'd had the right source to begin with, he might never have taken up with a stranger who was spreading a plague.

Verhoeven begins to wonder if such a service exists in Amsterdam. There must be plenty of travelers in the city for a day or a week at a time, he thinks, fellows like the Canadian, who want their pleasure and are willing to pay good money for a clean, high-class girl. Very good money! And The Hague is infested with diplomats who are always on the lookout for some discreet pussy. And the scientists and the professors at their endless conferences and meetings sniff around like anyone else. Intriguing possibilities nip rapidly at Verhoeven's brain, like hungry goldfish at feeding time.

Verhoeven reaches for another chocolate, leans back on the sofa cushion, and closes his eyes. Even if such a service does exist, who is to say there's not room for another? The world is shrinking every moment. Schipol Airport is always busy. All one would need is imagination and a modest expenditure of capital. And, of course, the right kind of girls. By the time he goes to bed, Verhoeven is convinced that his encounter with the Canadian was fated.

Mei-ling walks briskly in the cool air, head high, comfortable in a body that is her own again. Juliana has begun to drink from a bottle and has learned to take a few sips from a cup. Mei-ling swings her arms as she walks, lightly, in rhythm with her stride. She turns into a narrow street, on her way to an appointment with Berthe, who has turned out to be a professional masseuse. Once a week now, while Emma cares for Juliana, Mei-ling lies on a padded leather table as Berthe's strong hands dig into the muscle and sinew that knit her bones together.

When she arrives at Berthe's office, Mei-ling goes into the changing room, removes her clothing, and folds it neatly into a basket provided for the purpose. She then takes one of the light blue cotton robes stacked on the shelf, but not before inspecting herself, recalling Berthe's words at the end of her previous visit: "Well, you have your figure back, that's for sure. No sagging in the breasts or the belly either . . . like some I've seen after the child comes. Not even a stretch mark." Mei-ling places three fingers underneath each breast and lifts till they bounce lightly and settle into place. Nice. Berthe is right. She is herself again . . . whoever that may be.

While she waits her turn, Mei-ling is preoccupied with Berthe, who has intruded on her thoughts during the week since the last massage. Idly, almost languidly, she'd said, "That feels wonderful, Berthe. Your husband's the lucky one. He can have you work on him at home whenever he pleases."

She had never met Berthe's husband but felt as if she knew him. A good man. Berthe had said nothing at first, just seemed to dig her fingers a little deeper. She had asked, "Do you give him a massage often?"

Berthe had lifted her hands from her back then. "Oh, no. We've been divorced for many years now."

"But I thought you said . . . after the camp . . ."

"It was all true what I said, but everything changes. We were happy in the beginning. I think really he was sorry for what happened to me and decided he was feeling love." She hesitated before speaking again. "I'm not sure anymore if I loved him either. I was so grateful . . . and his parents were so kind. But when we were already married for a few years, he began to seem a little bit boring . . . and we had no children to be interested in together."

"Did you leave him?"

"No . . . only inside my head a little . . . I thought I needed him to take care of me . . . I was afraid to be alone without a man or a family of my own. Then he met someone else who was younger and Dutch like him. She could have children . . .

so he has two of them now. I was hurt in the beginning, but I don't hold it against him any longer. He was very good to me when I needed someone."

"What did you do? To take care of yourself? Did he give you money?"

"Some for a year, and we had a little saved that he said I should take. He was feeling guilty. But I didn't like taking money from him and I wanted to work. That's when I trained to be a masseuse. It pays enough to keep me going, and I like the work."

They had stopped talking about it after that, but Mei-ling fretted, considered, is still considering a week later as she waits for Berthe to work on her: Juliana is a baby, Mother is getting older and has never completely recovered from her wounds. They are my only family. Can I count on Dirk, my husband? I never know what he is thinking. He has begun to look a bit sickly. What if he should collapse and die? Or fly back to Hong Kong without us? What would we do? All I have is the jewelry.

Money, she thinks, that's what makes everything possible. She tells herself: I can't depend on anyone but myself for it. Who knows what Verhoeven will do? And Juliana's education will be expensive. And we must have a nice place to live.

Before Mei-ling's mind can race further ahead, the door to Berthe's workroom opens and a white-haired woman with a cane limps her way into the changing room. Mei-ling wonders: Who looks after her? It would be terrible to be old and poor and dependent upon others. It must never happen. Mei-ling arches her back and sits straighter, as if to confirm her resolve. Berthe pokes her head out and calls for Mei-ling to come in.

Mei-ling strips off her robe and stretches her slender body on the table. Berthe kneads her flesh as if she were a bread being readied for the oven. How good Berthe's fingers are, how strong, how penetrating! The silence is sweet. The room is quiet, white, and unadorned. Mei-ling's mind drifts and wanders. To Verhoeven. He has been staying with them less and less, sometimes no more than a day or two in a fortnight. Yet he takes care of everything. They are warm and well fed. All the bills are paid. She has money when she needs it. He comes at random in the evening . . . without notice . . . brings a toy for Juliana, a trinket for her, more rarely flowers, as if he is making up after a quarrel, though they never exchange harsh words.

He does and does not live with her. When he stays overnight they share a bed, but he is careful to leave a space between them, careful not to touch her. He wakes often in the night. She detects a faint unpleasant odor when he is beside her. It is hard to tell because he has taken to dousing himself with scented colognes and powders. An odd change of habit.

Has he been sleeping with other women? Even in Hong Kong, when they made love often, sometimes in the Mercedes because of Emma, when he could not have enough of her, she understood that he had other women from time to time. It did not bother her then, nor does she feel the least pang of jealousy now. She has always understood that they do not love as lovers do. Not that she hasn't . . . at times . . . after a fashion . . . cared for him and appreciated his attention: the pearl necklace and earrings for her birthday, the gold cat with emerald eyes at Christmas, the silk scarves, the embroidered lingerie, the flowers, the fine restaurants. Occasionally, she had enjoyed him as a lover, though most often she forced a passion greater than she felt. It was not a lie, more like a performance, as if she were an actress, Verhoeven her audience of one. Her life . . . and Emma's . . . had depended on how well her performance was received.

But now she is not required to perform at all. Why should he continue to pay and receive nothing in return? It is not the way he does business. And he has little enough interest in Juliana, though he smiles and gives her his hand when he sees her, brings her stuffed animals to play with.

What if Juliana had been a son? Would that have been better? In the instant of thought, Mei-ling is grateful for her daughter, relieved. There is no cord connecting her to Verhoeven. Once Juliana is older, in school perhaps, she will find work and care for them both without him. But what work can she do if their life is not to be drab and mean?

"All over." Berthe has finished rubbing scented lotion into her skin. Her voice seems to come from a distance. "You can get up now. I'm finished."

Mei-ling rises from the table slowly and slips into the cotton robe. She breathes in the scent of the lotion. Spice that reminds her of China, but she can't remember the name or what it would be in English. She says, "Next week, Berthe?"

"Good." Berthe smiles at her fondly. "It's good to work with a healthy body like yours instead of so many old and sick."

"I'm depending on you to keep it healthy," Mei-ling says. "I'm going to need my strength."

Montreal

DAVID LEVY DROPS the black case stuffed with books and papers on the floor before the door has time to close behind him. He calls out, "Val?" No answer. For the first time since their marriage, he is happy not to find her at home. He wants this time to himself.

Levy tears at the corners of the white envelope embossed with the Harvard logo in the upper left-hand corner. Squeezed in above the logo is the familiar P.P. He pulls out a letter. It is handwritten in a sprawling scrawl that covers several pages of lined yellow paper. As he shuffles through the pages before reading them, Levy sees that there are almost as many sketches and doodles as words. Pete's style! Five years since he's seen it, but he'd know it anywhere.

Dear "Prof" Levy,

So you've gone and done it—joined the establishment—a professor no less (even if you haven't quite finished a few bits and pieces of the—what do they call it up there?—anyway, what we call a dissertation—we won't quibble—your students are past the puberty and groping stage, so you can call yourself professor). And a married man! The question is—Does she deserve you? Take that any way you like.

Very clever sending the letter care of my parents. I've been doing some wandering around these few years—trying to "do good" and stay out of the slammer at the same time. I've managed the latter but I'm not sure about the former. Things are weirder here all the time. Do you get all the news of what's been happening in the States? This country is a disaster—except for the war being more or less over. A great thing! Years and lives too late. Nixon is getting loonier all the time. Even my father is beginning to wonder if the man has a screw loose. Do they report on Watergate up there? Our own ranks seem to be accumulating a generous quota of weirdo freaks—a fact, but I can't seem to face it. I bumped into Carrie, who now sports a couple of tattoos. Not flattering, but she claims they put a hex on cops. ?????? Everyone is tripping on something or other, mostly acid. Len M. had a bad trip and is in the "hospital"—probably for keeps. Not exactly the old days when a few joints were a great high. Trouble is, nobody can do anything useful for the struggle while all this personal discovery shit is going on. All they do is talk and trip.

Which brings me to my big news. No, I'm not getting married and "settling down." Most of the femmes with brains have turned hostile and grown fur—and truth is I have a warped sexual nature—an aversion to smelly armpits and hairy legs, not to mention the occasional aggressive mustache—a definite turnoff. The not-so-brainy femmes are needy, needy, needy, by which I mean all they want is—hold your breath—sex, the wilder the better. It's so frantic. Why does "free love" (as the enemy calls it) turn me off instead of the other way around? Hey, I must be basically a shy guy. (Stop laughing, people change.)

Back to my big news. Better sit down if you aren't already. I picked up my last semester at Harvard and have the "parchment" all rolled up and tucked away. For some reason I can't fully divine, Harvard Law let me know they wanted me. (Painful knowledge—those old ancestors of mine still seem to have some clout ****** not my fault!!!) Why, you ask, have I taken this step? It has finally dawned in my dim brain that if I really want to have an effect on this sick world, I need to know how the law works—and how to work the law. Otherwise, everything we do amounts to senseless heroics that lead nowhere.

Great to hear from you, Dave. Let me know if and when a junior Levy makes the scene. If—make that when—you write again, send it care of my parents. I'm still not permanently anchored down. Wouldn't want anything important to lose its way. Hey, can you believe that thirty is starting to creep up on us. By the time I'm working at the law, I'll have crossed the great divide. What rough beast waits on the other side? I leave you with that happy thought.

Peace, brother,
Pete

So, Dave thinks, Pete's going to land on his feet after all, a Harvard lawyer at that. Like me in a way, slipping into Canada to avoid Vietnam and five years later teaching at a university. Meant to be. We're programmed. It's inside our heads.

He glances through the letter again before putting it down on the table. No word about visiting him in Montreal. He's sure he asked, is disappointed, would like to see Pete. Still a stranger in Montreal, Levy sometimes has a hankering for Cambridge and New York. Even the bagels and corned beef are different in Montreal. Good, but not as good. He thinks about visiting New York when the political climate changes for the better. See friends. Introduce Valerie. Save his folks a trip north. His dad's health is not great. His fault?

He goes to the refrigerator for a beer, wonders when Valerie will be home. A note is propped against a bottle of beer on the center shelf. Cute!

Hello love,

Sorry I won't be home till after dinner. May be late. Do whip up one of your special omelets to fill your tummy. Some good cheddar if you want it is in the cheese box and a tomato is in the vegetable bin. Don't wait up.

Val

Levy is hurt (unreasonably?) that Pete isn't coming. He wishes Valerie were home for dinner. Still, she has her own life to live. They agree about that. As for Pete, he'll write to him again.

Amsterdam

~

T HE DOORBELL RINGS just as Mei-ling has settled down to
read after putting Juliana in her crib for a late morning nap. She
is startled, cannot imagine who it might be. They've never had
a visitor other than Berthe that one time.

As she rises to answer, Mei-ling thinks of Berthe rubbing her
shoulders and back and buttocks and legs with the scented lotion, saying, admiringly, perhaps enviously, "With a body like
yours, you'll never have to worry. There will always be a man
to look after you." Berthe's admiration has become unsettling,
as if the older woman were usurping her for some private dream
life of her own. Mei-ling hopes that Berthe is not waiting at the
door.

When she opens it, Verhoeven is standing there with a bouquet of pink-tipped yellow tea roses wrapped in green tissue
paper. He is smiling, healthier-looking than at his previous visit.
She says, "Dirk, what are you doing here at this hour? You
surprise me."

Obviously in good humor, he reaches for the small of her back
and walks her into the living room, saying, "You think I don't
belong here still? I believe you are Mrs. Verhoeven, and if I peek

into another room, I will find a daughter who would like a visit from her father."

"She's just fallen asleep."

"Then we can chat before she wakes. I want to talk with you. Why don't you make some coffee?" He hands her the flowers. "And put these in some water."

"They're beautiful." She brings them to her nose and inhales. "The fragrance is delicious." She can tell from the way he looks at her, how his eyes follow the outline of her body, that she is in his favor again. Has something happened?

Verhoeven follows her into the kitchen and stands beside her, placing an affectionate arm on her shoulder as she fills a vase and prepares the coffee. The heavy odor of his cologne invades the lingering sweetness of the roses. Mei-ling's pleasure is clouded, she grows wary, watchful. What does he want?

In a few minutes the coffee is ready. She pours, prepares a tray with a plate of butter cookies and a cream pitcher. She carries it into the living room and places it on the table in front of the sofa. They sit. Mei-ling is silent, waiting for Verhoeven to speak.

Verhoeven takes her hand and says, "Have I told you, my dear, that motherhood becomes you. You are more beautiful than ever."

She wonders if he is about to embrace her, but, no, he reaches instead for his coffee and brings it to his lips. He leans back into the cushions of the sofa like a cat resting comfortably, tail between his legs.

Mei-ling says, "You're looking much better yourself, Dirk. For a time, I wondered if you were unwell."

He doesn't respond to her implied question. Instead, he says, "Tell me, what have you been doing with your time? Have you found a way to enjoy yourself?"

She is bewildered by his renewed interest in her. She says, "Most of the time, I spend with Juliana. We go to the park and take walks. But I'm able to get out on my own when Mother takes care of her. I look in at the shops, I enjoy the museums, I visited Rembrandt's house. We learned about him at Miss Richardson's school." She picks up a book from the table. "I bought this at the Rijksmuseum. Rembrandt. Have you gone to see his work?"

He laughs. "When you've grown up in Amsterdam, you get tired of everyone telling you how wonderful he is, and I can't say the museums are my first choice of entertainment, but I'm glad you like them."

Suddenly, Mei-ling recalls her father, his great treasure of Chinese art books . . . probably scattered ashes now. Her father, so much the better man, knowledge and virtue in every pore . . . for all that so defenseless . . . so unlike this sturdy Dutch husband whose only thoughts are wealth and pleasure. How different, too, was her brown-faced friend, the strength of his hand as he pulled her aboard the train, sacrificing himself to help her, his blood drying on the road like a dark puddle of mud. So long ago. She sips her coffee.

"You must be bored being cooped up with a baby. You need to get out at night and enjoy yourself."

"I suppose you're right, but I'm not bored. Juliana is interesting . . . more interesting than you imagine."

"You must come to my party. I'm going to be entertaining a few business clients at my new office. You've never seen it, and I want you there."

Mei-ling is not expecting this. Is it a command? She has never been involved in his business. Even Emma claims she never understood all the little packages that she picked up by hand from hotel clerks or the bills for general merchandise that she tucked into folders or the sealed envelopes of cash she delivered to ship captains and airline pilots. Mei-ling is intrigued and a little excited. "A party! When will it be?"

"Tomorrow night at seven. We'll have some refreshments and then go out to dinner afterward. Your mother can stay with Juliana."

"Yes, of course. She'll be glad to."

Mei-ling watches as Verhoeven reaches into his inside jacket pocket and pulls out a tan leather wallet from which he removes a wad of bills. He peels off several and presses them into Mei-ling's hand. "Buy something special to wear. I want you to look splendid. And wear some of your diamonds. A woman never looks cheap if she is wearing diamonds. Anyone who says that is an envious hypocrite."

Mei-ling looks at the bills. "I'm sure I can find something that will please you with this . . . and perhaps have something left over to surprise you with."

"Good. Take a taxi. I'll be there before the guests arrive, but you can arrive a little later." Verhoeven picks up his coffee cup and drains it. Then he stands up. As if it is an afterthought, he says, "You should wear the emerald pinky ring rather than your wedding band. No need for anyone to know our personal business."

A thin wail sounds from Juliana's room. Verhoeven says, "Well, that is my cue to be going. She needs you."

Mei-ling thinks: a business visit. She says, "Don't you want to see your daughter?"

"Perhaps for a moment, but not too long. I'm working on something new. You'll understand later on."

"I have to change her diaper. She's always wet after a nap."

"I'll wait here. I can't stand the smell of soiled diapers."

"I'll bring her in as soon as I change her."

Mei-ling notices then that he has not brought a toy for the child, only the roses that had mingled so unpleasantly with his cologne. She is disappointed . . . though she tells herself she shouldn't be. He takes care of them in his own way. If she expects more, the disappointment will be greater.

She picks up Juliana to quiet her. Then she spreads her on the changing table, removes her soaking diaper, and impulsively smells it. The ammonia stings her nose a little, but the smell pleases her. Impurities the body washes away. The smell of the body working as it should. Healthy nature. Not repulsive at all. A better smell than Verhoeven's cologne.

When she brings Juliana to her father, the child's eyes grow wide. She reaches her hand toward him as if he were a large teddy bear who has appeared unexpectedly. She begins to smile and tests his ear with her fingers. The tip of her nose and her cheeks are still pink from sleep. He takes her hand and shakes it for a moment. But only a moment.

Verhoeven turns to Mei-ling: "Remember, a little after seven o'clock. I'll be expecting you." He starts to leave, hesitates, then nods toward the child. "She looks well. She'll pass for pure European, don't you think?"

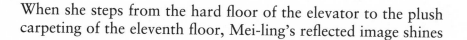

When she steps from the hard floor of the elevator to the plush carpeting of the eleventh floor, Mei-ling's reflected image shines from the mirrored wall opposite the elevator doors. Dirk, she thinks, will be pleased. She raises her hand to her right ear and adjusts the clip holding a cluster of small diamonds. A thin chain of diamonds circles her wrist. Her fingertips end in graceful red talons. A pinky ring, a square emerald set in gold, sits like a brilliant hummingbird on a delicate stem.

She removes her coat and places it on her arm. She turns from side to side. He will like her choice of dress: a sleek purple sheath. A round gold choker with its diamond clasp just under the point of her chin sets off her face. She smoothes her dark hair and nods at herself in approval. Dirk's business friends will envy him. Without her wedding ring, they'll not know she's his wife, think only that he has a beautiful young woman at his command. No doubt the effect he is after. And close enough to the truth.

Her inspection completed, Mei-ling turns to the corridor on the right as Verhoeven has instructed. She sinks her feet into the thick blue carpet, admires the silver-and-gray-striped wallpaper, the cool white hexagonal glass of the light fixtures glowing softly on the ceiling. Expensive, she thinks. Dirk Verhoeven must be doing well to have his business here. The door to Verhoeven's office is dark blue, a deeper shade than the carpet. She pauses, listens to the low, raspy whiskey laughter that comes from behind the door, thinks she has just missed a joke. It is Verhoeven himself who opens the door when she rings.

"Come in, my dear." He raises his voice. "Everyone is waiting to meet you." He takes her coat and drops it on a chair near the door, then takes her hand and propels her toward the reception room from which she hears the sound of glasses being filled, more laughter. His arm sweeps the air and points toward her. "Here she is, gentlemen, the Miss Wang I told you would be here soon. Worth waiting for, isn't she?"

Mei-ling cringes a little, but she holds Verhoeven's hand and smiles at the men, who seem to be taking her in greedily. When they smile in return, their teeth look large, as if she were seeing them through a magnifying glass. Why does everything appear distorted? Where are the other women? It cannot be that she is to be the only woman here. Or can it? What had she been expecting?

Verhoeven presses a glass into her hand, says, "Drink up. We're all ahead of you." She does, and in a moment she is feeling better, able to smile more naturally and exchange a few words.

The men begin to take on distinctive shapes. There are four of them: three old enough to be her father, and one, a tall, portly, silver-haired fellow with a slightly mottled skin who looks old enough to be her grandfather. He, she thinks, is what Verhoeven will look like before too many years have passed. All the men are wearing well-tailored business suits in dark colors, striped ties, polished black shoes—a club of gentlemen. Their fingernails are short and smooth. Their hair is carefully barbered and creamed. They have the sheen of the prosperous. She wonders what business Verhoeven has with them.

He is busy refilling their glasses. One of the men, a fellow whose fringed, indented bald spot reminds her of a monkey's behind, turns and raises his glass to her. "To a most beautiful young lady!"

Before they can drink, the old fellow offers a further toast. "To all the beautiful young women. May they never grow old!"

A third chimes in. "Even if we do!"

They all laugh at this. Finally, they drink. Mei-ling, sipping the ice water remaining at the bottom of her glass, thinks of Emma and of Berthe, the lines in their faces, what it must be like to grow old and lose one's power over men.

Verhoeven says, "Well, gentlemen, the ladies are waiting, and a fine dinner is waiting too. What you do afterward is up to each of you."

All the men laugh again. Mei-ling doesn't understand. Has he told a joke? She notices that Verhoeven is handing each of them pieces of paper and telling them not to be late to the restaurant. They leave in pairs, apparently to meet the ladies Verhoeven spoke of.

Only at dinner, when their party has been joined by four women, all very young, all as beautiful and well-dressed as herself, all eager and attentive to their partners, does Mei-ling begin to think she understands the joke. But what is she doing here? She is, after all, Verhoeven's wife no matter what he has led the others to believe.

It is late. Verhoeven and Mei-ling are seated side by side, not touching, on a sofa in the reception room where Verhoeven's party had begun earlier in the evening. The place smells of stale smoke. Cigarette butts are still piled like slag heaps in the ashtrays. Heavy glasses, their ice cubes melted to puddles, mar the tops of the sleek designer tables. For a brief moment, Mei-ling wonders who will clean up the mess, then decides that Verhoeven has probably made an arrangement to have everything taken care of. As always.

She is disappointed. The party had not been at all what she'd expected, though it was a lively enough affair. The ristafel was a great novelty for two of the men who were in Amsterdam for the first time. One, who spoke a peculiar kind of English, kept referring to himself as the delegate from Coca-Cola who "hailed" from Georgia. The other, the one whose head reminded her of a monkey's behind, was a dealer in furs from Canada. They had both stuffed themselves. The two others drank more than they ate. The older man and his colleague were Swedes who visited Amsterdam often. She remembered him saying, "Our business is to serve humanity." Everyone laughed when he said that, but he and his fellow Swede insisted that they were quite serious, that they had to take their pleasure when they could; burdensome humanity made heavy demands on them. Because they were already a bit drunk, it was hard for her to tell if they meant what they were saying. Where, she wondered, had Verhoeven found them?

And the girls? They were well-dressed beauties in their twenties: three tall, slender, high-bosomed Dutch blondes and a dark, generously proportioned French girl whose lively breasts quivered whenever she stood up or sat down. It was hard not to look at them. She was paired with the older man, the Swede who was not nearly so interested in the food as in getting back to his hotel with the girl. When they were only partway through dinner, he grasped her hand and said, "Time to go."

His colleague, smirking and laughing, had said: "Don't be in such a rush at your age. The Hague will still be there waiting for us. The meeting doesn't begin till late morning. It's only a short trip from here."

But the tipsy old Swede and his French girl had been the first couple to leave. On their way out, he had leaned on Mei-ling's shoulder, squeezed it hard, said something to Verhoeven that had sounded like, "You win both ways." She didn't know what he meant, thought the old fellow too drunk to make sense. The others left soon after. She had not been sorry that the party ended early.

Now Mei-ling rests her head on the back of the sofa and closes her eyes. She had wanted to go home, but Verhoeven insisted she spend the night with him. He'd said, "Juliana is safe with your mother. I need you here."

Mei-ling would like to go to sleep, but Verhoeven has just pressed another glass into her hand. A liqueur. She sips it. Creme de cacao.

He says, "You were at your most beautiful tonight. Did you enjoy the party?"

"I didn't understand it."

He takes her hand. "Just what didn't you understand?"

"Everything. Who the people were. What business you have with them. Why did you want me to come?" She pauses. "What about the girls? Were the men paying them? It seemed so."

"You understand more than you think, my dear girl. Actually, I was paying the girls and the men were paying me."

She turns her head and looks into his face. He says, "I have decided to try a new business, and it is off to a promising start." He pats her hand. "Actually, it's a very old business . . . thousands of years . . . but I want to give it a new style . . . an international style. You're going to be my business associate."

"Me?"

"Yes, you. Who better than my wife? No more Kung and Coelho, where I lose control of the situation and the money. This way we keep the money in the family."

"But what do you expect me to do?"

"I want you to understand the way we'll work. We'll have only the highest class of people . . . the sort of men who expect to pay very well for what gives them pleasure . . . and clean, healthy, beautiful girls who know how to behave in public and please a man in private . . . girls just like you, the kind of girl who knows how to use the body God gave her and likes to live well. I can assure you, there are plenty of them right here in Amsterdam. My girls will earn a very good living, and with the kind of customers we'll have, they can enjoy themselves in the bargain."

He takes a breath and spreads his arm in a grand gesture, as if he were presenting a new opera to the public. "Expensive hotels, the finest food and wine . . . the company of men of affairs who appreciate their gifts . . ."

Mei-ling, recalling the drunken old Swede, can't conceal a smirk, but Verhoeven, caught up in his plans, doesn't seem to notice. She says, "Where do you find them?"

"Why, I advertise, like any businessman. Most of them fancy themselves models or actresses to begin with. They already understand their beauty will make money for them. It's only a short step to work for me, the best work they can find, to be sure. You should have seen how eager they were to take their clothes off so that I could see what they looked like . . . not embarrassed for a moment. They're proud of their bodies. It's only petty moralists who find fault with the business . . . who expect girls to do it from the goodness of their hearts."

A sigh escapes from Mei-ling's mouth. "I sometimes wonder if I have a heart . . . and if you do. Are you doing this business *only* for the money, Dirk? Or is there something else? And what is it you expect me to do as your partner?"

Verhoeven doesn't respond immediately. He seems to be considering. Then he says, "Stand up and take off your clothes. It's been a long time since I've seen you naked."

"Is that why you wanted me here? To look at me?"

"Please, stand up and do as I say."

Wearily, Mei-ling stands. She looks directly at him, sees a shadow flicker across his face. She tries to please him. She raises her chin and arches her back while she reaches for the zipper behind her. Her dress slips easily over her head. In a moment her bra and panties and stockings are on the floor. She stands before him clad only in the gold choker with the diamond clasp that sits just below the point of her chin. She expects him to reach for her.

Verhoeven looks appreciatively, mouth slightly open, but he doesn't move. "My dear, you have a face created for jewels and a body that will get them for you."

Mei-ling brings her fingers to her neck. "Do you want to unfasten the clasp for me?"

He remains sitting and doesn't answer.

"Don't you want me, Dirk? Isn't that why you asked me to stay?"

Verhoeven continues to look at her and lights a cigarette. He says, "My dear, I think you should know that I can no longer do more than admire your beauty with my eyes . . . and feel regret. No matter what the doctors do to help, the greatest of the world's pleasures is denied me. I seem to have become impotent."

Still naked, she sits down beside him, somehow relieved that a mystery has been solved. Before she can say anything, he says, "The delights you provide so well must now be for others to enjoy."

A chill passes through Mei-ling then. She reaches for her dress and slips it over her head, not bothering to fasten it. She looks at Verhoeven in the soft lamplight. "Do you intend for your own wife to be one of your girls?"

"You weren't such a narrow moralist when you were hungry and dirty. You were happy to eat my food and wear the clothing I gave you. Besides, you'd be more than one of my girls, more like my partner. A very well-paid partner who can watch over the others." He has an afterthought. "Like the first wife in a Chinese family . . . someone with status . . . not a mere concubine."

Mei-ling flinches at the word. "You want me to have sex with your customers. The head of a Chinese family does not expect that."

"Well, you're half European, and it's time you started earning your keep. Did you think I would pay for you forever and expect nothing in return? Especially since I can't fuck you myself."

Mei-ling flinches. He rarely uses coarse language with her. "Yes, Dirk."

"Try to understand. This is a business like any other . . . better than most. The men you'll meet will be entirely respectable. Many are wealthy and generous if a girl pleases them. Before long, you'll have as much jewelry as the queen. And it will look much better on you than on that silly old woman."

He stands up. "Now, let's go to bed. I can at least think about the way it was when I first saw you in Hong Kong. Even in those rags, I saw your beauty."

When they are in bed, he is soon asleep. But Mei-ling is awake, wondering about what lies ahead. She is oddly calm, considers the possibilities. She could, of course, refuse, take Juliana and Emma and leave. He would not try to stop her. But they would be poor forever. Emma's health is troubling. And,

she thinks, there are far worse ways to earn a living, far worse
ways to survive. Many have done it and gone on to other lives.
Soon, at least in thought, she is reconciled. She understands that
for a few years she will be meeting many men whom she will
entertain, that they will be businessmen and politicians who
travel the world, and professors with generous expense allow-
ances who are attending conferences in Amsterdam, and international civil servants who do their work in The Hague and find
their pleasure in Amsterdam. They will be acceptably "high
class," as Verhoeven had said. She will accompany them to restaurants, theater, concerts—the pleasures of Amsterdam. Then
she will spend a few hours or perhaps a few days in the finest
hotels, pleasuring them in quite another manner. Emma will
look after Juliana. She will be able to put a considerable amount
aside. Before too many years, she will have enough money to
strike out on her own without fear of the future. And she is still
young.

Part Four

1983

Montreal

⌐⌐

JACK RAMSDEN IS diverted momentarily by the splendor of the flowers. It is the middle of May, and the Botanical Garden is springing up in early bloom. Brilliant colors dance in the sun: late-blooming lilacs, lush assemblies of pink and white azaleas, masses of yellow, white and purple perennials, short, sturdy scarlet tulips beside tapered pastels that lean like ballerinas.

A reward, he thinks, for enduring the endless Canadian winter. It seems to grow harsher with every passing year. Or does being over sixty make an enemy of the cold? In either case, he's happy to have the winter behind him. He resumes his walk down the path to Grace's office. Then, in the shimmer of the late afternoon sunlight, a mirage appears. But when he squints and shades his eyes, it is not a mirage at all.

She is standing there, small and beautiful as the flowers, in a navy blue dress and red linen jacket. Her dark hair is styled differently than the picture in his memory; it is shaped like a fan that opens from a straight center part. The breeze catches it for a moment, then stops. It falls neatly into place. She is studying a bed of yellow tulips whose ruffled petals flutter slightly in the mild breeze. Sensing his staring, she looks up. Jack sees that she recognizes him immediately. Her face composes itself into a poised smile. He approaches her unsteadily, the ground shifting under his feet as he shortens the space between them. He holds out his hand. She takes it and speaks before he can.

"Here we are in a garden again, Mr. Ramsden. You must be very surprised to see me."

"Surprised to say the least, Miss . . ." As happens more and more often, his memory of names fails him. Her name has been erased, temporarily he hopes.

She helps him. "Mei-ling, Mei-ling Wang. It has been a long time."

"Yes, of course. Forgive me. I don't remember names as well as I should." He is conscious of a blush rising up. Embarrassed, he can't think of what to say next, blurts out, "What brings you to Montreal?" He regrets his words instantly, fearing she is with a client.

"I've been in Canada a few months now . . . you might say beginning a new life in the new world." She smiles.

"Then you'll be living here permanently?"

"Oh, yes, my bridges have been burned."

Her English is even more colloquial than he remembers. He wonders what she means about burning her bridges. Has she changed her way of earning a living?

"Are you going to remain in Montreal?"

"That is my plan."

"And how is Juliana?" The child's name comes easily now that they are speaking together.

"How nice that you remember her. She is very well and has adjusted to school nicely. She likes Montreal."

"A delightful little girl, though probably not so little now. And is your mother with you as well?"

Mei-ling's eyes redden and grow a little moist. "She died at the end of last year."

"I'm so sorry." He has never met the woman, was being polite, searching for neutral conversation, yet he feels a stab of sorrow. "Is that what brought you here, Mei-ling?" Her name, spoken softly in his own voice, thrills him.

"Perhaps her death hurried things along, but I was preparing for a change long before. I had hoped we would be here together."

"Do you have anyone in Montreal . . . any friends?"

"Not yet. That will take some time. But Juliana already has friends, and she can speak French almost as well as English."

"She must have her mother's gift for languages."

Ramsden wants to know more about Mei-ling, but given the nature of their acquaintance, he feels awkward. How can he inquire without seeming to have a prurient interest? Scarcely aware of what he is doing, he looks at his watch, realizes Grace will be waiting for him, is perhaps looking out of her window at that moment, wondering about the young woman with whom he is speaking.

Mei-ling notices the gesture and says, "You must go. Don't let me keep you."

"I'm afraid that I do have an appointment."

She extends her hand. "I'm pleased to have met you again, Mr. Ramsden."

He takes it, regrets having to leave. "Do you remember in Amsterdam . . . my promise?"

"Your promise?"

"I said that if ever you were in Montreal, I would be your guide."

She smiles. "I release you. I'm certain you never expected me to be here."

"Ah, but I insist. A gentleman always keeps his promise. You must let me know where I can reach you." He hesitates a moment, wondering how to reassure her of his intentions . . . assuming he himself knows what they are. "And bring Juliana if you'd like . . . if she isn't bored by adults now. She must be quite grown."

"As tall as I am." She smiles again.

This woman has changed, Ramsden thinks, less guarded. "That's not very tall, is it?"

Ramsden recalls his first sight of Mei-ling, her tiny perfection. A shudder of pleasure surprises him. He takes one of his cards from his wallet, turns it to the blank side, and reaches into his jacket pocket for a pen. He hands it to her. "You must give me your address and telephone number so that I can reach you. Permit me to keep my promise."

She hesitates, then takes the pen and writes. She hands the card and pen back to him. "I'm causing you to be late for your appointment."

He looks at the card. "Near the university, are you?"

"Yes. I will be a student there in a few months." She smiles again. "Odd at my age."

Ramsden, remembering his surprise at her knowledge of art and architecture when they first met, can't help feeling pleased, reinforced in his judgment by this bit of news. He wants to encourage her. "Just where an intelligent young woman belongs. I'll want to hear all about your plans when we tour the city."

"I would be happy to share them with you, but I won't hold you to your promise if you're too busy."

At that moment he has no intention whatever of being too busy. He fully intends to be Mei-ling's guide to Montreal. The situation may be a bit awkward, but he's certain they can get beyond it.

They shake hands again. Finally, it is she who turns away from him. He watches her go, studies the curve of her shoulders and hips, marvels at what has so unexpectedly happened. Then he hesitates. How is she earning her living? Might she consider him a prospective client? How would he feel about that? And what about Grace?

Ramsden looks at his watch again. His encounter with Mei-ling has taken only a few minutes, yet it seems as if hours have gone by. He hurries to find Grace. She will be waiting, looking forward to his arrival. They plan to have dinner and spend the night together. Only moments ago, he had been eager as a schoolboy.

⌒‿

Since her divorce, Grace hadn't been involved with many men, none she found attractive till she met Jack over a year earlier at a benefit flower show for Victoria Hospital. It was held in the middle of winter in the conservatory of the Botanical Garden. He was attending as a patron, his bank having made a large donation. She, of course, was working.

Mingling with the jeweled and chattering crowd, barely nibbling the canapés, sipping sparkling wine, she had spoken with him only briefly, but she was pleased when he steered their conversation away from fund-raising for the hospital to the Dutch bulbs she had chosen to decorate the event: royal purple hyacinths and huge golden daffodils forced into premature bloom to grace the occasion. She had wanted the guests to feel as if they were in a spring garden while the lawns outside the conservatory were still covered in snow. He applauded the effect she had achieved, had said, "I feel as if I've been transported from winter to spring. It's marvelous."

Grace was surprised at how much he knew about bulbs: that they were botanically related to common onions and garlic, that tulips had originated in Turkey, that they were an important factor in Holland's economy for centuries, that the markings of some of the most beautiful were actually the result of a bulb disease.

He had said, "I visited Keukenhof Gardens near Amsterdam once. They were very beautiful. You should visit them someday."

Aloud, she said, "I intend to." To herself, she said, *with you.*

She was charmed, attracted, could be interested in a man who cared about flowers. But was he married? All the really nice men she met seemed to be.

After he called her at work the following week, her spirits had risen like sap in springtime. He asked her to dinner. He was a widower. They had warmed to each other immediately. Had a whole year gone by since then?

Grace's divorce had been like the onset of a mysterious paralyzing disease. She had lain about for months in a kind of stupor, shrouded by the vast emptiness of a household crowded with precious objects. The porcelain vases, the hand-tinted prints from England, the silver candlesticks and tea service, the antique tables, the tapestry cushions, the Persian rugs, the jade inlay ebony box from China that held her jewelry: her delight in these had shriveled to a fine dust. It was as if she had been entombed with objects from a previous life.

Family and friends urged her to "get out of the house and do things." But what? She had no desire to grow fat eating lunch with widows and divorcees who were just marking time. Finally, because she had always enjoyed gardens and flowers and had collected and read a fair number of books about horticulture, she decided to volunteer a little time at the Botanical Garden. She poured herself into her work and, in only a few months, found herself employed three days a week at a modest—no— absurdly low salary. But money was hardly the point. Her check, which she looked forward to at the end of each month, was more like a trophy than a salary. It was the symbol that counted; the money was meaningless. She had so much of it already.

Shortly into her second year at the gardens, a bit of luck fell into Grace's lap: a post coordinating benefit-planning and fund-raising. Between the grander occasions, there was work, work, and more work. But the splendors the garden held were a daily pleasure for her. Even in winter. At Christmas, when the out-door gardens and trees were blanketed in silver and white, she invited the more generous donors for small private tours through greenhouses that looked for all the world like tropical islands. But she was still lonely, and the nights were long. Till she met Jack.

On this particular May day, while she is waiting for Jack, Grace stands at her desk, arranging her papers for the next morning. When she looks up, she sees him through her office window. He seems preoccupied. He is making his way toward her. Although it is still early, she feels the first pangs of hunger and anticipates a leisurely drink, a stroll and dinner together, then all the pleasures of affection—no, she thinks, not affection, more a lazy kind of lust—that will follow when they return to her house afterward.

In the restaurant, somewhere between the deviled shrimp and the lemon mousse, Jack changes things. He says, "I'm terribly sorry, Grace, but I'm not going to be able to stay tonight. Something's come up at work that I simply must prepare for. No way out of it."

She is disappointed. But later, as they walk together down the flagstone path from his car toward the house, her house, the marvelous Tudor with its leaded glass windows, its clipped and tailored shrubbery, its solid front door of weathered oak and wrought iron, she feels quite happy. At dinner Jack had said very clearly, "We're so comfortable together, aren't we, Grace." A statement, not a question. It wasn't like him to refer to their relationship at all . . . though they both took it for granted by this time. She was touched.

The light of the amber lantern hanging by the door illuminates the entrance. Before they reach the circle of light, Jack embraces her and kisses her affectionately on both cheeks. "Good night, Grace. Too bad about tonight. Next time to look forward to though."

"Good night, dear." Yes, she thinks, he is dear to her. They had been so delightfully intimate for months, as if they were already married. Well, it would not be long. December wasn't very far away.

Grace had always appreciated dignified men, men who didn't come at you like tigers, men who took their time getting to know you. She had liked that about Jack and, she was forced to admit, her former husband. It still pained her to think of him, how, without warning, he had taken off with a mere girl, a secretary twenty years younger than she. A cliché. A stab to the heart she had miraculously survived.

But now she has a man she can care for and trust, a man who has some money of his own, who isn't lusting after hers, who loves her for herself, who can talk about something other than banking and business, who enjoys concerts and museums and French wine and fine cheese and—she may as well admit it—sex with a woman not so very much younger than he. In his sixties he may be, she thinks, but definitely a man who needs a wife more than he needs a nurse.

Grace is already inside her house by the time Jack drives off. She feels a bond to the wonderful old place, an inheritance from her grandfather. Railroad wealth had built it sturdy and grand, like the Canadian-Pacific itself. She is the third generation of her family to live in it. But of all the family and the life that had been, only she is still holding the fort in Montreal.

She no longer feels quite at home in the city of her birth but has not been able to bring herself to leave. Now she is glad of it. Both her girls have settled in Toronto, having fled from the rage of Quebecois separatism. No future now for English-speaking young people in politically incendiary Quebec, French dominating everywhere . . . the street signs, the shops, business. It was like being taken over by an occupying power. At times, in the months after her daughters left, she thought of herself as a relic of some earlier civilization. But not anymore. Jack has changed everything for the better.

She locks the door behind herself, puts her purse down next to the bouquet of red tulips that fills the Delft vase on the entry table, and looks into the entrance hall mirror. It is an antique, a glass oval framed in walnut, kind in the soft overhead light. The person who looks back at Grace is a well-groomed, still attractive middle-aged woman in a quietly fashionable beige wool suit. Slim and long-waisted, she wears clothes well. She always chooses simple styles cut of fine cloth, the kind that last and don't go out of style.

Is her hair white or silver? The words are important. White means old, silver means beautiful. Friends have urged her to color it, but she is adamant in refusing, wanting to remain, as she puts it, "the person I am." Yet she is not without vanity. Quite the contrary. The turquoise silk scarf she wears complements her blue-green eyes, heightens their color, hides the new fleshiness of her neck. "The neck is the first part to go," her hairdresser had told her, a tip she has taken to heart.

Grace's face is finely shaped, an elongated oval topped by a corona of thick, glossy hair swept back and high into a smooth knot. Her forehead is unlined, her nose straight, her cheekbones high, her chin slightly pointed. Her pale skin is still soft, the gratifying result of years of rose water and glycerin diligently applied.

It is too bad, she thinks, that Jack wasn't able to stay. Not like him to change plans on such short notice. But there would be other times, many times. The years lay ahead of them. They are far from old. Grace decides to go to bed early and read, perhaps plan a little of their wedding trip to London in December.

In another part of Montreal, closer to the downtown heart of the city, David Levy has come home to an empty flat on the top floor of a three-story stone house. The house has seen better days, but, like the surrounding neighborhood, it has about it a touch of Paris or Greenwich Village before McDonald's and Benetton. Trees on the sidewalk soften the hard edges of stone façades; small shops and a restaurant brighten ground level and basement quarters. Guided walking tours pass through the street regularly; Levy has occasionally looked out his street-facing windows into the upturned faces of strangers: tourists earnestly studying the eroding pattern of the carved stone cornice above him.

David is disappointed but not surprised that Valerie is nowhere in sight, that he will once again scramble a few eggs for a solitary dinner. They had quarreled that morning, but even when they do not quarrel, she often contrives to be busy elsewhere when she knows he will be at home. She has taken to reminding him—"Women were not put on this earth, David, for the sole purpose of feeding and breeding"—as if he needed reminding.

Her hostility bewilders him; until she had begun attending her women's group, they rarely disagreed about anything. There was so much they enjoyed together: books, films, hiking in the Laurentians, Indian curries. Politics? Perhaps not for him any longer, but his work is itself a kind of politics, more important than endless boring meetings or futile demonstrations . . . and he never tries to stop her . . . though some of her notions have begun to seem harebrained. And some of her friends look as if they're in drag; they'd be bald if they cut their hair any shorter.

How can she possibly think he considers her a breeder or a feeder? He does more than his share of the housework and wants her to have a career every bit as much as he wants her to have a baby. He admits to himself that he has silently chafed at her skipping from one thing to the next—painting to teaching to pottery to social work—as if it were the idea of doing something that was serious and the work itself unimportant. But he has never thrown it up to her, especially since he makes enough to support them both, given the way they choose to live. Many people take time to find themselves. Then why, if he is so admirably reasonable toward her, does she make him feel like a criminal because he wants to be a father? Isn't it the most natural thing in the world? He can't very well do it on his own. David Levy passionately desires a child, and his wife with equal passion refuses to bear one . . . "at least for now," she says. But, he wonders, if not now, when? Valerie is in her mid-thirties, and nature, indifferent nature, has seen fit to limit women's procreative years. *The Great Mother may have screwed up,* he thinks, *but she must be obeyed.* Soon the decision will not be Valerie's to make. Is that what she wants?

Mechanically he scrambles eggs and prepares toast. He pours a glass of milk and sits down with a newly arrived copy of *The New York Review of Books.* But it is not sufficient distraction. Can this cold, obstinate Valerie be the same person who picked him up just over the border from Derby Line in Vermont? So many years ago, it hardly seems possible.

He sees her as she was then, a lanky, self-possessed blonde with long hair and a long stride who arrived five minutes before he had been told to expect her. How grateful he was that she hadn't made him anxious—simply walked into the small café where he was waiting, picked him out from among the stocky, chattering, middle-aged French couples, stuck out her hand and said, "Hi. You must be David. I'm Valerie Hume. Welcome to Canada."

The nervousness that had cost him in sleep and sweat drained away. He put himself in her hands, literally grabbing hold of them as he stood up to leave with her. He'd said, "Thanks. I got here early. I'm glad you didn't keep me waiting."

"You'll find that we're pretty organized. I'll take you to Montreal. We'll have you set up in no time."

He remembers how she held on to one of his hands as she led him toward her car. "You have plenty of company," she'd said, "more and more Americans are coming over the border every day. If the war doesn't end soon, Canada's going to fill up with them."

He saw that she was looking him over and hoped (with a boyish intensity since lost) that he measured up. She had the same sedate blond prettiness that Carrie had, the same quiet confidence, but with Carrie he was always uncertain, off course, lost in a storm. With Valerie he felt immediately secure. She was so strong. Was that why he fell in love so fast and so hard? No, he thinks, there was more, stuff he felt but can't remember now. But the way she seemed to rescue him had to have been part of it.

When they reached Montreal, she settled him into the apartment he was going to share with another American who was not expected to show up for a few days. As she was getting ready to leave, he said, "Can I have a phone number where you can be reached. I don't know anyone else here."

"It's on the pad next to the telephone along with a few others in case I'm not around. And there's food and some beer in the refrigerator."

"You do think of everything. Hey, I can't thank you enough."

"Thank me? Don't even think of it. It's you fellows who are the heroes."

Did she think he was a hero? He, who had no intention of fighting in the war or going to jail as a draft resister? He was glad someone thought he was a hero. He wasn't at all sure of what he was, except that he was scared.

Valerie was so pretty and such good company. He didn't want her to go. "How about something to eat before you go?"

"No thanks, but I'll stay a little if you want me to."

"Great. Let's have a beer."

Later, when she was getting up to leave, he took her hands into his again and said, "Hey, I want to see you some more."

She put her arms around his shoulders then and leaned into him. "Sure," she said. He was hot right away, hotter than he ever was before—like a hound in heat. No control anymore. She was putting her hands in all the right places. He was pulling her clothes off. She made it so easy for him, opening herself up, pushing him into her. When it was over, she whispered to him, "You haven't ever done this before, have you? Nice, huh?"

"Amazing. How did you know?"

"Just knew." She ran her fingers down his back. "But don't think I'm criticizing. You definitely have talent. Keep at it."

He laughed and kissed her again, a big, juicy, delightful kiss. Remembering, David sighs and finishes his milk. He puts the dishes into the sink and switches on the television. The mountain of paper waiting for him will have to wait longer. Finally, he goes to bed.

Valerie has not yet come home when he turns off the reading lamp clamped to the headboard and drifts into sleep. In the morning her place next to him is empty. He knows better than to worry about her safety. But this is the first time she has been away all night without telephoning. It is early—six A.M.—three hours before his first class. He washes up quickly, slips into his shorts and running sneakers, fastens the sweatband on his head. He does a few stretches to loosen up and leaves the flat.

The streets are almost empty when he begins to run. The few people who are out to work early are used to his familiar presence dashing past in any weather—even snow. This morning is not cold; his lean, compact frame begins to sweat long before he finishes his usual five miles. He is soaking wet by the time he lets himself back into the flat.

When he gets out of the shower, he hears noise above the radio. "Val?" he calls out.

"Hi, David. Can you stand some toast and coffee?"

Her voice is warm and friendly, as if nothing is amiss between them. He is relieved, does not relish a confrontation. He smells the coffee, pokes his head through the bathroom door, and says, "That would be great."

David throws a terry robe over his naked body and goes to the kitchen in his bare feet. The floor is sticky. Neither he nor

Valerie are much into cleaning, and they are both opposed in principle to hiring a once-a-week housekeeper because they will not exploit anyone else's labor. In practice, this means that he does enough to keep them from sinking into squalor and Valerie ignores the mess. He is beginning to think that they are being silly, that plenty of immigrants would welcome a job, that he and Valerie would pay better than the going rate. But this is not the time to broach the subject of housekeeping.

Valerie smiles up at him from the table. She is holding a cup of coffee and puts it down. "Hope you weren't worried. The session lasted so long, I decided to crash with Garnet. I didn't want to take the chance of waking you by calling."

"Thanks," he says, and helps himself to the coffee and toast she has set out for him. He hates Garnet, who affects dark red clothing and jewelry to complement her name. If indeed it is her name. David thinks it is probably false, like the stories she tells about the legion of men who have violated her. Their world has suddenly become populated by perverts and rapists. Does Valerie believe all this? Does any rational person? What was Garnet doing while the brutes had their way with her? Knitting?

How like the new Valerie, he thinks, treating him badly and turning it into a virtue . . . not wanting to wake him. It wasn't always like that. She used to be so direct . . . so admirable. David is beginning to hate the women's movement and feels guilty for hating it, thinks he should try harder to understand what is happening to Valerie, to all women. They have, after all, suffered and been violated. He smiles at her across the table and demolishes his toast.

She asks, "Another slice?"

"Thanks."

He sees that she is eager to please, to smooth things over. He will go along. Why not? She is prettier than ever—slim and lively—and he loves her. Will he always? When she places the hot toast in front of him, he puts an arm around her waist and squeezes. "You make the best toast," he says.

For a moment he thinks it is the wrong thing to say, that she'll accuse him of thinking she's a "feeder." But no, she leans down and kisses his forehead. He runs his hand over her backside, and she rewards him with a smile. Then she says, "You'd better finish up or you'll be late for class."

Translation: Don't get any ideas. No sex. He tries conversation. "How was the group?"

"Okay. Good turnout."

He is not interested enough to inquire further, and she does not volunteer anything more. He dresses and kisses her on the cheek before leaving for the university.

In the afternoon, after his final class, he goes to his office, where student papers are piled up on his desk, waiting for him.

Mei-ling rests before breakfast in lazy solitude. Nestled in comforts—an ivory silk nightgown embroidered in the Philippines, smooth paisley bed linens, plump cushions, a woven cotton coverlet—she is contemplating her future and Juliana's. More and more since they have come to Canada, the future seems to hold agreeable possibilities.

Juliana is happy, flourishing, safe now in the company of friends at summer camp. She is learning to swim. Montreal is pleasant, a bit of old Europe in the new world to judge from the parks and the architecture and the various bakeries and the good French food in even the most modest restaurants. Surprisingly, several of the Chinese restaurants are quite acceptable, though crowded with tourists since the weather turned warm, and not to be compared with those in Hong Kong.

Classes at the university will begin in less than two months. Already the old life with Verhoeven, the parade of men, repellent and charming alike, is disappearing in the brisk wind that blows from the St. Lawrence River. And the past, she thinks, however disagreeable at times, has served a purpose. It is essential to have money. About that, Verhoeven was absolutely right. Without it, how would she begin again? What choices would be open to her? Odd though, to have crossed paths with the old life, that nice Mr. Ramsden, in so large a city.

Mei-ling is not surprised that Ramsden has not called. In the rare moments when she thinks of him at all, she is relieved. A misunderstanding on his part would have been embarrassing. Yet she cannot help being slightly disappointed that he has not kept his word. He had seemed the sort of man one might trust. There are so few. But she brushes thoughts of him away with

the flick of her hands in her hair. There is so much to do before
summer ends and university begins.

Mei-ling rises and showers. As she dusts herself with powder,
she notices a few dimples on her thighs where they had never
been before. But she doesn't dwell on them. The smoothness of
her thighs no longer matters very much. She looks through the
packed closet and selects a tailored white cotton dress that is
piped in green, crisp and comfortable enough for a Montreal
summer day, yet suitable for the pleasure of business. It is most
agreeable, she thinks, to no longer be in the business of pleasure.

The sandals she fastens to her slender ankles are a web of thin
green straps. Though low and comfortable for walking, they
manage to complement the curve of her legs. She appraises herself in the full-length mirror and approves. A few strokes of the
hairbrush, a light layer of powder, a delicate touch of lipstick,
a tracing of eyeliner: she is almost ready. She fixes thin gold
hoops in her ears. Daytime jewels.

Mei-ling pulls a small wooden ladder over to her closet and
climbs to the top step. She stretches her diminutive frame to the
right-hand side, reaches up to the second shelf, and pulls out the
gray metal box that holds her papers. Not the irreplaceable ones.
Those are safely ensconced in the vault at the bank. She inspects
them only occasionally, adds to them, watches her assets grow.

Mei-ling opens the box and removes her records: a precise
running total of her assets, the due dates of her dividends, the
rents received on the property she still holds in Amsterdam. She
checks the record carefully. Two of the coupon bonds stored in
the vault are due. She slips a pair of tiny clipping scissors into
her purse before sitting down to a light breakfast. She doesn't
want to forget them.

The fresh peach she slices is not as sweet as those she remembers eating in China when she was a child, but peaches are still
her favorite fruit. She enjoys their tart sweetness, enjoys too a
cup of tea and toast spread with orange marmalade imported
from England. Before leaving the apartment, she replaces the
metal box on its shelf, smoothes the bed linens and coverlet,
rinses her breakfast dishes. Only when all is tidy and orderly
does she take a final look in the mirror, smooth her hair, check
her purse, and leave.

It has been Mei-ling's habit when the weather permits to walk
through different sections of the city. Street by street, boulevard

by boulevard, each park and square and monument: she has explored, examined, evaluated. She knew what she was looking for: a piece of good, solid property.

Today she has a more fixed purpose. Previously she had come upon a little tucked-away street on a pleasant square not very far from Mount Royal Park. The neighborhood was a mix of commercial and residential: tall office and apartment buildings, small stores, a few restaurants, rows of older stone residences, the survivors of better days. Better than decent but not posh, on the way up, she guessed, with the next upturn in the economy.

The square itself was a pretty picture. Bordering the north side of the green, in a perfect row like uniformed sentinels, was a group of charming two-and-a-half-story gray stone houses, slate roofed, with small front and rear gardens marked off by iron gates. Their front windows faced south toward the sun. The angle of the roofs, the solidity of the structures, reminded her of Amsterdam, but these houses were wider, more spacious, more like the new world than the old, or perhaps more like the English than the Dutch in the way they settled into their space. These, she decided, were what she had been searching for.

One of the houses had a realtor's sign in the front garden. That house, she fancied, would be only the beginning—a home. Then, one after another, as they became available through the years, she would acquire as many of the others as she could. A legacy for Juliana, for future grandchildren. Perhaps, one day, the square might take the Wang family name. Stranger things had happened in the world. Had she not known them? It would take many years, of course, but the Chinese are accustomed to being patient, to waiting for an advantage.

When she first saw the house, Mei-ling decided to wait a week before calling the agent. She wanted to return and evaluate the property and the neighborhood in a more dispassionate state of mind. If the house were sold, she would of course be disappointed. However, if it were not sold, the price might be negotiated lower, much lower. After all, she calculated, Montreal was in turmoil, with so many English-speaking Canadians and English-owned business relocating from Quebec to Ontario to escape the heavy hands of the French. If an English speaker owned the house, she might get it at a very good price indeed. She would take her time.

But Mei-ling has been able to wait only a few days before

returning for a second look. Now, when she turns into the small street, the row of houses is as she remembers it: a finely executed architectural rendering brought to life. Privet hedges and broad-leaved hydrangeas poke through the iron gates. The square to the south is open and green; a few benches are occupied by old men soaking sun into their bones and young mothers with babes and toddlers in tow; a fountain at the center sends a spray of water toward the sky that forms colored crystals in the sunlight.

The agent's sign is still posted on the fourth house from the corner. Mei-ling permits herself a moment of joy, then sets to work. She calculates the dimensions, the apparent condition, the price she would consider. The housing market is in a down-swing; she might catch it at the bottom. She steps across the street to gain perspective. The solid stone house is a jewel, old and intrinsically valuable as the Wang family jade that she will never again see. Mei-ling is determined to have it. It will be the first of her properties in Montreal.

Before calling the real estate agent for an appointment, Mei-ling sets out for the bank. The sleek marble substance of the bank's plaza and lobby give her a feeling of well-being. The building itself testifies to financial soundness. Her jewelry, her deeds, her securities, her envelopes of reserve currencies, are safe in its deep underground vault. She descends by elevator, claims her box of valuables, settles herself in a cubicle, and clips the bond coupons for redemption. She glances quickly into the silk pouch that holds her jewelry, smiles, draws her tongue across her upper lip. She looks again and fishes out a gold chain that holds a single jewel, a tulip pendant, gold enameled in red, an antique. She no longer wears it. Perhaps she will give it to Juliana when she is a little older?

In less than half an hour, Mei-ling completes her transactions at the bank and is ready to go. As she leaves the building, her eye catches sight of a familiar-looking figure stepping out of an elevator in the lobby. Only when she is outside does she realize it was Ramsden. An odd coincidence, she thinks, their paths almost crossing again in so large a city. She remembers now why the tulip pendant caught her eye. It was he who had given it to her. Fleetingly, she wonders if he saw her.

Mei-ling goes straight home from the bank. A letter from Juliana is waiting in the mailbox. Despite the noon heat and all her walking, she is still fresh when she closes the door of her flat. She turns on the air-conditioner and makes herself a cup of tea. As she sips it, she reads Juliana's letter.

Dear Mother,

Camp is very much fun. Jill and Margaret are in the same cabin. We went swimming this afternoon and tomorrow we are going to ride horseback. I am not afraid. The food is disgusting but I am so hungry I eat tons of it. Margaret was stung by a bee the first day but she was very brave. I hope it doesn't happen to me. I hope you are enjoying yourself and don't miss me too much.

Your daughter,
Juliana

Mei-ling smiles and folds the letter. After finishing her tea, she goes to the telephone and presses in the real estate agent's number. She expects to hear English, but the answering voice reminds her that French is now the law for everyone.

"*Bonjour.*"

"*Bonjour.* Do you speak English?"

"Yes, may I help you."

"I'd like to inquire about a property you have for sale. The sign said one should inquire of Betty Bloom."

"One moment."

Mei-ling holds the receiver to her ear with her left hand and has a pencil poised in her right.

"Betty Bloom speaking." The voice is strong and professional.

"I'm calling about the house a few blocks off Dorchester . . . on the square . . . in a row . . ."

"Oh, yes. The Owen house . . . gray stone with the slate roof . . . black trim . . . a choice property . . . fine condition . . . beautiful row of homes . . . harder and harder to find something like that."

"Perhaps it's too expensive, then, not what I have in mind."

"Why don't we speak about price if you decide you like it. When would you like to see it?"

"I don't want to waste your time if it's more than I can afford. What is the asking price?"

"Just a moment." There is a pause. "At this point, the owner says he won't take less than $300,000. It's a wonderful home, well worth it."

"It did look lovely, but that's very high. Perhaps we'd better not bother."

Betty Bloom catches a hint of a foreign accent but can't quite place it. More and more of her customers are from abroad, and some are drowning in cash. It would be a pity to lose a live fish.

"I'd be happy to show it to you. The interior is impressive . . . high ceiling . . . stone fireplace . . . recent bathroom and kitchen renovation." She scans her file as she speaks. "If you see it and like it and are willing to put in a bid, I'd be required to take it to the owner. A serious offer might convince him to come down."

Mei-ling can tell from what she says that there is room for maneuver. The owner's name is Owen . . . not French . . . perhaps on his way to Ottawa or Toronto.

"Has the house been on the market long?"

"Actually, I'm not sure."

Mei-ling wonders if she is being truthful.

"But a gem like that will be grabbed up soon. It's the sort of place you fall in love with."

Mei-ling says, "I suppose I can look at it so long as you understand that the price is more than I'm prepared to pay."

"Name a convenient time. I'm available mornings Wednesday and Thursday and on Friday from noon to two. I have the key."

"Oh, doesn't the owner live there?"

"His primary residence is in Toronto."

Now Mei-ling is certain the house will be hers. An absent owner is usually eager to sell. She might be able to secure an advantageous mortgage from the owner if she offers enough cash as a down payment. She confirms a date with Betty Bloom. "Wednesday morning would be fine. Shall I meet you at ten at the house?"

"Good, but I'll need some information now for my records. Let's begin with your name."

"The name is Wang, W-a-n-g."

"Wang?"

"Yes."

Betty Bloom smells a serious customer. She's already sold several commercial properties to Chinese immigrants. Many are pulling their cash out of Hong Kong, afraid of the Communists taking over. This one speaks marvelous English, probably well educated and well off.

"Will your husband be coming to look at the house with you?"

"I'm not married."

Betty Bloom has never sold a house to a single woman, only to couples and men. She is not against the idea in principle so long as the woman can afford it, but she hopes this Miss Wang is not about to waste her time. Still, more and more women are buying property. And a commission is a commission, what with the separatists wrecking the real estate market. She says, "Let me take your address and telephone number for now. We can take care of everything else on Wednesday."

When she hangs up the telephone, Mei-ling is happy. With careful planning, she will have the transaction completed by the time she begins classes at the university in September. Her interest and dividends are accumulating nicely. The value of her jewelry is climbing. It is safe in the vault. She and Juliana are safe.

And one day they will be wealthy. Mei-ling thinks of Verhoeven, who is gone, and Ramsden, who did not bother to call, their pretended kindness. They no longer matter, she thinks. Men no longer matter. She does not need them. It is a great happiness.

Ramsden is emerging from the elevator on his way to a lunch meeting with Claude Boisvert when he catches sight of a petite, shapely woman in a white dress and green sandals. She hurries past him and is outside the building before he realizes who she is. Although he had only a partial view because she was walking so quickly, he is certain it was Mei-ling.

Ramsden is relieved that she didn't notice him. It would have been awkward if she discovered that he was an officer of the bank. He'd been careful in Amsterdam. He remembers clearly that he never mentioned what he did or where he worked, had made only vague references to business. She was not curious then, not nearly as inquisitive as he had been about her.

A wave of guilt sweeps over him. He'd promised to call and had not done so. What choice did he have? Given the terms of their acquaintance, they couldn't possibly meet on a casual footing, and as far as he is concerned, anything else is out of the question. It would be a betrayal of Grace.

Grace. There are times when he finds her devotion almost too intense, more of a yoke on his shoulders than wings, but he is grateful for her all the same. It's such a good fit between them, like the title of the old movie he and Celia had enjoyed so much: made for each other. Even the nights, a gift at their age.

Running into Mei-ling at the Botanical Garden—breathtaking as it was—had served a purpose: It forced him to consider all he would lose if he veered off in another direction. He does not want to lose Grace. That much is certain. They will be married in early December: a small church wedding just for family, then London for theater and shopping and some nightlife, home in time for Christmas. How could he even consider allowing a dalliance with Mei-ling to interfere with all their lovely plans? There is no denying the woman had been a high-class call girl. For all he knows, still is.

"Jack, you're gathering wool. Didn't you see me? I could have sworn you were looking straight at me."

Ramsden is always mildly irritated when Boisvert uses one of his more-English-than-the-English phrases. Irritated now with himself as well. What is the matter with him, standing there like a statue when there is business to be done over lunch with an important client of long standing?

"Claude! Sorry. Have you been here long?"

"Arrived this moment. You seemed light-years away."

"No, only a few years and an ocean." He touches Boisvert's shoulder and propels him forward. "Shall we go?"

Remembering the white dress disappearing through the glass doors, he decides to tell Boisvert while they are having lunch about his coming marriage to Grace.

~

David Levy has always liked September: the sweetest corn, the juiciest tomatoes, new crisp apples and tawny cider. The heat is less intense, the breeze fresher. School begins. Even as a small boy, he felt most at home at school, probably because the work came so easily. Everything else may have changed, he thinks, but not that. He wonders if it's a Jewish thing.

Reading and writing are as natural as breathing. Teaching is second nature. He feels good in the classroom—hatching his brood. At the end of the semester they fly off and soon a new brood takes their place. Agnostic, skeptic, he suspects he has found a religious calling in spite of himself. Or a life's work that passes for one. Teacher/rabbi: synonymous in the language of his ancestors.

At the beginning of September, every year for the past six years, David has made his way down the same corridor to his office. On the door is a small, unobtrusive sign that spells out in white block letters against a black background: PROFESSOR D. LEVY. On that first day, the sign always evokes a rush of mingled pride and pleasure. Then he forgets himself in the press of work to be done. He must prepare.

Levy teaches American Literature of the 19th Century and a few introductory writing courses. American literature has gained a measure of respectability in Canada, where it was once viewed as a delinquent child. He has also begun to teach an introductory course for immigrants new to Canada. They are entering the university in increasing numbers. His students are a pre-tested group, literate in English but needing to hone skills that will bring them to university level. It is the kind of work he enjoys.

His office is little more than a cubby, but he has turned it into a comfortable nest. Tightly packed bookcases line one wall. Two upright wooden chairs face the battered oak desk that he prefers to metal. His brown leather desk chair is on wheels and can tilt back when he wants to rest with his eyes closed for a few moments. Poster portraits gaze down from the wall behind him; the soulful eyes of gray-bearded Walt Whitman, Herman Melville, and Frederick Douglass look deeply into the faces of students who arrive for conferences. The posters and a large rubber plant near the window make the room Levy's own.

The rubber plant is an heirloom of sorts, a descendant of his grandmother's original. His parents brought it to Montreal on one of their visits. Its progenitor once rested at the base of the living room window in the walk-up apartment in the Bronx where his grandparents lived. Family legend has it that as a small boy his father was sent scurrying after the few remaining horse-drawn wagons that traveled their street so that he could scoop the horse droppings into a bucket. Dried and deodorized on the outdoor fire escape, the manure nurtured the fabulous matriarch of generations of rubber plants now spread throughout North America by the clan Levy. David faithfully tends his own portion of the original stock by feeding it with store-bought sterilized manure and cleaning its broad, shiny leaves with damp paper towels. He keeps the miniature tree in a deep tub near the office window, where it manages to thrive in an alien climate. Once, fleetingly, he had pondered his grandmother's plant, its unknown ancestor sprung to life hundreds of years ago, uprooted perhaps from a rubber plantation in the Indonesian jungle, where it caught the fancy of a plant-loving imperialist who transported it by sea to the European continent. Or perhaps it first sprouted in the fecund forest of Brazil, where it caught the eye of a Portuguese trader who thought it might be of some commercial value. Whatever the original source, these beauties had found their way to North America, immigrants, like his grandparents, like many of his students.

Now it is almost two weeks into the semester. Today, as always, Levy's office door is open. He prides himself on being accessible to students, closes the door only when he leaves for the day or when a troubled student shows signs of spilling over into a tantrum or tears. But that is not the only reason for his open door. During the last few months he has become uncomfortable in small, confined places. In elevators he sweats and feels queasy, so he avoids them if at all possible. He uses the stairs. He tells anyone who asks: "Stair climbing is the best exercise. You should try it." But he is afraid of his fear.

Levy spends long hours at his desk: preparing for classes, grading papers, conferring with students. He knows that he neglects the scholarly work that is expected of him and is uneasy because he has yet to complete his book about the "epic impulse" in American literature, though several of his papers have seen print in respectable publications. He worries about the creeping lethargy that has overtaken his research, worries about where he is headed. Yet all this would be manageable if he were not distraught about Valerie.

Valerie wants a divorce. She has gone to live with Garnet, probably permanently. "David," she had said, "think of this dialectically, a new synthesis we'll all be the better for."

She'd been so calm, as if she were trying to reason with a recalcitrant child. "Nothing remains static throughout life, and that includes sexual identity. This is not a break; it's simply a change in the nature of our relationship. Garnet and I both want to be your friend. It's just that I'm *her* lover now, not yours."

He had shrieked when she said that. He was her husband, not some casual lover. They had been together almost fifteen years.

Didn't that count? He wanted to stuff his fist down her throat, break a few of her expensive teeth in the process. But, of course, he held back. Stupidly, he'd wept. It was as if they had traded sexes, he the weepy woman, she the rational, self-possessed man.

For how long had she been carrying on about the oppression of women? Years? A decade? At first he thought he understood, but he had grown deaf to her . . . well . . . ranting, probably because the women he knew who were most obsessed with the cause had the least to complain about. Or they had deliberately made themselves homely and hated men for not loving them in spite of it. Too many had turned into harpies and harridans.

Is that what struggle does, he wonders, even in a good cause, turn the oppressed into the oppressor? He feels violated by Valerie, is furious at her for leaving him, furious because a man in his middle thirties should have a family to come home to, a child rushing to greet him at the door, a pleasant meal and conversation with his wife. It doesn't seem too much to ask.

Now he has the apartment to himself. Valerie's gone, taken her things, disappeared—right down the drain, like the dirt in television commercials. She is dirty, he thinks, cruel, and dishonest, even with herself. He will not "come to terms" as she had put it, change his "retrograde attitude toward sexual identity." It is disgusting, women poking their fingers and mouths into each other's private parts. Even more disgusting when it is Valerie doing the poking and licking. She is no more a homosexual than he is, David thinks, just a smug radical out to make a political statement. So what if it ruins his life. She doesn't give a damn. Sexual politics! A kick in the ass is more like it. No, he decides, not a kick in the ass at all. A kick in the groin, his groin. A direct hit. Game over. He loses.

David struggles to free himself from his thoughts. He has work to do. He knows that everything will change when he is in the classroom. A charge of energy will take possession of him. He will be suddenly witty and captivating. The students will cohere into an attentive group. They will laugh at his jokes and try to please him with their work. To them he appears in control of his life, in an enviable position, a man possessed of knowledge.

When he is teaching, Levy's penumbra of red curls bobs to the rhythm of his speech. The jets of sound that burst through his lips, the emphatic smiles and frowns, the uninhibited enthusiasm of his moving hands, the bouncing energy of his feet: these engage and amuse his students. The students in his class for immigrants, recent arrivals in Canada, are unaware that the loud, harsh, New York–accented English he speaks marks him as a fellow immigrant, a wanderer like themselves, sprung from a tribe of wanderers. The native Canadians, by far the majority of his student load, find him exotic: funny, unconventional, not boring. Most of them enjoy his enthusiasm, his quirky erudition. His classes are sought after. He is an established if not establishment figure on campus. No small consolation in his darker moments.

Unable to ignore the tall pile of papers on his desk any longer, he picks them up and arranges them. The first work he assigns to the newcomers is to write about a transforming event, an experience that changed their lives. The papers help him judge their level of competence, the nature of the effort that lies ahead for him and for them. But beyond that, he knows they will be forced to think and structure their thoughts, use material that's of importance to them.

"Let me discover who you are through your writing, and remember," he assures them, "everything you write is in complete confidence. I'm the only one who'll read your work and then I'll return it to you with my comments."

Then he asks, "Any questions?" If nobody answers or raises a hand, as happens most of the time, he smiles and says, "Of course, please don't tell me if you've murdered anyone. I don't want to know." A few of the students laugh aloud and a few others smile. Some look bewildered, but he is confident that they will grow used to him soon enough. At the very least, they'll pay attention.

Levy riffles through the papers on his desk, the transforming experiences. Most are three or four pages long and held together by paper clips. A few are in transparent binders. One is different. It is very thick, at least fifteen neatly typed, double-spaced pages in an opaque green binder. In the lower right corner of the title page is a pen and ink drawing of a tree branch covered with blossoms and a Chinese character, meaningless to him but graceful and attractive. Searching for the student's name, he finds it at the end of the last page: *Mei-ling Wang*. A gesture of modesty, he wonders, putting her name on the final page . . . a Chinese custom? He decides to save this one for last and begins with the shorter ones.

The world outside his desk settles into silence. It is late in the afternoon and the corridors are empty. Only the occasional scratching of his pencil intrudes on the quiet. When he is finally ready to read Mei-ling Wang's "transforming experience," he is bushed. He packs the paper in his briefcase to take home with him.

At night, after his solitary dinner, he takes her paper out of his case, idly speculating about why her "transforming experience" requires so many pages. She has titled her work "Red Harvest." Familiar? Of course, the title of a detective story by Dashiell Hammett, written in the thirties. He wonders what this red harvest is about. Isn't red a lucky color to the Chinese, the color brides wear? He begins to read.

Red Harvest

The year and place of my birth were auspicious. The East dawned red in 1949. Like a great flood, the Communists surged through the land, hoping to cleanse it of the evils of the past. Poverty, corruption, prostitution: All were to be swept away finally and forever. My parents were busy sweepers and showed others how to sweep. They were good people. They were dedicated members of the Communist Party.

I remember the red star on my father's blue hat. When I first saw it, he was holding me above his head, smiling. His words linger in my ears, echoing, like the bamboo wind chimes that hung outside my window during the good years. "Very pretty, very pretty." A consolation. He had wanted a son. Did he know even then that I would be his only child?

My father had been away for a long time, so his visit home was an event. I am not sure if I was four or five years old. My mother dressed me in a red flowered jacket and tied a red silk ribbon in my hair. But she and my father were dressed like twins in their padded blue jackets and blue cotton trousers. All our neighbors wore identical jackets and trousers as well. Even when I grew older, I did not think it unusual. A great mother had given birth to a multitude. That her children resembled one another did not surprise me.

Yet I could tell them apart easily; I had solved the puzzle of their voices and faces and gestures long before I was old enough to go to school. Only one face, the one closest to me, was more mysterious than the others. Her hair was the color of ginger and her eyes were sometimes green like leaves, sometimes blue like the sky. All the others—my father, my grandmother, my cousins, my aunt and uncle, the neighbors—had hair and eyes alike, the color of earth. When I looked in the mirror, my hair and eyes were the color of earth too. Years later, when my mother and I had both grown older and had passed through great sorrow together, her eyes seemed more the color of jade, like the jewels she had carefully hidden from me, hidden even from my father. Perhaps especially from my father. Relics of the capitalist past, he might have given them away. She was more practical.

"It is good she is her father's child and does not look like the foreign woman." The words were piercing. I knew it was me they were speaking of, me and my mother. But why was it a good thing? What was a "foreign woman"? Why did my great-aunt dislike my mother? Why did she speak so to my granny?

Our house was comfortable and quite large. I slept in a room with my grandmother Wang, my father's mother. We each had our own bed. My parents had a bedroom for themselves. The family ate and worked in another room, but my father was seldom home and my mother often stayed late at the university. My grandmother and I spent much time together. I looked forward to the days Mother returned early enough to share our evening meal.

"Your nose in a book again!" My mother's voice sounded happy when she spoke. I had not heard her enter the room, so intent was I on studying the horses and sheep on the page before me. The paper was shiny and the characters strange, different from signs at the market and in my parents other books, the ones on the lower shelf I could reach easily. Even the trees were different, round and thick like balls of twine.

"Do you like the pictures?" She pointed to them and

spoke in a language I did not understand. "Horse, sheep, tree." Then she pointed again and told me the names in Chinese. "This is England," she said, "where I was born. I lived there when I was a little girl like you and rode on the back of a horse." I had never heard the word "England" before, but I understood it was a different place, the place of my mother's birth. I knew by then that my mother was a "foreign woman."

My teacher was stern and serious. "You are the most fortunate of all the world's children. You are the comrades-in-arms of Chairman Mao. Each one of you is a builder of the new China." It was from my teacher that I learned of the great responsibility that was mine in the world, the important life I was to lead. Like myself, all my classmates were the children of Party members, privileged, worthy. But most could not read as well as I, nor write as well either. My mother taught me before I was old enough to enter school. Often, she woke early, before going to work, so that she could read with me. When I recognized characters, she smiled and squeezed my shoulders. She said I was her "pride and joy." She said those words in English. But in everything save an occasional utterance in English, even going so far as to adopt a Chinese name, the "foreign woman," my mother, had given herself completely to her husband and their common cause.

My father was sent to prison for the first time in 1957. Having been among the earliest of Mao's blooming flowers of thought, having uttered his thoughts in articulate speech that was noted by others, he found himself in a cold cell, where he spent his sleepless nights listening to rats scuttling across the cement floor and rattling the metal slop pail with their unsuccessful assaults. By day he "criticized" himself at sessions thoughtfully provided by his jailers. His self-criticism must have been effective, because he was mysteriously released three years later. Still a devoted son of the revolution, still thinking himself a comrade-in-arms of Mao, he assumed that an unfortunate mistake had been made which the all-wise Party had rectified. He was grateful to them for his release, or so my mother told me afterward.

I had hardly noticed his absence. He had been away so often fulfilling the many tasks the Party had assigned him when I was small that his absence was not important to me. If I was aware of the creases and grooves daily growing deeper in my grandmother's face, wasn't that how grand-mothers were supposed to look? If the rims of my mother's eyes were oddly pink and watery at times, weren't her eyes tired from the strain of her work? Wasn't that perhaps how a foreign woman's eyes looked?

Despite my father's imprisonment, my mother's loyalty was not questioned—perhaps for pragmatic reasons. They needed her. Her skill as a translator of English into Chinese was useful to them; her record of service to the state was without blemish. Like my father, she wanted nothing so much as to be of use, a vehicle carrying passengers on the road to heaven. In their zeal and self-abnegation, my parents were much like Christian saints. Years later, I wondered if they had chosen celibacy after my birth, a priest and a nun in service to the great god Mao. Was that why I was an only child, a daughter at that, long before the one-child family became a policy of state? Or was it more simple? Did they not desire another child because their lives were elsewhere?

By the time my father was released from prison, Mao's Great Leap Forward was hurtling in reverse. The "twenty years in a day" he had prophesied were a grim irony. He had plunged the country backward into the crisis and fam-ine of the war years with Japan. But at school my teachers did not speak of failure or of hunger. Indeed, *we* were not hungry. While the workers and peasants were sipping gruel and eating grass, the Communist cadre and their children in Beijing were feeding on noodles and vegetables . . . in di-minished quantity. Though we were sometimes hungry, in my school there were no children with swollen bellies. I could not imagine children suffering in the new China. Only later did I learn that millions had died in the famine.

I was eight years old, and Mao still reigned. His revo-lutionary comrade, Liu Shaoqui, was made head of state while Mao controlled the Party. "Now all will be put right," my father told my mother as we were eating a rare meal together. Words escaped my mouth. "What is wrong?" I asked. My parents looked at me, perplexed, sur-prised at my curiosity. "Nothing," my father said, "nothing is wrong." Was there a hint of fear in his voice as he said this? But of what? The moment passed.

My father did not go away again. My grandmother's step quickened and my mother's eyes were clear, but darker than they had seemed when I was small. Sometimes my father came home in the evening with a peach or a piece of candy for me. He was given a post at the university. Comrade Wang became a professor of foreign language. At night, while I was busy at my own studies, he spoke to my mother as if I were not present. He said, "The years away were a useful lesson in humility. I was becoming too arrogant, thinking more of myself than of the Party."

"I don't think so" was all my mother said. I remember, because it was the first time I heard her disagree with him. I still did not know that the years away had been spent in darkness, in a dank cell with rats for company.

After some time we had meat on our table, pork and chicken. My mother and father were busy at their work. He had a western suit and she had a new flower-printed dress that she wore to foreign receptions, where they met old friends from their university days in England. It came as a great surprise to me that my father had lived in England when he was a student, that he had been a classmate of my mother's. They had never spoken of how they met. For some reason I did not ask. Why did I not ask certain questions? Why did I banish them from my thoughts? One night, when I was in my room trying to sleep, they returned late from an embassy reception. I heard her say to him in English, "It was almost like a visit home." Wasn't this her home?

Great sorrow entered and took root in our house when I was thirteen, already a woman with breasts and monthly bleeding. My grandmother became ill and died of pneumonia. The gasps of her breathing and the heavy rumble of her coughs—low, like distant thunder—pains me still. My father's grief was silent and stoic, but my mother's weeping was an ocean of salt tears, uncontrollable and mysterious and frightening. Deferring in her own home to the rituals and wishes of her husband's mother, she had taken it upon herself to be a proper Chinese daughter-in-law. She felt a deep obligation and attachment. Against tradition, her marriage had been given a blessing by my grandmother, who was able to accept a "foreign woman" as her beloved son's wife.

Only once can I remember seeing my mother lose control of herself. It was the day my grandmother died. My mother's grief was like a great rock splitting and breaking in two before my eyes. How could the death of my grandmother in the normal course of old age break my mother in two? Was my own grief insufficient, lacking in honor, or was I simply more like my father, reserved, stoic? Or were my mother's tears not only the emblem of her love for my grandmother, but also some other loss I could not fathom?

At night, in my room, I could sometimes hear my parents talking, but their voices were low and I could not understand everything. Once, I clearly heard my father explaining in a louder than usual voice, as if for emphasis, as if to himself as well as my mother, "Gaining power was hard. Our struggle took every breath. How could we have known that using it well would be harder still, and more painful? There are bound to be errors. We must be patient." My mother said something then, but she spoke softly and her voice was lost.

I am ashamed to say that I soon left my sorrow behind in the busy days of my life. Although I was lonely at home and required to cook the evening meal and clean the house in my grandmother's absence, at school I won prizes for my poems and high grades in everything I studied. If some of my classmates were jealous of my honors, others were drawn to me as satellites circle a planet.

The son of my father's associate at the university asked me to walk with him in the park. He was older than I, tall for a Chinese, much taller than my father, and already a prodigy of science. He was determined to be a doctor, one who would combine the best of modern and traditional medicine, one who would bring China to her rightful place in the great world.

Zhang was a very serious boy. He liked to lie silently on the grass with his eyes closed. I would sit nearby and close my eyes too. Sometimes our clothing touched. Sometimes we shared a peach. The juice dripping sweetly from our mouths and down our chins made us both laugh.

Although my parents were always hard at work, they were never too busy to follow my progress in school. They were pleased with my accomplishments. My mother no longer told me I was her "pride and joy," perhaps because she was afraid I might grow too proud, perhaps because she was just afraid. She may have understood before others did that it would no longer be safe for the intelligent children of intellectual parents in Mao's China. But she loved my poems and placed each one in a book, carefully noting the date it was written. The book is lost, like everything else from that time.

On my fourteenth birthday my father took me by the shoulders, pressing them hard enough for me to feel pain, and spoke in a solemn voice: "You have a gift for language. I think you have the ability and background to enter the diplomatic service. I see you, my daughter, as a representative abroad of the new China, a woman of the new China. You will do great things in the world. Your work will bring honor to the family and the nation." I did not know how to respond to such a compliment with words. We embraced. I felt myself a pearl plucked from the many grains of sand, lustrous, a jewel. I began to learn French with the help of a tutor. Great-aunt said my parents were in error encouraging me in things foreign.

My sixteenth and seventeenth years brought storms and winds that swept through every city, every village, every house in China. Loudspeakers blared "The East Is Red" from every corner, a siren song racing through the air, a swelling chorus for marauding bands of youth, first my age, then younger and younger still. We were the Red Guards, "revolutionary path-breakers," the vanguard of the Cultural Revolution. Yes, I was a Red Guard.

We were proud, my friends and I in our uniforms, costumes for the great drama in which we all had a part. Dressed in our green jackets and pants in imitation of the People's Liberation Army, red scarves fluttering at our necks, red bands on our arms, Mao's Little Red Book in our hands, his words in our mouths, we fled our schools, stopping only long enough to parade our cowering teachers through the streets. We tied them together with rope, hung their necks with humiliating signs—I AM A FOOL, I AM A

PIG, I AM DIRT—and pelted them with stones and excrement. When the streets were fouled with our teachers' blood, and sometimes their urine as well, we cleaned them and chanted together, "We are washing away the dirty water." The great river of tears many of us shed in the years that came later cannot wash away the shame of our evil deeds. But at the time we felt no shame, only pride and power.

Idols were toppling in all of China. President Liu, Mao's comrade-in-arms on the fabled Long March to the caves of Yenan, author of *How to Be a Good Communist*, was denounced as a "capitalist roader." He lay as crushed and broken as the ancient temples and tombs that littered the cities and countryside in the wake of the Red Guards' assault. Great fires burned, fueled not only by foreign books like my mother's beloved *Pride and Prejudice* (a strange favorite, I think, for a Communist), but by the great classical poets and sages of China.

One idol remained unshakable on its base. Chairman Mao. I worshipped him. We all did, we young Red Guards. He was our guiding star. Mao, the god we were told had been the son of peasants, became our father and mother. We carried his banners: THE FARTHER FROM HOME, THE NEARER TO CHAIRMAN MAO; THE PEASANTS ARE CLOSER RELATIVES THAN MOTHER AND FATHER. Above all, he exhorted us to criticize and destroy the Four Olds: old thought, old customs, old culture, old morals. With great passion, I believed in his words and tried. . . .

⌒

David Levy is about to turn the page but he stops reading. He drops Mei-ling Wang's paper on his desk. He tries to picture the class. There are only two Chinese in it, and one of them is a man. But, he thinks, the tiny beauty sitting quietly in the second row, the one with the slightly rounded black eyes, can't possibly be old enough to be writing about what happened in the sixties, doesn't look more than twenty-three, twenty-five at the most. Yet it has to be her story . . . the only one in the class it can be. She has to be in her early thirties if she was born in 1949 . . . the year the Communists took over.

Amazing, he thinks, to have been a Red Guard . . . gone through all that and wound up in Montreal in his class. And she writes English like a native, only better. Why is she in Canada? It couldn't have been as direct a route for her as crossing the border was for him.

He remembers her dark eyes fixed on him, the small earrings that caught the light when she tilted her head to one side. She had been hard not to notice. A familiar warmth rises in him, nice but not completely welcome. His firm rule is never to come on to female students, even when they come on to him. And he doesn't intend to begin. Besides, Levy thinks, it will be a while before he wants to come on to anyone, let alone a student, even one as intriguing and attractive as Mei-ling Wang.

But the story she tells is so powerful, so evocative. It must be 1967 or 1968 that he is reading about now. She was probably chanting and waving her Little Red Book and worshipping Mao and tormenting her teachers. He remembers an old magazine photograph: thousands and thousands of assembled Red Guards—kids really—holding their books in the air as if they were pieces of the true cross, looking coked-up or hypnotized, depending on who was doing the looking. It is hard for him to imagine the beautiful woman in his class as one of those fanatic faces. Were they idealists or lunatics or just young and easily led?

Those were crazy years, he thinks, remembering the war and the protests, the Democratic National Convention in Chicago that turned his life inside out . . . students not much older than the Red Guards, the chanting and singing, the cops clubbing and gassing, Pete finally coming through the door late with his face swollen and purple as an eggplant. Yet by 1969 everything had changed. The antiwar movement was split up, fractured every bit as much as Humpty Dumpty, and there was no putting it together again. He and thousands of others went over the border; Pete and who knew how many others went underground or into some other danger zone. The Weathermen . . . days of rage . . . explosions . . . communes in Vermont . . . the same time that Mei-ling Wang was waving Mao's Little Red Book. Not to mention Russian tanks rolling into Prague and student riots in Paris. David wonders what Pete is doing now. It is a long time since they have been in touch.

Levy is certain that there are connections in all the events of 1968, but they are loose and hard to figure out, even if you were there. Perhaps, for him, because he was there. Mei-ling's story about the Cultural Revolution has made him uncomfortable—the marching, the slogans, the anger, the righteousness. Levy's throat is dry. He goes to the sink and fills his glass. While he drinks, leaning back a little in his chair with his eyes closed, a line from a new novel he is reading forces itself into his thoughts: . . . *the image of . . . evil [is] a parade of people marching by with raised fists and shouting identical syllables in unison.* Milan Kundera, a Czech who was there.

But that's not true either, David thinks, at least not always true. There's more to it—the purpose behind the marching and the words you were chanting. In 'sixty-eight they were *right* to be against the war and for civil rights. That's what the marching was about. The war *was* evil, a vicious, stupid war with people being blown to smithereens, incinerated, and crippled, Americans and Vietnamese. That had to be stopped, he thinks, reassures himself, and we stopped it. Or at least we helped.

Levy hesitates: Was it us and our protests, or was it the body bags coming home, or the endlessness of the damn thing? Probably all of that, a lot more complicated than it seems when you're eighteen or twenty. But that doesn't mean we shouldn't have tried to do right. And it went double here at home with civil rights. The KKK *was* blowing up black churches and killing innocent kids, and blacks *were* getting shot for trying to vote. Levy tells himself: Vietnam was over sooner because of us, and blacks vote and are elected to office. The movement wasn't like a bunch of Red Guards worshipping a single great leader, no pack of screaming fanatics. The bank robbers and bomb makers in the movement didn't come till later, and there were never many to begin with. Mostly, they killed themselves. He hesitates . . . and a few innocents in the wrong place at the wrong time. David wonders if Pete had ever been involved in any of it . . . even for a little while. God, he thinks, it would be ghastly to have stuff like that on your conscience.

He is still leaning back in his chair, eyes closed but trying to see. Were they always as right as they thought they were? There was a darker side to the movement, and not just the heavy drugs. While the Chinese Red Guards were chanting and getting rid of the Four Olds, they had their own mantra: *Never trust anyone over thirty*. Levy can't help thinking the ideas were pretty much the same: Throw out the civilization we've got because it's not worth keeping . . . we can make a better one fast and easy . . . and have fun doing it. Yippee! But it wasn't fast and it wasn't easy and it wasn't fun. Good things happen—when they do happen—in small, painful steps. The only revolution that succeeded in a big way, he decides, is the sexual revolution. And his life is a mess because of it.

He retrieves Mei-ling's paper and goes back a few paragraphs to pick up the thread. He hiccups when he comes to the part about the teachers wearing signs saying they were fools or pigs. He remembers the shouts and the slogans in '68: OFF THE PIGS. That was tame compared to some. He hated the cops and they deserved it, but had he ever wanted to "off" anyone? He just can't shake the idea that he and his "brothers and sisters" were counterparts to the Red Guards, no matter how inexact the comparison, how clean his conscience, how well they all meant. *Why did so many young people the world over chant and demonstrate and bring entire countries into chaos during the same few years? In France, in Czechoslovakia, in China, in Chicago, even in good old Montreal, everything was blowing apart at the same time. Why?* He can find no satisfactory answer. It is like trying to understand why Socrates and Confucius were doing roughly the same thing at the same time at opposite ends of the world over two thousand years ago. The results are plain enough: Civilizations happened, but the process and reasons are unclear. Are civilizations unhappening now?

Levy is surprised to find himself laughing in a low chuckle, turning over a notion that struck him recently: He thinks he may be ready for a try at the unexamined life. The examined one is proving too much for him. Then he chuckles again. Is that any way for a Jew to think? Might as well give up breathing.

Finally he calls a halt to examining and begins reading the final pages of Mei-ling Wang's paper. At least, he thinks, there will be a happy ending. He knows that because she is in his class and looks wonderful. Better than wonderful.

. . . criticize and destroy the Four Olds: old thought, old customs, old culture, old morals. With great passion, I believed Mao's words and tried to root out the old. We, my friends and I, had much time for rooting out, because our schools were now as empty as riverbeds in a time of drought. We smashed our school windows and toppled statues in the gardens, we burned our books, old and new. But for the most part we roamed the streets looking for something to do now that traditional Chinese thought and customs and culture and morals belonged to the past.

One day, as I was walking with my friend Julin to the canteen where we now ate our meals together, I saw a procession of dunces. One of those in front was my father. Another was my friend Zhang's father. I was frightened and ashamed, wanted to run but could not. In the instant, my shame was for my father, his disgrace. But soon my shame was for myself, my dishonor. What had I done?

The academic colleagues were trussed together with several others like pigeons on a spit and basted with what looked like a mixture of dirt and manure. Even at a distance I could smell the rank odor they gave off. Tall dunce caps rested on their heads. A banner—DESTROY THE FOUR OLDS—was carried by several Red Guards. Some of the miserable dunces' necks were hung with signs likening them to animals or vermin. But my father had something different around his neck: FOREIGN DEVIL'S SERVANT. I shrunk in fear when I saw it and knew at once that my life lay in ruins before it had really begun.

Suddenly a young man shouted, "Down, dogs!" The stinking and filthy dunces tumbled to the pavement, moving on all fours as the ropes would allow, some losing their hats, while the heroes of the Cultural Revolution kicked them and shouted orders, forcing the prostrate victims who were distinguished scholars to bark and howl like beasts.

Like a snake disappearing in the grass, Julin darted from my side. The gathering crowd swallowed her. I wanted to reach out to my father, but I was stunned and frightened by the grotesque injustice unfolding before my eyes. My father was a loyal Communist, my mother too. Now he was on his knees and she was called a "foreign devil." If only Mao knew, I thought, he would surely punish the wrongdoers. My parents loved Mao and the Revolution.

Too frightened to help my father, shamed by his shame,

shamed by my own complicity, I ran to my house for shelter. To my surprise, my mother, whom I had never before seen with a needle, was sitting and sewing, concentrating on her stitches as a spider weaves its web. She had cut the ragged sleeves from her old blue padded jacket and was binding the armholes with fat bulky edges. She raised her head to acknowledge my presence. Seeing the fear in my eyes, she said, "I know."

I began to weep but she did not rise to comfort me until she had finished with her needle and put on the odd-looking padded vest she had fashioned. Over this she drew a khaki-colored unlined jacket that reached to just above her knees. Her trousers, too, were of rough khaki cotton, old, remnants of the Revolution. I noticed for the first time that the ginger-colored hair that peeked from under her cap was now streaked with gray. Her face was grave and sagging. Her voice when she spoke was cold, as if frozen in her throat. "There is nothing we can do for your father now. He is being taken to prison. I am being sent to labor in the countryside, to learn from the peasants."

If her tone was ironic, I did not know it then. Incredulous, but trying to make some sense of it all, I asked, "As Comrade Mao says?"

She looked at me but could not seem to find words. Finally, she said, "Yes, I am learning my lesson from Comrade Mao." She clutched me in her arms then. "I am being sent away, but I'm not certain of our final destination. Be brave. I will return when they come to their senses. This madness"— she plucked at my red armband—"will end. The path of history is a winding one. If we are lucky, your father will be released soon and you can wait for me together. When I return, we will go on as before." She paused and considered. Her fingers shook. "Perhaps not as before."

There was no time to think or to talk. She slipped a cloth bag over her shoulder and stuffed some pumpkin seeds and rice cakes into the pockets of her trousers. Her arms circled me. She said, "The truck is waiting." She kissed me and whispered in my ear in English, "Be kind to others. Cruelty is a sin. Do not neglect your poems. You will always be my pride and joy." Then, as if the sun were in eclipse, her light was gone.

As I sat there alone, my sorrow and confusion were absolute. There were no words to express what I felt even if someone were present to whom I might speak. And, perhaps most perplexing of all, the red armband of which I was so proud, was, if my Communist mother was to be believed, the instrument of my family's undoing. Surely she was mistaken in some way, I thought. Surely my father would soon be home. Chairman Mao was still watching over us.

I had no time to mourn my parents' fate or ponder the cause. The whirlwind of events lifted me up rudely and forcefully. Within days of my mother's departure, my Red Guard unit was called to the countryside to learn from the peasants, as Chairman Mao urged. I was pleased not to have been cast aside because of the charges against my father. I reasoned that he, a loyal Communist and comrade of Mao, would have wanted me to learn from the peasants. I thought he would soon receive justice and gain release. (He did, but not as I had imagined.) Consider as well, what would I have done if cast completely adrift? With my mind clouded by fear and confusion, I welcomed action and travel.

We young people were exhilarated at the adventure and the opportunity. The leader of our unit, Comrade Chu, painted the prospect before us: "The peasants will welcome you with outstretched arms. They will share with you their thousands of years of knowledge. Learn from them how to plant and harvest, how to free the earth and its people from slavery. Seize the opportunity the Party is giving you."

We assembled at dawn. Loudspeakers were already playing "The East Is Red." The long train, a linked chain of passenger cars and boxcars, was resting empty in the station when we arrived, first in small groups, then by red-banded brigades, like a medieval Children's Crusade that I read about in later years. By that time I was relieved to discover that we had not been history's first army of fanatical children. At word from our leaders, we poured into the train, eager to be going, eager to secure a seat for the long journey.

Scrambling, jostling, climbing over one another, we squeezed into any niche we could find. The train was soon full, packed tight, the latecomers climbing to the roofs of the cars, others securing footing and handholds on the open platforms between the cars, still others squeezing into tiny lavatories. When the train finally inched its way out of the station, arms and legs dangling from every window and door, it must have looked to those remaining behind like a giant centipede crawling slowly toward some new territory.

Although hours had passed since I first arrived at the station, it was still morning when we departed. Because of my early arrival and place close to the train, I was one of the "lucky" ones, seated. Five of us occupied a seat meant for three. The crowds in the aisle, trying to remain balanced on their feet, loomed over us. I was not able to see out the window only a few feet away from me. Frequently disgusting sounds or smells escaped from the packed bodies. At first we were cheerful and sang patriotic songs. However, when, more than four hours after we had begun, the train slowed to a stop, I felt near suffocation.

"Rest stop, rest stop," someone shouted. Within a few minutes the train had emptied completely. So desperate were we to relieve ourselves that we lost our normal modesty, though males and females separated as best they could. Together with countless other girls trying not to look at one another, I crouched behind the cars of the train and watered the crushed stones and dirt beside the track. There was no way to clean ourselves. To my disgust, I was forced to eat my rice cake with the smell of urine in my nostrils.

Just as we were getting ready to board the train to go on, a great cloud of dust appeared in the distance. Trucks drove up. At least two hundred more young people wearing red armbands and red scarves jumped to the ground, as fresh and eager as we had been hours before. It was obvious they were to join us, but how could we fit them in anywhere, hundreds of them?

When the call came to board the train, the ground under my feet began to shake as if an earthquake had begun.

Uniformed bodies flashed past me. Standing there in the midst of the surging crowd, I felt frightened. Rooted to the earth, I was unable to run with the others. Just a few hours before, I had been eager for my adventure to begin. Now I was paralyzed in place, my body trembling like a leaf in the wind.

I felt a strong hand take mine and pull it. "Come, you'll miss the train and be stranded here." My feet began to move even before I looked at the young man who had propelled them into motion. I did not know him. He had a round brown face and a strong grip that carried me along.

As we neared the train, I heard a hiss of steam and felt the air shudder. Heads and limbs were poking out of the passenger cars like stuffing from a torn pillow. The car roofs were occupied by so many that I feared a lurch of the train would send them tumbling to the ground. Brown-face still held my hand and was dragging me along toward the end of the train. The crowd on the ground had already thinned to a few when we reached the last car.

"This is the best place," he said. He reached for an iron handle on the side of a wooden freight car and hoisted me through a narrow opening, then jumped in as the train began to move. In the faint light of the windowless car, we could see many boxes and crates in no particular order. A few shadowy figures sat on top and between them. A few leaned against the sides of the car. It was piled high with freight, but one could breathe and was not assaulted by smells. Brown-face found a space for us. If we pulled up our knees, we could wedge our backs against a large box, push our feet against the side of the car, and look out through the narrow cracks between the wooden slats.

The train began to pick up speed. As my eyes adjusted to the semidarkness, I looked around at the other passengers and was relieved to see there were not too many, no more than twenty. Although it was hard to be certain, they all seemed to be young men. That was natural enough. We city girls, many of us from good families, would not think to enter a freight car even if the comfort was greater. I had my brown-faced friend to thank for my breathing space.

He smiled at me in a friendly fashion. Even in the dim light, I could see that dark spots stained his teeth, a sure sign that he was not from an educated family like my own. I was disappointed. And ashamed of myself for my "old thoughts" that Chairman Mao had told us to root out. We were to learn from the peasants, not look down upon them or those like them.

As the train snaked its way through the countryside, we passed small rude villages. Often, slogans were painted on the sides of the dilapidated houses: LONG LIVE THE GREAT PROLETARIAN CULTURAL REVOLUTION and OUR RED HEARTS YEARN TOWARD THE RED SUN. Through the slatted spaces we saw children on the backs of water buffalo and barefoot peasants propelling themselves along like beasts of the field under the weight of the yokes on their backs and buckets dangling at their sides. We had been told the peasants would welcome us with open arms, but when they were within our sight, staring at the train from parched-looking fields, their blank-eyed, sun-browned faces looking sullen and perplexed, I wondered about the welcome that awaited us.

Much of the countryside we passed was without trees, just a few young saplings breaking the earth occasionally here and there. I later learned that the precious trees that held the earth in place had been cut down for fuel ten years earlier. Not fuel for homes but for Mao's steel furnaces in the home, perhaps the greatest failure of the "Great Leap Forward." Foolish, bubbling pot furnaces that produced little steel, but that resulted in immense flooded fields where the earth was no longer held by deeply rooted trees.

In this vast bare new world rushing by us, hours passed quickly. The outdoor light began to fade. Soon I heard laughter behind us. I could tell from their crude remarks that some of the young men were relieving themselves out the narrow opening of our car. Brown-face tried to divert me from them but was not very good at conversation. Nor was I. I wished the train would stop for our relief, though I had drunk little and could wait hours more if need be. My throat was dry.

The vulgar laughter of the young men came closer, and the remarks became clearer. I had never heard such coarseness before, and I soon realized it was directed at me. I was indignant, not fearful, affronted that such undesirable elements existed among the Red Guard. I vowed to expose them as soon as we reached our destination.

The train was rumbling along in the fading light. We were in near darkness. Brown-face was silent beside me. The laughter and remarks had stopped. The motion of the train was lulling me to sleep, when I heard a few of the young men forcing their way through to our nest among the crates and boxes. Brown-face suddenly shouted, "Stop!" His cry filled my ears as they were scrambling upon me. He tried to push them away. At once my senses were as alert as a beast's in the jungle. I saw the flashing blade of a knife and heard a groan that sounded like the cry of a wounded animal.

While they held me down, each in his turn violated me. I don't know how many. I lost consciousness. When, after what may have been hours later, the train came to a stop, I sensed my own breath and became aware of great pain. Beside me, brown-face lay not making a sound. I heard the others, my violators, and those who must have cast their faces in another direction, jumping from the car, their footsteps lost among hundreds of others milling outside. I was not able to move and may have fainted or fallen into a deep sleep.

I woke to daylight when two strange men in ordinary clothing without red armbands or scarves entered the car and began to unload the freight to the platform below. They reared back in fright when they saw us and jumped to the platform themselves. I was not surprised that they had made no offer to help us. Fully awake beside me, his eyes wide and stunned, brown-face sat with a blood-soaked rag to his ear. His mouth was black with caked blood and he seemed unable to speak. In the palm of his hand he held two pieces of flesh. In a moment I realized that the larger of the two was a piece of the ear to which he was holding a cloth. Sour bile rose in my mouth. I cast away my own pain.

"What have they done to you?"

When he pointed to his mouth, I understood and felt nausea. The second piece of flesh was the tip of his tongue. The need to vomit seized me, but I suppressed it. I managed to rise and help him to rise. I straightened my clothing and, in order to cover my shame, pulled my jacket down over my torn trousers as far as it would go. I took some saliva from my tongue and wiped the blood as best I could from the caked mouth of brown-face. He seemed numb. I said, "Let's try to find a doctor for you." He shook his head. I arranged his clothing, and pulled him toward the doorless opening through which we had climbed the previous day, innocent steps that had changed our lives forever.

When we emerged into the daylight, my eyes were stunned by the milling hundreds oblivious of our fate. Freight was being unloaded by somber men in ragged clothing. Trucks were standing in a line, forming a long fat snake whose end I could not see. Some were empty, but many had already been loaded with youth chanting Mao's slogans and singing "The East Is Red." They were all to be transported by truck to the small villages where the peasants awaited their arrival.

In all the excitement and traffic, I wondered how to find a doctor. However, my task was soon unnecessary. A truck loaded only with boxes and bundles and crates was moving quite rapidly down the road alongside the row of stationary traffic. People jumped aside as it picked up speed. I stepped back as it drew near, but my companion dropped the cloth from the bloody remains of his ear and before I could grasp the full horror of his mutilated head ran into the path of the oncoming truck. It crushed him, but the truck drove on unaware or uncaring. Screams arose from those who saw what had happened.

The routine was broken for a short time as the body was carried off, but soon the young people clambered aboard the waiting trucks again. Then each truck drove off in turn with its cargo of red-banded youth chanting and singing, ready to "learn from the peasants." Brown-face, whose name I did not know and never learned, was forgotten.

For all my pain and wounds, I felt no despair then, only a kind of numb curiosity. My innocence was surely lost forever. My nameless friend had run under the wheels of a truck after a vicious assault and mutilation. Who would mourn him? Would his family ever learn his fate? Was his death a matter of little importance compared to the great task at hand, a sacrifice for the glorious future? I could not believe that any longer. And what I believed or did not believe was of no consequence.

Standing there, unable to move, I began to think of the world in a new way. The most horrible things imaginable can happen, but then they are over, and if you are still alive, you go on, just as the earth goes on, because there is nothing else for you but to go on living. Each of us is no more significant than an insect or a bird or a flower. We prepare ourselves as best we can for what fate holds in store. We do what we must until we die. If good fortune smiles, as it does at times, we snatch at happiness.

This was when my first life came to an end. Years later, fortune smiled at me. My daughter was born. She is my happiness, my pride and joy.

Here the paper ends. Her first life! Levy reaches for his handkerchief and blows his nose. He fights back tears but they come anyway. He hiccups several times and tries to hold his breath, but it is no use. The hiccups will not go away. He remembers when he was a little boy, how he used to have an attack of hiccups if he was frightened because he had done something bad, how his mother told him to hold his breath till they went away.

Levy tells himself he is wrong to feel guilty, to think himself complicit somehow in Mei-ling's fate, an accessory to the evil that befell her. When some Red Guards raped her, he was a young student living on the other side of the globe. And she had herself been a Red Guard.

But, he wonders, didn't he and his friends once believe, if only in a childish way, that Mao's was the world to come? That the Chinese Reds were good and building for the future, that the Vietnam Reds deserved to win because they were good too, that the United States was bad, the capitalist imperialist behemoth who wanted to selfishly exploit the world for its own evil ends? Were they wrong, then, even those like himself who weren't revolutionaries, just innocent idealists?

Levy catches himself up short at the word "innocent." Is innocence possible any longer? Can innocence itself be complicit in evil? It is hard to remember another time as it was, you as your younger self. Had he naively, inadvertently, with the best of intentions, become an unknowing accessory to the suffering of millions? Did his innocence absolve him if it were so? Possibly. And hadn't he helped shorten the war, save lives? He thinks so, but is glad he doesn't believe in heaven or hell.

The Cultural Revolution. The words themselves seem grotesquely ironic. If what happened to Mei-ling and her brown-faced friend had anything to do with culture and revolution, civilization itself must be doomed. Yet, people are out there every day, working, raising their families, often enjoying themselves, doing what they must—as Mei-ling Wang said.

He wants to know more about Mei-ling Wang, much more. How did she find her way to Montreal? Is she still married to the father of her child? Was she ever married to him at all? How terrible to have been raped! It used to ruin a woman's life entirely, as if it had been her fault and not the rapist's. Plenty of places in the world, they still felt that way, even killed the woman. He sighs. At least civilization in Canada has advanced beyond that kind of primitive belief. He laughs at himself—as if all his worrying about the decline of civilization made the least bit of difference. But if it doesn't, why does he still go on teaching and loving what he does? Because that is what people do, go on?

He packs Mei-ling's paper into his briefcase. Her writing is excellent, but he will not place her in the more advanced class, where she so clearly belongs. He wants her for himself.

Winter begins early in Montreal, in November. Inside the small restaurant, steam forms a broad arch on the wide street-facing window when the heat of the pizza oven condenses on the chilled pane of glass. The aroma of olive oil and garlic wafts through the room. But Mei-ling, her pale pink sweater innocently provocative beneath her dark eyes and hair, doesn't notice the pattern on the steamy window or the pungent odor of the food. Her eyes are focused intently on the smaller arch formed by David Levy's curly reddish head. He is sitting opposite her in the booth they share.

Mei-ling and David are warm now and have been eating their
fill. Oblivious of time, they have been chatting endlessly over
pizza and Coca-Cola. Mei-ling loves his talk. When they're
alone together, he seems anything but a professor. He jokes
about "a sugar fix" and "a grease blast" being good for "what
ails you." She catches his humor only at a slant, finds it easy to
laugh though, is enjoying herself. Mei-ling isn't used to laughing.
It makes her hungrier. She says, "I don't know why I'm so hungry. I must have another slice."

"Allow me," he says grandly as if they were dining in fine
style. He tears a slice from the two wedges remaining on the
round, oily pan and is about to hand it to her. Instead, he
folds it in his fingers and reaches across the table, offering her
a bite. She takes it and chews, then he takes a bite and chews.
She notices that his hair has been trimmed and combed back,
tamed a little. They smile and finish a bite at a time, wipe the
oil from their lips with fresh paper napkins, hungry again for
more talk. At this moment, in this place, it is the aphrodisiac
of choice.

Mei-ling and David talk about themselves, talk about New
York (where she wants to see the Statue of Liberty, and the
Public Library that looks like a Greek temple guarded by
stone lions, and the art museums, especially the small jewel
she read about that houses paintings by Vermeer and Rembrandt and Hals . . . she can't remember the name . . . he
squeezes her hand under the table and says "Frick" as if it
were a magic word). They talk about Hong Kong (where he
wants to sample Chinese delicacies on a floating restaurant in
the harbor and gawk at neon palaces and buy a shirt made to
order for himself and silk scarves for his parents . . . another
magic word . . . "parents" . . . he loves them, they love him . . .
he is an only child, like her, like Juliana). Mei-ling offers him
a sip of Coke from her glass.

He asks her about Amsterdam (where he wants them to ride
bicycles together and bargain at the Saturday flea market and
visit the museums and take a trip to the tulip fields . . . and tilt
at windmills if there are any left to tilt at . . . she doesn't quite
understand . . . thinks she knows what he means anyway . . . has
any man spoken to her this way before?).

Mei-ling doesn't smile when David talks about Amsterdam,

does not join in his plans for them there, but is not sad. How could she be? It is where Juliana was born. She's told him about Juliana. He says he wants to meet her. David has not asked for many details about her husband, accepts without question that she is the widow of a man much older than herself, a Dutchman who did business in the Far East, a man who had helped her mother in Hong Kong after they had fled China, after her father's death. It is all quite true. She has not lied to him.

Bite by savory bite, they finish the last slice of pizza. She notices a crumb on the front of David's shirt, reaches over, flicks it off. She would like to kiss him, but there are so many people around. How delightful the moment is: this sudden yearning, this unfeigned desire, urgent as hunger. Love . . . this must be what she feels, has been feeling . . . so different from anything she has known before. Detached from time, they talk on and on . . . about, of all things, poetry. On what vessel did they sail from Amsterdam to poetry? Mei-ling is not sure . . . perhaps on the wind alone. It is like that with David. He is interested in what she says, what she thinks.

He asks, "Did your father write poetry?"

She tries to remember but is not sure she knows. There is so much about her father that eludes her. She says, "I don't know if he wrote poetry himself. He was a scholar . . . like you." In her mind's eye, she sees her father's many volumes side by side on their shelves. Then scattered. Swept away. Ashes. She tries to explain. "He treasured the Chinese classical poets and collected them, but when I returned our house had been ransacked. Only empty shelves remained. From what we were able to learn, his books had been burned. We couldn't find a single one. And then we had to leave." Her eyes are suddenly full.

David reaches for her hand. "It's hard to imagine Communists burning books."

She withdraws her hand, doesn't reply. What can he be thinking? Only a moment ago they understood each other perfectly. How is it possible that anyone so knowledgeable and clever as David, a professor at a university, could still be this naive? Of course it is possible! Wasn't her father intelligent, even brilliant? Yet a faithful Communist to the end, loyal to

Mao and the Party even as he crawled through the streets covered in filth.

David had never been a Communist in any formal sense, she knew that. At her first conference in his office, when they talked till it grew dark, he had taken pains to explain the difference between "the new left" and "the old left," phrases she had never heard before. Very few Americans or Canadians his age had been Communists, but he had come to realize that many, to one extent or another, were shaped by Marx's vision ... had fallen under the spell of faith, the faith that after a great struggle there would be eternal peace and plenty and justice for all, a kind of paradise on earth. Of course, he didn't believe it anymore, didn't believe it in quite that way ever, had always been "hooked on democracy," didn't see a contradiction. Still, Mei-ling thought, some remnant of faith must remain, or he wouldn't find it hard to accept that Communists burned books. Mei-ling is relieved her faith was cauterized early. But David's naivete is troubling.

Was the power and beauty of a vision sufficient to both deny reality and transcend it? Often to some good purpose? Millions of people believed the impossible for millennia: the voice of God from a burning bush ... the virgin birth of a savior ... eternal life for the deserving ... reincarnation in the next life as a bird or beast or flower. Perhaps the communist vision of a perfect future was one in a long line, an updating of the old necessary fictions in keeping with the scientific spirit of the times—a reformation of the Reformation. Of course, the old religions had a distinct advantage: Their beliefs could be confirmed only in the world to come—if it existed—but the communist faith had been tested in this one. It had failed. Her dear father was a martyr to his faith. Though if Emma were to be believed, the Communists had done much that was good ... especially for women, who had been little better than slaves ... and would again now that Deng had taken the helm. Emma had died happier knowing Deng was in power.

She will speak to David about all this, but not now, not when she most wants to touch him across the comfortable silence between them. As if reading her mind, he takes her hand again, kisses her fingertips. He doesn't look at all like her father, but he reminds her of him at odd moments. Her father rarely joked, but David does . . . all the time. Once, when she asked him why, he seemed puzzled. After thinking about it, he'd said, "I suppose it's the way I see things. Anyone who takes this world completely seriously could wind up jumping off the nearest bridge. Since I don't intend to do that, I try to joke my way out . . . salvation through cosmic kidding."

Her father would never have said anything like that . . . so American. Still, the two of them are alike . . . intelligent . . . good . . . innocent to a fault . . . the only men she has ever been able to trust . . . among so many. She shudders, fearing for David, for herself for loving him, thinks suddenly to look at her watch. Where have the hours gone? She squeezes David's hand. "I promised Juliana's sitter that I'd be home no later than eight."

"Let me take you."

"No. I'll take a taxi."

They leave the pizza place together dressed for the cold. He hails a cab for her, remembers how Valerie would have bridled at such a gesture, is relieved and pleasured by Mei-ling's grateful smile. With the cab door open, she says, "Remember, I'm expecting you on Saturday. Juliana can't wait to meet you."

"Me too. One o'clock, right?"

David runs his hand down her back over the thick wool of her coat. She turns and kisses him lightly on the lips before getting into the cab. "Saturday," they both say at once.

When the door slams shut, Mei-ling settles into her seat, notices that a fine white powder has begun to fall. Will her first Canadian winter be as long and arduous as everyone says? It is hard to believe that she's been in Canada almost nine months, that she owns her own home, that she is studying, that she finally knows the joy of love. She had not been able to imagine that possibility, yet love has overtaken her.

It seems only yesterday that David had returned her first paper with the comment that so moved her: *Your experience and your rendering of it goes beyond anything I had reason to expect from a student. Had it been written in blood instead of ink, it could not have affected me more. I wish you well in your life here and look forward to discussing your work with you.* She had not expected such drama, such emotion, from a professor. He had understood and cared about what had befallen her. Had she fallen in love with him then, before they had touched or spoken?

A thicker snow begins to fall, casting feathery shadows across the street lights. The taxi is moving slowly. She is pleasantly warm, thinking still of David . . . his red hair . . . his liveliness in class . . . one of the people of the book, as Berthe had once remarked . . . like some of her parents' college friends . . . talented, but a little apart. "We're really like everyone else," he had told her, "only more so." She had smiled at that—one of his jokes? what he felt to be true? She couldn't tell . . . but she could not agree either. He was unlike other men. He would not hurt her or try to use her. She was certain of it.

The unwelcome ghost of Dirk Verhoeven invades the cocoon of the taxi like a chill wind. So few years really that they had been together . . . only a small part of her life. Those years are behind her now. No need to think of them. No need to burden David with them.

The world has turned white when Mei-ling steps out of the cab in front of her sturdy stone house. A fine line of snow frosts the iron gate and windowsills. The windows are brightly lit from the inside, glowing like festival lanterns. She has journeyed long. China is at the opposite end of the earth.

When she opens the door, Juliana is waiting for her, leaps up, hugs her—eager, self-confident, a new-world child—bubbling over: "Mother, it's snowing. Can I have ice skates for when the lake freezes? The girls want me to go skating with them. We can't wait."

"Ice skates? That sounds like a good idea to me."

Mei-ling kisses Juliana, notices that she is wearing her flannel pajamas printed with ballerinas. Juliana loves her ballet classes. Mei-ling marvels: ice skates, ballet, Barbie dolls, furry hats, hot cocoa, ice cream . . . these are the children of a dream place. Mei-ling asks the ritual question. "How was school today?"

"Very good. I forgot to tell you. One of my poems won second prize and it's going to be printed somewhere. They're going to send you a letter. You'll have to come when they give out the prizes. They said I'm one of the youngest ever."

Mei-ling takes Juliana's hands, notices again how tall she has grown. Something of Verhoeven in her bones. Even this reminder doesn't dim Mei-ling's pleasure. As always, though, it frightens her a little. She looks Juliana in the eye, holds both hands in hers. "You are my pride and joy."

The sitter, Anna-Marie, a girl who lives a few houses away, is standing awkwardly, a sallow fifteen-year-old chewing on a cookie, waiting to be paid. Mei-ling pays her and thanks her.

Before Anna-Marie has closed the door, Juliana says, "Is he coming on Saturday? Did he say yes?"

"He's coming. He's looking forward to meeting you."

"I hope he likes me. Maybe he'll want to marry you and be my father. All my friends have fathers. It's not fair. I should have one too."

The breath goes out of Mei-ling. Has Juliana been unhappy all these years? It hadn't seemed so. She never asks about her father, accepts that he is dead.

"I'm sure he'll like you. How could he help it? But it's much too soon to talk about marrying."

"Why? Don't you love him? You said he's the nicest man you ever met."

Mei-ling tries to choose her words. "He is a wonderful man. I think I love him. But it's too soon to talk about getting married."

"Why?"

Mei-ling taps Juliana's behind. "You ask too many questions. And I don't know why. Now, don't say anything about this when he comes. Let's just enjoy ourselves."

David hesitates before ringing the bell. It has never occurred to him that she might have such a house, that she might be well off, that her husband—he dimly remembers they'd been married only a few years before he died—might have left her with a good deal of money. What does he know about her? One moment everything . . . now, it seems, nothing.

She's an enchantress from the East . . . wonderfully clever, mysterious, seductive . . . like Cleopatra . . . and who was Cleopatra? . . . an errant projection of a Roman conqueror's desire? . . . the issue of a scribe's imagination? What would we know of Cleopatra if not for the Romans, Shakespeare, Shaw?

Why doesn't he just ring the bell, stop thinking so damn much, forget about the Romans, who have nothing to do with any of this? It's a curse, all this thinking, a Jewish curse. Discomfited, he comes face-to-face with the obvious: He is no Caesar or Marc Antony . . . no conqueror . . . only David Levy . . . a decent enough Jew without money. And he is wild about her. And she seems to love him back. He doesn't want anything to go wrong.

The house looks like a wealthy dowager, corseted, silver-gray trimmed in white fur. A soft mantle of fresh snow adorns the roof and window ledges. The crystalline winter sunlight gives the granite façade a jewellike sparkle. He would have much preferred a dowdy, needier look to the place. He feels small, a supplicant rather than a protector ready to shield Mei-ling from the harshness of the world, make up with love for all she has suffered. He knows he is foolish to feel so, yet he can't help himself. Don Quixote Levy!

David had been elated on the way over, marveling at how relieved he is to have Valerie behind him, the divorce final. He doesn't miss her for a moment, is perversely grateful to her for his happiness. When has he ever been so happy?

David rarely thinks of Valerie, is drunk (besotted? . . . a word they use in romance novels) on Mei-ling, on the future they'll have together. He has seen Juliana's picture, has spent days anticipating their meeting. Absurdly, though he and Mei-ling have yet to speak of marriage—they don't need words, he thinks, so certain is the event—David has rehearsed the finer points of being a proper stepfather. When he and Mei-ling have children, he will be careful not to favor them over Juliana. She will want a brother or sister. He himself had longed for a brother or sister. He and Mei-ling will give her one quickly. They will be happy together. He will love Juliana as if she were his own daughter. She will be his own. He will adopt her. It has all been settled before he reaches for the brass knocker on the front door.

David has come prepared with a gift, a book, *Little Women*, just right for a bright ten-year-old. Mei-ling has told him Juliana likes to read. He had wondered if the charming old chestnut was readily available, but there it was on the bookstore shelf in a newly minted illustrated edition that transformed Jo into a ravishing beauty, Marmee into a svelte homemaker, and Professor Bhaer into a rakish charmer. He hopes the text has been spared.

David is not supposed to be standing there with a book in his hand. He and Mei-ling had agreed to wait till the semester was over before visiting each other's homes. He would no longer be her professor . . . he would be her proper lover . . . though they hadn't used those words. Finally, they decided that a few short weeks could make no difference.

It was an oddity in Juliana's usual routine that had hurried things along. A couple of months into the semester, he and Mei-ling were having coffee together in a small place far enough from the campus so that they wouldn't attract attention. As usual, he had asked about Juliana. When Mei-ling said, "She can't talk about anything but a birthday slumber party at a friend's house on Saturday," a bell sounded sweet and clear as a soprano's high note.

Impulsively, he'd grasped the opportunity. "I know a lovely little place in the Laurentians. It's quiet and beautiful. It's French and the owner cooks the world's best food. The season is slow now. They're sure to have a room for us, even on a Saturday night. Let's go together."

She had hesitated only a moment before saying, "Yes, of course. I want to."

Had she planned for it to happen that way, for him to say what he said? What difference did it make? They would be together . . . share a bed . . . infinitely better than breathy pawing and frantic kissing behind his closed office door . . . foolish to wait. She was no casual student affair. She would be his wife.

It had already begun to rain heavily when they arrived in the late afternoon. They were both glad. They didn't have to pretend they were eager for a walk in the fresh country air. Their room was small: a double bed covered by a pink chenille spread, an old Empire chest with white drawer pulls, twin milk-glass lamps atop spindly plant stands that did duty as night tables, a worn pink-and-green boudoir chair tucked into a corner, a bare wood floor. But there was a fireplace and the fire had already been lit. The room was warm and cozy and smelled pleasantly of wood, but it would hardly have mattered if an icy draft had been blowing through. They spoke very little. Love sounds were all they could manage.

When they woke afterward, still wrapped in each other, he melted at her first whispered, sleepy words: "I never loved any man so much as I love you."

Playfully, he'd teased. "Not even your first husband?"

She allowed his mistake to pass. "No." She had laughed a little before adding, "It was like being a virgin again . . . loving the one man I was meant for."

Momentarily, David entertained the wildly improbable notion that he and Mei-ling had been destined for each other from birth. He was somehow regenerated, restored, a virgin himself, . . . as if everything that had happened before this had been wiped away.

The pungent smell of dinner cooking distracted him. Suddenly, he was ravenously hungry, but loath to untangle himself from the warmth of Mei-ling's flesh. Looking for graceful words, not finding them, he'd said, "That makes two of us. Two hungry virgins. We'd better get some clothes on and get something to eat."

Dinner was delicious and rich—sausage en croute to begin, duckling in plum sauce, butternut squash with apples, salad— so rich they couldn't finish the vanilla soufflé their host served for dessert. It sat on their plates, deflated, wasted, while they emptied their wineglasses and lingered over their coffee in the almost vacant dining room. The auberge had a small game room, but they weren't in the mood for games. The rain had become a fine mist. He'd said, "Let's go out for some fresh air. I'll get our coats and hats."

They could walk only a little way. Within a short distance of the small parking area, country darkness closed in. The fallen leaves were slippery under their feet. They'd leaned into each other for support, giggled, kissed with their lips, kissed with the tips of their tongues, decided to go back to their room.

After the cool damp outside, the warmth of the room was welcome. Embers were still glowing in the fireplace. David tossed another log on. Mei-ling ran a hot bath in the small, old-fashioned oval tub perched on sturdy claw feet. They'd squeezed in together, sudsing and caressing till the water began to turn cool. The towel bar was heated, the only touch of luxury in the room. As they rubbed themselves dry with thin towels, David couldn't keep his eyes off Mei-ling, her dark petite shapeliness, so unlike Valerie's lanky blondness. Standing, he'd eased himself between her legs, cupped her buttocks in his hands, drew her into him. He'd heard his own breathing, felt her fingers touching him, went for the bed.

They were late for breakfast the next morning. The kitchen was already closed, but their host, relaxed in a slow season, heated croissants and made fresh coffee for them. After breakfast they packed their few things and left. The slumber party was scheduled to end at noon. Mei-ling did not want to be late for Juliana. A remembered pleasure . . . she was a good mother . . . conscientious about her daughter. She would be a wonderful mother to his children as well. Perhaps there *were* happy endings here and there . . . if you tried hard enough . . . and had some luck.

But this handsome house he is standing in front of, that he hasn't yet found courage to enter, is more luck than he wants. He'd had no idea when she gave him the address, had expected only a modest little place of the kind he lived in. Only now he remembers vaguely that she mentioned owning, preferring to pay off a mortgage than rent. But this? Certainly not a mansion, but far grander than anything he or his parents ever lived in.

Finally, he knocks twice. It is Juliana who answers. She is dressed in red woolen pants and a red-and-white-striped sweater; a stretchy red headband keeps her long brown hair neatly in place. She looks at him directly, openly. Pretty as her picture, he thinks, Europe and Asia competing in her face, Europe winning except a little around the eyes . . . not the serious beauty of Mei-ling but pleasing to look at. In what seems like a single breath, she says, "Hello, we've been waiting for you, but don't worry, you're not late, we have plenty of time. Please come in."

The small foyer is white and inviting, freshly decorated: glazed ceramic tile floor, striped white-on-white wallpaper, a graceful white globe hanging from the ceiling. David says, "I'm not the least bit worried." He extends his hand to take hers. "I'm David, but I guess you know that by now. I'm very glad to meet you. Your mother talks about you a lot."

Juliana, all smiles and bright, even teeth, takes his hand and shakes it. "Wow," she says, "your hand is freezing. Don't you have gloves?"

"I don't like gloves. I always lose one."

"Not me. I stick them in my pockets every time. I hate losing things."

"So do I. That's why I don't wear gloves."

Juliana looks a bit puzzled. "But that's why your hands are cold."

David winks. "There ain't no free lunch."

She laughs. "I don't know what you're talking about. My mother says you joke a lot. Do you know any riddles?"

"Sure. Lots of them."

Before he can dip into his reserve of riddles, Mei-ling, in dark green corduroy pants and white sweater, comes to the door. "Are you going to keep David standing there, Juliana? Let's go in."

She takes him into a living room that has about it a feeling of costly comfort. A fringed Persian carpet, red embellished with designs of cream, gold, blue, and green, covers most of the dark oak floor. The walls are ivory white. A sofa and two chairs are upholstered in hunter-green velvet and strewn with tapestry cushions. The patterns pick up the colors of the carpet. Two black inlaid chests serve as lamp tables. The lamps are large, urn-shaped red vases that glow with the luminous finish of porcelain. They're shaded by ivory-colored silk, fringed all around. Large framed prints hang over the sofa and on the walls on either side of the tall front windows.

David smells chocolate. Mei-ling is handing him a cup of steaming cocoa that she has taken from a large round brass tray that rests on black lacquered legs to form a coffee table. He has seen pictures of tables like it in magazines. She smiles at him and reaches down for another cup that she hands to Juliana with a soft admonition. "Be careful."

With calm dignity, Juliana responds. "Don't worry. I'm a very neat cocoa drinker."

David decides that he likes this child, who is already almost as tall as her mother and bright and pretty to boot, decides that all will go well between them. A few photographs of Juliana at various stages of growth are displayed on a hanging shelf above a mahogany cabinet whose surface is covered with oversized books.

Mei-ling notices David glancing at them. She says, "Come and look at these. I brought them from Amsterdam. They're my treasures."

The painters are all Dutch, from the Renaissance to the moderns—landscapes, portraits, still-lifes. David realizes that the prints on the walls are all Dutch as well: a Vermeer here, a van Ruysdale there, a quivering van Gogh, a stark Mondrian looking out of place in this company, a Rembrandt self-portrait. She jokingly apologizes, "I can't afford an original just yet."

David laughs. "Someday."

"Perhaps. One never knows."

"Why only Dutch?"

She hesitates. "I don't really know. I enjoyed the museums in Amsterdam, and I fell in love with some of the paintings. They spoke to me when I needed them . . . a kind of company."

David and Mei-ling have hardly begun to leaf through the books, when Juliana says, "When are we going?"

"Soon. When we finish our cocoa. Do you have to go to the bathroom first?"

David watches a cloud cross Juliana's face, hears the resentment in her curt "No." He remembers his embarrassment whenever his mother mentioned going to the bathroom in front of strangers. He thinks that Mei-ling should be more sensitive to Juliana's feelings.

Soon they are bundling themselves into their jackets. They are on their way to an exhibition of puppets and dolls that Juliana's teacher has told the children to see. The museum is nearby. Because it is crisp and sunny out, they have decided to walk. Mei-ling and Juliana wear white furry hats and warm fur-lined gloves. David does without either.

When they are outside, Juliana says, "Your hands are going to be freezing."

"Then you'll just have to hold on to me to keep my hand warm."

"What about the other one?"

"Your mother can hold that one."

The three of them swing down the street hand in hand, turn the corner, lose their breaths in a cold gust of wind, start to run, laughing till they turn again and face into the sun. David thinks: We're like a family already. Juliana is asking if they can have hamburgers and french fries afterward. He says, "Sure. Among my favorite killer foods."

David has already forgotten—no, merely set aside in a less present area of consciousness—Mei-ling's expensive stone house and the comforts that surround her, the kind of comforts only a considerable amount of money can buy, the kind of comforts people get used to and finally can't live without.

Mei-ling is sitting on the green velvet sofa and leafing through the newspaper. The winter sunlight filters into the room through a thin layer of clouds. Though it is late on a Sunday morning, the room is in shadow. Mei-ling reads by lamplight. She turns the page and takes a sip of coffee from a cup that rests on the brass table, then studies a page of advertisements for children's toys. Christmas is only two weeks off.

She and David have decided to celebrate "a heathen Christmas,"—David's words—so that Juliana will not miss out on the gifts and food and merriment that accompany the holiday. She searches the advertisements but can find nothing suitable for Juliana, who has begun to tire of ordinary toys and already has the ice skates she had longed for.

When David arrives later in the afternoon, she'll talk to him about what to buy. He'll think of something suitable. Juliana is in her room preparing a "surprise" for him. She insists that he is the "best" father for her, that she must have him, that it is "only fair" since she has had to do without one for so long. Mei-ling worries about what might pop out of her mouth.

David has promised to cook "a decent Chinese meal" for them this afternoon rather than go to one of the Chinese restaurants in Montreal that he disdains. He has assured her: "They're nothing but a pale imitation of what you can find in New York." Explaining his culinary talent, he claims that he has learned to cook Chinese food "in self-defense," as if he were talking about martial arts. It is still hard for her to understand his peculiar way of saying things, joking and serious at the same time.

Mei-ling, an indifferent cook, is content to eat in restaurants. But David says he likes "a home-cooked meal." She suspects he eats at home in order to save money. He has made plain that he has only his teaching salary, has tried to make a joke out of it. "If you hook up with me, you'll be getting a Jew without money." Then, more serious, "Are you sure you can live with that?"

Before she was able to reply, before she knew what she wanted to say, he'd cracked, ". . . the money and the Jew part both." It was odd, the way he spoke of his being a Jew as something she would have to overcome, like poverty or bad lungs. Didn't he understand how much she loved him? And why did he keep reminding her that he wasn't rich? She had been tempted to say: I have plenty of money for both of us. But she held back. Would he be foolish enough to insist that they live on only what he earned? Would she consider it? No matter how much she loved him? Only children thought that money didn't matter. It mattered a great deal.

Mei-ling returns to her newspaper. She is turning a page of jewelry advertisements and social announcements, when a photograph catches her eye. Surely it is Mr. Ramsden with an attractive, white-haired woman. They're smiling into the camera. Mei-ling reads:

Grace Todd-Taylor and Jackson Ramsden Wed
Mrs. Grace Todd-Taylor and Mr. Jackson Ramsden, both of Montreal, were married on December 8, 1983, in an Anglican ceremony at Grace Church. A reception for family and friends was held afterward at the Botanical Garden, where Mrs. Ramsden serves as the Director of Special Events. Mr. Ramsden is Senior Vice President of the Commonwealth Bank. After a wedding trip to England, Mr. and Mrs. Ramsden will reside in Montreal.

So that pleasant Mr. Ramsden who broke his promise to call was a vice president of the Commonwealth Bank, her bank. And he was married now to a woman who worked at the Botanical Garden, where they had spoken to each other. He was probably meeting her that day. That explained why he didn't call when he had seemed so eager, eager enough for her to be apprehensive. He had wanted to be faithful to Grace Todd-Taylor. A good reason not to have called, she thinks.

She will always be faithful to David. She smiles to herself. *If* she decides to marry him! Which she probably will, though she has sworn that she will never marry again. Perhaps not exactly that . . . sworn only that she will never be dependent again . . . upon any man. Not at all the same thing. But doesn't loving someone make you dependent?

Mei-ling's mood has been darkened a little by Ramsden . . . a shadow of her other life. She hopes David will come early so that she doesn't have to think about anything or anyone else. Just as well Ramsden never called her, even if it was only as he said, to be her guide to Montreal. Best to leave the past far behind her.

Shortly before two o'clock, David arrives. He is carrying two large brown bags filled with the makings of a feast. Mei-ling takes one from him, but not before raising her face for a kiss. "Let's go right into the kitchen with these," she says. They start unpacking the bags. Soon the kitchen counters are full: fresh water chestnuts and snow peas, bok choy, garlic, green onions, dried mushrooms, fermented black beans, cellophane noodles, chow fong noodles, sesame oil, bean paste, bean curd, hoisin sauce, soy sauce, ground pork, chicken breast, large shrimp . . . a few condiments even she does not recognize. "David," she says, "did you think all of China was coming to our feast? This is enough food for a month. What will we do with it?"

"Trust me," he says before spreading his arms wide, then circling her with them. "When I said we were going to have a feast, I meant it. I always keep my promises."

An unfortunate echo Mei-ling might not have noticed if she hadn't been thinking of Ramsden earlier. Even if he meant to keep his promise, Ramsden had broken it . . . and he had seemed a man who could be trusted.

She gives herself over to David's embrace, buries herself in his warmth. He whispers in her ear, "I can think of something I'd rather do right now, but we better put the meat and seafood away or we'll wind up with ptomaine poisoning." He brushes her ear and neck with his lips, reluctantly distances her at arm's length. Mei-ling's face is glowing light pink, a faint blush underneath the ivory of her skin. She is the color of the Peace roses he remembers seeing in the Bronx Botanical Garden when he was a boy. They were his mother's favorite.

While they are still putting the food away, they hear Juliana on the staircase. She runs into the kitchen and gives David a hug. "You can't come into my room because I have a secret surprise for you. I'm making it myself."

"How long do I have to wait to see it?"

"Christmas."

"That's a long time to wait."

She draws her lips together, considers. "Maybe I can give you a hint. It's made of leather."

"I know," he says, "a new pair of shoes."

She laughs. "I can tell you're joking."

"No, I'm not. I can use some new shoes."

Juliana casts a knowing glance in Mei-ling's direction. "Maybe somebody else will give you shoes."

Mei-ling says, "David is going to make a Chinese feast for us."

"How come? He's not Chinese."

"He wants us to have a treat. And we're Chinese."

"Only part."

Mei-ling says, "The most important part."

David steps back. He has heard words like this before, only they were about Jews . . . Jews with mixed blood . . . but somehow it was the Jewish part that mattered most. Proportion and logic weren't the point. But Juliana is too young to understand . . . and has grown old enough to question her mother about everything.

They change like chameleons at her age, David thinks, especially girls. Two weeks ago she was an adorable kid, all woolly and furry and cute, like a teddy bear. Now she seems like a budding adolescent . . . something about her clothes. Juliana is wearing a stretchy green turtleneck and tights. A slight swelling, smaller than half an apricot, has risen on either side of her chest. Budding breasts. David wonders if she will begin to menstruate soon.

While Juliana and her mother are having their mild joust, David has been busying himself with the food. He says, "If we're going to have this feast today, the two of you had better clear out and let the master chef go to work." Playfully, he brandishes the chopping cleaver he has brought with him. "Juliana, you'd better go back to my leather whatever. I expect it to be ready by Christmas."

Juliana laughs and says, "Okay. As long as you don't make me eat any terrible food. I don't like globs."

As soon as she is out of the room, Mei-ling puts her arms around David. "She thinks you're wonderful."

"An insightful child."

"She is indeed."

Later, when they are at the table, amid the plentiful remains of fried wonton, and chow fong noodles in a mushroom and vegetable broth, and lion's head, and shrimp in red spicy sauce, and minced beef and eggplant in black bean sauce, and bean curd with green onions, and steamed chicken breast with crispy vegetables—Mei-ling and David mellow with wine, the winter night closing in, the brass chandelier lending a pleasant glow to the room—Juliana turns to David, an expectant look on her face. "Aren't you going to ask me what I want for Christmas?"

Mei-ling says, "Juliana, it's not polite to ask for a present."

"But I'm going to give *him* a present."

David says, "It's okay. She knows that I'm going to get her something."

Juliana turns to Mei-ling. "See."

David says, "Don't you want it to be a surprise?"

"No. I know exactly what I want."

"Okay. Tell me. If it's possible, I'll try to get it for you."

Juliana bends her head toward David, smiles coyly, almost flirtatiously. In a low, fluttery voice, different in tone from her usual high-pitched child's voice, she says, "I want you to marry my mother. Then you could be my father. That's what I want "most."

Mei-ling is aghast. "Juliana, you shouldn't say that."

David reaches across the table for Juliana's hands and squeezes them. "That's exactly what I want too. Do you think we can convince your mother to get it for us?"

Mei-ling, wide-eyed but smiling, says, "This isn't fair. We should take more time to get to know each other better."

David and Juliana form a chorus. "No."

"The two of you are ganging up against me."

David says, "Gang? You can join. We'll be the gang of three."

Juliana says, "Yes."

Mei-ling frowns. "David, that *is* a bad joke. It sounds like Mao's wife and the Gang of Four, and you knew it when you said it."

"Isn't it good to laugh at them? You're safe now."

Juliana says, "What are you talking about?"

Mei-ling looks at Juliana. "Oh, just something that happened in China. It's all very far away and a long time ago."

In January, after the end of the semester, after the excitement of the holidays is over, Mei-ling and David are married in a simple civil ceremony with only Juliana in attendance. Mei-ling and Juliana both wear red, the color of good fortune. Mei-ling carries a bouquet of pink roses and baby's breath.

For a fleeting moment, she recalls her first wedding ceremony . . . Juliana already turning and kicking inside her, impatient to be born . . . Emma, solemn . . . Verhoeven, moody and eager to be done with it. But the moment passes quickly. Despite herself, Mei-ling is suffused with joy, overflowing with expectation.

Part Five

1986

Montreal

MEI-LING WATCHES AS David runs his fingers through his scalp, sculpting peaks and valleys in his wiry red hair. It is shorter now than when she first saw him in front of the class, but still on the wild side and only slightly flecked with gray. He starts to scratch hard and fast, as if he were being bitten by fleas. A drop of spittle forms in the corner of his mouth. He hisses at her in a tight, hoarse voice: "Why didn't you tell me instead of jerking me around all this time?"

Mei-ling says nothing, sits stoically at the kitchen table that is still littered with the remains of breakfast, rinds and crumbs and crumpled napkins. She clenches her teeth, waits. Perhaps the storm will pass.

"How could you fuck me over like that . . . even letting me think there might be something wrong with me?"

His spider eyes are staring at her . . . dark centers glowering . . . red lines radiating through the whites like charged wires. She has forgotten how to be afraid; still, in the habit of long ago, she retreats into herself, tries not to hear his voice. But the old way doesn't work. David's hissing will not stop. He is furious and vulgar; he has never before spoken to her like this.

"Didn't you think you should have told me right from the

beginning? We loved each other. We had Juliana. I could have taken it. Why the hell didn't you lay it all out for me?" A red blotch the size of a quarter erupts between his eyes. "What else don't I know about? Tell me the truth."

Mei-ling shrinks from the roughness of David's voice. It is usually mellow with affection, a blanket that warms her in a cold climate. She has never known such warmth as in the time they have been together. She turns away from him, not knowing what to say, suddenly fears she will weep if she tries to speak.

A splinter of irritation begins to nag at her. Easy for him to prattle on about the truth. What does he know about it . . . how dangerous it is . . . how it can destroy . . . how it must be gotten around . . . how at certain times it is best left alone. He has not been tested as she has. What right does he have to judge her?

Perhaps she had been wrong in talking Dr. Westerveldt into the operation. It had seemed right at the time . . . necessary. It had been Verhoeven's idea, of course, though she had given her consent willingly enough after he'd prodded a bit. "Get it over with once and for all," he'd said. "Then you won't have to worry about pills or sheaths or pregnancy. It's all a big nuisance."

Perhaps it was as simple as his not wanting her to have another man's child. Not that she'd had any intention of doing so. Juliana had been love enough. As for another man . . . any man . . . until years later when she met David, men were simply a matter of business.

Dr. Westerveldt had tried to talk her out of it. "You're so young," she'd said, "you might want more children later on. That old reprobate of a husband isn't the only fish in the sea." Then, in a lower voice, though they were alone in the examining room, "Besides, he's not going to be around forever. He doesn't own you. By the time you're thirty, you can be free of him if you play your cards right."

She'd been surprised at the doctor's frankness . . . how much an echo of her own thoughts the doctor's words were. But she'd decided to go ahead, as if some irresistible fatality had been driving her. Tying off the fallopian tubes was a simple enough operation. Quite safe. Verhoeven would stop nagging her. There would be a gift afterward; it was his way when she pleased him. When it was over, she had added a ruby and diamond cocktail ring to her collection.

After a brief period of recovery, she scarcely thought about it. Pleasure in Amsterdam was busier than a hive of bees. Everyone seemed to be happy: the girls, who were paid exceptionally well, who lavished themselves with perfumes and silks when the clients weren't doing it for them, who drank vintage wine and ate the finest food; the clients, wallowing in lovely, expensive flesh, giddy in their play, naughty but not too naughty when they chose; . . . even Verhoeven, at those moments when he was free of pain and fear . . . when he could remind himself that he was growing rich again and driving about like a lord in his splendid Mercedes.

Yet, Mei-ling, remembering herself as she was then, had not been happy. Dirk had misled her, used her badly, insisted she "fill in" more and more often. Except for spots of delight with Juliana, happiness was an elusive and mysterious thing far back or far forward in time. She didn't quite understand what it was, imagined a hollow place behind her heart waiting to be filled. With what?

Yet she had not been unhappy either: Her bank account was increasing nicely; Juliana was growing tall; Emma was finally resigned and always helpful, though a little lacking in energy. The men and their occasional peculiarities—what they did to her, what they wanted her to do to them—began to seem ordinary. A few were quite pleasant and surprisingly thoughtful, a few were coarse and boorish, most were merely forgettable. None were like the Red Guards on the train who still loomed in her thoughts without warning, like menacing shadows dancing in firelight.

It never occurred to her then that she might marry again someday, that she could love a man, any man, as she loves David, that he would want a child. Why hadn't David said something about having children before they married instead of afterward? She never intended to hurt him. It was he who had insisted on rushing everything. He had simply assumed she would want more than one child. What right did he have to assume?

He is so pleased with Juliana. She adores him, clings to him. That should be enough. Doesn't he understand that it's not possible to have everything one desires . . . that most often it is necessary to settle for less, that limitation is inherent in life? Why have they never talked about such things? She runs her long fingernails along the palm of her hand and up her arm, sees the red lines but is not conscious of pain.

The room is quiet except for David's footsteps. He has stopped hissing at her. No, Mei-ling thinks, he probably *doesn't* understand much about her. He is, after all, an American. Americans assume that anything they desire—money, love, success—is within their grasp, if only they try hard or are lucky. No price to pay, always a way out. Most of them never grow up. David, she thinks, knows little enough about the lure of wealth, still less about the urge for sexual domination or degradation that rules so many men. Men unlike himself. How can she expect him to understand her years with Dirk Verhoeven? She has been blinded by love and should have known better.

Now there is pain. Love, she thinks, is like a drug. When it grabs hold, one must have a continuous supply. One is probably better off without it in the long run. But how could she have known in advance? She had never loved another man . . . except her father . . . never thought she could. Now it is too late. Mei-ling doesn't say any of this to David. She sits there, waiting for the storm to pass, knowing nothing will be the same between them again. David goes to the sink for some water, is chugging it down in great gulps, glass after glass. She would like to explain why she had gone ahead with the operation—in a way he could understand, in a way that would not disturb other history best left unspoken, in a way that would not put more distance between them.

Something else. It is not only her inability to bear a child that is at the root of his fury. It is the failure of trust that wounds him, that and the fear of all he might lose. Not her alone, not their home. Juliana is his child now as well as hers. Wasn't it he who wanted a legal adoption almost immediately? Parting with Juliana would be worse than an amputation.

Mei-ling drains the last of her coffee, feels the dregs on her tongue, lukewarm and bitter. She should have found a way to tell him she was not able once he began to press her for a child, before he felt himself violated. She vows to make amends. But how much should she reveal of her years with Verhoeven? Will he understand how urgent the necessity that drove her, how precarious her hold on survival? Isn't it best for him, for both of them, for Juliana, not to open a window on that other life?

David does not sit down at the table, will not look at her. He

paces the room as if he is determined to wear out the floor.
Finally, when he does sit down, he plainly has other grievances
to air. "And what exactly was all that bullshit about devoting
yourself to your studies for a few years till you graduated? Why
didn't you level with me at the beginning and tell me you
couldn't get pregnant instead of inventing some cock-and-bull
story that you knew would hit my soft spot? If it were up to
you, I'd be in the dark for months thinking I must be sterile . . .
and you would have let me. It was just a fluke when that jerk
of a doctor's secretary called and you weren't home."

David mimics the secretary's lame effort. "Oh, Mr. Levy,
thank you for taking the message. The office is so busy. The
doctor asked me to call Mrs. Levy to answer her question about
reversing the surgery she had in Amsterdam, you know, on her
fallopian tubes. Dr. Silverman says that after so much time you
can't reverse it like some vasectomies. Mrs. Levy asked him
about it."

Mei-ling struggles to keep her voice neutral. "I spoke to the
doctor because I wanted to know if what was done could be
undone . . . because I loved you and wanted to please you and
didn't want to hurt you."

"Didn't want to hurt me! Thanks, thanks a whole lot."

"I cared enough about you to see if the surgery could be re-
versed. Don't you understand?" She is beginning to feel his be-
havior is excessive. Perhaps only a shade irrationally, she says,
"You shouldn't have taken *my* message. You shouldn't always
poke your nose into my affairs. I have a right to some privacy."

"Your affairs! Have you gone nuts? As if this doesn't concern
me . . . it's just a fine point of etiquette. I'm your husband, in
case you've forgotten that unimportant detail. And as long as
we're laying things out on the table, what other little details
haven't you mentioned? Any more sweet surprises?"

Mei-ling is silent. Not now, she thinks, not now. Her bladder
is suddenly urgent. She goes to the bathroom to relieve herself.
When she returns, David is wearing his windbreaker. Although
it's already well into May, the warm weather is late in coming.
He says, "I'm going for a walk. I can't think around here."

Once David is out the door, Mei-ling fights off hot tears that
run down her cheeks . . . the first since Emma's death . . . an indulgence she decides she cannot afford. She dries them and begins to take stock. Literally! It is her custom in time of anxiety,

a reminder that she and Juliana can survive on their own if they must.

She goes to the office behind the kitchen that she and David share. It is a medium-sized room formed by knocking out a wall between what was once the breakfast nook and a maid's room. A blooming Easter cactus and two green but blossomless Christmas cactuses sit in brown and green majolica pots atop a three-shelf bookcase that divides the space neatly into his and hers. David's space is piled high with books and papers and office paraphernalia, but Mei-ling's is orderly: desk surface bare of paper, pencils sharpened, Lucite receptacles for postage stamps and paper clips, a stapler, Scotch tape, a photograph of Juliana on ice skates in a Lucite frame, a photograph of the three of them in front of the Parliament buildings taken during a trip to Ottawa, a computer and its components at right angle to the desk. Mei-ling seats herself in front of her computer and turns on the power.

As she scans the record of her holdings—all meticulously up-to-date as of the previous week—a faint (if unconscious) smile forms as it often does when she is sitting in satisfying contemplation of her assets. The stock portfolio is up sharply, and dividends are accumulating; the certificates of deposit are earning gratifying interest; the utility bonds and foreign holdings are doing well enough; only the gold stock is disappointing, but worth holding on to in the event of catastrophe. Yet it is the listing of jewelry and property that is most reassuring, that brings another closemouthed smile to her face. Precious gems, diamonds, sapphires, her ruby ring, the antique jade she sought out in a futile attempt to replace the irreplaceable, her pearls, a number of semiprecious jewels of good quality ("gifts from clients"), even the antique enameled tulip given her by Mr. Ramsden, all catalogued and appraised and insured, all going up in value. Most are in a vault at the bank.

Perhaps now would be the time to consider investing in an original painting, she thinks, if she hasn't already missed the market—also skyrocketing. What she craves is beyond her reach still. Should she aim for one of the lesser-known artists, a modern who will increase in value? A Chinese perhaps? A few like Shi Hu have done fine work and are crossing the border to Hong Kong and Singapore, working their way into American and European collections. Perhaps his work would be a good place to start . . . a brilliant craftsman and colorist . . . Chinese with an overlay of European . . . a hint of Picasso, a whisper of Klee . . . a brilliant synthesis of East and West. Yes, Shi Hu might be a good beginning.

She will graduate at the end of May with a degree in art history. "Take time off," David had said. "You've been working like a dog, summers and everything. We can make a baby and then you begin graduate work a year or two after that."

He had it all worked out for himself. "You're a natural, a born scholar," he'd confided warmly, as is his way . . . or was. "It wouldn't be fair to expect you to devote yourself completely to a baby. I'll help out as much as I can." She'd had to bite her tongue when he said that. Goodness can be such a burden.

Mei-ling is not at all sure that the path of scholarship David seems to have selected for her is the right one, though it would have pleased her parents. She loves her studies for their own sake . . . as her father loved poetry . . . not as a means to some practical end. She has no desire to teach. Why should she pursue a more advanced degree when she can continue on her own to wherever her fancy takes her? For David, the university, his students, may be a way of life, but is that the case with her? Other matters interest her . . . investments, real estate. She enjoys making money. David would not understand, but he has not been her only teacher.

Heresies and daydreams had been deepening their roots long months before this crisis. Had she known it was coming? Even as she diligently sat at her books, she had begun to consider the notion that she would undertake business as the occupation of her days, the pursuit of art as the companion of her years.

Mei-ling never speaks to David about her property . . . the deep pleasure she finds in the accumulation of wealth. She knows it would make him uncomfortable, as if she were indulging in a vice. But it is not a vice at all, she thinks, simply an awareness of her own reality. If she is not to be at the mercy of others, a woman *must* have money. Mei-ling read that somewhere . . . agreed almost violently with the rightness of it.

Should she reveal more of her former life, she wonders, the "truth" David claims to want . . . the years with Verhoeven that have rested as quietly as the statues in Emperor Qin's tomb? Would he leave her? Of course, she need not reveal everything . . . might soften the edges. But perhaps it is best not to live with secrets between them? And shouldn't David find a way to understand why it was necessary to do as Verhoeven wished? It was, after all, that which had made all this . . . their happiness together . . . possible.

She turns back to her computer, absorbed again in her financial affairs, her property, the key to real wealth if one is careful not to overextend oneself. She has been cautious in Montreal because the real estate market fluctuates like a barometer of political pressure. But when Betty Bloom called her about a small building that she could have at rock bottom because the owner was leaving Quebec and needed to raise cash—a shop at street level, four flats above—she was not able to resist. Now a tidy return on the property is coming in regularly. She had been able to lease the entire building almost at once to a large Chinese family from Hong Kong. They needed commercial space for their import business and living space for three generations of family. Mei-ling smiles thinly: If they are successful, they will want to purchase the building from her. She will get a good price.

And there are future prospects. With the British lease on Hong Kong coming to an end in 1997, only a decade away, many of the prosperous Chinese, terrified of losing everything, are leaving the territory in droves. Quite a number are pouring into Canada with bulging pockets, most to Vancouver but a surprising number spreading east to Montreal and even into the Maritime Provinces. She will buy as much property as she can safely manage. Chinese prefer to deal with other Chinese. The value of her real estate will rise if wealthy Chinese buy in the area, especially if the Quebecois make more of the English too nervous to stay. Chinese from Hong Kong could be a stabilizing force . . . or better.

Mei-ling hears the door open and close. She shuts down the computer. Should she go out and greet him? He has not called out to her. Does he want to be alone now? Before she can decide, David enters the room quietly. His face is red and sweaty in spite of the cool weather. He looks as if he has been running instead of walking. He makes no attempt to touch her. In a flat, uninflected voice, he says, "I think we need a break from each other for a while. Right after graduation, I'll go visit my folks in New York . . . maybe see some old friends . . . take time to think about where we go from here. You can do some thinking yourself. When I get back, we'll try to see what we can do with this."

"How long will you stay?"

"I have to be back for my summer course, but that—"

They both look up startled when the door slams. Juliana calls out, "Hi, Mom. Is Dad home yet?" Without waiting for an answer, she rattles on at the top of her lungs. "He's going to love this . . . the poet he said I should read . . . Emily Dickinson . . . I wrote my essay-of-choice on her. An A-plus. Miss Everhart says I'm a sensitive reader and have a deep appreciation for language. Do you believe it?"

By the time Juliana is in the room, Mei-ling and David have composed their faces, facsimiles of smiles outline their lips.

"Great, you're here," Juliana says, tugging at David's sleeve. "Do you want to see the essay?"

"Immediately." He smiles, genuinely now, and strokes her hair.

"I'll show it to you later, Mom," Juliana calls out . . . almost an afterthought.

London

JACK RAMSDEN UNZIPS the shoe bag and fishes out the black
dress pair he's brought to London for evening wear. As he bends
over to put them in the closet, the plum color of the carpeting
sparks a memory . . . that blissful week in Amsterdam with the
lovely little Chinese . . . the tiny, voluptuous body, the porcelain
skin . . . sends a tingle through him even now . . . can't consider
her a prostitute . . . wasn't really, even if money did change
hands . . . a call girl? . . . beautiful and intelligent . . . altogether
charming . . . knew about art and architecture . . . an artist at
her own trade . . . but beneath her, of course . . . went on to
something better. How on earth did she get involved in such a
thing in the first place? Strange how she turned up in Montreal
so unexpectedly . . . looked absolutely smashing. Just as well
that he never called her though . . . impossible situation. That
little girl of hers . . . delightful child . . . must be a teenager by
now . . . like his grandsons . . . soon be off on their own. Grace
is speaking. What is she saying? He should pay attention, not
let his mind wander all over the place.

"Not quite the same as before, I'm afraid." Grace wrinkles
her nose, runs her finger along the top of the night table, where
a rather thick layer of dust has escaped the eye and hand of the

chambermaid. "The housekeeping is not what it was, though, I suppose, I'm being picky. Still, for what they charge . . ."

"The Victoria's probably changed ownership. There's been so much turnover in London. They may have cut back on personnel."

"Too bad," Grace says. "This place was a perfect jewel the first time." She gets up, unzips a tan tapestry-and-leather suitcase—new for the occasion—and begins to unpack. When she opens a bureau drawer, the scent of rose sachet wafts out. "At least things smell nice."

Jack removes a navy blue worsted from a bag hanging on a brass rack, shakes it out, and places it in the closet. "Several of the quality hotels have been bought up by the Arabs and Japanese the last few years, not to mention prime chunks of London real estate."

Grace sits on the bed again and folds some underclothing and blouses before putting them in the drawer. "Is that so? I don't really keep up with things as I should." She shrugs. "Why bother? Everything's spinning out of control anyway." She pauses, looks at Jack. "Especially Montreal. Do you think the separatists can possibly have a chance? I can't imagine Canada broken in two."

"I won't hazard a guess on that," Jack says as he shakes out a second suit, a gray one this time. "It would be irrational, but since when has that stopped any fanatic nationalist? Of course, we're small potatoes in Canada. The Far East and the Middle East . . . that's where the fanatics and the money are now. Amazing how it happened so quickly. England once counted for so much. Now it's a kind of theme park peddling royal kitsch and stately homes. The mighty have certainly fallen."

Jack walks to the window and looks into the distance to catch a glimpse of a remembered Gothic church, but the view is almost entirely obstructed by a new commercial tower. "When I was a boy," he says, "London was the magic city and the sun never set on the British Empire."

Jack and Grace are in London for a combination second honeymoon and retirement celebration, though he isn't at all sure retirement is something to celebrate. He feels too young to spend his days out to pasture. Still, it will give them freedom to travel . . . they're looking forward to it. Afterward, he'll think of something in business . . . consulting . . . perhaps investments. No sense letting all his contacts and all those years at the bank go to waste.

Although he hasn't wanted to admit it to Grace, Jack began to feel a bit depressed soon after they landed. It was the taxi ride from Heathrow to the Victoria that had done it to him. The weather was surprisingly pleasant for London, and they were both cheerful after an easy flight, but London didn't seem like the London he remembered from their wedding trip. It was as if an old friend had broken out in pus boils. The streets were dirty, trash everywhere. Too many of the people didn't look English at all. They weren't really . . . more like survivors of a shipwreck . . . tossed up from foreign shores into the bosom of "the mother country" . . . darker even than the immigrants in Montreal. It wasn't that he was racially prejudiced or anything like that . . . not in any crude way anyhow . . . though most people are more comfortable with their own . . . look at the Japanese. It was just that London didn't seem all that English anymore, not like London used to be, polished brass and swept stone, solid, dependable, polite.

As the taxi wove through traffic, it crossed his mind that the Brits were paying for their sins . . . real and imagined. But that's not quite it, he thinks, hanging his ties on the closet rack. It's not only the Brits it's happening to . . . more of a global shifting of people. We won't understand the impact till fifty or a hundred years from now, he thinks. Wasn't Montreal and every other big city in Canada changing dramatically from month to month? Only recently, Boisvert, who had been visiting France, told him that Paris was beginning to look like an Arab invasion had taken place. "The revenge of the Saracens," he'd said.

"Well," Grace says, cutting in on his thoughts, "let's hope the Victoria tea hasn't deteriorated. I still remember the wonderful little sandwiches and lemon and strawberry cream tarts they had the last time. I do love a good English tea."

Jack looks at his watch. "They won't begin serving for at least an hour. Why don't we try for a nap. We'll still have time to shower and dress and take tea. Do we have theater tickets for tonight?"

He leans down and kisses the back of Grace's neck. He always leaves arrangements to Grace. She handles them so well. He's happy with the way things have worked out between them. Two good marriages . . . against the odds . . . luckier than anyone has a right to expect, he thinks. He's thankful to be one of those men who are comfortable with monogamy, who don't itch all the time, who choose the right women! He laughs to himself. Certainly makes life less complicated.

"We're seeing a new play by a Pakistani who grew up in England. They say it's first-rate." She catches the frown cross Jack's face, laughs lightly, circles her arms around his waist. "Don't look unhappy. It's supposed to be quite witty. We'll catch the musicals later in the week. I arranged it all with the agent in Montreal, so there's no need to frown. This is going to be a wonderful vacation. Let's stuff ourselves at tea and have something light to eat after the theater. We can try some of the Indian restaurants later in the week."

Afterward, when they enter the Victoria's dining room, Grace and Jack are rested and refreshed. They are a handsome, polished, older couple of the sort that one finds in venerable and expensive London hotels. Grace's silver hair is swept back and twisted into a French knot. She wears a shadow-striped black suit and white silk blouse. The diamonds that were her wedding present from Jack sparkle in her ears and rim the collar of her blouse. Jack, by virtue of a twice-weekly workout at his new health club, is slimmer than when they were married and looks quite elegant in dark gray and a striped silk tie. His remaining hair is a pleasing mixture of brown and gray, well trimmed, and his eyes are clear, his bearing just short of distinguished.

A formally attired maître d' escorts them to a pleasant window table set with crisp white linen, gold-rimmed white China, and bone-handled cutlery. A well-trimmed hedge that is set inside wooden flower boxes separates them from the pedestrians walking back and forth on the busy street outside the window. A waitress wearing a starched white apron over her serving dress brings their tea, a platter of artfully arranged sandwiches, and a sectioned tray of assorted condiments and relishes.

Before they begin to eat, a passerby, a well-dressed older man in a black Derby—he could be anyone from a stockbroker to a retired haberdasher—looks in at them, smiles, then crosses his eyes, tips his hat with his cane, and goes on his way. Grace and Jack look at each other and laugh. The London they both remember, complete with harmless eccentrics, part of the charm of the place. They turn their attention to the tea and scarcely notice the passing foot traffic or the cars and small trucks that pull toward or away from the curb, parking briefly for the time the law permits.

Grace bites hungrily into a sandwich and sips her tea. She smiles at Jack. "Now, this is the London I've been looking forward to."

Jack is feeling better now, more relaxed. The sandwiches, cut in neat triangles and spread with herbed mayonnaise, are savory and delicious. Although the sky has turned a bit gray, it is still quite light outside, no sign of rain. Jack says, "There's plenty of time before the theater. We can take a walk after tea. I'd like to look around."

As he speaks and turns to the window for yet another glance at the sky, he notices a brown van pull up to the curb. The driver, an ordinary-looking workman—tan shirt and pants, reddish hair, a pale, freckled face, narrow eyes, and a thin, pointy nose—opens the door and steps down to the curb. Irish, Jack thinks. The driver slams the van's door shut and saunters down the street away from the hotel.

The waitress brings a fresh pot of tea and the cream tarts they remember fondly. "Mmm," Grace says, biting into the rich confection of strawberries and custard in a flaky crust. "These are as wonderful as my memory of them."

Her fork is poised in midair, a spot of cream on her lip. Jack is cutting into his own tart with the side of his fork when he feels a vibration and his chair begins to tip. In the instant, a booming noise rends the air and deafens him. His ears are suddenly tightly sealed under pressure, like champagne bottles about to pop. The chandeliers inside the dining room darken; the window fractures into a thousand particles and rains in on them. Jack sees Grace rise up in a shower of glass and then fall, a jagged piece of glass fastened to her throat like a crystal brooch, her neck turning crimson, as if she had thought to tie a bright scarf around it. She is still clutching her fork.

Jack doesn't know how long he has been lying there when he hears again, first the eerie hooting of ambulances, then the moans and shouts echoing from near and far. "Over here," someone shouts, "this one's alive." Hands reach for him and lift him on to the stretcher. He opens his eyes briefly, sees nothing but dust and shadows moving about. He closes them again against the grit and smoke. A terrible smell—rotten eggs? gas?

shit?—makes him gag. His throat is parched and dry, but nobody offers him water. He can't speak above the noise.

In the hospital afterward, his ears throb like a beating heart and wake him from what seems a long sleep. There is a sudden bright flash of light. Jack opens his eyes in time to see a nursing sister with skin the color of caramel brandishing a pole—a mop?—and chasing a photographer through the ward. She shouts: "Out of here this moment. Parasite. Leech. How dare you? I'm calling security if you're not gone in seconds."

Before sinking again into a web of drugged sleep, Jack remembers Grace and the piece of glass that looked like a jewel at her neck . . . the blood scarf. He's not been so lucky after all. Poor Grace.

Montreal

JULIANA HAS ALREADY left for school. David's place at the breakfast table is empty, body and spirit having fled to New York. Alone, Mei-ling is sipping her coffee and reading the newspaper. She scans the front page, decides that she has no patience for another article about whether the separatists will prevail. Perhaps if Canada were her birthplace . . . but it isn't. There is nothing on the front page from Beijing or Shanghai or Guangzhou or Hong Kong, datelines that still draw her. Of what concern is any of it to her now? The only energy left her on this sunny summer morning is focused on David . . . where he is . . . what he is doing . . . when (if?) he will come back to her . . . what he will say when he does.

She finishes the last of her toast and is about to turn to the business and real estate pages, when she sees a photograph in the bottom left-hand corner that puzzles her: Jackson Ramsden and his wife, the same picture that was featured in their wedding announcement several years before. She knits her eyebrows together, quizzical. What is it doing on the front page? She reads:

IRA Blast Takes Life of Montreal Native
Grace Taylor Ramsden, a socially prominent native of

Montreal, was killed yesterday when a bomb believed to be the work of IRA terrorists exploded in the heart of London. Mrs. Ramsden, wife of Jackson Ramsden, recently retired vice president of the Commonwealth Bank, was vacationing in London with her husband. Mr. Ramsden is hospitalized in stable condition and is expected to recover fully. Mrs. Ramsden, who was dining with her husband when the bomb exploded, was one of seven people killed. Scores were injured, some seriously. The powerful explosives were believed to have been detonated inside a van that was parked in front of the Victoria hotel, where Mr. and Mrs. Ramsden were staying. Funeral arrangements are incomplete at this time.

Mei-ling's hand shakes when she lifts her coffee cup. The saucer rattles when she puts it down again. Why is she so upset? It has been years since she saw him at the garden and at the bank . . . coincidences that amounted to nothing. She remembers her last bank statement, the newsletter enclosed for customers, a small formal photograph, the announcement of his retirement after long years of service. The bank and all its employees wished him well. Absently, she had wished him well. He had been kind to Juliana . . . plainly had cared a little for her as well. He looked fit and healthy for a man his age, too young for retirement. For a moment she wonders if she should write a letter of condolence.

If only David were here. But he isn't. When will he be back? What would he think if he knew about Mr. Ramsden, how they met in Amsterdam? Would he be able to absorb that and go on? He is so innocent. Can one ever be sure how another person will react? Isn't that why secrets are so often necessary?

She nibbles on a piece of toast. David will come around, she assures herself. There is too much between them for it to be otherwise. She remembers their eager lovemaking . . . David's breath tickling her ear . . . his whisper . . . the words . . . "my destiny" . . . a mantra . . . his mouth on her breast . . . the heat of their coupling . . . both of them sinking into safe, warm sleep. Never with the others had it been like that . . . never any passion . . . only business. Good business and bad business.

It is true, she thinks, what David said about destiny joining them together. Perhaps she should tell him everything. Perhaps

he will admire her courage and her honesty, fathom her help-
lessness . . . how young and vulnerable she was . . . how much
she and Emma had been through . . . how desperate their need.

Mei-ling raises her coffee cup again. This time her hand does
not tremble and she is able to drink. She feels a quick charge of
caffeine, drains the cup. Once more she stares at the photograph
in the newspaper. Mr. Ramsden and his wife, looking so safe
and happy together. Blown apart.

New York

⌒

THE AMTRAK MONTREALER, nearing New York after its overnight run south, slows down in the dark tunnel that leads to
Penn Station. David, groggy from his long night of troubled and
elusive sleep, stands up in the aisle and stretches. He reaches for
his blue canvas bag stashed in the overhead rack, but the train
suddenly lurches and tips him off balance. He grabs hold of the
seat and steadies himself, decides to sit down till the train comes
to a full stop. What's the hurry?

He wipes his face with his handkerchief, straightens his blue
cotton shirt and tan chinos, runs a comb through his hair. The
train finally stops, but he waits till most of the passengers have
exited before retrieving his bag and making his way out. No
sense rushing. His parents don't expect to see him till tomorrow.
He won't be meeting Pete until dinner. He can check into the
hotel anytime.

Morning rush hour is over and the station crowd has already
thinned out. The day stretches ahead of him, a day to himself
in Manhattan. Strange how once the political climate cooled
down and the amnesty was declared, he wasn't all that eager to
visit, wanted his parents to come north instead, as if it were a
holiday for them. "It'll be like a European vacation," he'd urged.

"Everyone speaks French." Maybe he wanted to unload the guilt
. . . not being there for them . . . not wanting to watch them
grow old alone together in the apartment . . . no grandchildren
to play with.

When he first went over the border, they drove up for visits,
but when the long drive got too tough for them, they flew. Every
time they came north, they were a little slower, as if their bat-
teries were running low. Should he urge them to move to Florida
like their friends, spend the summers in Montreal with him and
Mei-ling? A rock in his chest! Mei-ling . . . the reason he's here.
Now that he's finally back in New York . . . it's not even to see
them . . . just trying to run for a while from his fucked-up life.

David sighs, wonders what New York will be like after so
long. His bag's not heavy, just summer stuff. If it's not too hot
when he gets out of the station, he just might decide to walk to
the hotel, take a gander at what's going on in the Big Apple.
The words—Big Apple—seem strange, foreign. People didn't
call the city that when he was growing up. It was just the city,
a cornucopia.

David is a little hurt but not all that surprised that Pete didn't
invite him to crash at his place. It's years since they saw each
other. Only a letter or telephone call once in a great while,
barely managing to keep in touch. Yet neither of them seems to
want to cut the cord. So close in the college years . . . remem-
brance of things past . . . hot blood cooled down to warm pud-
ding and doubts now. They hardly know each other, mostly
memories, but such memories . . . the best years of their lives . . .
brains on fire, music, arms and legs and hearts and minds drifting loose in smoke and sound, cramming together, heavy on No-
Doz and a joint for relaxing, endless yakking, imperialism and
Marxism and anarchy, who has sold out and who hasn't . . . do
they or do they not try LSD in the name of science and doing
your own thing (no for him, a coward, once for Pete, who
wouldn't admit afterward he was scared shitless, who had nightmares for a while) . . . long-haired Carrie and the clever Chinese
girl, the rich Boston doctor's daughter Pete dated for a while.
Funny how he and not Pete wound up having a Chinese wife
. . . something hard to imagine for either of them when they
were born. The only Chinese most people met back then ironed
shirts or cooked chop suey.

Bag in hand, David steps onto the escalator that will let him off near the street exit closest to uptown. He looks up a long way toward the landing. The escalator that parallels his moving in the opposite direction is almost empty, just a couple of people. He rests his bag on the moving stair, waits. Before he understands what is happening, a kid, a teenager, a light-skinned black wearing a red-and-green knit hat on his head even though it's June, reaches across the hand rails and lands a glancing blow on his cheek. It hardly hurts, but he's startled, guard up, in hostile territory. He looks back down the moving stair to see where the kid is. The kid grins up at him. "Motherfucker," he hoots, "goddamn motherfucker," then runs down and out of sight.

A tall gray-haired man with a thin nose and lips and skin that looks like it never sees the sun is about to get on at the top of the escalator. He hesitates, adjusts the brim of his straw hat, waits. More to himself than to David, he says, "They're killing the city. You're lucky he didn't have a knife or a gun."

David nods, rubs his cheek, picks up his bag, and walks toward the street exit. The last time anyone called him a motherfucker was in Chicago in 1968 . . . and that was a cop. Just reverse the last two digits of the years . . . shazzam . . . damn near a generation gone by. What exactly happened? And what *did* he have to show for all that time? Well, the war finally came to an end and he may (just may) have had something to do with it; a middling but good enough career; one absolutely failed marriage, maybe another in the making; an almost grown daughter he never laid eyes on till a few years ago when he married her mother . . . whom he might lose if he and Mei-ling can't get past . . . if *he* can't get past what he can't get past. What else hasn't she told him? Something's in the dark—sharp teeth and claws. He can feel them ripping into him.

When David reaches the street, it is the kind of rare June day that makes Manhattan look spiffy and okay, especially if you haven't seen it in almost half a lifetime and have been reading all the bad news in the newspaper and your folks keep telling you long distance about how much has gone wrong. It looks good even if your jaw still tingles from where a black kid who should be in school socked you because he's either crazy or just hates anything white. Even the air smells good, like pizza. The pizza stand on the corner of Seventh Avenue is open for business. A man is tossing disks of dough into the air and painting them with tomato sauce and grated cheese. David looks up at the Empire State Building. His mood lifts as he heads across town on Thirty-fourth Street.

The taxi and bus traffic is loud and slow. Bicycle messengers dart like lizards through any spare inch of space. There's enough of a fast-moving crowd on the sidewalk to make it feel like the New York he knows: tourists and shoppers gawking, business-people hurrying, teenagers playing hooky and popping bubble gum, a couple of equal opportunity hookers, black and white, big hair, micro-mini skirts, twitching asses as they walk and turning into a doorway. David looks at the sign on the wall of the entrance. An arrow that points upstairs says: MASSAGE YOUR TROUBLES AWAY. No thank you, he thinks, not my cup of tea.

Sex workers, Valerie used to call them. He tried to tell her nobody had to be a whore, that there was other work if anyone wanted it, but she wouldn't be convinced, just admonished him, insisted saying "whore" was like saying "nigger" and not to be tolerated, that no man could understand what being a woman was like, how powerless it made you feel. Valerie powerless?

A frowning, bedraggled, gray-skinned woman of indeterminate age is coming toward him. She wears enough heavy mis-matched clothing to keep any three people bathed in sweat on such a warm, sunny day. She carries two shopping bags in each hand and wears two hats on her head, a loosely knit fitted job topped by a tattered summer straw. The columns of people heading east and west take no notice . . . a bag lady . . . released, he suspects, from a mental hospital to a happier life on the streets, where she can exercise some self-determination. David grimaces. He used to believe in all that horseshit. Anyone with half a heart would have wanted to help patients stuck in a men-tal hospital. But, he acknowledges, ruefully and not for the first time, the best-intended help sometimes (*not always,* he assures himself) makes things worse. Why do you have to be pushing forty before that finally sinks in?

As the bag lady comes close to him, about five or six feet away now, she drops her shopping bags abruptly, hikes up her skirts, squats on her haunches, and pees a rushing river onto the sidewalk. Except for a few teenagers who giggle loudly and turn to watch, most people avert their eyes and move on. But David is transfixed, watches her urine run down the sidewalk. She

cackles in gibberish at the giggling teenagers, but when she notices David stopped in his tracks, she stands with feet wide apart,
like a bridge over the river of her own creation, doffs her hat,
and in a surprisingly cultivated voice, says, "Welcome to New
York, sir. Enjoy your day."

Nonplussed, David, in the most respectful tone he can muster,
replies, "Thank you." She continues to stare at him. He says,
"Have a good day yourself." She smiles, satisfied. Without ceremony, she picks up her bags and moves on.

David, sweating in the sunshine now, sagging under his lug-
gage, hails a cab and tells the driver, "Gramercy Park Hotel."
When he sees the puzzled look on the driver's face, an East
Indian face, he says, "Just take me to Twenty-first Street and
Irving Place . . . it's downtown near Lexington."

The square surrounding Gramercy Park—elegant brown-
stones, tended gardens, ironwork, polished brass—still gives off
a whiff of old-moneyed New York. The hotel, tall and thin, tries
to keep up a façade of elegance—a liveried doorman, a formal
portico, a bright restaurant—but the grandeur has faded. The
lobby, with its frayed carpets and worn upholstery, exudes an
aura of faded gentility just bordering on shabbiness. But the
hotel is in a quiet part of town and a walk to almost everything.
His room is clean and comfortable if not luxurious and has a
sweeping view of lower Manhattan. He looks out the window
all the way to the eastern end of Greenwich Village. The rates
are cheap by New York standards. Cheap counts.

David likes the agreement he insisted on when he and Mei-
ling were married: He pays half their expenses, including Juliana's camp and lessons. Mei-ling pays for her own clothing and
extras. Of course, the house is hers from before they were married, swell, okay with him. What's not okay is keeping him in
the dark that way. A betrayal, no getting around it. But they've
been so happy . . . more than he thought possible. His mind goes
blank when he tries to imagine being without them, Mei-ling
and Juliana both.

David calls his parents to tell them that he will be up to see
them the following morning and will spend the day, that he is
tired after the long trip, that he is having dinner with his Harvard roommate, Peter Parsons. Did they remember meeting
Pete? He is not prepared for his father's tart "We're not senile

yet, Dave." But his mother, always the peacemaker, says, "It'll be a wonderful visit. Come early for breakfast."

Why is he depressed when he hangs up? He's been looking forward to seeing them. Knocked out, he lies down to rest, sleeps for two hours. It's already near three in the afternoon when he is ready to go out, but he doesn't have to be at Pete's till seven. Plenty of time to walk around Union Square and head toward Greenwich Village. Maybe he'll find a little something for Juliana. She loves it when he buys her the odd gift for no reason in particular.

Pete lives several blocks north of Washington Square Park in a venerable old apartment house just off Fifth Avenue, the kind of building that has two big apartments to a floor, that has well-tended gardens out back and on the roof, the kind that doesn't scream money but that you can't afford to live in unless you have plenty. Must be doing well, he thinks, even for a Harvard lawyer.

When he was still in high school and went down to Washington Square to listen to the guitar playing and folk singing and meet girls, David always wondered about who lived in places like that, what it was like to be rich, to have two bathrooms in an apartment, to have a service entrance for deliveries . . . how bad you had to be to make that much money, how much virtue you had to lose.

He enters the lobby through a heavy iron-and-glass door being held open for him by a man of about sixty in a green uniform and peaked cap, feels himself an impostor, an intruder, as if he should be holding the door for someone who belongs there. The doorman calls Pete through the intercom, then turns to him. "Mr. Parsons is expecting you. Eighth floor." What, no elevator operator?

Pete, tall and impressive-looking as ever, is standing beside his open door. "Hey, come on in, buddy," he says, draping a long arm around David's shoulder and ushering him inside. "Great you finally made it."

Pete is smiling, looking good, looking rich. He is dressed in a style David dubs high-key casual, soft fabrics and colors that mix like gin and vermouth . . . the very things lined up near a bottle of scotch, a bottle of bourbon, a small bowl of olives, and a Lucite ice bucket and tongs on top of the minibar that partially divides the entrance hall and living room. Pete propels him forward with one of his huge hands until they are standing in a large, attractive, uncluttered living room. Pointing to the bar, Pete says, "Before we get started, how about something to drink?"

David laughs, feels easy. "Do you have a cold beer in the fridge? I never took a liking to the hard stuff."

Pete smiles. "Once a prole, always a prole. Wait a minute."

He goes to the kitchen and comes back with a bottle. "Labatts okay?"

"Great. Good Canadian brew."

Pete, talking, mixes himself a martini. "So, you're a Canadian now."

David, swallowing the chilled beer, settling into a deep sofa that seems to shape itself to him, says, "Not exactly. I never gave up my citizenship, but I'm an official immigrant to Canada. I don't see myself coming back. My work and family are in Montreal. I don't have much left here except my parents."

"They okay?"

"Pretty good. I'm seeing them tomorrow."

"How come you didn't bring the wife . . . Mei-ling, right? Didn't she want to see New York?"

David tries to hurry past this. "Our daughter's still in school. She couldn't leave her."

"Ah, yes, the ready-made model child, from what you said."

"She's thirteen now."

Pete's mouth turns down playfully. "Teenager, eh. How's it working out? Angel or devil?"

David forces a smile. "Mostly angel. She's a great kid." Quickly, before Pete can say anything, he changes the subject. "What about your folks?"

"Dad died. My mother lives most of the year at Hilton Head. She comes up a few months in the summer. But enough of this. How does the kid from New York feel being back in the Big Apple?"

"New York didn't exactly open its arms wide. I was hardly off the train before a black kid on the escalator socked me, apparently just for the fun of it, and a crazy bag lady let go a river of pee on the sidewalk in front of the Empire State Building."

"Welcome to New York."

"That's what she said. I must look like a tourist by now."

Pete laughs. "Have a pretzel." He points to a wooden bowl on a teak end table. David reaches for a few and licks the salt before popping one into his mouth. Relaxed now, he looks around. The room appears professionally done: off-white walls, plush charcoal-gray carpet, contemporary sofas in a lighter shade of gray set at right angles, Scandinavian tables in warm-toned woods, an Eames chair in black leather and chrome, recessed lighting and white sculpted lamps, abstract paintings. A high-class pad, David thinks. Very high-class.

Pete says, "Our reservations are for seven-thirty, but if I remember correctly, you won't be able to hold out without a little something solid."

"You know me well, friend, but the pretzels are plenty good enough. Can I steal a couple of olives."

Pete brings them from the bar. "Help yourself."

"Hey, who's the beautiful lady in the picture?" David points at a dark-haired, long-necked woman in tennis whites, an Ali MacGraw look-alike, smiling up at Pete in a photograph on the end table.

"Clarice? I guess you could say she's a special friend."

"Are you planning to get married?"

"I don't seem to be the marrying kind. At least not yet. She does the tennis circuit and I don't want to be tied down. Suits us   both."

"Don't you want a family?"

"There's time. I'm busy as hell at work. Takes everything I've got."

"I've heard about the eighty-hour weeks lawyers put in down here. What kind of cases are you doing?"

"Didn't I write when I joined Hayworth, Harrison?"

"Yeah, I was surprised when you joined a firm in New York instead of Boston, but the name didn't ring any bells. Should it have? They can't be doing civil rights if you can afford digs like this."

Peter laughs. "Corporate law. Mergers and acquisitions. We handled the VPC Cross deal."

"I confess. I don't know what you're talking about."

"God. Don't you read the papers? It was a three-*billion*-dollar deal. Hayworth, which is to say me and three other attorneys, did most of the legal work. It was the most interesting and complex acquisition I ever worked on."

David can't resist a small puncture. "Not to mention the dough must have been pretty good. Somehow I never pictured you for corporate law."

"It's the most challenging stuff around. And I make out. That's the beauty of the situation. Everybody does."

David can't conceal some unease at Pete's heady enthusiasm . . . as if nobody lost. "Don't a whole lot of people lose their jobs when one of these huge mergers takes place?"

Pete manages a laugh and a grimace at the same time. "Hey, what are you, one of those unreconstructed radicals? That was supposed to be my bag." He throws David a wink, letting him in on a joke. "Besides, if you're trying to make me feel guilty, you're not going to succeed. People wind up getting other jobs if they're willing to work at it, sometimes better ones. Haven't you heard, good buddy, the economy is booming. You can't still be serious about the decline of capitalism and all the college-boy stuff. This is the real world we're talking about. If anyone has a chance to beat out this country, it's Japan. Even little guys in Asia like Taiwan and Hong Kong and Singapore have rolling economies. They're fantastic. Real competition and a terrific work force. Believe me, they're not taking any cues from socialist economics."

"So I've heard." David digs a toe into the thick carpet, thinks: *Neither is Pete.*

"If any country goes into decline and fall sometime soon, it's going to be the Soviet Union, and if by chance you're still harboring the delusion that some kind of socialist paradise is in the cards anywhere, you're in for a rude awakening. Even the Chinese are starting to move because Deng is opening the back door to private production and distribution. He's smart enough to keep channels open in Hong Kong and not scare them to death . . . let the golden goose go on laying its eggs. The best Gorbachev can do is paper-over the cracks. He means well, but there's not a helluva lot he *can* do. I wouldn't be surprised to see the whole place collapse in the next few years. Right now, it's not much more than a Potemkin village. I visited a few years

back; half the buildings were crumbling and more than half the
men were drunk, and plenty of the women too. It wasn't the
least bit pretty. If you're looking for omens, think Chernobyl.
They'll need a miracle to save them. And Gorbachev, despite
what many people think, does not walk on water." Pete takes
a short breath. "Want another beer?"

"Okay. One more. Taciturn as ever, I see." He reaches for a
few more pretzels as Pete gets up and ambles to the kitchen. It's
almost like old times, David thinks, Pete propelling the talk forward like a freight train . . . but there's a different flavor. Saving
the world is not on the agenda.

Pete hands David his beer and pours a second martini for
himself before folding his long legs into a seat and taking a
swallow of his drink. David, watching him, thinks: Pete can hold
his liquor better than most, it's not the alcohol talking. He really
thinks the Soviet Union is going into free-fall. How could he
think that with a new breed like Gorbachev in charge? Wrong
about China too. Deng is making socialism work, not getting
rid of it. And to cavalierly wave away thousands of people losing
their jobs in this country . . . not the Pete he knew . . . not by a
long shot . . . and instrumental to boot. God, he wonders, can
he have voted for Reagan? What happened?

As if reading his mind, Pete says, "We thought we knew
everything when we were in college, but we didn't know much.
The bad war—and I still think it was a bad war, in case you
were wondering—it made the good things seem simple. Well,
they weren't. When it comes to civil rights, which you have
cleverly observed does not form the bulk of my practice, the
whole business is a lot more complicated than we thought. We
can't just make nice, open the doors, hand out a few dollars, set
up a few programs, and expect everything to turn out just
swell—cute little black kids trotting off to school and turning
up a few happy years later as doctors and lawyers and engineers
and schoolteachers. Plenty have, but it doesn't work that way
most of the time. Sometimes the programs are wrongheaded or
the people who run them are corrupt; sometimes I think nothing's going to work until we can figure out how to solve the
drug problem. Have you heard about crack? Our newest plague
in the big city . . . not to mention the welfare system . . . which
is hopeless . . . unless you think kids having kids is a good idea.
It's easy for someone who doesn't live here to think I've grown

a callus on my heart or a tumor in my head, but all I'm trying
to do is see things as they are, not in some rosy haze. And just
in case you're thinking the worst, I haven't turned my back on
all the stuff we believed in when we were college boys. I just
learned something about how the world works." He taps his
finger hard into his own chest. "*I'm* not in college anymore."

"Ouch!" David can't resist a smirk. "It's all those leftist college professors doing the damage."

"If the shoe fits, buddy . . ." He takes another swallow, rev-
ving himself up. "If you want to accomplish anything, demonstrations don't mean diddly anymore . . . except maybe to the
demonstrators, who are trying to convince themselves they have
brave hearts and pure souls . . . or maybe trying to fuck up
everything to high heaven so nobody has anything and the revolution comes quicker. So what if everybody—"

"Take it easy, man."

This time Pete's finger pokes at David's chest. "You are my
witness, Dave, nothing good or lasting happens without a solid,
thought-out program with tight controls and money to back it
up. Making money is nothing to be ashamed of, Dave. Money,
well-handled, is what makes things work. Which brings me to
the subject of what you probably consider my ill-gotten gains."

"Hey," David says, trying to get a word in.

Pete, ignoring him, plunges ahead. "We've gotten together, a
few of us in the firm, who, selfishly of course, don't want the
city to go down the tubes. We set up an organization with corporate sponsorship to spot twenty talented black or Hispanic
kids and take them in hand and see them through college. I don't
claim to be a philanthropist, and the amount of time and money
is small potatoes compared to what we pull in, but it's something, and in the end twenty people who wouldn't have had a
chance will have one . . . a good one."

"Hey, wait," David says, knowing as he mouths the words
that they are not quite what he means, "you don't have to apol-
ogize to me for anything, let alone your life." Truth is, he can't
help wondering how many thousands lost jobs in the VPC Cross
deal Pete worked on. How can he be so sure they'll get others?

Pete downs the last of his martini. "I wasn't apologizing. Just
wanted you to know the way things are." He looks at his watch.
"We'd better grab a cab or we'll be late." He calls downstairs
to the doorman. A taxi is waiting when they step out of the

elevator. "You won't be disappointed with dinner," Pete says as the door slams shut behind them.

The restaurant is better than good. It's terrific. David takes a deep breath when he looks at the menu. It's expensive, shockingly expensive. He doesn't say anything; it won't break him. When the food comes, it lives up to Pete's promise. The bread is crusty and hot; the salad is crisp and cold with a slightly sweet dressing that has bits of lemon peel and a mix of spices in it; the sole bathed in a buttery shrimp and herb sauce is ambrosial; the wine Pete orders without consulting him is a gift from Bacchus. A family could live for a month on what this meal is going to cost.

They eat and they talk. More precisely, David listens and eats while Pete talks between swallows. Most of Pete's table talk is about money . . . the getting of it, not the spending . . . (Pete used to say money didn't matter, that it would be obsolete in a hundred years) . . . the magic of accumulating wealth, the energy and brainpower it takes, how few men are up to the challenge . . . (Pete used to say that half the guys in his prep school were too dumb to tie their shoelaces but they stood to inherit fortunes anyway, get jobs on Wall Street, and wind up drunks) . . . that government should do nothing to impede business except protect against out-and-out crooks and provide safety standards and "a certain level" of job protection . . . (God, can Pete be halfway through the second bottle of wine on top of a third martini before dinner? If anyone can hold his liquor, it's him. Does he really believe this stuff?) . . . the stockmarket boom in the second Reagan administration shows no sign of stopping . . . Reagan . . . "admittedly the man has faults but he has an instinct for the big picture even if he's fuzzy on the details," an "instinctive intelligence" that gives people and the market "confidence," that lets "the experts" deal with the nitty-gritty of "implementation." (Can Pete be speaking approvingly of Reagan while the debt is showing signs of going through the roof and whole industries are going down the tubes, not to mention people's jobs. Doesn't he know how much of this is smoke and mirrors, voodoo economics, in Bush's phrase? Aren't the rich getting richer and the poor getting poorer?)

David strains to say something, challenge Pete. The words won't come though. He doesn't know enough, has been away too long, too used to playing Socrates with undergraduates and hanging out with academics who think the same things he thinks

. . . or who don't think at all about anything much except their own specialty. Money seems to be Pete's specialty now. Maybe it's a class thing, Pete becoming what he was destined to be all along, with a little noblesse oblige to the ghetto thrown in. A clean conscience and a big bank account. David struggles to pay attention. Does Pete know something he doesn't? Like Mei-ling and her cauterized tubes.

Over dessert—a lemon-and-orange tart that looks like one of van Gogh's sunflowers—Pete says, "It's amazing, even to me, the Dow has jumped past 1800, up over 350 points in a few months and no sign of slowing down. That's the kind of confidence out there. No matter how much you might not like Reagan or some of his policies, Dave, you've got to give credit where credit is due. This country is working, and the people who put him into office are working people, not just the rich the left is always rattling on about like a stuck record. Nobody says there aren't problems."

David is uncomfortable and a little woozy from the wine. Too much of Peter's argument is plausible, if not acceptable. He should say something even if he's not sure he can put the words together . . . something right. "Your scenario is too rosy to be true, good buddy. Let's see how the wealth is spread around a few years from now . . . how well the country is working with big bucks as the driving force, how happy the voters are. I'll reserve judgment for a while."

Pete says, "I'm not making bets that nirvana is around the corner. I'm just saying things are a helluva lot better than guys like us thought they would be. Nobody can predict the future." He hesitates. "Especially not the folks who spend their whole lives theorizing on college campuses or communing with nature in Vermont when the action is everywhere but."

David, surprised but not stung, a little tipsy, digs his fork into the tart, lets it sit there while he tilts the conversation slightly. "Just so people won't think I'm a complete ignoramus, and since you, living in the real world"—he winks at Pete as he says this—"know more about Wall Street than I'll ever know, how about giving me the dope on some of these insider trading scandals even I've read about."

Pete frowns, as if David is missing the point of all he's been saying. "There's always a few greedy bastards out there who aren't willing to play by the rules, who'll kill it for everyone if we let them. And the news media is like a bunch of piranha once they pick up the scent." He fills their wineglasses again, looks at David with eyes full of regret, commiseration, and fine red lines. "I'm sorry to say with regard to the whole insider trading business that several of the worst offenders are among your brethren, and all the rest of you will be shouldering the blame in the public mind. It's a damn shame."

David is suddenly very tired, not at all in the mood to deal with the turn in the conversation. He says, "Let's finish our coffee. I'm really bushed. I couldn't sleep on the train last night and I've got to be up early to see my parents. They're way up in the Bronx."

"That's right," Pete says. "I remember . . . a cooperative . . . teachers and people in the bureaucracy."

"Civil service."

"Right." He signals for the check.

David asks, "What's my share of the tab?"

"Don't even think about it. You're the visiting fireman. You can pick up the tab when I come to Montreal."

David knows Pete isn't coming to Montreal, acquiesces anyway, thanks Pete, drains his coffee cup. It was an excellent meal.

Once they are outside the restaurant, a cab pulls up almost immediately, as if the driver knows a heavy tip is waiting at this particular door. Pete insists that David take it. They give each other a quick, boozy, man-to-man hug and swear to do it again soon, not let so much time go by.

Inside the cab, David, unsteady but clear enough to think reasonably straight, tells himself that what he and Pete once had in common was being thrown together in a terrific place . . . serious politics in an exhilarating time . . . both in the past. Most likely, they will never see each other again. Unfortunate, a little sad perhaps, but not tragic.

Tragic is something else . . . the loss of something good to believe in. Tragic is war. Tragic is early death. Tragic is the death of a family. Mei-ling and Juliana, his family . . . shouldn't . . . can't . . . turn into a tragedy. He's here to work things through about that. Why should he give a shit about whether Pete sold out or caved in to Wall Street? Nothing but words. Nothing to do with him. To hell with Pete. To hell with politics.

The sky is a little overcast the next morning. David looks up at clouds that promise to be thunderheads before long, hopes he won't get caught in a storm. He walks the two blocks to Twenty-third Street and then heads east toward the subway. He has to navigate the sidewalk. Yesterday's fruit rots on the cement like a moldy excrescence, and sticky candy wrappers skip around in the humid breeze. Cigarette butts are scattered everywhere.

Before David reaches the subway, "the homeless" appear, not entirely unexpectedly. He's read about them, even in Montreal, the feral men and women who've devised a new architecture for the New York landscape: corrugated cartons fashioned into crude shelters; "discarded packaging for discarded people," the headline read. But reading about them is one thing; the reality is something else.

Two men are on their asses leaning against the wall of a building a few yards from the subway station. New meaning, David thinks, to the word *lowlife*. Their legs are splayed on the sidewalk beyond the edges of their adjacent cartons, their heads lolling over the sides, their mouths either grinning or grimacing, he can't decide. They remind David of a toy he had broken, a jack-in-the-box whose spring he had popped till it couldn't pop anymore. He had cried, refused to let his mother throw it away though it was useless and took up shelf space. He couldn't have been much more than a baby when that happened.

The men's faces and hair and clothing are so worn out and grimy that David can't imagine what they might have looked like in a more fortunate time. They seem to be attempting to groom themselves, but their efforts consist largely of scratching—scalps, backs, ears, armpits, feet—the saddest and most terrible feet he has ever seen. Their shoes, filled with newspaper, are on the sidewalk next to them. David is not sure if the smell that rises from them like a noxious cloud comes from the shoes or the reddened, oozing eruptions on their feet. He had expected panhandlers in New York, but not this. *This* is tragedy. He remembers the previous night's menu. Or is it some kind of grotesque farce?

Trapped between revulsion and pity, he can't wait to get away. But one of the men calls out to him, "Hey, Mister . . ."

David doesn't wait to hear the rest. He takes a couple of dollars from his wallet, crumbles each one into a ball, and tosses them to the men, who grab the air to catch them. He rushes away, his throat gagging. He runs down the subway staircase as if he were escaping from the plague. His ride is uneventful.

When David leaves the subway and walks toward the Union Park Cooperative Houses in the northeast Bronx, where his parents still live, the sky darkens and hangs low overhead. Rain can't be far away. David is relieved to see that the neighborhood is holding up fairly well . . . stores, park areas with benches, kids whizzing on skateboards . . . friendly, safe enough for walking and shopping . . . still a refuge for the city's working people . . . a precious and precarious balance of black and white but noticeably darker than when he was growing up. Good, what they always wanted—as long as it doesn't tip. The city's unions have done right investing in projects like these, he thinks.

Yet it's all so charmless, so institutional. The buildings rise above the flat terrain like monoliths, looming rectangular mock-ups of the future, concrete and intimidating. David feels no surge of nostalgia; he can't imagine himself living in this place again, though it had pleased him as a boy. He passes a familiar playground . . . his. It is strangely empty. Of course, he thinks, the slums or mean streets aren't his alternative. Instead, he lives in cushioned comfort in his wife's beautiful stone house in one of North America's loveliest cities. Would the men living in the corrugated cartons next to the subway find happiness in this decent place? Not easy to say unless you can look inside their heads. Maybe not then. Complicated . . . like everything else.

"Davey," his mother says, hugging him into the apartment, kissing his cheek. His parents seem shrunken and faded since their last visit only a year before. The visit had been a good one. They spent a day in Old Montreal and ate lunch in a French restaurant. Mei-ling had gone out of her way to please them: tickets for a string quartet, a visit to the old Jewish section on St. Urbain, an afternoon at the Botanical Garden. She had been touched by their affectionate ways, their delight in Juliana, their effort not to intrude too much on her time, though she explained it was between semesters. What would they think now? Well, he won't ask their opinion. He won't mention anything at all. When they ask, he'll say everything is fine, say she couldn't leave Juliana, who will be at school till the end of the month, the same thing he told Pete. That, they can understand, a mother unwilling to leave a child.

David's parents had embraced their late grandparenthood eagerly, sending birthday and holiday gifts, books they thought appropriate, suggesting flute lessons. Juliana, who had been denied grandparents—so young when Emma died—felt the absence keenly. She enjoyed being doted upon during their infrequent visits and spoke to them willingly and at length on the telephone. She kept a snapshot of "my family"—the five of them—on her bulletin board. A good kid, he tells himself for the thousandth time.

It is so long since he has seen his parents in their habitat. David notices that his mother has stopped dying her hair: It has turned gray, almost white, and bits of scalp shine through where once it was thick as a fox tail. Her arms, uncovered in summer, are speckled with brown spots as large as dimes. The flowered cotton dress she wears, crisp and clean as always, seems more of a container now than an adornment of the pretty lady he remembers. His father's clothing hangs neatly on his slightly stooped frame; the alligator on his blue knit sport shirt sits low on a chest that seems to have bent in on itself. But they are both bright-eyed and happy to see him and seem in good health. His mother plants a few more kisses on his cheeks, takes his arm, and pulls him toward the table. "You must be starving," she says.

"As a matter of fact, I am."

The three of them tuck into the lavish spread David knew would be waiting for him: fresh-squeezed orange juice, small platters of smoked fish and cheese, sweet butter, pickled herring in cream sauce, sliced tomatoes and cucumbers, a bread basket piled high with warm bagels and cinnamon-nut rolls, and a carafe of fresh-brewed coffee. After they have swallowed down a few mouthfuls and relaxed into their chairs, more easy with one another, his father asks, "So, Davey, how does it feel to be back home?"

David smiles, takes another bite of bagel to give himself time for the lie he will speak. "Great, Pop, like old times."

The guilt of leaving them and remaining in Canada still weighs on him. They are getting old; they need him; he is their only child. He wants his return to be a happy occasion. He won't tell them about the punch from the grinning black kid who wears a wool hat in the summertime, or the crazy bag lady, or the men with running sores on their feet who live in cardboard boxes. They probably know it all anyway, have avoided telling him. He won't even tell them much about Pete, who has fallen in love with making money but who makes a disquieting kind of sense.

As if on cue, his mother asks, "And how's your friend from college, your roommate . . . ?" She struggles to remember the name, finds it, smiles. "Pete . . . the tall one with the good manners."

"Rich. He's very rich. He asked to be remembered to you."

"That's nice he remembers us," says his mother.

"It's nothing so terrible to be rich," says his father. "I used to think it was more important to be good and that you couldn't get rich without doing something bad. Maybe I was wrong. Maybe you just have to be smart." He hesitates. "It's nice to be rich when you get older . . . makes you independent."

"Anything wrong, Pop? Tell me if you're short of money. I can help out without it hurting me any." Not true. He would have to let Mei-ling's money take up some of the slack, the wrong time for that.

"Hell, no." His father laughs. "I was just talking philosophy. Between my pension and social security and Medicare and my false teeth under the dental plan and your mother's good cooking, we're sitting pretty. Maybe you need some help. Just ask."

"No, Pop, I'm fine."

His mother asks, "So what's doing with Mei-ling and Juliana? How are they?"

"Fine. Mei-ling is finishing up. Juliana's studying like crazy for her final exams." He adds this last because it will please his mother and it has the additional advantage of being true.

"I remember when you used to do that . . . getting almost all perfect grades." She fills his coffee cup again. "She's like a chip off the old block."

"Her mother's no dummy either," David says. "That's where most of the credit belongs. I came along late in the game."

His mother counters. "I suppose you think it's not important having a professor for a father, setting an example."

His father says, "Does she say what she wants to be?"

"Depends when you ask her. We go from movie star to brain surgeon. She writes wonderful poetry. I'd like her to be a writer, but I get the feeling she has a more practical turn."

"If she's so good with oooowords and she's so intelligent," his mother says, "maybe she should think about being a lawyer. There's lots of opportunity now for a woman lawyer, not like in the old days before the women's movement."

David laughs. "Too bad it didn't come along soon enough for you, Mom. You would've knocked them dead."

By the time he finishes his cinnamon-nut roll and coffee, he is stuffed to the point of discomfort. He is not used to eating so much but wanted to please his mother . . . Lord! . . . still pleasing his mother. Well, why not? For better and worse, he is what he is because of her . . . because of them both . . . but more because of her . . . usually okay . . . nothing to be ashamed of . . . sometimes better than okay even if he hasn't saved the world or set it on fire with his great works.

David sneaks a glance at his watch. Only an hour has gone by. He realizes that the long day may be as heavy as the clouds. What are they going to talk about for seven or eight hours? What are they going to do?

"It looks like it's going to rain later," his father says. "How about we go for a walk in the old neighborhood now so you can look around? Then we can drive to City Island for a good fish lunch, even if it's raining."

"Sounds good to me, Pop. What kind of car are you driving now?"

"Whatever the rental agency has handy that's cheap. All those years I drove a Chevy . . . now I don't care . . . I have no loyalty to General Motors . . . a bunch of greedy bastards with no pride in their products anymore . . . just raking it in by the millions for the guys at the top . . . squeezing the workers. Let the Japanese squeeze them out. It'll serve them right."

Ah, this is the father David remembers, spilling over with righteous indignation, a flash of the working-class radical, a whiff of the Old Testament prophet. But over a rental car?

"Besides," his father continues, "it pays to rent when you need a car once in a blue moon. Who wants to pay car insurance in New York? Should I become bankrupt for the sake of a drive once in a while? How often do I drive anyway?"

This, too, is the father David remembers . . . turning statements into questions. David begins to feel as if he is a visiting anthropologist studying the folkways of exotic people. In Montreal, when they visited, his parents were the mother and father he was happy to see. Here they are a faded remnant of the New

York that is no longer his. An alien city has risen in his absence, a cold, shriveled heart at its center, a spectacle of high and low life, a freak show. He doesn't love it anymore.

His mother has been clearing the table. She looks up. "Before we go, I promised Gladys Washington that we would say hello. She always asks about you. Is it okay if I call her?"

"Sure, Mom. Boy, how old is she? I didn't know she was still alive. She must be getting on."

"Wouldn't I have told you if she died?"

"Sure, Mom." He hadn't meant to offend.

"Age is relative, Davey. She's only about ten years older than I am."

While his mother dials, David remember Gladys's husband, Frank, an organizer for the electrical union, who died of diabetes in his fifties after going blind and having one leg amputated. He had been a square block of a man with a sensitive face that looked like an African carving: noble forehead, broad nose, full lips. He had managed to remain both sweet and stoic in his illness. Sometimes David read to him from newspapers and magazines, taking turns with his mother when he wasn't cramming for exams. Friends from the union came to visit from time to time. But the heavy load had fallen on Gladys. They had no children.

Once, Frank had said to him, "You could be a kid of my own, Davey. That's how much I enjoy your company."

He'd been embarrassed, didn't know what to say.

Sensing his discomfort, Frank slid from the personal to the political, where they were both comfortable: "When you're part of the labor movement, though, you don't really need children. You're responsible for everyone's children. It goes double if you're opening up opportunities for your own people . . . bringing them into the mainstream . . . helping them have something to look forward to . . . goals."

David, remembering, winces. Nobody talks that language anymore. It's like a voice from the tomb—*the labor movement, helping them, goals*. What would Frank think of the crack kids, the kids who don't or can't learn, the boys with guns, the girls who give birth before their thirteenth birthday? Does anyone from the union remember Frank Washington?

When they reach Gladys's apartment after riding down to the third floor, she opens her arms wide and gathers David into her bosom. "You've been gone too long," she says, "but I keep up with you. It's good to have a professor in the family." She laughs. "For a while there, when you first left, I was worried you might land in jail. I was getting ready to send you a cake with a file baked inside."

"Glad I didn't need it, but anytime you want to send the cake . . ."

The four of them spend an awkward but pleasant half hour together, chatting about old times, but they run out of much to talk about once they get past Mei-ling and Juliana and the shows on television. They seem to have made a pact not to speak of anything sorrowful. What would be the point? More pain?

"Take care of yourself," David says as they leave.

"You too, sonny," Gladys says, hugging him again. "Come back. Don't wait too long."

By late afternoon the sky opens up. Potholes turn into ponds. The summer storm drenches the streets and water runs along the gutters like rivers in flood.

"Stay over and stay out of the rain," his mother implores him. When he insists on returning to the hotel—he tells his mother the room is reserved and paid for and that he has things to do in Manhattan early in the morning—his father wants to drive him. "That would be crazy, Pop," he says. "We'd be stuck in traffic for hours. Just drop me at the subway. It'll be a whole lot faster."

"But in a downpour like this, even the subway could get stuck."

"It'll be okay, Pop. Don't worry so much."

His mother insists on driving to the subway station with them. Trying to cheer her up, he kisses her, says, "Next time in Montreal." Then he opens the door and runs past the puddles to the subway entrance.

Back at the hotel, he takes off his soaking clothing and showers. Then he picks up the telephone and dials through to Montreal. Juliana answers. He says, "Hi, honey, it's me."

"Dad, it's great to hear from you. Did you see Gram and Grampa?"

"They send you love."

"What else did you do?"

"A few things. We can talk about it when I get home. Is your mother there?"

"No. She went out."

"Do me a favor. Tell her I'll be taking the train for home tomorrow morning."

"Great. I can't wait to see you." She gives him a loud smooch into the telephone.

David wonders if she will turn on him and on her mother when she is deeper into adolescence . . . or if he has been given a special dispensation having come to fatherhood so late in the game.

Montreal

⌒

THE HOUSE IS cool and pleasant. Peaceful. It will welcome David home. While the sun beat down during the day, Mei-ling kept the windows closed and the blinds drawn, managing to shield the rooms from summer heat. Now she raises the blinds and opens the windows to bring the fresh evening air inside. A lingering June twilight casts a pleasant lavender glow. Insects buzz in the shrubbery. Venus is already shining in the distant heavens. A world away, China is the shadow of a shadow, Hong Kong the echo of an echo, ghosts. She doesn't believe in ghosts, flicks them away like motes of dust. David is coming home . . . gone only a few days . . . a good sign.

Mei-ling switches on a lamp so that David will see a light in the window. Her gauzy blue dress is the color of a robin's egg. She has taken pains to prepare some of his favorite food: chicken in lemon and garlic sauce, rice pilaf, and strawberry shortcake made with real whipped cream and the first local berries of the season. Beer and wine are chilling in the refrigerator. The dining room table is set for three, but it has the look of a dinner party complete with white linen, buffed cutlery, crystal wineglasses, and yellow lilies in a blue and white vase: a still-life waiting for a painter to set up his easel and brushes.

Mei-ling and Juliana are both waiting dinner for David. The turn of his key in the lock signals his arrival just as the last of the twilight disappears. As soon as he sets his suitcase down, Juliana hugs him and smooches his cheek. She says, "I'm glad you finally got here. I'm starving." She casts a glance at Mei-ling. "Mother said we had to wait. Let's eat."

"Don't you want to see what I've brought for you first?" He hands her a small package wrapped in flowered paper and tied with a bright red ribbon.

Juliana has the package open by the time he finishes his sentence. The book is bound in heavy colorful cloth, a paisley print in variations of red and gold borrowed from an antique Persian design. "Oh," she says, "the cover is so beautiful." Flipping through it, she hesitates, not exactly disappointed, a little puzzled. "It's all blank. It's not a diary with dates and stuff. What am I supposed to use it for?"

"It's for whatever you want to write . . . thoughts, poems, ideas . . . whatever you want."

Possibilities suggest themselves to Juliana. She brightens. "Perfect," she says. "I can use it to keep track of what's inside my head. Sometimes I forget how I want to say something if I don't write the words down right away."

Mei-ling has been watching them, the sprouting plant and the gardener. Dirk Verhoeven's opposite pole, she thinks, the most loving of fathers. She sighs inwardly, regretful, not penitent; what has been done cannot be undone. Should she kiss David as Juliana has—freely, openly—or should she wait to see what he does? He has come home to them quickly . . . a good sign. But best to wait, take her cue from him.

David looks at Mei-ling, at the gauzy blue of her dress, the slope of her neck and shoulders, the welcome in her dark eyes. He smiles tentatively, wonders how it will go between them.

She says, "I'm very happy you're home."

David, in one continuous motion, squeezes her shoulder, slides his arm to her waist, leans into her a little, and brushes her lightly on the lips. The kiss is like a flower petal. She feels her breath catch. He whispers into her ear, "It's where I belong. We'll talk some more and work things out."

"Yes," she says, a blush rising in her cheeks, guilt driving a wedge into her heart. Wrong, she thinks, to have kept anything from him.

"I think you'll like this," he says, handing her a package similar to Juliana's but larger. She snaps the ribbon and tears the wrapping off. She leafs through the book of bird and flower prints—graceful pen strokes, clear, delicate colors, feathery wings, and luminous petals—so different in feeling from the Dutch prints in her collection that are saturated with paint, solid, real. She has seen prints like these long ago, in China, when she was a girl.

"Where did you find this, David," she asks. "It looks like a book from my father's library . . . though the paper is different."

"There's nothing you can't find in New York if you're willing to search. Look at the imprint in front. It's made in China . . . reproductions of famous antique prints. They're doing this sort of thing more and more now that the scholars and artists aren't kept busy hauling bricks and tending pigs . . . at least the ones who are left. From what the salesman told me, there's quite a worldwide market for work like this."

"It's a treasure." She kisses his cheek.

Juliana asks, "Can we eat now? I may starve to death."

While David goes to wash the travel grime from his hands and face, Mei-ling puts dinner on the table. She feels lighter. Other men have given her jewels. Only David presents her with books that might have belonged to her father. It will all work out, he will understand, a matter of how she presents everything to him. She has thought of little else from the moment Juliana gave her his message, chosen her words carefully, rehearsed.

It is very late when they finish their strawberry shortcake.

"Nothing less than perfect," David says, putting his spoon down and wiping his mouth with his napkin. "When did you take up gourmet cooking?"

Mei-ling smiles. "Last night."

"Great," says Juliana, licking cream off her lips, "but I still have biology to study for tomorrow. I'm going up. I'm setting my alarm for early." She leaves them at the table . . . calls out moments later on her way to the stairs . . . "Thanks for the book, Dad. It's gorgeous." She has taken to superlatives, he thinks, a sure sign of adolescence.

David says, "We're lucky she has a cheerful disposition. At this stage she could be saying everything is horrible in this worst of all possible worlds, especially us."

Mei-ling smiles. "It didn't work that way in China. It never occurred to me to criticize my parents. In this country children are encouraged to speak their minds even if it shows lack of respect for their parents or teachers or even the law. Have you seen the bumper stickers that tell you to question authority? Sometimes when I hear Juliana and her friends together, when they don't know I'm listening, I think a little respect for authority might be a good thing for these blessed and naive children. It's what keeps them safe. Remember the poem by Yeats? 'The Second Coming' . . . 'the center cannot hold, mere anarchy is loosed upon the world.' "

A thrill runs down David's spine as he does indeed remember. No wonder he has come home to her . . . not family as an abstraction . . . not only how she looks (wonderful as that is) . . . the inside of her head is the real turn-on. And there's the mysterious something he can never quite touch . . . the essence he's always reaching for . . . foreign. His own Cleopatra. She is not boring. She never will be.

Alone together, they put away the remains of dinner and load the dishwasher. Mei-ling asks about his parents, wants to know how he spent his time. He tells her his parents are well, aging noticeably, that they send her their love, that they enjoyed reading Juliana's poems, that his mother thinks Juliana should be a lawyer. He tells her about the depressing street scene in New York. He tells her about seeing Pete but doesn't go into detail. She seems a bit distracted by then, slightly tremulous . . . the mysterious something. He wonders what she is thinking. They will have to talk, but not yet. It can wait. It's late.

Mei-ling wipes the surface of the stove while David rinses the sink. The kitchen is clean. There is nothing more to do. When they go into the living room, David says, "They sell compact disks in bookstores now. I bought us one while I was roaming around."

"What is it?"

She expects something classical, Mozart or Mendelssohn, his usual preference. And hers. Miss Richardson's was not remiss in her musical education. When they first married, David still listened once in a while to Bob Dylan or Joan Baez or James Taylor or Joni Mitchell, and rock groups with names she couldn't manage to remember, old stuff that left her indifferent but that he carried with him from a previous life, the way soldiers safeguard a regimental flag.

David slips the new disk in, says, "This is very New York . . . Broadway . . . the way it used to be before we were born. Gershwin."

"What?"

"Not what, who. Gershwin . . . George. You never heard of him?" There are great gaps in her knowledge of things American. It always takes him unawares. "He wrote a lot of popular music in the 1920s and 1930s. They're reviving it now, but it's been around forever. You'll recognize some of the songs even if you don't know who wrote them. They're wonderful."

They listen to the introductory medley, the strong piano riffing through "Stairway to Paradise," "I've Got Rhythm." Mei-ling, lilting to the captivating tunes, takes David's hand and tugs him out of the chair. They rarely dance, but she wants to now. It was the only part of her work in Amsterdam she enjoyed, going to one of the clubs, dancing till the real business of the evening got under way . . . though she wishes she hadn't thought of it at this particular moment. And most of the men were clumsy.

David tries to dance but is not very good at it, never has been, his feet get in his way. After a minute or two he pulls her into his lap on the green velvet chair and on cue they cling to each other while the singer—a young man whose name escapes David . . . Feinberg or Feinstein or Feingold . . . something Jewish—charms his way through "Embraceable You" in a pleasing androgynous voice. Mei-ling is like a kitten, soft and warm, seeming even to purr. Her breasts rise and fall to the sound of their breathing. He nuzzles them with his cheek and lips, strokes her arms and her legs, the wonderful firm roundness of her behind, kisses her neck.

Mei-ling clings to him. They will talk tomorrow.

Mei-ling is still asleep when David wakes, but as he eases himself quietly out of bed, the mattress shifts beneath her and prods her into consciousness. She hears his padding footsteps, the whoosh of running water in the bathroom, the closet door opening, the rustle of clothing. There is whispering in the hallway. Juliana must be awake. She said she would set her alarm. Mei-ling still hasn't opened her eyes, but she turns in bed and reaches for the place where David slept beside her. It is still warm. She lies there feeling good . . . safe . . . drifts off again into sleep.

David's hand on her shoulder wakes her. "Time to eat," he whispers. "I made us some breakfast."

Juliana calls out from downstairs, "I'm going." The door slams behind her.

David's hand is moving slowly up and down her back. She says, "I smell the coffee." Her mind is alert now. There's important work to be done between them this morning. She sits up, the taste of sleep still coating her mouth. "Let's have breakfast. I'll wash up."

When they have finished eating and are lingering over a second cup of coffee, Mei-ling, loath to break the mood but eager to have everything she must do behind her, says, "David, there are things I have to show you. Afterward, we can talk. I don't want to wait. Let's begin now and get everything over with."

This isn't the way he thought it would be. He had been rehearsing on the train all the way from New York, everything he would say, how grateful and relieved she would be to have him forgive her and understand her. He expected to take the lead, do most of the talking, tell her how disappointed he was about giving up the idea of a baby, how angry he was because she had kept something so important from him, but that Juliana was his daughter as much as any child could be, that they were lucky to have one like her, that they were a family, that family counts more than anything even if damage has been done, that she should never keep anything from him again no matter how much she thinks it might hurt him, that he loves her as he had never loved anyone, including Valerie, that life without her would be a paltry thing, that they should begin again and leave the past behind them. On the train his generosity and largesse had comforted him so well, like a down quilt in winter.

But now she's cut him off at the pass, so he doesn't *say* anything . . . though his mind and heart are suddenly racing and jumping like squirrels and his sweaty armpits are leaking halfmoons on to his yellow T-shirt. What can she possibly want to show him? He wishes he were somewhere else. He can't think of a joke to take the edge off. Why does he feel as if he is about to fall off a cliff?

It takes them a few silent moments to stack the dishes in the sink and clear the table. Mei-ling wipes her hands on the dish towel, then cuts the silence. "While you were gone, I've been able to think. You're right. There should be no secrets between us." She takes his hand and turns toward their office. "There are parts of my life you know little about . . . I feared wounding you."

He leans his head to one side. "Wounding me?"

"If you've grown up in the West, you can't imagine the struggle my mother and I had just trying to survive while finding a way to get out of China. The Cultural Revolution drove everyone insane. You can't imagine what it was like to be hungry and dirty all the time . . . so terrified of being caught at any moment that every day was a twenty-four-hour nightmare. Then the fear and isolation when we got to Hong Kong."

"I know all that. Don't think I haven't thought about it from the moment I met you. But what is it you're trying to tell me? What's going to wound me?"

"When we finish, David, you'll know me almost as well as I know myself." She gives a dry, mirthless laugh. "Assuming I know myself at all . . . assuming any of us does."

"But you haven't said what it is you want me to know. Can it wound me more than knowing about the men on the train?"

"I didn't understand it at the time, but I suppose everything followed from that."

"It's long behind us."

She kisses his cheek. "I'm glad you said 'us.' " She smoothes her hair back with her hand. "Try to put yourself in my place. You haven't been there, so it's difficult. I'm going to count on you and trust you with my life."

Mei-ling points to a motley assortment of books and papers in an orderly pile on her desk, some almost new and others frayed and dirty, stained by the abuses of age and the insults of transport. "I've arranged all this in rough chronological order," she says.

David recognizes the green folder on top but can't imagine what on earth she put it there for. He's already read it . . . her "transforming experience" . . . and his.

Mei-ling, with a lift of her eyebrows and a tiny smile that softens her otherwise grave expression, says, "Here is my life." She taps the top of the pile. "You said you fell in love with me when you read my story, even before you spoke to me. But the life of the girl you fell in love with ended when I was seventeen.

I was terrified afterward, as if a tornado had swept me into its funnel and kept me whirling there in permanent suspension. For a long while I barely spoke." She hesitates, runs the palm of her hand over her hair again. "Afterward, I kept most things to myself. It became a habit. When I met you I was able to be more open . . . I could trust you with bits and pieces about my mother and Juliana when she was little . . . fragments of my life in Hong Kong and Amsterdam . . . my schooling . . . the food and flowers and art museums . . . and even Berthe. You always wanted to know about the Jews in the war."

He tries to remember . . . Berthe. Of course . . . the neighbor in Amsterdam who was Jewish, a survivor of the Holocaust. She had been a prisoner in a camp . . . forced into grotesque surgery that left her unable to conceive a child . . . the one who married badly and earned her living as a masseuse. David remembers Mei-ling telling him about her, but why was she talking about her now?

He goes over to the pile. "Why do you want me look at all this? What is it?"

"I want you to sit down and read these papers. I'll leave you alone with them. After that, we can talk."

"I'll read it all if it's so important to you. But why don't you just tell me what's on your mind?"

"Everyone has things we can't bring ourselves to talk about or even remember if they hurt too much. It will be easier this way."

A series of loud, painful hiccups seizes David. He holds his breath to silence them. "Nerves," he says. "All this mystery is making me nervous."

"Don't be. Sit down and make yourself comfortable. It's going to take a while. I have a few errands, but I'll be back before one. We can talk and have lunch."

A quizzical half-smile crosses his face. "Will I have any appetite left after all this?"

"It won't be easy, but I'm counting on you. When you look through," she says, pointing to the pile, "consider what it took to make it happen."

A new appeal springs to mind. She says, "What kind of people survived the concentration camps? Were they the most virtuous or those who did whatever they were forced to do to hang on to life . . . to last long enough to be rescued?"

David considers, sits down. "You ask scary questions, Mrs. Levy."

⌒

After wading through the formidable pile a little while, David begins to wonder if there is any mystery at all, if his fury about her keeping the tubal surgery from him hadn't caused her to imagine secrets where there were only innocent omissions. Except for the paper in the green folder that revealed her early life to him, he has seen none of this before. It is like reading a documentary novel, bits and pieces of paper taking on a life of their own, gradually unfolding the whole story. It is oddly compelling, a vicarious tragedy, a survivor's tale.

A thrill of sorrow sweeps over him as he skims Mei-ling's "transforming experience" once again. He knows what is coming: the severing of the family . . . the humiliation of her father . . . the long train . . . the rape . . . the nameless man who tried to shield her . . . his ear and tongue severed . . . the terror and blood . . . flinging himself in front of the truck . . . dying before her eyes. But he has seen none of the other documents before.

Emma's handwriting is precise, but he feels himself a scholar deciphering an ancient manuscript when he reads her journal. The paper is dry and crumpled and the writing faded. Why had Mei-ling never shown her mother's journal to him? She must have known he would want to see it. But there is no mystery here, no terrible secret, only confirmation of much that he knows and an unexpected love story, poignant, a bittersweet ending . . . like an old-fashioned movie.

Perhaps, he thinks, Emma's journal should be included in an anthology along with the testimony of other victims of the Cultural Revolution. Perhaps he should edit such a collection. It would be a proper memorial to Professor Wang and Mei-ling's mother and old Dr. Kung . . . all the others.

What, he wonders, would Juliana make of her family story? Mei-ling should share it with her. Juliana should know about her grandparents' lives, how much they suffered and sacrificed for their beliefs, how they were betrayed by them. At least on her mother's side.

David props his elbows under his chin. The grandparents on her father's side must have been long dead if Dirk Verhoeven was deep into his fifties when he married Mei-ling, probably near sixty when Juliana was born. Dutch people. Mei-ling professes to know almost nothing about them. Wasn't she curious? Perhaps she was more her husband's child than his wife?

It is hard for him to imagine young Mei-ling the willing bride of so old a man? Perhaps she longed for a father. Plenty of times she said he reminds her of her father. How could Emma Wang have given her consent to such a match? No doubt the man helped them when they desperately needed it. Mei-ling told him that much. How much more can there be? David can't remember if Mei-ling ever mentioned how long they'd been married before Verhoeven died. In truth, he preferred not to dwell on the matter. He would have had to imagine her in bed with the old man . . . making love. His mouth tastes sour when he thinks of it.

David rearranges Emma's journal carefully so as not to damage the already-fragile pages. He will tell Mei-ling to put them into a secure folder that will preserve them. It would be wrong to allow the words of a witness to disappear.

The next item on the pile is an eight-by-ten manila envelope that is fastened with a piece of red string. He opens it and pulls out the contents. Miss Richardson's School for Girls in Hong Kong . . . report cards. He scans them. All excellent grades. Hardly surprising. A few essays in her neat handwriting, all with laudatory comments. Does Mei-ling mean for him to read them? He skims the pages . . . Shakespeare, Milton, Wordsworth, Disraeli, and Queen Victoria . . . the curriculum of an English schoolgirl. The papers stop in the nineteenth century. He won't read them now. He can always go back.

There is a photograph, a group of schoolgirls lined up in front of an iron gate, and a few women, obviously teachers, standing to the side, unsmiling. The girls are wearing white blouses and dark skirts. Is this a graduation photo? Perhaps, but he can't say for sure. It is easy to find Mei-ling, one of the few Chinese faces in an embroidery of English young ladyhood, solemn faces, passions, if there are any, hidden beneath their prim blouses and skirts. Mei-ling seems hardly to have changed at all from the grave and proper girl in the photo, though she is certainly more fashionable. Her delight in new clothing has bewildered him at times, charmed him . . . so winningly female, so unlike the spartan Valerie. It is still hard for him to believe that Mei-ling is the mother of a thirteen-year-old. The virginal photo sparks a surprising flash of lust, hardly the pain Mei-ling has led him to expect this morning. Yet, he remembers anxiously, his mouth dry at the thought, she was no innocent schoolgirl when the photo was taken, however much she looked the part. The rape . . . the gang rape . . . was already in the past. David slides the school memorabilia back into the envelope. He must move ahead if he is to finish before Mei-ling returns.

He has begun to enjoy the unexpected journey into Mei-ling's past, though he feels a bit of a voyeur peeping into windows. Next on the pile is an embossed folder of heavy paper with the outline of the Eiffel Tower stamped in front. Oddly, it is a menu from a Hong Kong restaurant . . . in English . . . but the food clearly has pretensions to French. Why, David wonders, with the best food in the world around every corner and on ships in the harbor, would anyone want to go to an ersatz French restaurant in a climate so hot and wet, the walls sweat? The wine list on the last page is in French, but it is partially blocked by a photograph, probably a Polaroid, in color. David is startled. He has never seen the man before, but he knows at once it is Dirk Verhoeven. And Mei-ling is sitting next to him in a dress that is very sexy, cut just low enough to reveal emerging breasts, and a necklace reaches to the V where the dress begins, and earrings that dangle to her shoulders. She looks anything but virginal, yet she can't be much older than the girl in the school photo. She is holding a glass of wine in her raised hand and smiling a bit stiffly.

And the man . . . Verhoeven . . . not yet her husband . . . they were married after moving to Amsterdam . . . also raising his glass. He looks entirely satisfied with himself. He is wearing a cream-colored suit and a broad, smug smile that displays a mouthful of even teeth set in a firm chin and jaw . . . Juliana's teeth and jaw. David grimaces involuntarily. He dislikes the look of the man and hates the sight of him with Mei-ling. Verhoeven is handsome enough, only slightly puffy around the eyes and under the chin, but he is old . . . a randy old man. Where was Emma in all this? Why did she permit such a match? Something is clearly wrong here! David thrusts the menu and picture on to the small but growing stack he has finished. He is glad to be done with it.

How long has he been looking at this stuff? David checks his watch. It will be a while before Mei-ling returns, but the pile is growing smaller only slowly. His throat is dry. He goes to the kitchen and pours a glass of grapefruit juice, gulps it down, and goes back to the desk.

When he begins to look through the next batch, David finds himself in Amsterdam: postcards of landscape paintings and windmills and tulip fields, small, cheap prints of works by Vermeer and Franz Hals, a larger, better print of van Gogh's irises, several programs from the Concertgebouw, folders from Rembrandt's house and Anne Frank's house.

When David first sees the Dutch lettering on a piece of official-looking paper, he cannot make out what it is he's looking at, but after a bit he is able to figure out the names and enough of the words to know that he is looking at Mei-ling Wang and Dirk Verhoeven's marriage certificate. It has an official stamp, the signature of witnesses, the signature of an official, probably the person who performed the ceremony. The date catches his eye and brings him up short . . . only a few weeks before Juliana's birth.

Why does he feel as if he's been decked by a punch that came out of nowhere? He has never been one for middle-class conventions. He and Valerie had lived together before marrying . . . everyone did. A new convention, he realizes ruefully. But a picture shapes itself in his mind that forces a belch of grapefruit juice back up into his throat: a greatly pregnant Mei-ling and the toothy man in the cream-colored suit going through the marriage ceremony. A revulsion he can't control shakes him. But, still, there is no great mystery here, just pictures and documents that manifest a reality he finds unpleasant but hardly shameful, nothing he couldn't have imagined if he let himself.

David is relieved when he opens the white baby book. Mei-ling has cared for it so that it looks new. Why hasn't she shown it to him before? She must have known he'd want all the little details about Juliana before he knew her: her first smile, her first tooth, when she sat up, when she crawled, baby pictures. He leafs through the pages. Here is a snapshot of Juliana as an infant raising her head and peering through the bars of a crib, a lock of her dark hair in a transparent envelope, a tracing of her tiny hand, another snapshot, in her pram being pushed by her . . . grandmother? It must be. The famous English Emma, whose journal he has just finished. He has never before seen what she looked like, this Emma who married a Chinese student and joined the Revolution, who wound up a still-young widow hauling stones in some godforsaken spot where she was the only westerner for miles around, who plucked up courage to flee the countryside, find her daughter, and escape to Hong Kong from the mainland . . . who seems to have stood by, either in ignorance or complicity, as a man older than she took possession of her daughter . . . a daughter who had already suffered a grotesque violation.

Wait a moment! Did Emma know about the *rape*? It occurs to him that Mei-ling might not have told her . . . that she held back what was too painful to reveal . . . just as she held back from telling him about her surgery because it would cause them both pain. Even when they first met, Mei-ling was reluctant to actually talk about the past . . . though she was able to write about it in class. Selectively. But he is puzzled about Emma. Whether she knew about the rape or not, why didn't she just get another job to support them after they were settled in Hong Kong? Mei-ling, the Mei-ling he knows, couldn't have been in love with a man like Verhoeven. Emma must have known that.

It doesn't cross David's mind that what *he* calls love may have been beside the point, that for a woman who lived in revolutionary China for twenty years, who was in ill health and without resources, who knew no one, just getting another job might not have been a realistic option. As he is about to go on reading, he suddenly thinks: *papers,* they had no valid papers . . . birth certificates, citizenship, nothing . . . illegal aliens . . . stateless . . . subject to deportation or imprisonment. The worst kind of trouble. Mei-ling is right, he decides. How could he, even in his darkest times, understand what it had been like for them?

David returns to the baby book. Past the listing of first steps and first word—he is not surprised that Juliana was precocious—there is a final photograph: a birthday party, Juliana, age one, a cake in front of her, Mei-ling smiling behind her, Emma on one side and a stranger on the other. He doesn't know who she is but tries to guess. It must be the neighbor, he thinks, Berthe—she doesn't look Jewish, but not Dutch either, dark, somehow sad. A good face if not a pretty one. Finally he closes the book. As he puts it on the finished stack, it occurs to him that there was not a single photograph of Juliana's father in it, not even at her birthday party, unless it was he who had taken the picture. Somehow, he doubts that. He cannot imagine himself absent from his daughter's first birthday.

The baby book complete, David takes the next papers in sequence, but he has a hard time deciphering them because everything is written in Dutch. Still, with some difficulty and lapses here and there, and a surprising bit of help from a smattering of German and Yiddish that he didn't know he knew, he deciphers two deeds and leases on property in Amsterdam, the owner being one Mei-ling Wang Verhoeven. He is surprised. Still, he can't blame her for keeping this from him. From the start he had insisted that he wanted none of it, that everything should go to Juliana. Still, he had not expected her to own properties in Amsterdam, accumulating income, a fact that is confirmed on bank stationery clipped to the leases and deeds.

How is it possible to be part of someone, live intimately with them, yet not be privy to another life they lead? It's as if he and Mei-ling are Siamese twins joined at the spine, always vitally connected but looking out at the world in opposite directions. Does she feel as he does, that separation would be a kind of death, that they are destined to be together always?

He sighs, looks at his watch, then takes up the next batch of papers. Death certificates . . . plain enough in any language . . . two of them . . . less than a year apart . . . first him . . . then her . . . as if Emma had held on to stay by Mei-ling's side till Satan had been vanquished. Satan? Wishful thinking. Mei-ling had told him Emma died of liver cancer that spread quickly. And the enigmatic Mr. Verhoeven? Apparently some kind of infection that wouldn't respond to treatment, that left him vulnerable to the pneumonia on the certificate.

David shuffles through the papers, expecting to find a will or a copy of a will along with the death certificates. But there is none. Instead, he sees an official-looking paper, complete with a raised seal and date and several signatures, that he thinks confirms that Dirk Verhoeven died intestate. The legal language eludes him, but there is Mei-ling's name as wife and Juliana's name as daughter, something about their entitlement to inherit, something about taxes and fees due and paid out of the estate. It seems pretty straightforward. David puts it aside.

The next document is puzzling. It seems to be a legal contract selling something—the closest he can come in translation is "Happiness or Pleasure or Joy in Amsterdam"—Mei-ling Wang

Verhoeven, the seller, and a peculiar name that must be Dutch (though possibly German or Scandinavian), the buyer. He'll ask Mei-ling about it when she returns. She wouldn't have included it if she didn't think it mattered.

At last, papers written in English and French. These he can dispense with easily . . . they are straightforward . . . airline tickets on KLM from Amsterdam to Montreal (David wonders why she bothered to save old tickets) . . . entry and immigration documents (Verhoeven must have legalized his wife and daughter in Holland), certification that she brings the minimum assets (the amount is a shock, a high-class bribe for entry?) for an immigrant of her status . . . copies of health histories . . . Juliana's school records.

He is almost finished now . . . only one large reddish envelope tied with a string remains. Inside, he finds a series of folders each with its own label: bank certificates; securities; real estate; jewelry; miscellaneous. David is uncomfortable about looking through all this. Mei-ling says he must know everything about her—faulty memory!—it was *he* who insisted on no secrets between them. She is giving him what he wanted. But, David thinks, financial worth has nothing to do with why he married her. It's not a matter of importance, only bookkeeping. Still, he begins with the first folder.

"Holy shit," he whispers to himself when he is only part of the way through, after the cash and securities but before the real estate and jewelry. He knows, has known from the start, that Mei-ling is well off, but he is not prepared for real wealth, wealth he can scarcely keep track of from item to item, surprising reserves in unexpected places like Switzerland and Hong Kong. Where did it all come from? She and Emma had been penniless when they fled. Was Dirk Verhoeven's estate so large? How the hell did he make his money? And some of the stock purchases are quite recent. Mei-ling seems to buy and sell on a regular basis . . . and make money most of the time. She is good at this!

Mei-ling has always taken care of their finances and taxes, a chore he hates. All he ever had to do was sign his name. Was his ignorance deliberate, a way of not knowing, a way of not having to ask where the money came from? Why does he feel frightened, when any sensible man would be happy? Does she give any of it away . . . as he surely would . . . as he sometimes does . . . the only politics he practices nowadays, an amputee who feels a pain in his missing limb now and then.

He and Mei-ling live quite simply, but well, unusually well by the standards he grew up with. He adds it up in his head: a comfortable home . . . good food and enjoyable wine . . . taxis because neither of them likes to drive in the city, an occasional rental car for weekends . . . nice clothing . . . restaurants, concerts, books, lessons and camp for Juliana . . . weekends in the country . . . expensive bicycles . . . a cleaning woman once a week . . . a self-indulgent but rather ordinary, comfortable life. And for the past three years, ever since they were married, Mei-ling has spent most of her time studying. She pores over her books as if they were the Rosetta Stone and writes papers of lapidary elegance. He has never known a more conscientious student. Yet, when he opens the real estate folder, he sees that she has purchased property . . . a substantial property . . . within the past year. Where did she find the time?

The jewelry folder consists of only two pieces of paper, a listing of items, their approximate value, and where each item is located. There's no total of their worth, but a quick estimate leaves David's jaw hanging loose. She doesn't even wear most of it, he thinks, only the few pieces he remembers with pleasure: thick gold hoop earrings, pearl button earrings, delicate gold chains she wears singly or together, a double strand of pearls that gives her skin the luster of porcelain, a choker of iridescent blue stones (the list says sapphire!) fastened by a diamond clasp, an antique jade pin and earrings that Mei-ling once told him reminded her of her grandmother, the wide gold band he gave her when they were married. The rest of her substantial collection, including diamonds and other precious stones, seems to be sitting in a safe deposit box at the Commonwealth Bank in downtown Montreal, increasing in value from year to year. The jewels alone are a small fortune. Correction! A not-small fortune.

Is this what she wanted him to know? Why? He was never interested in her money. All this cash and property makes him nervous. He is somehow disappointed in Mei-ling's character, embarrassed by the piling up of wealth, as if he had discovered an unexpected flaw in a perfect diamond. What gold mine did Verhoeven stake a claim to if he could leave her so much? And with the husband dead all these years and the money puffing up

like popcorn, how come she doesn't do anything good with it
. . . the child of Communists! She should give some of it away,
let it do something useful . . . help people who need it.

The Chinese, he thinks, have heads for business, like the Jews,
but they aren't as quick to give money away to strangers. Family
maybe, but not strangers. Or perhaps it's Mei-ling . . . still too
frightened to part with any . . . still thinking despite all the evidence to the contrary that the wolf is always at the door. He's
come across people like that. It's something he can understand.

Mei-ling, back for lunch as promised, looks into the office. David's head is on the desk, his arms stretched out in front of him,
sleeping. The documents are piled up on the right side of the
desk instead of the left. He has finished reading them. Mei-ling
breathes in and out, alternating currents of anxiety and relief.
When he wakes up, they will talk. Nothing will be hidden any
longer.

Mei-ling steps quietly to the kitchen and begins to prepare the
lunch she bought. She arranges a plate of Brie and country pâté,
slices the baguette, rinses a cluster of green grapes and puts it
in a glass bowl, and finally sets a small block of halvah near
David's place. He has a special fondness for this odd middle-
eastern candy—sesame seeds ground to a fine paste and sweetened. It is readily available since Arab shops opened in
Montreal. She tried it once; it reminded her of sticky sand.

Mei-ling is pouring iced tea when David appears. He says, "I
didn't hear you come home."

She turns around to face him. "I didn't want to wake you."
She laughs a little. "My life seems to have put you to sleep."

He only half smiles. "Not quite. More like it knocked me
out."

"Why don't you wash up. We can have lunch and talk."

When he comes back, they sit down to eat. Mei-ling's throat
is dry. She drinks some iced tea. David is looking down at his
plate, carefully spreading some Brie on a slice of bread. Neither
of them seems ready to speak, or perhaps neither knows how
to begin. Finally, David says, "I didn't know you were so rich."

"I tried to tell you, but it seemed as if you didn't want to
know. When I used to say anything about money, you said you

weren't interested . . . you had your hands full with teaching and keeping up with the new scholarship. You said you wanted everything to go to Juliana anyway. Remember?"

He remembers. "Yeah, but how could I . . ."

"You said you weren't crazy about the idea of inherited wealth, but that she should get whatever I had, that you had enough income from teaching and we didn't have to worry about health care the way people did in the States. Remember?"

David nods his head, looks at her directly. "Where are we going with this?"

She takes his hand. "I loved you more because you didn't want it. You reminded me of my father. Sometimes I think I fell in love with you because of that." She pauses a moment, drops his hand. "But my father was a naive and impractical man. Because *he* was incorruptible and virtuous, he thought most people were, especially Party people. In his mind, personal wealth was a thing of the past. If he were alive today, he might think Deng was a traitor for encouraging people to go into business and make money. I don't intend to repeat my father's mistakes."

"But why do you need so much," he asks, "and where the devil did it come from to begin with? Your mother had nothing left after you reached Hong Kong. That was pretty clear from her journal." He takes a large bite of bread and cheese, feels it form a lump as he tries to swallow, washes it down with a little tea. "I feel as if I know her now . . . though not as well as I'd like. I used to read about people like her in books."

Mei-ling says, "I should have shown the journal to you sooner."

"Take care of it. You ought to give it to Juliana when she's older. She'll probably think it's a treasure." He pauses. "I think it is." He reaches for a branch of grapes, pops one into his mouth, and feels the sweet juice on his tongue. "Anyway, how the hell did you come into such a bundle?"

"Let me explain something first . . . you know a lot of it already. People like my parents thought money wasn't important . . . they would work for the good of all and the state would provide for them. They were idealists, no doubt noble but sadly mistaken. It was all a lie. The state—or at least the Red Guards and the Cultural Revolution—stripped the family of all we had, including my father. Unless we could accept a life of virtual slavery, there was no choice except to flee. If it hadn't been for my mother's courage and the family jade, we might well have died. So many did.

"Once we were past the worst of it, when we were in Hong Kong with a roof over our heads and food in our bellies, I understood in my bones that having money means having freedom . . . and independence . . . and comfort and beauty . . . as much as anyone can have in this world. Money is useful. It means being able to bribe your way out of a perilous situation. It means being able to pick up and move when you want to or need to. It means being able to begin again. It means being able to enjoy the world."

She feels as if she is giving a speech, stops a moment, peers into David's eyes as if she were trying to see inside him. "I make no apology for wanting money. You of all people should understand this. How many of the Jews who escaped the Nazis were poor?"

He looks puzzled at this new turn. "But the Nazis killed Jews indiscriminately . . . and what does it have to do with us now?"

"Don't you see . . . some escaped before being taken . . . they escaped because they had money for bribes and transportation . . . and to pay people who would give them food and shelter along the way . . . usually at a very high price . . . except for the rare saint. That's how it was for my mother and me. Berthe once told me about a woman she knew whose infant son had been carried through the woods by a Polish peasant for something like ten thousand dollars American . . . and they were glad to pay it. If they didn't have the money, they and their son would have gone up in smoke."

David thinks a moment, sips some tea, says, "Even if you're right, you have enough by now for anything that could happen."

"I don't know what enough means . . . and there is nothing sinful in that. Enough for what?"

"But what do you need it for?"

"How can I know what the future will bring? A painting, perhaps. I have been thinking of buying a painting. But I can't afford what I want. I'm not quite ready yet. Is it bad to want to buy a painting?"

"Of course not. But I always thought that if you have really satisfying work and someone to love, you didn't need much else. Am *I* wrong to feel that way?"

"Not if you live in a place like Canada, where the government

is stable even in the midst of political turmoil . . . and not if you
don't lose your job and can't find another . . . and not if the
earth doesn't open up one fine day . . . or the wind or the tide
sweep everything away. Sometimes I think dying would not be
a terrible thing . . . but then I remember Juliana with her life
ahead of her and how much she still needs me."

"And me? Don't I need you?"

Mei-ling's face turns pink. "I hope so. But we're not children."

Suddenly, tears run down her cheeks, not ordinary sobbing,
more of a gentle stream overrunning its banks after an unexpectedly heavy rain. The tears stop almost as soon as they have
begun. David hands her a tissue. "Tell me what's going on.
There's something else here."

She catches her breath and says, "Life is never easy, David,
. . . and we've been happy for three whole years. I'm sometimes
afraid that's all we'll have. In China, three years of happiness
would be the greatest of gifts. Americans are so innocent and
spoiled . . . even now after the war in Vietnam. In China, what
you did . . . what you did here . . . avoiding the military . . .
might have cost you your life or an exile so terrible, you can't
begin to imagine it. Here you can return to visit your parents.
How can I expect you to understand what it was like for me
and my mother? We were caught in an earthquake. The whole
landscape of life shifts completely in something like that. You
suddenly do things you might never have done." She wrings her
hands as if she were washing them under the tap.

David feels his stomach knot. The halvah on the plate beside
him looks disgusting. "Easy now." David puts his arm around
her, but it's he who is uneasy, aware that she is trying to prepare
him for a blow.

Dry-eyed, forcing her hands to remain still, she goes on. "As
you probably noticed, I have most of my assets here in Canada,
but I also keep some in Amsterdam and Switzerland . . . and I'm
not without some resources in Hong Kong in the event that I
return to the East someday for whatever reason."

He smiles at her a little. "You seem to have covered all the
bases."

She sips her iced tea. The hard part of all this lies ahead of
her. She says, "Why don't we go into the office. You can speak

to me about what you went over this morning. Ask anything you like."

David pulls a chair over to Mei-ling's desk and they sit together side by side. Hoping he will draw the past out of her so that everything seems entirely reasonable, even inevitable, she says, "Now tell me what you want to know." She smiles at him. "Except why money is so important. I think I covered that."

"But you never told me where it came from, did you?"

"No. Actually, it was more than one place. Dirk left us quite a bit, but even before then and later on . . ." She smiles. "I seem to have a knack for business. Most of what you saw this morning comes from my own investments."

"Whew. How did you do it?"

Before she can answer, David pulls the baby book out of the pile. "I loved seeing this," he says. "It made me feel closer than ever to Juliana. I'm sorry I wasn't there to watch her grow up."

"So am I, David." Tears threaten to well up again, but this time she manages to suppress them. Tears should not become currency between them.

"And I liked seeing the picture of your mother wheeling the baby carriage, especially after I read her journal. It was strange not to find a picture of Juliana's father or a family picture of the three of you. Of course, I saw what he looked like . . . at least I assume that was him . . . the one that was taken in the restaurant in Hong Kong."

"Yes. It is the only one I have of Dirk. He didn't like to have his picture taken. He probably drank more than usual that night. I don't know why I save it . . . except that he *was* Juliana's father."

"I'd hate Juliana to see it. You didn't look like yourself . . . tarted up like that."

Mei-ling winces. "I wasn't myself. I was the person he wanted me to be. I can explain that if you want, but as far as Juliana is concerned, you should know that he was her father only in the biological sense. You're more of a father than he ever was. Dirk Verhoeven wanted a son very badly . . . to carry on his name. That was why he married me. You must have noticed that we married only shortly before I delivered. I know it doesn't make sense, but he was absolutely certain the baby would be a boy. When Juliana was born, he was so disappointed, he paid scarcely any attention to her. If he were a Chinese peasant, he might have drowned her. And he died when she was still young, only six."

"And left you the money."

"He didn't leave it to anyone. We were the legal heirs."

"How did he make his money?"

"He was a businessman."

"What kind of business?"

"At first, in Indonesia—I told you he spent most of his life in Indonesia—before he came to Hong Kong. Didn't I?"

"You mentioned it."

"He was a trader, a kind of middleman, all sorts of products, I never knew exactly what. I wasn't terribly interested and he was a great one for keeping secrets. Dirk told me he knew Sukarno and had an inside track on some lucrative deals. He made a lot of money and managed to take enough of it with him when Sukarno was forced out. In Hong Kong he dealt in jewelry and other things. He had very good connections in the Chinese community. That's how we met him. My mother's lover, old Dr. Kung"—David blanches when she says this, as if the spoken word casts a different light on the romance, carnalizing it—"he told Mother his nephew would help us in Hong Kong. Actually, the nephew was nothing like the old doctor. He tried to cheat us. But Dirk happened to be there that day and intervened. He seemed to be helping us out. We were desperately hungry. I still remember the lunch he bought us . . . dumplings and crab and prawns . . . the best food in the world. It always is when you're starving. Dirk hired my mother to work in his business and gave us a place to stay. We were very grateful."

"Of course." David is beginning to see how it must have been for them . . . alone and friendless as they were. But he is sweaty with apprehension. He says, "How long did you know him before . . ." David's voice trails off. He's not sure of how to say what he wants to say. He looks at Mei-ling sitting beside him, lovely as when he first met her, lovelier by far than in the picture with Verhoeven, when she was still so young, a different woman.

"We became intimate when I was eighteen. He had given us food and shelter and nice clothing and was paying for my education. To Dirk Verhoeven, everything was a matter of business. He expected to be paid back. I was too young to understand much about the world . . . except how terrible it could be . . . I didn't care . . . I was no longer innocent. He was much nicer than the men on the train. He didn't force me."

"But what about your mother?"

"She had great courage . . . it took tremendous courage for her to escape with me in tow . . . it was very dangerous . . . I was in a strange state when she found me . . . numb and silent as a corpse . . . she was unwell . . . still in pain. My mother was innocent in the ways of the world outside China. Mr. Verhoeven—that's how I always spoke of him then—offered her a job. It seemed an incredible stroke of good fortune. We would be safe and have a roof over our heads. She wanted me to have a chance at an education. He made it easy for her to avert her eyes. I think it took a long time till she understood—or was able to admit to herself what she should have known and perhaps could have prevented. By then it was too late to do anything. Besides, where would we have gone without money and passports? When the time came for us to leave for Amsterdam, Dirk arranged everything for us. He was a very resourceful man, not altogether a demon."

"Did you care for him?"

"Try to understand. I didn't mind him. He was not brutal, and he was good to us in his way. It wasn't a very nice way. We had a comfortable life." She averts her eyes from David, who is looking at her in a kind of grim fascination. "But I didn't feel anything, David. Sex had nothing to do with love; sex was what a man wanted. I didn't know what real love was and I never expected to find it. It was all just words till I met you."

He grasps for her hand, then lets it go. "I suppose that should make me feel better, but I don't know what I feel. You've dropped some of this here and there, you didn't exactly keep me in the dark, but it all seems more mysterious than it did before, as if there's something underneath you expect me to figure out and I can't manage it. Exactly why *did* the three of you wind up in Amsterdam after living in the Far East all those years? Was there a reason you had to leave?"

"Dirk wanted his son to be born in his own country. I don't know what gave him the idea. He had always claimed he couldn't wait to leave Holland because the climate was so terrible, but there may also have been business reasons—a big crackdown on corruption in Hong Kong a few months before we left." She smiles wanly. "Dirk wasn't the sort of man who would welcome that." She hesitates. "I suppose it also had something to do with his growing older. He was less interested in sex by that time . . . that I can tell you . . . though he always had many women. I was never the only one. Being his wife didn't change things. I didn't expect it to and didn't much care. I don't think he believed in abstractions like love and faithfulness that many people here think are so important. With Dirk everything was a matter of business. Women were creatures who would cost him something for the satisfaction and pleasure they provided. Don't many men think that? I didn't mind so long as we had a roof over our heads and Juliana had a secure home."

David blanches. He is hard pressed to imagine such a marriage, though he knows in some distant way that it is common. He runs his fingers over his scalp and scratches it. Mei-ling's casual complaisance coupled with Dirk Verhoeven's random amorality stabs him . . . as if he has suddenly pierced the truth of the doctrine of original sin after having believed all his life in human perfectibility. He asks, "Were you sad when he died?"

"We were never in love. He wanted me and helped me survive. There was a price to pay. He was hardly a father to Juliana. I felt very little when he died." She pauses. "Except one thing. I knew I was free to lead my life as I chose. I knew I was not poor, because I had put aside money and jewelry of my own. I knew that even after taxes on the estate, Juliana and I would probably inherit quite a bit of money and that Verhoeven's business and other assets could be sold."

"You never told me exactly what his business in Amsterdam was." When she hesitates slightly, he says, "It wouldn't shock me if you said he was on the wrong side of the law . . . or something equally rotten. I'm prepared for anything."

Mei-ling doubts that, chooses her words carefully. "Dirk's business was perfectly legal if not always what some people would consider respectable. He owned a service that provided attractive young women who would serve as hostesses to reputable business and professional men who were visiting Amsterdam and wanted to enjoy female company."

Mei-ling hears the intake and exhalation of David's breath . . . sees the color rise in his face . . . watches a few beads of sweat pop out on his upper lip . . . the innocence drop from his eyes. She continues: "The clients were from the highest class of people: wealthy businessmen, diplomats, dignitaries of all kinds." A distant echo of Verhoeven's description of his business seems to be prompting her. "They wanted to spend long hours with attractive women in both public and private. The women expected to be paid well and be treated well . . . and they were. Most of them liked their work because the men were often interesting and generous. They ate in the finest restaurants and stayed at the best hotels. The men were usually pleased and recommended their friends. It was a successful business that made quite a lot of money."

When she finishes, there is a long silence. Finally, David says, "Just one big party. Everybody wins."

Mei-ling watches as his eyes close and he rests his head in the cup of his open palms. She says, "David, try to understand. The Dutch are tolerant of these things. They prefer everything out in the open." She pauses for the effect. "Like you. It's what you wanted."

David hears Mei-ling's words but absorbs them slowly . . . a blind man beginning to learn braille. He opens his eyes. He says, "No, not like me at all. I am in deep water here . . . way, way over my head. You seem to know a great deal about this business. Were you part of it?"

She continues to look at him. It is too late to go back. "Yes."

"How big a part?"

"Toward the end . . . when Dirk was quite ill . . . I helped manage things, but . . ."

Before she can continue, he breaks in. "And in the beginning?"

"I was Dirk's hostess at parties. Sometimes, when there was a demand, I was a hostess for one or another of the clients. The clients were always well-to-do and presentable and came through recommendation. If they weren't, we'd have nothing to do with them."

David sags. He leans forward as if he might fall, but catches himself and starts to drum rhythmically on the desk with his hands. She puts her arm on his shoulder. He flicks it off.

Mei-ling says, "It was nothing but business . . . ever. David, sex is different things to different men. For many, it's nothing more than a commodity that satisfies their desires. In my mind, my heart, the business had nothing to do with me as a person. Besides, as soon as Dirk died, I washed my hands of it."

In a terrible hoarse voice, David says, "Let me get this straight. Are you telling me I married a prostitute or a pimp? both? either/or as business demanded?"

She grimaces. "It's not as simple as you think."

"Yes or no? That's pretty simple."

"If you're asking me if I slept with men for money when I needed to survive, the answer is yes . . . and I wasn't very different from millions of other women who did and do the same thing under far worse conditions. I was biding my time."

David stands up and grabs her shoulders, shakes her hard. "Seems to me survival stretched out over a mighty long period of years, my dear wife."

His fingers are digging into her arms. Mei-ling shouts, "Stop this. You are hurting me."

"Not as much as you're hurting me." David drops his arms, then flings them aside. The majolica flowerpot standing in the way crashes to the floor. Broken branches and damp soil litter the polished oak. Potsherds scatter like matchsticks. They both ignore the mess as if they agreed they were not to be distracted.

"I suppose this explains why you had to be certain you couldn't become pregnant." David rustles through the papers on the desk, picks one out and hands it to Mei-ling. "Is this what I think it is? It was hard for me to understand the first time around."

She looks at the contract for the sale of Pleasure in Amsterdam. She says, "I wanted you to see it. I expected you to ask me about it. I wanted you to know everything, including that it was sold soon after Dirk's death, as soon as it was mine to sell. One of the clients bought it. He was a Swedish official of some sort. He fell in love with a French girl who worked for Dirk. They were going to run the business together and were willing to pay a good enough price. I wanted to be rid of the old life as soon as I could." She stops speaking and there is silence in the room.

David has his eyes open now, is trying to take in everything she is saying, but makes no attempt to speak.

"Juliana was getting older. My mother was showing the first signs of her illness. She used to speak of Canada from time to time, that it might be a nice place to live. When she died, it seemed the right place for Juliana and me to begin again. They welcomed immigrants with means. I wanted nothing more than to get away from the old life." She puts her hands on his shoulders, forces him to look at her. "I don't believe in miracles, David, but finding you was a miracle I never imagined."

David hears the plea in her words, wishes he could make things right for them, but he is disconcerted by static buzzing inside his head. He gropes for logic, for a way to cope. He says, "You know Valerie would have no trouble understanding any of this. She thought women who were paid for sex were workers like any other kind, exploited by men and not all that different from the average housewife, just better paid. I'd like to convince myself of that."

"What Valerie thinks isn't important. What do you think? Now that you know everything, you have to decide if you can put it behind you. I can't spend the rest of my life apologizing or thinking of myself as a kind of fallen woman. The only thing I'm guilty of is surviving and learning how the world works at an age when luckier people had the luxury of being virtuous."

David is silent, but he looks at her with an expression as vulnerable as an abandoned child. He wonders how she can remain so self-possessed through all this while he would like nothing better than to drop suddenly into a dreamless sleep that would last a year. His head refuses to stay up straight. "Look," he says, "I'm so exhausted from this stuff, I can't even think straight, let alone talk straight." He points to the papers on the desk. "Why don't you put this stuff away. I've seen it all. We can decide whatever we decide later. Right now I need sleep. Okay?"

"Okay."

Upstairs in the bedroom, David looks at the queen-sized four-poster that he and Mei-ling share every night. It seems the only real object in the room—white summer linens, four soft, downy pillows with scalloped edges, crisp dust ruffle, thin patchwork quilt covered with blue and yellow and orange butterflies—everything else in shadow. Usually so inviting, the bed is reproachful in its prettiness and perfection, dangerous, as if it might smother him were he to sink into its softness. There will be no sleeping here.

Instead, David drags his leaden legs to the small guest room in the back, the place his parents stay when they visit, or, rarely, the occasional passer-through, a vacationing cousin or a child-hood pal from the States who needs a place to crash in Mon-treal. The room's bland beige-and-brown geometry, solids, stripes, and checks, are a comfort, neutral territory, a place to rest. It crosses David's mind that their few guests belong only to him. Mei-ling has nobody outside the family, only casual friends she sees at school. Except for Juliana and himself, she is quite alone in the world. Even if he wanted to, which he doesn't, how could he leave her? It would be heartless. But how can he stay? He sucks on the heavy air. She sold herself. There's no way around it.

David sits on one of the twin beds and leans over to take his sneakers and socks off. His fingers move in slow motion, like caterpillars, but they achieve the desired result; his sweaty feet are free and cool. He stretches out on the checkered bedspread, closes his eyes, and prepares to sink into sleep. But sleep is an elusive thing . . . like truth.

His thoughts twist and turn, tumbleweeds caught up in a strong wind. Looked at one way, Mei-ling kept her secrets bur-ied inside herself . . . but did she actually lie to him? No. In the same situation, might not anyone, even he if he were a woman, have done the same? She was, after all, the *victim* in all this, on the run, illegal, hanging on by her fingernails from minute to minute till she was safe . . . as safe as anyone could be after be-ing raped and God knows what else. He decides that he, David Levy, onetime admirer of Mao, is in no position to blame the victim. From the start she was more sinned against than sinning . . . a miracle she and her mother survived at all. But did she have to stay with that bastard husband? live the life she lived? It had to have gone on for years.

Though he is stretched out on the bed, every bone and muscle in David's body seems to be standing at attention. He can't fall off to sleep. This is not the truth he wanted . . . better never to have known . . . better to have been sentenced to hard labor hammering rocks. He'd be able to sleep and forget what he knows.

How not to judge her harshly? Mei-ling isn't the first or the last beautiful woman who wound up in a tight spot and found that particular way out. If he were reading Mei-ling's story in a book . . . or watching it in a movie . . . the suffering, the fear . . .

he'd be rooting for her . . . not moralizing. He'd be on her side completely, think any man who didn't stick by her after all she'd been through was a fool, worse, a betrayer . . . a deserter.

Besides, he thinks, everybody knows (he's not exactly sure who everybody is) that half the movie stars in Hollywood were call girls (his stomach turns over as his mind forms the words) or involved in some other reward for sex when they were on their way up (all the gossip about Joan Crawford and Marilyn Monroe, a legion of others whose names he can't remember, the wives of prominent businessmen and politicians whose money spreads a neat veil over the past). If he can't get past this, what kind of man is he? No man at all, just your basic tight-ass Jewish boy . . . a virgin (he reminds himself) till Valerie came along and did it for him. Where was the virtue in that? Isn't it time for him to grow up? see the world as it is? the way it was for Mei-ling?

David sighs aloud. The devil whispers in his ear. Nobody *has* to be a call girl . . . they're not chained to the bed . . . they're chained to the money . . . some of them maybe to the kicks. Not Mei-ling! He knows her too well that way, or hopes he does. How can he be sure? Can't.

In a haze of exhaustion David pulls himself into the fetal position and finally drifts off to sleep. A trickle of spit runs from the corner of his mouth down the lower part of his cheek and drips onto the beige bedspread, where it leaves a small wet stain.

David is wearing his navy blue bar-mitzvah suit, but it pinches his waist and is too short at the ankles. He is sweating. Bottles of wine and whiskey, platters of meat, bunches of red and green and purple grapes, and silver trays of chocolate truffles are piled high on a table in the center of the room. A single spoonful of food or drink is certain to make him vomit. He can feel the heave forming in his throat. What is this place? He looks around for someone or something familiar that will tell him where he is. Everyone is ignoring him as if he were invisible. He wants to run away but he is dizzy. The noise is so loud now that his eardrums are pounding like cannons. Boom, boom, boom. He wakes with a jolt. He is sweating and miserable. He has a pounding headache.

It's all so sordid, David thinks. If he leaves now, he can begin again. He's not too old to meet someone else, have children, maybe move back to the States, even Florida, make his parents happy in their old age. But what does he want? David sighs. He wants Mei-ling. He wants Juliana. They're his life.

⌒

Mei-ling thinks it must be a miracle. David *does* climb into bed beside her that night. Habit or desire? She's not sure, but when he reaches for her, the simple gesture of his arm transforms her. Her breasts swell and a quick hot dampness forms between her legs. A shudder of delight moves her. If it could speak, it would say: *You love me still. I will make you very happy.* Mei-ling feathers his shoulder and arm with kisses, waits for him to stiffen and press into her quickly, seal their union . . . their reunion. When nothing happens, she slides her hand down and touches the alarmingly flaccid flesh that seems to shrivel where it should swell. She draws her hand away.

"I don't know what's wrong," he says. "I guess I'm totally knocked out from all this."

She pats his shoulder. "Don't worry about it," she says as she once did with befuddled clients. "Next time."

Soon David is breathing beside her, his arm flailing occasionally, his body twisting, lost in dreams. But Mei-ling is awake . . . aware . . . preparing herself. His body, she thinks, has spoken for him. The hollow of loss encloses her. The feeling is familiar, oddly comfortable, like meeting a childhood friend in a strange city. You still know each other well, have much to tell each other. She is oddly calm, determined to look beyond this moment, console herself, decide what she must do. She takes stock. She is educated, wealthy, and has Juliana. Life is not over. Her eyes sting. It will be hard to lose David.

⌒

Juliana sits at her desk, dry-eyed and solemn, concentrating. The beautiful blank book David gave her—was it only a few days ago?—is open. She holds a pen in her hand but she does not write. She pokes the pen into her cheek hard, as if she were intent on giving herself a dimple. When she removes it, a red mark remains in its place. She puts the pen down, scratches her head, puffs up her cheeks, exhales, then takes up the pen again. This time she writes: *I have no luck when it comes to fathers.*

That is the absolute truth. David left the house today and took a lot of his stuff with him, boxes and boxes that he piled in a taxi. I don't know if they're getting a divorce. My mother says not now anyway. David says I'm still his daughter and nothing will ever change that. He says that we can see each other a lot and he gave me his new address and telephone number (temporary) in case I need him. He says that he loves me and he loves my mother and that nothing will change that either. His eyes were red when he said it, so I guess it's true. I never saw a man cry before. He kept blowing his nose as if he had a bad cold. He looked awful with his nose swollen like he had been in a fight. My mother looks better but she can hardly talk. Her voice is so quiet, I have to strain to hear what she says—which isn't much. I hate this whole thing. My life is cracking up and I haven't even done anything wrong. I don't think I have.

Dense white clouds scud through the chill October sky like migrating birds. Jack, who never wears a hat if he can help it, runs his hand over the bald center of his head, which is a little red from the morning cold. He wraps his gray cashmere scarf around his neck, tucks it into his brown corduroy jacket, rubs his hands together, and sticks them into his jacket pockets, where he finds a convenient pair of gloves. Probably been there since last winter, he thinks, pulling them on, not like Grace to overlook them. At times, she is still quite alive to him, off on an errand from which she will soon return. He shakes his head, and the moment passes.

The Botanical Garden is almost empty at this late-morning hour in midweek. Children are at school, grown-ups are working, tourists have taken their leave of the city. Only Jack Ramsden and a couple of young women with sketch pads in their hands are walking the paths between the flowers. The combined labors of gardeners and weather gods have yielded splendor: broad beds of chrysanthemums are blooming long and late. With every break in the clouds, brilliant waves of glowing autumnal color—yellow, gold, copper, burnt orange, dusty red, deep maroon, warm brown—ripple through the grounds like a flower-decked flotilla. He comes here fairly often, almost once a week, a sad errand, but close to Grace.

"The chrysanthemums are in their glory."

Her voice is familiar . . . only the barest hint of an accent. Surprised, not astonished, he turns to the pretty little woman standing nearby and raises his arm toward her as if he were tipping an imaginary hat. "Indeed they are . . . glorious."

"We seem destined to meet in this spot, Mr. Ramsden."

"What better place for flower lovers?"

Glints of sun dance on the blossoms like fireflies. Mei-ling kneels down a moment to look closely at a tufted specimen. She says, "Chrysanthemums have been cultivated in Asia for over two thousand years. They're highly prized . . . especially in Japan . . . the symbol of the emperor."

"My dear girl, is there much you don't know?"

"Books full, I'm afraid." She looks up, directly into his face. "I was very sorry to read about your wife's death. It was terrible. I thought of writing to you, but it was so awkward. It seemed best not to."

"You're very kind to have thought to write at all."

They are comfortable opposite each other over their steaming bowls of crusty onion soup, well-worn friends though they're scarcely acquainted. Jack says, "If nothing else, the French know how to cook."

"Better than the English but not as good as the Chinese."

He smiles. "I yield to your superior culinary knowledge, but you must admit the soup is delicious."

She takes a steaming spoonful, blows on it, tastes it. "Delicious."

He nods. "Now you must tell me about yourself. If I recall correctly, you are attending the university."

"Not any longer. I graduated this past June. Art history."

"My congratulations! A perfect choice, as I remember. But how is that possible? It seems like only yesterday you began."

"Three years ago. I studied summers. My husband helped with Juliana."

He had seen at once, as soon as she drew her gloves off, that she wore a wedding band. "Is your husband Canadian?"

"Yes and no. He was my professor at the university." She

smiles wanly. "He came here from the United States during the war in Vietnam and decided to stay."

"Many did, and quite a number wound up teaching. Some Canadians say too many." He takes her hand for only a moment. "I'm happy for you."

She shifts her eyes away. "I'm afraid we're separated now."

Ramsden puts his spoon down. "Oh, dear. I'm so sorry."

"It's quite strange meeting you today, Mr. Ramsden . . . as if fate somehow had a hand in the matter. Do you believe fate brings people together for a purpose?"

His lips tighten a little. He says, "I try not to think very much about fate at all."

"Nor do I as a rule, but let's pretend that we do, that we were meant to meet at the garden as friends."

He laughs. "I'm not sure I follow what you're getting at, but we can if you like. Friends." Not how he would describe them . . . yet there's some truth in it . . . how well they got along in Amsterdam when they met . . . all so strange. She is, he thinks, still very lovely, hardly changed at all, if anything, for the better. And so bright, good company in more ways than are obvious.

"I bank at Commonwealth and get their newsletter each month with my statement."

Ramsden wriggles in his seat a little, suddenly wary of his privacy. "Really?"

"I read that you had retired."

"Yes. It was time. Grace and I intended to travel. But now . . ." His voice trails off.

"Have you made any other plans?"

Why is she asking about *his* plans? He's old . . . retired . . . twice a widower. What interest can she possibly have in him . . . unless she wants something . . . unless she's financially strapped. "Actually, it's too soon to have made plans. I'll have to find something to take up the time though . . . can't spend my days wandering the Botanical Garden."

"I hope I'm not being presumptuous, Mr. Ramsden, but with your years of experience, have you considered business and financial consulting?"

Has this young woman been reading his mind? "Only in the vaguest way. A few special clients perhaps. Why do you ask?"

She hunches over the table, serious, focused, her hands

stretched out on the table in front of her, the remaining soup in her bowl growing cold. "I've decided to concentrate on managing my money. I've ventured into real estate. I already own some property in Montreal." She pauses. "And I have some property in Amsterdam as well. Perhaps you're in a position to advise me about the Canadian tax structure and investment opportunities . . . more than real estate. Surely you know all about these things . . . and I feel as if I can trust you. Fate, instinct, call it what you want." Her face reddens. "For a fee, of course. Purely a business arrangement."

What an interesting notion . . . advising this delightful young woman . . . work along lines he'd been thinking of himself. It would be a business arrangement. Nothing more. She's made that clear. Without waiting to think, he says, "Of course, if I can be of help."

Part Six

1990

Montreal

AUGUST 28. DEPARTURE day. Juliana stands with her hands on her hips, surveying the dust balls gathered in the corners of her closet, the scattered bits of paper and plastic dotting the dark oak floor of her room, the brown paper bags filled with outgrown and discarded clothing leaning against the wall next to her bureau. Waiting side by side at the doorway, her old black camp trunk and navy blue duffel are packed, labeled, and ready to go. The Apple computer David gave her for graduation is on top of the trunk. Simon will be coming soon to help her carry everything downstairs to the Chrysler minivan they are taking to Boston, a graduation gift from his parents. He's told her that they own Chrysler stock and think of such things, that their minds are too much on the dollar. She is glad Simon feels that way, that he has ideals. What's the use of being alive if you don't want to do something really important with your life, make the world a better place? Still, Juliana thinks, it is nice to have the van for the trip . . . so comfortable . . . roomy enough for all their things.

The room is stuffy, but Juliana doesn't want to turn on the air conditioner. She lifts the window as far as it will go. The dog-day heat of August has broken and a light northern breeze blows through. With a dustpan and brush she gathers the mess on the floor and mashes it into the overflowing wastebasket. The housekeeper will take care of the rest when she comes on Monday. Juliana's hands are shaking slightly. Why is she so jittery, vibrating like a violin string? She's been looking forward to this day for months.

Juliana stands on her toes and stretches her arms toward the ceiling, then wide and back to relieve the strain on her shoulders. Slim and sturdy in jeans and blue chambray shirt, taller than her mother by a full five inches, dark hair pulled back and caught in a thick braid down her back, high-cheeked and faintly almond-eyed, she could grace the cover of an outdoor magazine. Barefoot, she arranges herself lotus-style on her bed and begins stuffing the last of the belongings she is taking with her into a red canvas knapsack. A gift from her mother, one of several. When she'd taken it out of the box and started poking in all the compartments, she'd found a check for a thousand dollars clipped to a note that said, "Good fortune on your journey, dearest daughter." It had been tucked into one of the zipper pockets. The amount had been overwhelming, unfair, she thought, when so many people all over the world were poor and didn't have enough to eat. But she'd been afraid of hurting her mother's feelings if she seemed anything but grateful. It crosses her mind that she might give some to a worthy cause. Later. When she's settled.

Juliana tosses in a plastic case of toilet articles, extra glasses and lenses, hairbrush, birth control pills, camera and film, a Tony Hillerman mystery that Rachel gave her at their farewell lunch with Blair, pen and paper, pocket Kleenex, small flashlight, and personal documents and instructions from Harvard that she places in a separate pocket with money and credit cards.

Juliana picks up the paisley writing book from her bed and holds it in her hand. Cardboard corners peek through the worn fabric. Foolish to take it, she thinks, only a few pages left . . . be too busy studying anyway . . . might get lost. She runs her hand through the pages, pauses here and there, stretches her legs out, and leans back on her pillows, begins at the beginning.

"I have no luck when it comes to fathers." Not true, she thinks! How could she have said such a thing? David loves her . . . sticks like glue. That's the trouble. If only he weren't always

after her to see more of him, always inviting her places. It was so complicated, having to make room for him when she'd rather be with Simon or one of her friends or practicing her flute or dancing. And when was she supposed to study? There are never enough hours in the day. He said he understood, knew what it was like. But he was always a little sad . . . even his jokes.

More pages. Schoolgirl stuff from freshman year that seems trivial now: impressions of teachers . . . a sudden passion for a brainy boy named Ronald who had red hair and was good at biology . . . disillusionment a few weeks later when he said he was going to be a surgeon and move to California, where surgeons made lots of money and could play golf all year. Golf!

"Charles Dickens is the world's best writer." A Tale of Two Cities read straight through because she couldn't stop . . . the best and worst of times . . . love and pity and cruelty . . . important to be able to sacrifice yourself for someone you love or something you believe in . . . like the students at Tiananmen Square, she thinks. She had seen the old movie version with Ronald Colman on TV but it wasn't as good as the book.

"We're like three musketeers." Rachel and Blair . . . such different families . . . Rachel's mother friendly and inquisitive, always offering to feed them something, her brothers, the fat one always listening to opera even when he studied, the tall, thin one always on his way out to "shoot a few baskets," the father, a specter always "working at the store" . . . Blair, an only child like her, mother divorced, a sportswear buyer at Eaton's, reserved and quiet, no father . . . made her feel grateful for David even if he and her mother were apart. He *is* her father. Too much sometimes. She smiles and sighs simultaneously. Nothing's perfect.

"New York is the greatest city in the world. FANTASTIC!" . . . a trip with David to see Gram and Grampa, who lived in a small apartment in a tall building next door to a lot of black people . . . "more every month" Grampa said . . . shows and museums . . . *"The Museum of Natural History is amazing and not only dinosaur bones. It's like a Greek temple for a start."* Carnegie Hall to hear Itzhak Perlman play his magic violin sitting down because he was paralyzed . . . Little Italy, where they walked downstairs to eat spedini and veal and a cheesecake that tasted like rum at a restaurant called the Grotta Azura . . . Chi-

natown, where they walked upstairs to a huge room with big
windows looking out on the milling crowds in the street—*"I felt
as if we were in China"*—where they ordered fish fried in bean-
cake skin that was *"the best thing I ever ate."* Remembering,
the words smile at her from the page.

At a few entries Juliana stops skimming, lingers a while, and
reads carefully.

> October 1987. My mother has been raving about the stock
> market as if we were going to starve. I don't know why
> she's so hysterical. She keeps saying she should have sold
> everything when her financial adviser told her the stock
> market was overpriced—too hot. He's her old friend Mr.
> Ramsden, who says he met me once when I was little—
> may be true—I think I remember being in a beautiful gar-
> den in Amsterdam with Mother and a man who was nice.
> Well, she didn't sell everything. She was carrying on some-
> thing awful about being a foolish Chinese gambler. She held
> on to more than half and now she says it's not worth selling
> so she might just as well hold on. She was moaning that
> the Communists may have been right after all, that the mar-
> kets were failing all over. The stock exchange in Hong
> Kong closed down and might never open up. Mother is
> usually so calm and sure of herself. It's scary to see her like
> this. I keep telling her it's all going to be okay, but she says
> I'm too young to understand. That's also her major com-
> ment when I ask her about David. Maybe I am too young.
> At least they haven't gotten a divorce yet.

Still haven't, she thinks, and he's been gone from the house if
not their lives for almost four years. Juliana scratches her ear,
looks up at the ceiling as if seeking wisdom there. Too much
for her to figure out.

What a difference a few years makes. Her mother, who
thought she knew so much about investing, was wrong to panic,
and she, who wasn't supposed to know anything, was right. She
smiles to herself. Ignorant but right. Even Deng is pushing cap-
italist-type reforms in China. Her mother's stocks are doing just
fine. Too fine. It borders on the disgusting for them to be rich
when there are people who have nothing, but making money
seems to be in her mother's blood. How unlike they are, Juliana

thinks. Money means so little to her . . . basically unimportant so long as you have enough to eat and a roof over your head.

A fleeting thought creases her brow. She will not have to take out loans to get through Harvard. Neither will Simon. His father is wealthy. She thinks her mother has more money than she lets on. There should be a way to even things out—nobody super rich, nobody dirt poor. She wrinkles her nose and frowns, hears her mother's voice whenever she says anything political: "I know you intend well, but you're being naive." A variation on "too young to understand." But, Juliana thinks, she does understand. Her mother thinks she doesn't only because of what she went through in China . . . with her grandparents. Juliana can still conjure up a picture of Emma when she tries hard. It was an incredible shock to read her grandmother's journal. Her mother never talked about any of it until a few weeks ago . . . as if she had been saving it all up till they were going to separate . . . till she wouldn't have to answer too many questions. She hates to talk about the past. The journal was like a novel about her own family, about the terrible things that happened to them. Still, Juliana thinks, despite the terrible things that happened, the Communists had to have been on to something. In the beginning, after they first took over, millions of people supported them and they did many good things. Too bad they couldn't make their system work right . . . and so cruel to their own people . . . the students at Tiananmen Square . . . really boils the blood to think about it.

She flips through what now seems silly stuff . . . puerile maunderings . . . pauses . . . stops to read.

January 1988. The second new student in my class this month is named Simon Lee. He's straight off the boat from Hong Kong and speaks the smoothest English you ever heard, with an accent that sounds as if he is an actor playing English royalty. He seems a little shy but he is good-looking in a Chinese way and *very* intelligent. Some girls don't care about brains, but I can't work up an interest in a boy who doesn't have a damn good one. There will be more to come about this if he pays any attention to me.

Juliana smiles. More to come. How true. She turns a few of the pages and reads.

End of January. Simon can't believe I'm part Chinese. He got really excited when I mentioned it, as if it were the most important thing in the world. He said that it was natural to think anyone named Julie (no sense fighting it, everyone shortens the name without asking) Levy was Jewish and that he wasn't prejudiced against Jews. His father says they're good at business, almost as good as the Chinese. If he says that, he doesn't know David and Gram and Grampa. Simon thinks some Jewish people have Oriental eyes because their ancestors came from the eastern part of Russia and there was mixing. That's what he thought about me. How does he know so many things? He's like my mother, reading all the time. They must have good schools in Hong Kong.

Anyway, I told Simon my full legal name was Juliana (after the Dutch queen, which I don't tell many people) Wang Verhoeven Levy and that I was adopted by David after he married my mother when I was ten. Talk about eyes. You should have seen his open up when I told him that my mother was born in China and escaped to Hong Kong during the Cultural Revolution and went to school there. He was dying to know the name, so I asked her, but he said he never heard of Miss Richardson's. It was embarrassing when he asked about my father. I didn't know what to say except that he was Dutch and was a business-man. I don't know anything else and I don't want to ask my mother. I did when I was younger and she looked as if I had stabbed her. That's when she said he was in business and they met in Hong Kong before coming to Amsterdam, where I was born. That's it, except she said he was tall and had fair hair and beautiful, even teeth, like mine. I asked her if she had a picture of him, but she said no. How is that possible if you married someone? Not even a wedding picture?

Juliana closes her eyes. She feels a little sick, as if she's gorged herself on too much greasy food. It's a strange family she has, no aunts or uncles or cousins her own age, a lonely family, only her mother and David, who doesn't live with them, and his parents, her grandparents, blood or no blood, who are getting old. What if her mother never left China and lived through the Cultural Revolution okay till Deng came to power? Juliana thinks that she would like to visit someday. From what she sees on television, they really are leaping forward now. Maybe she and her mother and David can visit China together . . . the three of them . . . the way it used to be. Sighing, she flips through a few pages.

Simon likes to talk about politics. He says the Communists are going to take over Hong Kong and that they won't keep their promises. That's why his father moved the family to Canada even though they were very rich in Hong Kong. Simon says his father is angry because the British government won't let the Hong Kong Chinese who want to be British citizens move to England. He says they're racist hypocrites who don't keep their promises either. Anyway, even though his father travels back and forth on business, the family is here to stay. Lucky me! Simon's talk is a lot more interesting than all the blather about sports and clothes that goes on in school. Makes me glad I'm Chinese even if it's only a quarter. I wonder when he's going to get up nerve to really kiss me. He's backward in that department, as if he's scared of letting go of his feelings. Marty Mackler did the first time we went to the movies together, but I don't like him as much as I like Simon.

Flute recital, dance classes. Skip, skip, skip. Rachel jealous because Juliana and Blair have "steady" boyfriends. Skip, skip, skip. Gram knocked to the ground, her pocketbook stolen. Pause. She and Grampa moving to Florida. Sigh. Her fingers turn a few more pages.

I was walking with Rachel on St. Catherine Street. We were looking at the Christmas windows, and when I glanced away for a minute I saw David. He was holding a woman by the arm. She was wearing a red wool hat and Stuart plaid scarf and black boots with white fleece tops. I watched them cross over and walk into a store. He didn't see me. I felt nauseous afterward.

Couldn't have been too serious, Juliana thinks. He never says anything when she sees him, only talks about his students and movies and stuff, asks how my mother is in a polite way . . . they're still married . . . could go on like this forever . . . married but not married but not divorced.

January 1, 1989. Happy New Year, more or less. I'm glad the parties and craziness are over. Mother says that girls my age in China don't have enough fun and we have too much. She may be right. I need a rest and I am buried in work. I have my period and the usual cramps to go with it. As if that isn't bad enough, Simon says he has to study all weekend if he wants to make out well on finals. Sometimes he is a bit much. Does he really need to cram all the time? He's always at the top in most subjects. *Like me!* Since nobody but I will see this, I feel free to say we are probably the two biggest brains at our level—if grades mean anything at all. But he is fanatical about them. I wish grades didn't count, but if we have to have them, it's nice to be on top. David says that maybe Gram is right and that I should be a lawyer. He also expects me to be a poet. And Mother wants me to study art. Maybe I should learn to paint with a brush between my teeth while I write poems with my hands and study law with my eyes and what's left of my brain. I can exercise my toes while I'm about it.

Simon thinks we should go to college together. We were talking about trying for Harvard because they have good programs for both of us. He was impressed when I told him David was a Harvard graduate. He says that being his daughter will help me get in. Simon is thinking of combining economics and Chinese studies. I'm not sure yet because everything appeals to me. It's hard to decide what to do with my life. I just know I want to do something that counts. Mother wants me to stay in Canada and go to McGill. She says she'll miss me if I am too far away. One more thing. Simon has learned a lot about how to kiss and a few other things, but we're careful not to do anything dangerous. He has lost all his shyness.

The telephone rings. Juliana reaches for it, but her mother has already picked it up downstairs. In a moment, Mei-ling calls up to her. "That was Simon. He said he will be a little late."

She shouts down. "That's okay."

"Do you need my help?"

"No. I'm ready. I'm just resting a few minutes." Juliana sits up at the edge of her bed with her feet on the Oriental scatter rug, skips a few pages.

Sometimes I wonder if I really know my mother at all. She is full of secrets. Without saying a word in advance, she bought the most amazing painting and had it hung to-day while I was still in school. She said she wanted to sur-prise me, but I think she just won't talk about things in case they don't come true. She is always afraid bad things will happen. I wish she could relax. The whole huge canvas was mounted by the time I got home and takes up half the long wall in the living room. Down came a bunch of prints and up went Shi Hu, who is Chinese, but you can't quite tell from the painting. It is not exactly abstract, but not realistic either. You can recognize people and objects, but they're all folded into each other like people in fun-house mirrors. It's the colors that are truly amazing though—lit from inside like marigolds just before the frost hits them. I don't know what was more beautiful, the look on Mother's face or the painting. She was glowing.

She told me she bought the painting in Toronto at the Asian Art Gallery. She flew to Toronto and back on the same day just to see the exhibit. She should have stayed overnight and enjoyed herself. I know better though. She won't leave me alone overnight *ever* even though I'm more than old enough. I'm going to *have* to leave Montreal when I go to college just to get out from under. It's ridiculous. If Simon and I want to do something, we'll find a way whether she's home or not. Not that we will do anything. He thinks we're too young and should restrain ourselves. So do I. This is not easy, because once we start kissing and petting, it's hard not to go on to other stuff. Sometimes I can hardly breathe. God, why am I writing all this down when all I wanted to talk about was the painting.

Juliana screws up her face and scratches her head . . . doesn't remember writing so much about her mother and the painting

... this is supposed to be her own life. She realizes with a flash of curiosity and apprehension that there is more to come. She flips a few pages.

I think I understand Mother better now. Even though she's usually calm and busy working at something or other, she's sad underneath, lonely without David. When we were having breakfast this morning, she told me that she wants to buy another painting to keep Shi Hu company. Then she said, "Art lasts longer than love and it increases in value." She always has money on her mind. Then she laughed and looked at me, smiling as if she were going to say something funny, but she said, "And your children can inherit it." I felt like crying when she said that. I can't even imagine her dying.

Juliana feels the tears well up. Her mother is perfectly healthy ... and the way men look at her when they go anywhere together. Still, to even think about her dying. Maybe she should divorce David and marry somebody else. But who? She doesn't even go out with anyone ... except dinner once in a while with old Mr. Ramsden ... and that's just talk about money.

May 21, 1989. Here I am with final exams coming up soon and this year's grades most important for college, and I can't open a book. All I do is watch television with Simon and read the newspapers. He is in a bigger rage than Typhoon Brenda that shut down all of Hong Kong yesterday. But it didn't stop the demonstrators in Victoria Park. (I feel as if I know the place even though I've never been there. Mother says it's very pretty and so does Simon, but he says that even rich Chinese couldn't buy a home there till only a few years ago because the British restricted it to whites.) Over a million people turned out to support the pro-democracy students in Beijing who are on a hunger strike. Simon called Hong Kong and spoke to two of his friends. They said it was the biggest thing that ever happened there, that the Beijing leaders lost all credibility, even with their supporters in Hong Kong. When I called David to find out what he thought, he said the pictures of the Beijing students

in Tiananmen Square reminded him of an antiwar demonstration in Chicago when he was young. He still remembers the way the tear gas stung his eyes and his throat, but
he says it was worth it because they helped end the war
and they were part of history. I'd like to be part of history.
What's the point of just studying all the time? Simon and
I both think we should do something to help the students
in Beijing, but my mother thinks we would be wasting our
time. She said the Chinese leaders, even the good ones, rule
with an iron hand and have no mercy if they think they are
threatened. She says the students are intellectuals who don't
understand that the peasants will support the government
so long as they have enough to eat and are safe. She said,
"Except to the intellectuals, democracy doesn't count for
much in China." I think she's wrong. Democracy is as necessary as breathing. She said the students will be killed if
they keep on with the demonstration because everything is
on television and they're making the government look bad
all over the world—especially with Gorbachev coming. I
can't believe that's going to happen when the whole world
is watching.

Juliana frowns, grudgingly acknowledges that her mother was
right. It will be good to get away, she thinks, be on her own
without her mother hovering over her all the time. She looks at
her watch. Simon will be here soon. She should not be wasting
time reading, just throw the book in her bag and take it with
her. But she doesn't.

June 5, 1989. It hurts to say this, but my mother was right.
Again! I guess that if you predict that the worst will happen—as she always does—you're bound to be right at least
half the time. The Beijing leaders did kill hundreds of students and wounded thousands of others. It was a massacre.
I couldn't believe it was happening. I am disappointed in
Deng and the others. They were supposed to be better than
the old-style Communists. Not that there weren't some
higher-ups who tried to avoid the disaster. The head of the
Communist Party, Zhao Ziyang, was forced to resign because he didn't want to crack down on the students. He

actually went into the square to talk to them. I saw it on television. Maybe he remembered being a student demonstrator when he was young. According to Simon, there are many people in Hong Kong who were saying all along that the Communists will crack down whenever it suits them. Now even more people with money and skills are going to leave in droves because they're afraid of what the Communists will do when they take over in 1997.

Until almost the very end, when it was all blacked out, we actually watched the tanks and soldiers and the students on hunger strike and their huge white plaster Goddess of Liberty that they made themselves. Television is like an X-ray machine that lets you see clear through to the other side of the world. One fellow did the bravest thing I ever saw. He stepped right in front of an enormous tank that was moving into Tiananmen Square to crush the demonstration. He didn't move. The tank stopped inches away from him. One man alone defied the might of the whole army. My mother burst into tears when she saw it and couldn't stop sobbing. The picture was in the paper this morning and I cut it out to save. It's terrible not to be able to do anything to help. I've been too busy trying to catch up for my exams to write any poetry, but seeing that fellow in front of the tank did something to me, so I wrote a poem because I had to do something. I don't know if it's any good.

> Frail reed in raging tempest bends
> Low to earth. Tenacious roots cling,
> Suck marrow, worms, beetles, dung.
> The snarling tempest passes, ends.
>
> Earth nourished, urgent strength returns.
> Frail reed upright, erect, new green.
> Child of the golden sun breathes, leans
> Toward brothers, head to heaven turns.

Juliana reads her poem again and is disappointed. So much less than she thought it was when she wrote it. Maybe it would be better to be a lawyer. Something so much bigger than she is happens in the world every minute . . . yet she's part of it . . . it's part of her. She could do things if she studied international law. She turns the page. Only one day between her poem and the next entry.

I went to the first student demonstration of my life yesterday in front of the People's Republic legation. My mother didn't want me to go. She said that people who stick their necks out get their heads chopped off. I was sickened, really nauseous, when she told me the ugly stuff about how my grandfather was killed during the Cultural Revolution. She should have told me before. But when I said that, she said she wants me to be happy and forget the past. I told her we had to support the students in China. She said it wouldn't do any good.

There were close to two hundred demonstrators when we got there, mostly students, and almost all of them were Chinese. I never felt so Chinese before—as if I suddenly had a second soul I never knew existed. As far as I could tell, Simon and I were the only ones who weren't in college yet. He knew about it because a friend who was also from Hong Kong called and told him that it was going to happen and that we should meet him there. The organizers had lots of signs and banners prepared, and they gave Simon and me a banner to carry and put us in the line and told us to follow along with the slogans. At first I felt self-conscious to the point of foolishness and thought everybody in the street was staring at me, but people passing by were okay, even older people. And the police were keeping things orderly, not at all like what David told me about demonstrations in Boston or Chicago when he was young and the police were against the demonstrators and clubbed them. Canada and the U.S. *are* different. Some people stopped to speak to us and offered to give money to help, but the leaders wouldn't accept because they thought the Chinese government would say the democracy movement was corrupt. Television cameras were taking pictures of everything.

We were starving by the end of the afternoon when a whole new bunch of students came and took our place. We went back to my house to make spaghetti. Simon loves it with a thick tomato sauce. He says the Italians got spaghetti from the Chinese, Marco Polo or something. Sounds right. Mother looked relieved to see me walk in the door, but she didn't seem happy to see Simon, and I thought she acted a little funny. She said she didn't want spaghetti because she was going to dinner with Mr. Ramsden. She said, "We have some business matters to discuss, but he would like to see the new painting. He'll stop in for a few moments." Then she looked at Simon and said, "I'm going to be back quite early, as soon as Mr. Ramsden and I finish dinner. Are you going home to study after you finish eating?" She didn't wait for him to answer, just said, as if it were an invitation to leave, "You must be falling way behind." He didn't need that. He knows he's falling behind. We both are. She's scared to death I'll get pregnant. I can tell. But she never says anything direct. I think she must be a prude. In front of me she always acts like sex doesn't exist. Anyway, Mr. Ramsden came and made a fuss over the painting. They left while we were still cooking.

We did think we'd try to study, but it didn't turn out that way. I guess we were just too excited.

When we were cleaning up after the spaghetti, I was at the sink and Simon came up behind me and held me around the waist and pressed himself into me. He's the one who's always holding back, so I was surprised and I couldn't catch my breath and I couldn't move my hands to finish the dishes and we didn't say anything, just went up the stairs with him touching me from behind and my legs like jelly and wondering what was going to happen. We just flopped down on the bed and Simon's hand was like silk on the inside of my leg and he was kissing me under my blouse and finally unhooked my bra. I could feel his mouth soft and my nipples hard. Then, suddenly, it started and I was bursting and it was hard to breathe or even move. At first I didn't know what it was because it never happened before and we didn't go all the way and I thought you had to for an orgasm. Wrong again! All I could do was let myself go. Simon got off the bed and walked around the room, but I could still hear his loud breathing. By the time my mother got home, we were downstairs in the living room and really were studying, at least trying to. It was still light out.

Not many entries after that day. Juliana thinks, what was there to write that was worth the time it took? The weeks passed like minutes: the usual heavy schedule at school, filling out endless forms, hustling off to interviews, smiling and bowing like a circus animal. It *was* a circus going to college interviews, and she was one of the animals on parade.

With one flip of the page, more than half a year to the next entry. She remembers that one, short and sweet.

My acceptance came today. Harvard wants me. Simon too. Come the end of August, we're off to Cambridge. Together! PS: I think I would have gotten in even if I wasn't Juliana Wang Verhoeven Levy and the daughter of an alum. David is ecstatic (also thinks getting in had nothing to do with him). Mother is reconciled to my leaving and, I think, damn proud. She keeps talking about her father and the Wang family heritage.

And the next entry. Much shorter, almost as welcome.

My period finally came. Praise be to God—even if I am pretty sure I'm an atheist.

Juliana shudders, then laughs aloud. Okay to laugh now, she thinks, but it wasn't so funny then. She turns the page.

Last night belonged to my mother—the grand opening of the Plum Blossom Gallery. When she first told me about going into business like that, I didn't think she meant right away, but she had been planning it for months without telling me. She probably wanted to wait till we knew where I'd be going to college. That woman must have been born keeping secrets. Nobody does it better. It's great that she's going into business with something that she really likes. Since she practically lives in museums and other people's art galleries, she may as well have one of her own to keep her busy while I'm away. Who knows when I'll be back or if I'll be back except for visits. That's something we don't talk about.

The gallery is gorgeous. It's on the street floor of an old building she bought (at a fantastic low price, naturally!)—a few blocks from the Museum of Fine Arts, so I wasn't expecting anything sleek. Was I ever wrong. It looked like something out of the movies—high pale gray ceilings and moldings, white walls, white globe lamps hanging from invisible wires so that they looked like clouds suspended in space, a charcoal-gray carpet covering every inch of floor except for the entrance, where there was an area of red and white ceramic tiles that were copied from an old Chinese design. She thought of everything. The place was filled with the smell of roses, dozens and dozens of yellow and white blossoms in dark red vases that looked as if they belonged in a Chinese temple. They were set on narrow chrome-and-glass tables at a few places along the walls, where they wouldn't hide the paintings. And I haven't even gotten to what was hanging on the walls. One section was reserved for original works of current Asian artists. Mother says more and more collectors are going after it. Another section was filled with antiques—scrolls and sculpture and fine porcelains in Lucite cases and even a display of jade in a dark wood case. The antiques section was my favorite. I can probably get a course in Chinese art at Harvard. Up to now I wasn't all that interested—but all that beautiful stuff touched something Chinese in me.

It's hard to say what the most beautiful object in the room was, but it may have been my mother. Honestly! Even the tiny lines near her eyes looked like an artist put them there. She could have been one of the porcelain vases if she stood still for more than a few seconds. I never saw her so lively and happy except when she and David were first married. She really sparkled. Everyone was buzzing around her, dozens of people I never even saw before. Where did they come from? I recognized Betty Bloom, the real estate lady she does business with. Her husband was a fat, funny-looking man who smiled a lot but kept quiet while she talked. I saw Mr. Ramsden. He was with a gray-haired woman in a green brocade caftan down to the floor. Too showy for my taste. Now, Mother was something else again. She wore a simple midnight-blue sheath down to her ankles with slits on the side and a high Chinese collar. I think it's called a cheongsam. Very, very sexy. And that amazing sapphire necklace! Now, there's something I won't mind inheriting.

Juliana closes her eyes quickly on that sentence, as if a wind has blown dust into them. This bare hint of mercenary calculation and the possibility of benefiting from her mother's death seems deeply shameful to her. But the flash of shame doesn't last. It was the beauty of the sapphires that she coveted—and the way they looked on her mother—not their price. She knows that. It's okay to open her eyes.

Two waiters were carrying trays of champagne and miniature shrimp toasts and scallion pancakes that you could pick up with toothpicks so that your fingers wouldn't get greasy. I was sorry David wasn't there. He loves that stuff. I guess it was too much to ask. They do talk to each other pretty often though, mostly on the phone, mostly about me, so I kind of expected to see him walk in, but either she didn't invite him or he didn't want to come. Maybe he was out with the lady in the red hat. I hope not.

Anyway, Plum Blossom was a big success, the opening anyway. By the time everyone was gone, several of the paintings were sold, including a big one that cost thirty-eight thousand dollars that a Japanese man bought. A few of the antiques too. Mother seemed different from before. I don't know exactly what it was. She was happy the opening went well, but I could see she also enjoyed being with all those people and having them admire her and what she had done. I don't know exactly how to say this, but it seems as if she doesn't belong just to me the way she used to. Part of her belongs to the gallery and all those people. I suppose that's good, because I'm leaving and she needs other things, but it's also like losing something—that's how I feel.

Juliana sucks air into her chest and blows it out again. She runs her fingers through the remaining pages. Only one last entry followed by a few blanks.

Free at last. Graduated yesterday. Certified, shipped out—weighed down with honors, mainly history, English,

French, and Latin. The speeches were boring and humidity was intense, but I didn't care.

Took pictures with my new camera (a graduation gift from Gram and Grampa down in Florida)—a few shots of Rachel and Blair (both definitely going to McGill), Simon and his parents (he says they like me, especially after they met Mother, who *looks* Chinese). David took shots of me with Simon and me with Mother. Simon snapped several poses of David and Mother with me in the middle. When they're developed, we'll no doubt *look* like a family. Maybe we are. It isn't as if they've gotten a divorce. The three of us went out to dinner at night to celebrate as if we were a family. It felt wonderful, and I don't just mean the food, which was French and deliciously sinful. The wine was French too, and all three of us got kind of tipsy and we were laughing at David's jokes like we used to. I was woozy and tired when we got home, so I collapsed into bed without even brushing my teeth. Now the important part in this strange tale. When I woke up in the morning, David was downstairs cooking breakfast. My heart leaped up, as Mr. Wordsworth said. The truth is I have been worried about leaving Mother alone even though she keeps saying she won't be lonely and that she's busy at the gallery all the time. At breakfast they behaved like an old married couple—which they are and aren't—and it felt like we were a family again. But David left after breakfast and neither of them said anything about getting together again, at least not in front of me. I guess you could say they were celebrating my graduation.

Juliana runs her fingers through the blank pages at the end of the book. She tosses it into her knapsack. Probably won't have time to write, she thinks . . . so few pages left anyway. Still, you never know. Best to have it with her. It's her life.

⌒⌒

Mei-ling speaks quietly. "Simon's here."

Juliana looks up, startled. She had not heard her mother on the stairs. "Oh, good." She scrambles to her feet.

"He's waiting for you downstairs. Shall I tell him to come up."

"Not yet. I'll be down in a minute. I want to check the van before we bring everything down." There is a slight tremor in her voice. She hopes her mother doesn't notice. Then, without warning, her cheeks are hot with tears. She looks away.

Mei-ling wraps Juliana in her arms, is grateful to have her there, as if she were a child again. So much smaller than her daughter, she reaches up to wipe the tear-stained cheeks with her fingertips. "I'm going to miss you," she says, her own eyes brimming.

Juliana doesn't pull away. She drapes herself over Mei-ling's shoulders, clinging like a baby monkey. "I don't know why I'm crying," she says.

"It's all going to be fine. You're going to enjoy college." She takes Juliana by the shoulders and looks at her. "You're going to do very well." She laughs. "I'm proud to say you have the Wang family brain."

Juliana wipes her eyes and smiles. "Just born lucky? What about how hard I worked?"

Mei-ling laughs. "Yes, that too." She stands back, holding only Juliana's hands now. "You were always my pride and joy. It's hard for me to believe you're old enough to be going to college."

"If I don't get down to Simon soon, we may never get to Cambridge, let alone college."

Mei-ling drops her hands. "Yes. Let's go down." She hesitates, wants to say more. "I hope you won't think I'm an old Polonius if I give you some advice."

Juliana smiles and spreads her palms up. "Fire away. I can always decide not to take it."

"You'll probably think I'm being terribly harsh, but my life has taught me one great lesson. You'll do well if you expect a great deal from yourself and very little from others. That way you won't be disappointed . . . you'll have a chance at a good life . . . a much better chance than most people."

Juliana looks puzzled, doesn't know what to make of her mother's little homily, isn't sure what it means. Her words seem so cold. "I thought you were going to say something about studying and responsibility and not getting into trouble and that life is more complicated than it seems." She pauses. "Or that you love me."

"You know all that. Your happiness is what I hope for."

Suddenly playful, Juliana says, "In that case, I promise to be happy." She brushes her mother's cheek. "Don't look so sad. I won't be that far away."

"Not now. We'll see about later on."

Juliana picks up the red knapsack. "Simon's waiting for me, Mother."

Mei-ling takes Juliana's hand and squeezes it. "Yes."

"I love you."

Mei-ling nods and smiles. She walks out of the room with Juliana following behind her.

When Juliana opens the front door, she is surprised to see both David and Simon at the back of the van. They seem to be rearranging some of Simon's stuff.

David says, "More room that way."

Juliana rushes up to David. "I didn't think you'd be here today. I thought we said good-bye on the weekend."

"Couldn't keep me away, sweetie. I have to make sure you get off okay."

He turns to Simon. "No disrespect, you understand, but I have a habit before every long trip." He circles the car, inspecting the tires carefully. Then he nods toward Juliana. "Precious cargo, Simon."

Juliana grimaces. "For God's sake, Dad, I'm doing half the driving. I'm not just cargo." She speaks pointedly, only to Simon. "He worries more than my mother. Let's get out of here before they start feeding me baby food."

At this, all four of them troop into the house and two by two carry the trunk and duffel out and load them into the van. Juliana tosses her knapsack into the front seat and turns to Mei-ling and David.

"Time to go."

Part Seven

1997

Hong Kong

~

THROUGH THE SUNLIT sky, through the thin haze that hangs lightly over the island, the treasure towers of Hong Kong reach into the air like magnetic fingers. They draw Mei-ling's plane toward a spot of earth so small that it can be traversed by foot in a single day, so immensely rich that the world's financial centers wait and wonder: What will happen when it becomes Chinese soil once again? Hong Kong has been likened to Manhattan, that other small island fueled by energy and desire. Surely, Mei-ling thinks, the similarity is not lost on the powers in Beijing. Surely they will do nothing so foolish as killing the golden goose. She shakes her head as she peers out the window. With Deng gone, surely they might.

Mei-ling stirs in her seat. Only a short while, she thinks. At the stroke of midnight on June 30, 1997, the red, white, and blue Union Jack will be lowered over Government House and the red flag and gold stars of the People's Republic of China will be raised. How far her thoughts were from such things when she arrived long ago . . . a bloody scab, close to starving, scarcely able to speak. Impossible to imagine then that she would return one day after a life elsewhere. She fishes for her purse and takes out her compact. Looking at her face in the glass, she lightly powders her nose and cheeks, then spreads a thin layer of lipstick on her upper lip and rubs it against her lower so that only a faint blush of color remains. Scanning her image, she is pleased. She smiles into the mirror and mouths the words, *You'll do.*

The plane loses altitude as it approaches Kai Tak Airport in Kowloon and prepares to land. Mei-ling's ears plug up and her head aches, as if she is about to come down with the flu. She grimaces at a sudden stab of pain in her right temple. Flying is hateful to her. She is uncommonly sensitive to changes in air pressure, but, she assures herself, they will be on the ground soon enough. She sucks vigorously on the lemon drop she pops into her mouth, hopes that this will lessen the discomfort. It seems to work. She can hear and feel the rumble of the landing gear . . . catch the buzz of conversation in the cabin. She looks out the window.

Another stab of pain, in her right ear this time. She leans her head against the back of her roomy, comfortable first-class seat. It is well worth the price, she thinks, not to be squeezed together with strangers. Dirk Verhoeven's square face takes shape in her mind's eye; it was he, she realizes, who first taught her to enjoy luxury. How hard it is to force him from her thoughts now that the plane is about to land. Juliana was conceived in this place. Juliana lives and works here now.

Mei-ling closes her eyes, thoughtful, preoccupied with the strangeness of the world. Could either Queen Victoria, matriarch of empire, or Karl Marx, patriarch of communism, have imagined that the China of their day, disintegrating and opium-ridden, wreck of ancient greatness, easy prey to seizure of its southern tip by British gunboats, would rise again in the closing years of the twentieth century and insist, not very humbly, not very politely, on the return of the entire crown colony to Communists? The British "lease" on Hong Kong—its terms dictated by gunboats and opium—is up. After centuries of decline, China is ascending to an eminent place among the world's powers, perhaps preeminent before very long. Hadn't she read somewhere the words of an American Supreme Court justice who'd said that the twenty-first century would belong to the Chinese Reds because they had the "requisite number of geniuses." Hadn't she felt a surprising surge of pride at that . . . companion to a shudder of fear? What path would they take, she wonders, the unlikely pragmatists who rule the new China? All of Hong Kong is nervous. Most of those who had the means and the papers to leave have done just that . . . joining an exodus that has transformed whole cities in the United States and Canada.

During much of the long flight from Montreal, Mei-ling had been dwelling on other matters, mostly Juliana, a lawyer now, and Simon, an economist, both working in Hong Kong and earning an absurd amount of money. Not yet married. What are they waiting for? While eating her lunch, she thought also about how much the Hong Kong she left behind will have changed. Also about Jackson Ramsden, her old friend, whom she might never have met had it not been for Dirk. She shrugs. Well, she thinks, there are often unintended consequences.

Ramsden had seemed suddenly old this last year, all the spirit gone out of him. He'd confided in her one evening over dinner: "With Montreal under constant siege by the separatists, I feel as if I'm a displaced person. Eventually, they'll wear the country down with their endless agitation. I don't really mind being in the minority so long as things are sane and sensible, but the thought of Canada being broken into pieces someday fills me with dread."

But as Mei-ling remembers it, what had really brought him down was the transfer of one of his sons to Toronto. "It's all coming apart," he'd said, "the family, the country . . . maybe civilization for all we know." Then he'd said something else, odd and oddly personal for him. "You don't really need me anymore, my dear. You do me a kindness by remaining an old man's friend." It was, she supposed, true in its way—he had begun to lose interest in art and music, and he'd begun to walk slowly at times, as if each step were an effort, and he'd lost his sharpness about finance though she never let on that she thought so—yet there was still much that was solid about him. He was her friend. She didn't have many. Jack Ramsden's death had been so sudden, so unexpected . . . a heart attack in his sleep. A kind death for him, a loss to her. She'd wept at the news. Her deep feeling for him surprised her. She hadn't known it was there.

The timing of the funeral couldn't have been worse, only days before she was due to leave. She would have missed it altogether had she not spotted the obituary in the paper. As it was, she felt a stranger the moment she entered the church . . . which is what she was, of course, to everyone except Ramsden, who lay rouged and stoic in his coffin. She had never met his sons, his friends, or any of the cronies from his days at the bank. Her friendship with him had been nothing if not discreet, an intimate partnership neither of them felt compelled to define or disclose to others. His company—the occasional quiet dinner in a suburban restaurant, the visits to art exhibitions in Toronto or Ottawa, the auto trips to the Laurentians or Vermont when the foliage was glowing, quiet little excursions that suited them both, that made no claims on either—that's what she will miss, not the financial counsel she hasn't needed for years.

And up to the last few months he'd been so grateful for her small ministrations . . . a still rather virile old gentleman who purred when she so much as touched him or who simply sat beside her in creature contentment. For her, sex between them was never more than pleasant, sometimes not even that, nothing at all like what she and David still shared when it suited them. Yet it had pleased her to make her old friend happy. Unlike David, he had never judged her harshly.

A flight attendant's smiling voice breaks into her reverie. "We'll be landing shortly." Mei-ling smiles back absently, wondering if choosing Montreal as a place to live wasn't influenced by Ramsden's protective, courtly manner in Amsterdam. Or was it about family . . . perhaps that distant Cousin Sybil Emma had spoken of, the Canadian missionary's wife? Mei-ling had thought of England, but she remembered Emma saying that no family was left there. She wonders if she was drawn to a place where not everyone spoke the same language, where there was room for strangers.

At the funeral, the Anglican priest in his black robe had been a solemn fellow: fairly young, slightly balding, sandy hair, pale skin, light blue eyes, and lips drawn tight into a long, narrow face. "A real white-bread kisser," she remembered David saying about a man they met at a faculty do at the university, a man who could have been the priest's brother or near cousin.

David! She sighs audibly when she thinks of him. Wonderful that Simon managed to get him a seat on a plane. Every flight to Hong Kong in time for the transfer of power had been booked for years and the hotel rooms as well. Somehow, he'd managed. Luckily, he and Juliana had a fine flat in the hills near Victoria Peak that would be big enough for all of them. And air-conditioned! She breathes in relief, remembering the dripping heat of Hong Kong all too well. A sudden flash of memory . . . Dirk Verhoeven's Mercedes . . . the delight of its sequestered coolness . . . the price she paid. But no point in dwelling on all that. She is no longer young, not far from the half-century mark, dependent on nobody but herself, not Dirk, not David, not Jack Ramsden. He had been helpful to her in business matters, but she will manage quite well without him.

Mei-ling shudders slightly as the plane dips toward the water below. She forces her mind to concentrate on Ramsden. The priest's conduct of the funeral service had been traditional, as far as she could tell, which is to say it was vaguely interesting and faintly boring. She saw little overt display of grief among the many mourners in their dark suits and ties, their little black dresses and pearls, their discreet hats, their good leather shoes. Solemn faces, quiet murmuring, restrained.

Ramsden's son, the older one who had been transferred to Toronto, had delivered the eulogy. He was a man several years older than herself, a near replica of his father at the same age except for a neatly trimmed beard that distinguished him. Ramsden had spoken of his sons occasionally. She had remembered that this one, the eldest, had a wife and two grown sons. Until he rose to speak, they sat beside him in the front pew facing the dark walnut coffin with its spray of white lilies standing beside it. His voice had the same measured cadence as his father's, a steady progression of well-weighed words that fulfilled their obligation.

He began quite simply. "I've been thinking about my father and about the meaning of his life . . . if there is such a thing as meaning to one's life . . . as if we need to justify what needs no justification. When I say that he was a loyal and devoted husband to my mother, especially in the years of her illness, and to Grace in their short time together, that he was a supportive and considerate father to my brother and myself, that he was able and admirable in the service he rendered to the Commonwealth Bank and its clients during his long career"—a long pause for breath—"that he was a patron of the arts . . ." *Yes,* Mei-ling thinks, remembering. The son's eyes, Ramsden's eyes, had looked out at the mourners in their pews, then up into the luminous brilliance of the stained glass windows—". . . everything I say about him seems quite ordinary. Yet can anyone in our day and age still think that a devoted husband and father and a good and dutiful citizen is ordinary? We live in a time that no longer values very highly his unassuming and quiet virtue. He was born into a time that did . . . a time when the word *civilization* meant what it said . . . a community of citizens who subsumed their differences and social distance, who managed to be civil to one another, so that the community might flourish. I not only mourn my father's passing, I fear it."

She had watched in the hushed church as the son's eyes filled and reddened but did not brim over, listened as he continued.

"My father's life was, in its ordinary way, exemplary. So many of you being here today attests to that. Some of you grew up speaking French. Yet you are here. Some of you are from far-off countries. You too are here. For the most part, the Montreal my father was born into spoke only English or only French. But, as his generation entered a new age they often couldn't fathom, my father mastered French early and well. He chatted with his grandsons in French so that they would be able to function easily in a city that spoke more than one language. I fear that his efforts were thwarted by political passions that have little to do with reason. His grandsons will live out their lives elsewhere. That does not mean his efforts were worthless. My father managed to do what his family, his work, and his country demanded of him, and he did it well—certainly well enough for his life to need no justification. He was a good man and we all grieve at his passing. We will miss him."

Yes. Mei-ling opens her eyes and blinks. It's been a long, wearying flight. The attendants are belted into their seats. Her headache has disappeared. They must be very close to the ground. When she looks out the window, the waters of the harbor look back at her with the eyes of hundreds of vessels. More than she remembers. The plane hits the tarmac with a loud thump and a light bounce. Mei-ling grips the arms of her seat as the engines thrust into reverse. Her stomach lurches. She decides that she will swim back to Montreal when the time comes. The plane slows and coasts to a stop. A surge of mingled exhaustion and elation fills her chest so that she is slow to rise.

"Mother. Mother." Juliana shouts and waves, rushes to embrace Mei-ling as she walks past the gate. She must bend her head to kiss her. She has never before realized quite how tiny she is.

"Darling! How is my beautiful girl?"

"Frantic, if you really want to know. I've never worked so hard in my life."

Mei-ling laughs, hugs Juliana a second and a third time. "That's what happens when you're a clever lawyer with heavy responsibilities."

Juliana wrinkles her nose just as she did when she was a child. "Not to mention running around and getting to know the place and speaking the language. There's only so much Harvard can teach you. Simon wanted to be here, but he couldn't get away. You can't imagine all the work involved in the transition, even when you're working for an American company. He'll meet us at the flat as soon as he can."

They walk hand in hand amid a sea of Chinese faces, Chinese voices, mostly Cantonese but with an occasional snatch of Mandarin that surprises Mei-ling. I shouldn't be surprised, she thinks, with Beijing taking over so soon. "I had forgotten," she says to Juliana, "what it's like to be among so many Chinese."

"A lot more than when you lived in Hong Kong. It's ninety-eight percent Chinese now. They run the place already. The British haven't been much more than temporary figureheads for a while now. Lots of Canadians and Americans and Australians and Europeans doing business though, not to mention the other Asians. What a place for going after the dollar. It's the only thing that matters here."

"I remember my mother once said something like that. It couldn't have been more than a day or two after we came over the border. She thought Hong Kong lacked a soul."

"It does, but is it ever exciting, and things change every second."

Caught up in the crush of determined travelers, they press forward through the terminal. "You know, Mother," Juliana says, "I feel more Chinese living here. I feel as if I look a little more Chinese too. Isn't it strange?"

"No." Mei-ling reaches up and runs her finger over the jade disk that hangs from her ear. "And don't ask me to explain, because I can't . . . I expected it might happen."

"Mother, give me your baggage checks and wait here. I've arranged to have your luggage picked up and delivered. Otherwise, we'll be here forever. You can't imagine the traffic. They're building a new airport on Chek Lap Kok island off Lantau, but nobody knows when it will be ready for use."

Can she be only twenty-four, Mei-ling wonders as she sees the trim, self-possessed young woman run off . . . on her own, working and earning plenty of money . . . living with Simon as husband and wife. Though, she fears, there may be trouble there. Juliana's last letter had spoken of their "arrangement" as working out well "at least for the time being." It was hard to tell whether she was speaking about their relationship or their flat.

Mei-ling does not have long to wait for Juliana's return, only long enough to notice all the gun-toting security people patrolling everywhere. After so many years in Amsterdam and Montreal, she is not used to guards and soldiers in uniform anymore, their stiff carriage, their vague air of menace. It was all she knew while she was growing up, though, she reminds herself, at least they were disciplined, less to be feared than the marauding Red Guards. Juliana takes her hand and leads her through the oddly familiar yet confusing maze. Once outside, a veil of humidity envelops them so that Mei-ling's breath grows a little heavier. She looks up. The sky is as she remembers it, a sharp blue dulled at the edges now by an industrial haze. She puts on her dark glasses. They are immersed in a mass of scurrying people, most of whom seem to be headed toward the airport bus that will take them across the river from Kowloon directly to the hub of Hong Kong. Although the bus is air-conditioned, the crush of bodies builds up an odorous cloud very quickly. "I feel dizzy," Mei-ling says. "How did I once live in such a climate?"

Juliana takes her hand, notices a soft pocket of flesh forming under her chin. "You'll be used to it in a day or two."

Once the bus drops them off in Central, the heat of the day overwhelms Mei-ling. The heat and the shock of the new. Can this be where she lived for so long? Nothing is familiar. "Now I know what Captain Gulliver must have felt like on his travels," she tells Juliana. "Everything is so out of proportion. Why did they raise buildings so tall on this small island? It makes me dizzy. Even the few things I do remember are in the wrong place."

Juliana hangs on to her arm. "It's the land reclamation. Hong Kong is actually bigger than it was when you left here. They're building up and out. They need every inch of space."

"No wonder I made a handsome enough profit when I sold the tiny piece of property I still owned here."

"You had property here? You were so young?"

"I inherited it from your father. He had the habit of hedging his bets, holding on to things here and there just in case. It's probably worth even more now, from the look of things. Perhaps I should have held on."

"Probably. But everyone is waiting to see what happens after the takeover . . . if China keeps its promises. Then, who knows what it might be worth. You never told me he owned property here. I want you to tell me more about him."

"We can talk after I've settled in. Sometimes I feel as if we've never said more than hello or good-bye ever since you left for Boston."

"You exaggerate."

"Perhaps, but not by much." Mei-ling looks around at the traffic, shrinks at the crushing chaos of the streets. "Does the tram let us off anywhere near your flat? Your grandmother and I would ride it when we took picnics up to Victoria Peak on Sundays. We could cool off there."

"I want you to tell me more about my grandmother. I hardly know anything about my family."

"There's not any of it left, for one thing . . . at least that I know of. We can talk later, when we're out of this crush."

"Okay, but I know that you're putting me off."

Mei-ling smiles wanly and wipes her face with a handkerchief. "The heat is putting me off. I can't wait to bathe."

"Instead of the tram, I have something else to show you that will get us there faster. You'll be amazed when you see it. There's nothing like it anywhere."

Soon they are riding on a conveyance that one might find in a fantasy amusement park: the world's longest escalator-travelator, eight hundred meters, according to Juliana. It rises among skyscrapers and hillsides, alternating from horizontal to vertical planes, carrying them ever upward toward the heights as the city below recedes. Though it's still long before the evening breeze, Mei-ling feels cooler air brush the skin of her arms and neck as they ascend toward Mid-Levels, where Simon and

Juliana live. She is nearly speechless at being carried along so. Finally, she says, "This is like the world of the future . . . science fiction. How on earth did they do such a thing?"

"Oh, zillions of dollars and lots of imagination, not to mention all the labor. The construction jobs were sought after. Everyone loves it because we can live near the Peak without having to worry about being caught in traffic. People say it was a nightmare before."

"Only the English lived near the Peak when Mother and I came here. Chinese were kept out. Except for wealthy business families, most of the Chinese lived in wretched places." She waves her arm in an arc toward a group of luxury high rises. "This is like seeing a film."

"All of Hong Kong is." She points. "Look over there by that huge crane. Still more going up. I'm so lucky to have gotten a job here." Juliana squeezes her mother's hand. "I wouldn't have missed all the excitement for anything. It's great being Chinese in Hong Kong at a time like this . . . even part Chinese . . . even with all the uncertainty . . . not to mention the occasional twitch of fear." She laughs. "Even if the capitalists are unspeakably greedy and the Communists don't give two hoots about democracy and are corrupt when it suits them. It's like being at the center of the world."

Mei-ling smiles. "For someone who is only a quarter Chinese, you seem quite proud. I gather you're pleased you've come."

"It's stupendous. Don't forget, you once said that the Chinese part of me was most important."

Mei-ling takes her eyes for a moment from the wonderland of towers and hillsides that they scale as if by magic and fixes them on Juliana. "Yes, and you have a Canadian passport in case you have to flee from trouble. I suspect that most of the people here would be quite content with less excitement and more security."

"Oh, Mother, it's a great moment in history. Try to enjoy it. Hong Kong does by rights belong to China, not England. Though I have to admit that it was the English and the rule of law and political stability that made Hong Kong a favorable place for business and turned it into an economic miracle. But it's time for China to have it back. I know you have your reasons, but you're much too cynical about everything. Of course, there'll be enormous problems during the transition . . . perhaps for years after . . . but immense possibilities for the future are right here in this place."

Mei-ling looks hard at the daughter who is no longer a child. "I hope with all my heart that you're not disappointed." She squeezes Juliana's hand. "It's wonderful to be with you like this . . . and you're a grown woman. With everything there is to see, I can't take my eyes off you."

Juliana smiles and points up the hill a bit. "We get off here."

"Almost the top of the world." Mei-ling points toward the city below. "All before you, isn't it?"

"I feel that way now, but when I first came I was homesick. The training I got at Harvard was first-rate, but no matter how much you study, how well you master the language, nothing prepares you for the real thing. If it weren't for Simon, I would have been lost then."

"And you're not lost now?"

"No. I feel as if I've found something here . . . a Chinese piece of myself. Maybe more . . . I love my work." She hesitates, looks at Mei-ling, feels an involuntary flutter of her eyelids. "I'm not so sure about Simon anymore."

"Oh?"

The next morning, by the time Mei-ling wakes refreshed from an air-conditioned sleep on her comfortable bed in the second bedroom, Juliana and Simon are already gone. With elaborate apologies the night before, they said they simply had to work, that she should sleep late the first day to get over jet lag. Their solicitousness amused her. If she feels a trifle superfluous, there is compensation in it. How liberating it is not to be needed . . . not to feel someone else's life more demanding than one's own.

Mei-ling explores the spacious flat that looks out over the city, ponders the rental on such a place, remembers the two small rooms behind Dirk Verhoeven's office that she and Emma found refuge in, that are gone now because she sold the building to the syndicate of developers that had coveted it and paid her so well. She wonders if Miss Richardson's school with its black iron gate is still there. So many times she walked through that gate. So often he was waiting for her.

A note is on the kitchen table—short and sweet. *There is food in the refrigerator. Help yourself for breakfast. Don't eat too much for lunch because we're going to a wonderful restaurant for dinner. Have a fine day if you decide to go sightseeing. Don't wear yourself out. See you tonight. Happy you're here. Simon too. Love, J.*

Actually, Mei-ling is quite happy to be alone while Juliana and Simon are at work. She wants to explore the city at her own pace, try to retrace a bit of the past. When she mentioned it, Juliana had said, "You may be in for a disappointment. Things change so fast around here. The places you remember are probably gone. Except for a few of the colonial landmarks, if you want to see those." No, that isn't what she wants. They mean nothing to her.

More and more as she grows older, Mei-ling relishes her own company. More and more, like some ascetic ancestor whose temperament is woven into her, she savors a rather solitary life . . . though not a hermetic one. Jack Ramsden is gone. And they hadn't seen each other all that often. There is Betty Bloom, her only woman friend, but their common thread is real estate, and her husband is a silly clown. Plum Blossom, of course, where people come and go "speaking of Michelangelo." But that was Eliot's point, wasn't it—people's lives not really touching even when they chatter endlessly. In truth, she thinks, the paintings and antiques engage her far more than the people who come to see them.

And David from time to time . . . the odd little dance between them stretching out over the years. She wonders if she prefers it that way now, though for a long while *his* comings and goings were exquisite pain. Yet neither of them pressed for a divorce . . . and yes, she did love him . . . then and now . . . the only one. She will be happy to see him when he arrives later in the day . . . in time for all of them to have dinner together.

It must have taken some doing for Simon to get the plane reservation. Hers had been secured almost a year earlier and not without difficulty. She shrugs. Simon is nothing if not resourceful, but, if Juliana's mood is any indication, there may be a situation ahead even he cannot bend to his will.

Mei-ling looks through the dresses she had unpacked and hung in the closet the night before . . . remembers the first one she bought in Hong Kong . . . red and white. The beautiful lacquered saleswoman with the astonishing shoes and fingernails must be an old grandmother now. How numb with despair her younger self had been. The soft cotton and bright colors had made her feel alive again. She selects a cool pink cotton with short loose sleeves and walking shoes with thick soles. Her feet tire more easily than they used to. High heels would be a torture for what she has in mind.

Before leaving, she counts her money and tucks the various maps and instructions Juliana and Simon pressed on her into her purse. She had protested that however much Hong Kong may have changed, she knew it better than they did. "I hope you're not going to go on treating me like a child, Juliana," she'd said. "I speak Cantonese far better than you. No matter where I wander off to, I'll hardly be lost. What's the point of coming this far if I don't see all there is to see?" They'd let her be after that.

A cloud passes over Mei-ling's face. What will it be like, she wonders, when she crosses over to the mainland for a visit for the first time since she and Emma fled? . . . Hardly a homecoming. When Deng died in February, a shudder of fear shook her, but Jiang Zemin and the others in power have carried on as before. There is nothing to fear. Yet it's good that David has planned to come with her.

Mei-ling looks into the mirror, smoothes her hair out of habit. She smiles at an image still beautiful if slightly worn. It is reassuring. Like having money in the bank. She leaves a note for Juliana and Simon saying that she'll return before they arrive at the flat with David toward evening.

There is a futuristic splendor to the new buildings, an architectural passion that can't fail to impress—the interior superstructure of the Hong Kong and Shanghai Bank, clearly visible, pulses and flows like an overgrown robot's intestines; the blue-mirrored spheres and planes of the Stock Exchange soar into space like an interplanetary ship; the Central Plaza Building, seventy-eight stories, the tallest on the continent, seems almost as high as the Pearl River is wide. There is no denying that much was accomplished under the British. But Mei-ling soon wearies of the tall buildings and sleek exteriors. How much of this dubious progress can one marvel at? And for how long? There is too much to really *see* any. When a raging typhoon comes, as it must, she thinks, she would choose to be anywhere but inside such buildings. Unless, of course, the architects have found a way to control the winds.

Instead, Mei-ling goes off in another direction, makes her way past some of the familiar relics of British domination, colonial buildings with arches and columns that look quite out of place in the midst of this rampant modernity. They had so intimidated her when she was young. Then she walks in and out of a few of the old streets and alleys, the real Hong Kong that has almost ceased to be real. She used to explore them as a girl on lonely afternoons when her English schoolmates were busy at their play, when the few wealthy Chinese girls were secure in the laps of their families, when she wondered, as her mother worked and looked away, just what it was that Dirk Verhoeven had in store for her.

Thoughts of Verhoeven give way to a piquant nostalgia. It's fun to wander among the shops and stalls piled high with everything from bogus-brand wristwatches to fake antiques to mass-produced Buddhas to straw hats and sandals to hair ornaments and paper fans. The merchants and passersby hawking and spitting on the street when the spirit moves them is discomfiting but somehow familiar. She braces herself to dodge.

What's this? Mei-ling picks up a six-inch figurine, a ceramic replica of a Chinese boy, no more than five or six years old. He is wearing a Mao suit and wielding a pistol in his right hand. There must be thirty or forty of them in a plastic bin. She recoils at the random pile of lethal children. Where had the horrid things come from, these small defenders of the faith? She shakes her head. The mainland, of course. Are they surplus junk, she wonders, or do the men in power still count on an army of children to fight their battles.

It's almost noon by now, and bands of perspiration are moistening her skin and her clothes. She thinks longingly of an air-conditioned restaurant, but her stomach doesn't agree. It does not crave nourishment. Quite the contrary; keeping food down might be a problem. A family of American-sounding tourists is picking among the merchandise nearby. Their little girl, a sweet-faced child with curly brown hair, is twirling a paper bird on a stick. Round and round it goes, its tissue wings rustling in the heavy air.

Of course, Mei-ling thinks. She hurries to the Star Ferry terminal. There is always a breeze on the water. The ferry, the *Shining Star,* is a pleasant reminder of earlier trips taken to avoid the heat or to just get away. After buying a ticket to the upper deck, she makes her way through the thicket of noontime travelers and heads toward the prow, where the breeze is strongest. Just across the harbor, the transformed skyline of Kowloon looms up before her, a new magic city full of high rises where not so very long ago stood tumble-down shacks and decaying offices and shipping terminals. The ferry moves clumsily out of its slip and in seven short minutes docks in Kowloon.

Mei-ling looks around briefly at the hubbub of the terminal and spots quite quickly the For Hire sign on a red and silver taxi that will take her to Mongkok. After a brief haggle with the driver, who is surprised at her ability to play the game, they head up Nathan Road, which should look more familiar than it does. Despite the changes, though, there's an increasing familiarity to it all. There will be many days to go exploring, but just now she knows exactly what she is looking for and doesn't take long to find it. The Bird Market in the old Chinese heart of the colony is as she remembers it and just as marvelous: white cockatoo princes strut in their cages; green and yellow canaries practice their trills; jungle-hued parrots are proud in their plumage and tilt their heads and bark raucous commands through hooked beaks; their smaller and more charming parakeet cousins swagger on perches. So many rare and delightful creatures, acrobats ruffling their many-colored feathers, speckled and spotted and subtly shaded, comely in their cages. When she was young, she'd been entranced by them. And the wonderful cages! She had quite forgotten about them. Might not a few of the finer ones, carved in teak and bamboo, find a home at Plum Blossom? She would have to look into it. But for now she is content to wander the dirty, feather-strewn alley with the other bird fanciers, some of them holding their prettily caged pets beside them like children. Even the musty, sour smell of the old place is pleasant, companionable.

A vendor is feeding his flock. Mei-ling watches as one by one he lifts a lively grasshopper between chopsticks and holds it to each hungry beak in turn. Sacks of grasshoppers piled in a large straw basket are for sale to the bird lovers, as are packages of seeds. Treats for the precious creatures. How strange and how familiar this place after so many years in the West.

In her delight with the birds, Mei-ling had almost forgotten the heat and her tired feet, but it is afternoon now, heavy and humid. All of her is tired. And hot. She should leave time for a nap before dinner, time to shower and don her own pretty plumage for the Hong Kong night. Juliana had casually reminded her, "Everybody dresses to the teeth here, and the restaurant is very special. Wear your best."

It had been amusing to hear Juliana—always so serious and studious at home, so disdainful of mere appearances, so zealous in her legal studies, so eager during her undergraduate years to make the world right or at least better—warn to dress properly. Hong Kong had a way of doing that to people. It was, she supposed, a minor form of corruption, a relatively harmless one. Mei-ling laughs to herself. No, she decides, if Juliana were to be corrupted, it would not be by clothing or cars. She never wanted for those. Her passions would not be so easily satisfied. She would try to reach for some impossible ideal . . . inside herself and out in the world . . . like her grandparents before her. Mei-ling sighs. Could that account for her change of feeling about Simon? He is so practical.

⌒

Simon and Juliana have arrived with David in tow. How well he looks, showered and ruddy and surprisingly dressed in tropical white. Plainly, he, who rarely deigns to wear a necktie, has taken pains to rise to the occasion. He positively shines and is all smiles despite the rigors of flight. Perhaps his mood is so high because Juliana teases him about the fine dinner they're going to have, tells him that even he can't match it. Or perhaps his mood is so high at the simple rare pleasure of all of them being together in this special place.

Combed, scrubbed, and scented as the queen's corgis, the four of them step into the neon night. The hot colors blink and flash like mutant fireflies, but they are no match for Mei-ling: the sparkle and glitter of the diamonds that adorn her ears, throat, and wrist, the shimmer of lavender silk that cascades from her neck to her ankles along the curves of her still-slim torso. Simon, innocent, suddenly subdued, had whispered when he first saw her emerge from her room, "You look beautiful." Mei-ling had heard that tone before. It was not one young men used to compliment their beloved's mother. No, it was something else entirely, and it rather pleased her.

Juliana, attractive in an abstract turquoise-and-purple print and a gold choker and earrings that Mei-ling had given her when she graduated from college, had said in a voice perhaps a shade too tight for humor, "Before we start admiring each other all night, we'd better be going or we'll be late."

The Pearl River Palace is filled but not full when they step out of the teak-paneled elevator that whisked them to the panoramic top floor of one of Hong Kong's newest skyscrapers. Through the windows high above the city, the lights of Kowloon brighten the night, blinking and sparkling across the river. The harmonious elegance of the restaurant, suggesting an aesthetic impulse beyond the abundance of mere money that went into the making of it, takes Mei-ling by surprise. She says, "There was nothing so beautiful as this when I lived here. Why on earth does an investor build such a palace if they're so afraid of the Communists taking over?"

Simon, thoughtful, answers: "It may not seem to make sense, but there's so much money here that they keep on spending and hoping for the best, and you'd be surprised at how many of the Communists have a taste for luxury and the money to go with it. There was a scandal a few years ago when some Party officials in the south actually had gold dust sprinkled on their food. The optimists here in Hong Kong say that things will go on as before, at least for business. Just as Deng promised. The leaders in Beijing don't want to kill the golden goose."

Mei-ling laughs dryly. She brushes her hand across her throat. The hard surface of the diamonds is cool against her fingertips. How nice to have them out of the vault, where she can enjoy them, be seen in them. There are only a few such occasions in Montreal; in Hong Kong everyone seems to glitter . . . or try to. She understands a taste for pleasure and luxury, how it warms the blood, how it warmed her blood when she thought it frozen forever.

The Pearl River Palace doesn't shriek like most of Hong Kong; it speaks softly, a subtle fantasy of old and new China: pale shantung walls, a high graduated ceiling of teak beams and brass lanterns, burnished brick-colored floors set in hexagonal patterns, copies of Ming jardinieres sprouting wide-spreading jade trees and tall bamboo, generously cushioned rattan chairs and tables with legs shaped like elephant tusks. Mei-ling stares at them. Can they be elephant tusks?

An obsequious host in black tie shows them to their table, nodding and welcoming them all the way across the floor. They are seated at a round table set for four. A porcelain bowl filled with floating candles and baby orchids the color of apricots is at the center. Mei-ling, having some small notion of the price of luxury in Hong Kong, asks, "Have you ever eaten here before?"

"No, Mother, of course not. We wanted you to see how much things have changed since you left. All the important people eat here. It's the finest new restaurant in Hong Kong. Everyone says so."

Simon laughs. "Everyone who can afford it anyway. We won't be coming back often, even with both of us earning salaries of foreign nationals."

David chimes in: "I say we stop talking about money and start talking about food." He nods toward Juliana. "We'll see if they can best the master."

Juliana laughs. "I'm afraid you've met your match, Dad."

Mei-ling says nothing. She looks around the room. Several of the women wear jewels that rival her own and silks that would be the envy of a Parisian couturier. Most of the patrons are Chinese, but there are numerous Europeans and a sprinkling of other Asians and a number of mixed parties as well. So different from the rarely crossed custom of separation she remembers . . . that Dirk Verhoeven used to enjoy thumbing his nose at by bringing her to the better places . . . preening himself . . . showing her off. Several of the tables are occupied exclusively by men, some obviously in the colony for a few days business, others simply enjoying the prerogatives of the East.

"I ordered in advance," Simon says. "My boss told me a few things we shouldn't miss."

Mei-ling sips her water. "Very good. I won't have to make any decisions." She points a playful finger at Simon. "And I hold you responsible if the meal doesn't live up to its reputation."

"Not fair. Not fair."

"Well, nothing is. It's time you learned that, young man." Then, remembering Juliana's doubts, she would like to take the words back.

A steward brings the wine and fills their glasses. David says, "I would like to propose a toast." He raises his glass and nods toward Juliana. "To my daughter and her future." He turns to Simon. "And to yours, Simon."

Juliana sips her wine, leans toward David, and kisses him lightly on the cheek. "Thank you. I'm so glad you're here."

Just as their waiter arrives with a platter of scallion pancakes and morsels of crab and oyster in their own tiny fried noodle baskets, just as a flurry of servers spreads plates and dishes of sauce before them, a new party of diners is led to a nearby table.

Mei-ling says, "I'm not used to seeing so many men dining together in the evening. Except for bachelor parties once in a while, it's uncommon at home." *Home,* she notes, as the word leaves her lips. Montreal is her home now. She is only visiting.

"These don't look like bachelors to me," Juliana says softly. "Too old and stiff. I think they may be officials from the mainland."

"Oh," Mei-ling says, dropping her eyes unintentionally.

Simon picks up his chopsticks. "I don't know about you, but I'm ready to eat and I'm very hungry."

"I still remember my first meal in Hong Kong," Mei-ling says. "Dumplings and crabs, but I scarcely knew what I was eating. I felt as if I might never find food again."

Juliana stares at her. "You never told me that."

"You were too young . . . and it was a time I didn't enjoy remembering."

"But you met my father here."

David pauses with his chopsticks in midair and a tiny pancake falls to his plate. Juliana, noticing, reaches for his free hand, says, ". . . the first one, Dad, not the best. It's natural to be curious."

Mei-ling says, "It was Dirk Verhoeven who bought the food for us . . . me and your grandmother. I don't know how, but he knew we had escaped from the mainland. And he knew we were down on our luck. Anyone could see that." She laughs. "To put it mildly."

"So he helped you out," Juliana says. "I'm glad."

Simon breaks in. "My father said that Red agents were coming over the border back then to stir up trouble. There were big riots in 1967. The British got the message and started to improve things for the local Chinese."

"My mother and I escaped from the mainland in 1968," Mei-ling says, "and I can assure you we were anything but agents

. . . though my parents had been Communists. They could have stayed in England, but they went back in 1949 to help reconstruct the country. They had no way of knowing they were ruining their lives and sealing my father's doom. They thought they were building a new China."

"How did you live when you got here if you were too poor to afford food?" Juliana asks.

"My mother sold her last piece of the family jade, and Dirk Verhoeven gave my mother work and found a school for me."

Juliana's eyes form a question, but Mei-ling continues quickly. "Your grandmother was desperate to escape from China. The country was insane, completely insane at the time of the Cultural Revolution. You can't imagine it . . . the cruelty . . . the humiliation and the suffering. My parents and millions of others were cast into darkness by the country they served with such devotion. And people were hungry. Starving." Taken aback by the heat of memories long held in check, Mei-ling returns to more neutral ground. "But except for having found safety for a while, your grandmother thought Hong Kong a terrible place."

"In heaven's name, why?" Simon exclaims. "My parents thought it was the end of the world when we decided to leave. We never would have if it weren't for the takeover being on its way."

The waiter comes over to refill their glasses and remove their plates. Mei-ling continues: "But your parents were rich and looked to the future. My mother, unlike myself"—she smiles wryly—"did not fear poverty if her ideals could remain unsullied. She rather welcomed it as the outward sign of her inner goodness." Mei-ling pauses. "But even she had to eat." She looks down. "And there was me to provide for. And there's so much you can never understand. At times I thought happiness would be impossible." She looks at Simon and Juliana soberly. "The world disappoints. You should marry and have children. Family is everything."

Juliana looks at her wide-eyed. "Don't rush things so, Mother. I'm young. I love my career. I wouldn't give it up for anything. Besides, there's so much I want to do . . . so much I want to learn more about. I hardly know myself."

Simon, silent, sips his wine, looks down at his serving plate, studies the plumed birds on the rim.

Mei-ling sets her glass on the table. "I spoke out of turn,

Juliana. It's your life to do with what you think best. You and Simon both. I just want you to be happy."

David, less ebullient than earlier, says simply, "We both do."

"But I'm already happy," Juliana says, "as happy as I can be." She brings her face close to Mei-ling. "I'm not afraid, Mother. I don't need anything to cling to. If I want a child . . ." She pauses. "If Simon and I want a child, well, then, we'll have one. If not, we won't."

Just then the waiter brings two more platters. Juliana looks at Simon, asks warily, "What are these?"

"Taste them. Don't worry. I'm not passing off any snakes or dogs." He turns to Mei-ling. "Your daughter, madam, is afraid of perfectly good Chinese dishes. I keep telling her that if she wants to stay here for a while and go back and forth to China for her work, she'll have to be more flexible, especially her taste buds."

Mei-ling's eyes narrow. She looks at Juliana. "You never mentioned that. Are you thinking of staying here for a long time?"

Juliana says, "At least for a few years. If things go well and the Communists keep their word about leaving the Hong Kong economy alone for fifty years, the opportunity is too good to pass up. I'm qualified in international law, I speak Cantonese and Mandarin passably well, not to mention English and French. I'll be in demand. It's the chance of a lifetime. You wouldn't want me to pass it up, would you?"

David breaks the silence that follows. Looking at Mei-ling, he says, "You can't blame her. China's the place to be now."

Both pleading and consoling, Juliana says, "Mother, there's something for me in China, not just Hong Kong. It's important for me to find it."

The men at the nearby table are growing a little boisterous. Glass after glass is raised in a toast. Their Mandarin speech, familiar now in the Cantonese colony, is quite loud. Other diners glance toward their table, a few frown slightly, but nobody complains. Loud sounds are part of the scenery in Hong Kong.

Simon looks toward them. "They may be part of the transition team from Beijing. So many of them are here now. Most are businesslike, but some have an arrogance about them that can be unpleasant."

Juliana, lowering her voice, perhaps in subconscious anticipation of a new kind of rule, says, "Communists or not, lots of them have become enormously wealthy. They're up to their elbows in private *and* government enterprises. A few are as greedy and corrupt as any robber barons. There's a fellow who used to be a Red Guard who got as rich as Croesus in the Shanghai stock market. He's called Millions Yang, and ordinary mortals beg him for tips. Some of the better Party leaders in China are worried about the corruption that has come along with the economic boom. A few of the leaders have been sacked because they were so greedy, even the mayor of Beijing. But it may not help. The children of the Party leaders are all in on it. A few are doing big business in Hong Kong . . . they're seen in all the expensive restaurants. The head of the legal department told me all about it. Laws bend for people in power . . . unless their powerful enemies want them out."

Simon points discreetly with his chopsticks. "You see that table with seven of them, three on each side and one at the head of the table. The one at the head of the table facing us is the top dog and the ones farthest away from him are the least high up. It's easy to tell because of the seating arrangement. They always do things that way. Unfortunately, very predictable."

Mei-ling looks at the top dog and decides that he is not a very appetizing fellow, that she would do better to pay more attention to the succulent food before it grows cold. She watches David nibble away at some marvelous morsel, catches his pleasure. It's good that he's here. Then she steals another look at the top dog . . . the plumpness of his earlobes, fat as bird's eggs, the pitted cheeks, the scowl under his smile. He has a familiar look to him. A sickening sensation takes hold of her. "I know that man," she hisses, her mouth suddenly dry.

Simon and Juliana and David stare as Mei-ling's expression hardens into glass. In a voice dry as sand, she says, "He punched me to the ground." Her face burns in memory of the coiled fist as it struck her almost thirty years before. She turns to Juliana: "It was his kind that hounded your grandfather to death. Of course, it was the higher-ups who were really responsible, Mao and his detestable wife."

Mei-ling looks toward the man again. His chopsticks fly as he gobbles delectable tidbits. He reminds her of a voracious animal gnawing disgustingly at its prey. "Anyone who got in their way suffered," she says, choking out the words, "people like my mother and father . . . even Mao's comrades of a lifetime who had sacrificed everything for the people of China. Before she died my mother told me more than I could bear to know." Mei-ling waves a pointed index finger back and forth at Simon and Juliana. "It was the best of the Communists who died or lost their minds or their hearts . . . unless they found a hiding place till the storm subsided. Even then, many languished in prison or some remote exile for years afterward." Mei-ling smiles wanly. "My mother hated Hong Kong for its greedy, capitalist ways." She nods toward the gobbling man with chopsticks in his hand. "What would she think now seeing this piggish official stuffing himself with food that costs more than a peasant family earns in a year?"

Juliana asks, "How can you be sure it's him after so long?"

"Some things are too ugly to forget. He's one of them." Contempt creeps into her voice. "Just look at him, that overfed man, that man of such importance in the world, probably rich and expecting to become much, much richer. That hypocrite accused others of being capitalist roaders. They were imprisoned or worse. Now look at him." She sucks in her cheeks and purses her lips. "He has the blood of his betters on his hands. And there's nothing to be done about it." She pauses. "The irony, of course, is that despite the bloody past, and the past is always bloody, the people of China are better off than before. There's no denying it. But it is hard for me to swallow, seeing this fellow here."

The waiter comes to the table, removes their plates, and brings fresh ones for the next course. He notices how much food remains on Mei-ling's plate. "Is everything all right, madam?"

"Fine, fine. Thank you."

Simon and Juliana look somber. David, not knowing what else to do, pats Mei-ling's hand. She does not want to ruin their evening. She forces a smile. "We should not let that man spoil our reunion. He's done enough damage already." She turns toward the new platter being set before them. "Ah," she says, "what delightful thing have we here?"

The three of them go through their meal, eating, commenting on the food, trying to make conversation, but the festive spirit has evaporated. Coarse jokes in Mandarin drift over from the nearby table that their eyes try to avoid. Mei-ling must force herself to eat so that the others will be able to enjoy their food. As soon as they finish, she says, "This was wonderful, but I still seem to be suffering from jet lag. We should go."

In the marble-floored entryway, where Simon and David are still weighing the quality of the meal and its cost, Mei-ling says to Juliana, "I seem to have forgotten something. I'll be back in a moment." Without waiting for her to respond, Mei-ling strides across the long expanse of dining room floor as if she is returning to their table. But she turns slightly and heads to a nearby table instead, toward the men from Beijing. Small-statured as ever, but impressive in her jewels and silk, she stands in front of the man at the head, the top dog. "Comrade," she says in a low voice, smiling slightly, not wanting to attract attention, "do you remember me?"

Startled, slightly befuddled with drink, the man leans back. He smiles at her, pleased to have the attention of a beautiful woman. "Madam?"

"It was a long time ago . . . when we were together in the countryside . . . the Red Guards." She watches as an uneasy expression forms on his face. The other men are silent, watching them both. Their shark fin soup cools in their bowls. "Ah," she says, "perhaps you do remember."

"No. I don't know who you are, madam."

"Perhaps your memory is less sharp than mine."

"It was a long time ago." He sees from her change of expression that something is wrong. He is quickly sober and wary. "What do you want of me?"

"Let me see your ear."

He rears back. "What is this? Tell me what you want."

"Don't be afraid. I just want to renew our acquaintance. I will help you remember." Before he knows what is happening, she grasps the man's jacket as if she would embrace him and leans over as if to whisper in his ear. Instead, she opens her mouth and bites down hard on his earlobe till her teeth draw blood. Quickly, she spits her bloodstained saliva into his shark fin soup.

He struggles to stifle the cry he would utter. Too stunned to move, the other men remain in their seats. The seconds stretch like rubber bands. Then he slaps Mei-ling very hard, hard enough to leave the imprint of his fingers on her cheek. She wavers slightly but does not fall to the floor.

Suddenly, David is there, breathing heavily, pushing the very important man from Beijing back, forcing him into his seat, grasping Mei-ling's shoulders and pulling her away from the table. "It's not worth it," he says, trying to calm her. "Put it behind you. Let's get out of here."

He pulls her away. She is weeping. Diners stare. The head man holds a napkin to his ear. Several members of the staff are murmuring apologies to their honored guests from Beijing. Mei-ling and David are away from the table by now, but words fly back to them ... *unbalanced* ... *please forgive* ... *sorry for your trouble.*

Simon and Juliana, hardly able to take in all that has happened so quickly, wait anxiously at the entrance as David half carries Mei-ling toward them. Finally, more steady on her feet, more herself again, Mei-ling says, "They should be reminded, especially now, when they are riding high, that their victims are not forgotten."

The lapel of David's white suit is smeared with the red and black of Mei-ling's lipstick and eye makeup. Simon has the elevator waiting. As the door closes behind them, Juliana embraces her mother. "You'll have to tell me about what happened back in China. Don't try to protect me from everything bad in the world. It doesn't work." Meaning to console, but unable to restrain the note of reproach in her voice, Juliana says, "Don't keep me a stranger to the dark parts of your life. It's like not knowing you at all."

In the street, they stand together waiting for a taxi to take them home. A little behind them, unnoticed but watching, is one of the men who had been sitting farthest from the top dog, one of Beijing's many eyes and ears in the colony during the remaining few weeks till the transfer of power is complete. This lesser official, a man in his mid-thirties who was a small child when Mei-ling and Emma fled, is probably quite a decent fellow—educated, intelligent, fluent in several languages, devoted to his only son, loyal to his country—whose job at the moment is to learn all he can about this audacious, half-crazed woman who attacked his chief. Imagine ... biting his ear till she drew blood.

That night, David, who has insisted that Mei-ling take a sedative, cannot sleep himself. He lies awake thinking, remembering Mei-ling's words to him not long after they were first married, when everything had still been right between them: "You're just like my father . . . always trying to improve things. Thinking you can make things perfect. Life can never be perfect." She'd wagged her finger at him and laughed. "You'll come to a bad end."

Had he? With her? Leaving like that. Breaking up the family. He certainly hadn't been at his best. Who was he to judge her, he tells himself for the thousandth time, when he hadn't been in her shoes, nothing like it, when his most dangerous times had been child's play compared to her easiest? Plenty of men would have been turned on by a story like Mei-ling's, wanted to console her *and* wanted to fuck her. He, deluded fool, couldn't get it up with her once he found out. Well, he decides, certain, *I'm over it now.* How fucking complicated everything is. He can't help smiling to himself. How complicated fucking is. He moves restlessly, wishes he could sleep. But he's not even drowsy. His mind wanders to Juliana, how she's pushing for more and more about the past. He winces. *God,* he tells himself, *I hope she never finds out.*

⌒

The immigration official at the Hunghom KCR Station in Kowloon, scanning and stamping documents in his own good time, gives only a cursory glance at the endless stream of passengers he is processing. Mei-ling and David are only a few feet from him. David, near fifty, is still a reed of a man, white-haired and tan-skinned, almost handsome now in a trim, leathery way. He is irritated by the pace, the heat, the pushy crowd, the grating sounds of Cantonese surrounding him, the vigilance against pickpockets and thieves Simon drilled into him. He says, "Well, the Chinese invented bureaucracy. I suppose we'll have to get used to it." He glances at the armed guards in their uniforms. "And to them too. It'll probably be worse over the border."

"Keep your voice down," Mei-ling whispers. "Don't assume they can't understand. I'm sure the security people have English speakers stationed all around. This may not be China yet, but everything is in place. There's no point giving needless offense."

He lowers his voice and leans his face toward her. "You're frightened, aren't you. Are you sure you want to go through with this trip? It's not too late to cancel." He tries to keep his voice neutral when he says this, but missing out on China once he'd come this far would be a terrible disappointment. Still, since that awful scene at the Pearl River Palace, she seems so fragile, so unlike her usual controlled and capable self.

"I wouldn't consider canceling." Mei-ling's voice is low and not very steady. She speaks as close to David's ear as possible without appearing to tell secrets. "This is the best time to go. Even if Beijing keeps its word and allows Hong Kong to remain more or less free, there's no telling what will happen in the future if there's a power struggle in the Party or an economic failure. The Communists won't make any trouble this close to the takeover, but afterward, who knows? I was born in China. To them I'm Chinese forever. What if they were to detain me for any reason?"

"Easy now, no need for paranoia. You're a Canadian citizen with a Canadian passport."

"Not necessarily to them."

The line moves forward. The immigration official reaches for Mei-ling's passport. Her hand shakes a little as she pushes it toward him. He studies it, pauses at her name—Mei-ling Wang Levy—looks up at her, looks at David standing slightly behind her, frowns, drums his finger, flips the pages back and forth as if he is looking for something that is missing. He shuffles through some cards, picks up a pencil, and makes a note. Has he done this with others? Mei-ling can't remember. Finally he stamps the passport and shoves it toward her. He grunts in David's direction and extends his arm.

Once inside the express train that will whisk them over the border to Guangzhou in only two and a half hours, first-class, Mei-ling breathes more easily. She manages to smile. "I feel foolish being so upset there."

"Not hard to understand why. Borders make everyone nervous. You have more reason than most."

She looks around at the pleasantly upholstered train. "It wasn't like this when my mother and I came through. The truth is, I don't remember the details all that much. I suppose Dr. Freud would say that I'm repressing a horrible memory. He's probably right."

David puts his arm around her shoulder, squeezes. "Don't push yourself to remember. That's not what we're here for."

A bewildered look crosses her face. "What *are* we here for?"

He looks at her closely: thin traces of age beginning to make their mark, luminous green jade earrings fastened like medals to her delicate lobes . . . for wounds suffered . . . for bravery . . . for survival. David tries to think of comforting words that will ring true. "To see a hunk of the new China for ourselves. Canada and the U.S. aren't the new world anymore. Asia is. And maybe, just maybe, you can exorcise a few demons." He pauses. "And maybe we can get to know each other almost as well as we used to. It's not too late."

She rewards him with half an enigmatic smile and looks out the window.

Once the train begins to move, David and Mei-ling, alternately transfixed by the landscape and absorbed in each other, generally ignore the passengers, though it's hard to ignore the cigarette smoke that fills the car. David says, "I never knew the Chinese were such smokers. It's a miracle any of them live past forty."

"They say Deng smoked three packs a day into his nineties."

"Tough old birds, the Long March survivors. I guess if they got through that, they could get through anything."

Mei-ling brightens, teases lightly. "You'll take some adjusting to China. Wait till your first serving of monkey brains. It's a great delicacy in this region." Her eyes widen in mock curiosity. "Will that be a problem for you?"

"Don't try scare tactics. If I close my eyes, it's bound to taste like chicken liver. I like chicken liver."

The express doesn't stop when it passes through the Lo Wu border crossing as it leaves Hong Kong, but the track bisects the center of Shenzen City so that they know they are across the border. David leans forward to peer out the window. "Can this really be the mainland? It's hard to tell the difference from Hong Kong. The place is busting out with skyscrapers. It's unreal."

"And all in a few years. It's amazing what Chinese can do once their energy is let loose," Mei-ling says, an oblique note of pride creeping into her voice. "Back in 1980 Deng made Shenzen the first Special Economic Zone and allowed private business. It's been a fantastic success. Buildings and companies sprouted like mushrooms. People poured in from all over the country. Lots of foreign business investment too, not just Hong Kong. They even have a big McDonald's. Simon and Juliana say it's one of the biggest tourist attractions . . . people come from all over China."

"How long can it keep up?"

"Nobody knows for sure. Simon told me that the investors are nervous because of overbuilding and the power struggles in Beijing. He says it's all like a big gambling casino where nobody knows if the game is fixed, but they play anyway because they love to gamble and the stakes are so high."

Construction cranes loom like dinosaurs along the route out of Shenzen City as the train heads north toward Guangzhou. Tall commercial and residential towers compete with low-slung factories belching smoke. Dilapidated shacks stand cheek by jowl with startlingly large homes. David lets out a long, low whistle. "No zoning here. They'll live to regret it."

A pervasive drabness takes over soon enough, helped along by a haze of grainy pollutants suspended in the heavy air. But the clogged atmosphere is electrically charged: people appear along the rail line, standing, running, bicycling. Children wave at them as the train speeds through the countryside like a camera clicking its shutter, capturing the moment before it changes forever.

An isolated settlement appears here and there along the tracks, ragged and poor: wooden carts being pulled by callused hands, pigs, ducks, toddlers and teenagers, whole families, all jumbled together in the coarse grass of the village as they might have been a century before. But not exactly. Here and there, from what seems only a rude shack, a television antenna raises its long neck. A truck kicks up a cloud of dust. Mei-ling and David decide between them that some young boy or girl is sitting at a computer inside the red-flagged school building, marching double-time on electronic feet into the twenty-first century.

To the west as they near Guangzhou, a broad green swath of fields and low-lying hills appears in the distance. "Rice," Mei-ling says.

David cranes his neck. He has never seen rice growing except in photographs or paintings. "It looks like the pictures I've seen, but how can you tell?"

"I remember," Mei-ling says.

"In Hong Kong, I more or less knew what to expect . . . greed and glitz and hot-shot architecture . . . fun and profit. But this is different. I feel as if we're in a high-speed time machine. We can go back centuries . . . but any minute someone in a space suit could jump on board."

A certain elation, only slightly tainted by anxiety, takes over between them: excitement about their trip, two whole weeks . . . then, afterward, Hong Kong for the great occasion . . . the British chapter sinking into imperial history. Amazing luck, David thinks, Juliana and Simon taking jobs here. Maybe not only luck. The pull of home . . . even a home Juliana never saw, that can never be fully hers any more than Israel will ever be his. Yet it's there inside his head like a long-lost uncle, the way a piece of China must be inside hers. Secretly, he is happy she's had second thoughts about Simon . . . a nice enough guy and very clever . . . but he doesn't think much past his career. Soul, David thinks. He doesn't have much and Juliana has it to spare.

David looks at his watch. "We'll be there soon."

"It makes me dizzy to see how much has changed," Mei-ling says. And all I've seen so far is through the windows of the train."

Guangzhou

〜

DAVID AND MEI-LING are in their room at the White Swan Hotel on Shamian Island—not so much a true island as an appendage to Guangzhou proper to which it is connected by bridges. In the aftermath of the Opium Wars, the British and French had extracted commercial concessions from the emperor. Fearing and loathing contamination by foreign devils, he required them to build their warehouses and trading posts across a narrow channel of water on this small spit of sand just barely detached from the mainland.

But Shamian Island is larger than it was then. In the new China the very land under David's and Mei-ling's feet has been reclaimed from the sea by one of the mammoth construction projects that have transformed the landscape in this part of the world. It's as if the Chinese—on the mainland, in Hong Kong, in Taiwan, in Singapore—are determined to prove themselves not merely equal but superior to the European powers that had humiliated them a century and a half earlier.

Mei-ling and David have requested and been given a room on a high floor with a view of the river. Thirty-three stories up, their room is large and light and the appointments are luxurious: fine woods, rich fabrics, marble and tile fittings. The new China with a vengeance. "I can't decide if I like this or not," David says. "It's so opulent. Are you sure we're in China and not on some movie set? I thought only hotels in Las Vegas sported waterfalls and jungles of foliage in the lobby."

Mei-ling, no stranger to the seductions of luxury, yet not in thrall to them, scans the room with its sumptuous furnishings and carpets and wall hangings. "I wonder what my parents would think of all this? Of course, it's mainly for foreigners and higher-ups."

David says, "Isn't that always the way? Who stays at the swank hotels in London or Paris? Or New York for that matter? The peasants?"

Having had a chance to wash and change from their travel clothes into loose cotton robes, a refreshed Mei-ling and David step out to the terrace to take in the vast sweep of the Pearl River. They look down at a steady traffic of freighters and ferries and sampans and tankers that navigate the ancient maritime trade route. The June air is sultry, yet a light breeze plays around them at this height and cools them a little. The ageless gray river that has seen so much stretches into the distance. Mei-ling says, "It will go on forever . . . long after we're gone."

David runs his arm down her back. "Don't rush us." A sudden erotic current springs up between them. Like adolescents, they rush: kissing, touching, fondling, moaning, leaning against the terrace wall for balance, finally moving into each other. When it is over, they don't speak for a while, just stand there, moist and spent and years younger than they thought. At least for a little while.

⌒

Morning. "It's time to go to work," David says. "Are we tourists or aren't we?"

David is holding a map and guide with their destinations marked, but Mei-ling holds back. "Let's just stroll along the waterfront for a while and look at a few of the old places before they disappear."

They make their way through ancient streets and alleys and flyblown buildings that once were rife with the opium trade and sinister underworld wars. Now ordinary shoppers pick among stalls and baskets filled with ordinary household goods. David picks up a blue-and-white plate decorated with a tree and a little footbridge over a river. He smiles in recognition. "My grandmother had a whole set of these."

"It's old Canton china. They shipped it all over the world. It was a thriving trade. I saw some in Montreal."

His smile of recognition dissolves into a more somber expression. Without looking directly at Mei-ling, David says, "See, even when I was a kid in the Bronx and liked to eat off these pretty plates, you were part of my destiny. Then in Montreal, where neither of us ever imagined we'd be. Now here."

Mei-ling begins to walk toward the next stall. He grabs her arm and holds on. "Look, we never talked about it after I was jerk enough to leave, when I should have tried at least to work it out, and this sure isn't the place, but I'm sorry. I'm really sorry. We *are* meant to be together. It's crazy to go on like this . . . as if we're some kind of distant relatives who hop into the sack every once in a while. I want to be really married again." He relaxes his grip on her arm. "Hell, we may be grandparents one of these days whether or not Juliana marries Simon."

Mei-ling walks ahead slowly, thinking. Once, these words would have been like honey. Now she is not certain. Why *not* see each other only once in a while? Solitude, the other side of loneliness, has become a pleasant companion. Plum Blossom and her financial investments keep her busy . . . too busy. At times they're a bit of a strain. And poetry, the love of her youth, begins to form words on paper again. She is secure . . . wealthy . . . content. Why risk all that for the whirlpool of romantic love . . . old love at that? Still? A warmth not from the sun turns her cheeks rosy. He's the only man she's ever loved. He still is. There is no denying it.

"Aren't you going to say anything?"

"Not now and not here," she says, more troubled than she wants to be. "Guangzhou won't wait for us, and everything else will. It has for years. Let's go."

The two of them pick their way through the stalls quietly. At the corner of one of the alleys, a man squats in the street with a straw basket. They are about to pass by, when Mei-ling says, "Stop." She bends down and picks up a small statuette with what seems to be a suction device on the bottom. She shows it to David. "Look."

"It's a plastic Mao."

"The very one."

"What is it?"

She speaks to the vendor in Cantonese and breaks into a sardonic smile. "He says that if we put it on the dashboard of our car, it will prevent accidents and bring us good luck."

"You mean like the saints back home. This has got to be a joke."

"Not at all. He means it. He says that if I'm interested, he can find some Mao buttons left over from the Cultural Revolution. He says the real ones are very popular souvenirs, so they're more expensive than the imitations."

"After all that blood and suffering? It's obscene."

"No. It's China. Now I know I've come home."

"Put it down and let's get out of here. I want to see Sun Yatsen's monument. That's China."

"They both are." She fondles the plastic figurine and speaks to the squatting entrepreneur. Then she fishes some money out of her purse and gives it to him.

"You're not actually buying that thing?"

She drops the plastic Mao into her purse.

"Why not, for a keepsake? Wasn't it Mao who determined the course of my life? In truth, it was he who brought us together."

David frowns. "I guess it depends on how you choose to look at it. Let's get a cab or a bus or something to the monument. I want to get out of here."

A young woman walks up to them and speaks in English very slowly. "I hope that you not consider bad manner for interrupting. I hear you standing the blue-and-white plates. Perhaps would you be kind to speak English with me. For my practice."

Mei-ling shrinks back a little, doesn't answer immediately. Who is this person who undoubtedly was watching as she bought the little Mao?

The young woman's face is round and she wears large glasses with dark hornrims that give her a studious look, though she seems older than a student. Her clothes are very plain, a dark blue dress with a white collar, the dress of a nun or a modern-day Puritan, and the little black canvas shoes that can be found in discount shoe stores all over Montreal. She smiles eagerly, as if she is eager to be a friend.

David says, "Sure. What do you want to talk about?"

"Where you are from?"

"Canada."

"Very cold, like Beijing. This pretty lady you marry?"

"She is my wife."

"Nice. Chinese wife." She turns to Mei-ling. "Very nice Canada husband."

Mei-ling joins in. "Are you married?"

She looks surprised. "Me marry? No."

"What work do you do?"

"I work at bank. My name Yulin. I need make better English. More business now. I work higher up if English better."

"That's very nice," David says, "Good luck. We are going now to visit the Sun Yat-sen monument."

She smiles, evidently pleased. "Excellent," she says . . . a good word mastered. Yulin pinches Mei-ling's sleeve. "Wait. I show interesting thing first. It very near here. Famous Qingping Market. Very good. People have own business. Chairman Deng make it open in—" She gropes for what she is trying to say but finally resorts to a pencil and paper on which she writes *1979.* "Very big success. All people come see and buy."

Mei-ling and David look at each other. Mei-ling shrugs. David says, "Okay." Privately, he wonders if she expects to be paid for showing them around. How much?

Outside the enormous market, crowds of people mill around hunting for bargains at the small food stalls that dot the perimeter, but Yulin hurries them inside to an orderly pandemonium.

"Wow, look at this." David picks up a string of dried fungi and smells it. "Earthy. Nothing like it in Chinatown. Do you think we could take some home?"

"Ah," Mei-ling says, reaching for a bundle of dried golden curlicues, "you might want to try these as well."

He studies them, breaks into a grin. "Scorpions. Just the thing."

The market is alive with the screeches, slithers, barks, howls, and cries of live monkeys and owls and pigeons and snakes and dogs. They fuss in their cages while waiting to become someone's dinner. Several live carp frolic in a large tub of water as if it were a mountain lake.

"Hey," David says, turning to Mei-ling, "my grandmother had one of those swimming in the bathtub at home when I was a kid. Once a year before Passover."

"I thought you would find all this disgusting."

"It is in a way . . . the direct connection between you and the animal. But, hey, people fish and hunt and raise animals for slaughter. Besides, nobody's forcing me to eat monkey or dog." He looks around. "People here look healthy enough. It's all cultural when you think about it. What's the difference meatwise between a dog and pig? It's all what you're used to inside your head."

Yet David shrinks from the sight of bundles of limp frogs and blue-skinned poultry dripping warm blood to the floor. For the first time he remembers without pleasure the spicily fragrant glazed ducks hanging in the windows of New York's Chinatown markets.

"Is this what it was like when you were a kid?" he asks Mei-ling.

Her eyes jump from one place to another. "Nothing like it. I never saw such plenty in China . . . all this food and so many people who can afford it. It's so different from what I left behind. Even the people are different." She runs her eyes over the crowd of eager shoppers fingering and haggling. "Their clothing is better . . . they seem more confident."

Yulin smiles broadly. "China now rich. Plenty food to eat. Deng change everything. More for people."

David speaks slowly so that Yulin can follow what he is trying to say. "But what about the government . . . shooting (he thinks she will understand) . . . the students who were demonstrating for democracy? . . . putting people in prison who disagree with them?"

Yulin strains for the words, frowns, tries. "Tiananmen Square. I am student then. I protest . . . in Guangzhou." She shakes her head. "No good. Mistake. I think"—she struggles with the difficult word, a new one for people accustomed to millennia of Confucian morality and hierarchy—"democracy . . . no good for China now. Good food, good house, good health, good school . . . people happy . . . we make better now . . . maybe later . . . democracy." She shakes her head back and forth, as if she is a teacher impressing her students with what they must not do. "China and America not same. America sad ten people die for protest . . . China sad ten million die for hunger." As if the answer is self-evident, she asks them, "Who *more* correct?"

Mei-ling speaks to Yulin in Cantonese. "I think we should go outside now. We have other things to see and don't have very much time in Guangzhou."

Yulin says, "It is good you remember your language."

"When I was a child in Nanjing, I spoke Mandarin."

Yulin does not ask any questions such a confidence might inspire, just remarks neutrally, "Your Cantonese sounds like Hong Kong." She walks ahead of them, erect, sure of herself.

Mei-ling whispers to David, "I'm probably paranoid, but I wouldn't be surprised to find out that she's been assigned to us. Let's try to leave her here."

"Okay, but you probably are paranoid. It's interesting talking to ordinary people who can speak a little English."

"You tell her we're going on by ourselves. Your white western hair might carry some weight."

When they emerge at the other end of the market, the steamy air is ripe with the smell of decaying fruits and vegetables, but leaving the rank odor of entrails and droppings behind refreshes them both.

David takes Yulin's hand and shakes it. He speaks slowly and warmly. "You have been very kind to show us this. Thank you very much. We are going to take a taxi to Yuexiu Park. You must have many things to do now."

Yulin waves her hand as if her own concerns were nothing. "I take you. We go bus. Very cheap. See Guangzhou good."

When David, tempted by the offer, pauses, Mei-ling steps in and speaks in arm-waving gestures and brusque Cantonese, an exchange that results in Yulin's polite but cool departure.

David says, "I think you hurt her feelings. She was really nice to us."

"If she wasn't being paid for it. Let's find a taxi."

They look around at the jam of traffic and try to spot one.

"Hello, change money." The young boy who stands only inches away is persistent. "Change money, good deal."

To David, Mei-ling says, "Don't do it. Simon warned me about the black market. He said we should have nothing to do with them because they're robbers. We could get into trouble." She raises the palm of her hand toward the boy, and when he doesn't move pushes it toward his chest and dismisses him in a tone David has no trouble understanding. The boy spits and walks away.

"I've never seen you so tough."

"You've never seen me in China before."

"I thought they weren't supposed to have a black market here. Aren't the dealers afraid?"

"This is the south. There's an old Chinese proverb. 'The mountains are high and the emperor is far away.' Beijing leaves Guangzhou alone so long as it makes China rich. Why should they crack down if it's going to hurt them?"

Mei-ling finally succeeds in hailing a taxi. It is not air-conditioned, so they must leave the windows open in order to breathe tolerably. They drive past colonial buildings that retain a little of their former dignity but that have clearly seen better days. After Hong Kong, the entire city seems a little dingy, but it is lively . . . energetic . . . perpetual motion. David says, "I've never seen so many bicycles in my life."

"They look as good as the ones in Amsterdam."

Mei-ling has not been able to speak to the driver once she told him their destination. After that, he'd closed a thick plastic shield that separates the passengers from him. David says, "They have stuff like this in New York cabs to protect the drivers. I didn't expect to find it here."

"Did you notice what's hanging up front?"

David squints through the cloudy plastic and struggles to see a photograph hung just above the windshield, a smiling, benefricent Mao at the height of his power. "Not again," he says. "What is this, the second coming?"

Mei-ling, thoughtful, leans back on the sticky plastic seat. "That may be just what it is . . . the revolution Mao led without the memory of his terrible deeds. Prosperity cleanses everything. Maybe my mother was right after all . . . about the revolution being good in the long run for China . . . even if the making of it was bloody and terrible. That's what history is . . . bloody and terrible."

"That's what Yulin meant . . . if an ordinary person has more to eat and a better life than their parents or grandparents ever had, why should they concern themselves with an abstraction like democracy? Especially in a country that never had it." David squints through the taxi window at some children holding their kites. "Someone young as Yulin doesn't remember the Great Leap Forward or the Cultural Revolution. It's more real to her that she's eating good food and that women can have an education and jobs and a chance to get ahead and that if she gets sick she can get medicine . . . and that she won't have to worry about having her feet bound or becoming a concubine the way they did in the bad old days."

Mei-ling nods. "In my more generous moments, I can persuade myself that the Communists were like the early Christian martyrs . . . they were bearers of a great vision that in its time transformed people in ways we can't fully understand now . . . imperfectly perhaps . . . but better than they were in the past." She laughs. "I'm beginning to sound like my mother."

All the while they talk, they look at the rushing streets. David has not seen her as animated in years, speaking openly, as if the blood vessels to her heart and mind were finally flowing freely. The passionate bride he remembers. Always, after he'd left, long after they'd gotten past the worst of it and lain with each other from time to time, there'd been a tight reserve between them . . . even in bed . . . a too-silent coupling that brought them together only to remind them of what had been lost. But not yesterday. Not today. He puts his arm around her shoulder and pulls her to him, a gesture not sexual, meant only to reassure, as are his words. "After all the blood spilled, I hope you're right. Now if only Deng's heirs don't screw up too much in the next century."

Mei-ling smiles at him, sadly, ruefully. "They will. That's why progress"—she hesitates—"and I do think it exists, takes forever."

"At least we'll be getting an idea of where their heads are when we see what they do with Hong Kong. In my wildest dreams I never thought I'd be lucky enough to watch the close of that chapter . . . not that we'll see too much with all the crowds and the big shots getting the best places. Still, it's the last gasp of imperialism. Between British pomp and Chinese fireworks, it's bound to be quite a show."

Yuexiu Park in Guangzhou is, in the green heat of June, a widespreading oasis in the city—lakes, boats, gardens, sport grounds, a teahouse, an art gallery—too much for a single day according to the guidebook Juliana had thrust upon them. They will have to return another time, but at this hour they ask the taxi driver to drop them off at the Hundred Steps Gate so that they can climb to the Sun Yat-sen monument. The heat and effort of the climb coats their skin with a layer of salty sweat, but they enjoy the height and the fine view of the city. The memorial is a tall obelisk built of granite and marble, serious and unostentatious, fitting for the first president of the Chinese republic.

Mei-ling, though she has never lived in this place, has a proprietary air, assumes the role of guide and teacher. "Many of the early revolutionaries were from the south," she tells David. "After Dr. Sun declared the republic here in 1925, there were bloody massacres when Chiang tried to push the Communists aside and take power for himself. Did you know that Dr. Sun was a Christian? My mother told me that, not my schoolbooks. She seemed proud because some distant relative once taught at a missionary school . . . as if the English did some good here after all."

David looks at the inscription that is engraved in stone. He asks Mei-ling to translate it for him.

She studies it a moment. "These are Dr. Sun's words from his last testament in 1925. 'For forty years I have devoted myself to the cause of national revolution, the object of which is to raise China to a position of independence and equality among nations. The experience of these forty years has convinced me that to attain this goal, the people must be aroused, and that we must associate ourselves in a common struggle with all the people of the world who treat us as equals. The revolution has not yet been successfully completed. Let all our comrades'—she reads on to the closing words—'and abolishing unequal treaties should be carried into effect as soon as possible.' "

"Well, he didn't live to see it," David says, "but the last of the unequal treaties will be history right after we get back to Hong Kong." He thinks a moment. "Only three-quarters of a century from prediction to fulfillment. Not bad as these things go."

Shanghai

EAST AND WEST met and married for a while in the city of Shanghai, an unhappy marriage of unequal partners. Yet the marriage did have lasting benefits. Shanghai is a city of broad boulevards and still grand if faded colonial buildings. Neither the bombs of the Japanese during World War II nor the depredations of the Cultural Revolution a generation later have succeeded in destroying the grandeur of the place or the cosmopolitan air of the people. Around every corner new construction is transforming what was once a colonial jewel into a great Chinese city. Shanghai spreads wide and high, accreting like coral.

Mei-ling and David's first day strolling and exploring is a success, but afterward, back at their hotel, after a shower and change from their sweat-soaked clothing, Mei-ling says, "This heat is making me sick and I can't stand the flies and my stomach feels terrible. There's no point staying in a hotel all the time for the air-conditioning and the bathroom." She is out of sorts, looks into the mirror above the double bamboo chest that holds their clothes. "Look at me. I look like an old woman. Let's not go out to dinner, David. You can eat something in the hotel."

David stands behind her and holds her shoulders. "You do look a little on the crummy side now that you mention it."

She blanches, looks again.

"Only kidding," he says, "you look fine. Whatever you're feeling, it's probably no worse than a mild case of traveler's tummy. You might be able to take something for it. We can find a pharmacy."

But there is no pill or potion that is going to help. Mei-ling has begun to see Shanghai through haunted eyes, hers and Emma's. How weary and frightened they were in this place, scrambling to escape, never raising their voices above a whisper, heads kept low, Emma's hair tucked under her cap, both of them sinking invisibly into the crowds. Mei-ling remembers the clutch of Emma's hand pulling her forward as she furtively bargained away the beautiful family jade for scraps of vegetables and wet, bumpy rides south toward Hong Kong. Mei-ling feels again how their bones ached and the sorrowful eyes, the raspy coughs, the greedy hands of strangers. And the certain knowledge that the least mistake in judgment might doom them.

The hard ball in her throat is what Mei-ling remembers best, how large and painful it was, how difficult to breathe, how impossible to speak, the agony of forcing a bit of broth or a few grains of rice into her throat. And she remembers the fear when her period didn't come, when the silent screams she held inside herself threatened to escape and reveal to Emma everything about the men on the train and what they had done to her. At seventeen, how was she to know that she needn't have worried about the final crushing humiliation of pregnancy by rape, that it was terror and hunger, not a growing fetus, that kept the blood from flowing as it should have?

Still, for David's sake, Mei-ling tries to shake the sense of dread that clings to her. There is so much to see here. They want to shop for paintings and antiques and some of the better reproductions that might sell well at Plum Blossom.

When they do venture out in the morning, the sticky summer heat of the city has already coated everything. The gallery Mei-ling most wants to visit is not where the guidebook said it would be. They wander among the crowds of people, in and out of small shops that display curios and works of art. Mei-ling makes inquiry about particular pieces, especially a marvelous one of two birds fashioned from ivory and mother-of-pearl set in ebony, but the transactions come to nothing. The Shanghai dialect is not difficult for her, but everything else is strange, unyielding, unexpectedly foreign in this most cosmopolitan of Chinese cities.

Can she be imagining it, or is a thin young man in a blue cotton shirt and dark green pants following them? Like the woman in Guangzhou? Mei-ling grimaces. David will think that she is becoming paranoid if she tells him to look at the man. Nevertheless, she says, "David, I keep seeing the same man wherever we go. I think we're being followed."

"Why would anyone care about us? We're no danger to anything."

Mei-ling looks again at the man, who has stopped at a street vendor. "They don't need a good reason. They can invent one. And they're always suspicious of foreigners."

"So you consider yourself a foreigner?"

"What I consider myself isn't important. To them I'm Chinese when it suits them and foreign when they want me to be. I've always known what it is to be both. It's in my blood." She pauses and looks at the man again. He has begun to walk slowly toward them. "Let's move on," she says. "Now I'm sure that woman in Guangzhou was there to keep an eye on us. Like the man here."

"Well, we're not doing anything wrong, so what's there to be afraid of?"

Mei-ling sighs. "Spoken like an innocent American."

"Guilty! But there's no point hanging around worrying about it. There's so much to see, we won't be able to take in half of it in a few days."

A few hours later, they have a lovely lunch in a restaurant blessed with air-conditioning. But when they walk out into the heat and make their way down another street, the man is there again. They both see him. "David," Mei-ling says, "I want to go back to the hotel and I want to go now. Don't try to talk me out of it."

"Sure. But this is ridiculous. Why the hell are they bothering with us? It's loony."

"You may think it's mad, but they may think I'm their enemy. I may have given them reason to think so."

"Now you're being crazy."

"That night at the Pearl River Palace . . . I couldn't control myself . . . I regret it now."

"They didn't know who you were."

She laughs dryly. "They'd have no difficulty finding out if they wanted to. I'm afraid I provided more than enough provocation. An important man isn't likely to forgive or forget someone biting his ear like that . . . twice. We might have been tracked from the time we came here."

"So what should we do?"

"For now, let's just get back to the hotel. I've lost my taste for shopping and sightseeing."

When they try to spot him again on their way back to the hotel, the man in the blue shirt is nowhere to be seen. Even Mei-ling wonders if she was mistaken. But the next morning he is on the street in front of their hotel, perched on a bicycle. He is wearing the same clothing as the day before. He wants to be spotted. They want her to know that she is being watched. Well, she thinks, now they can watch her all the way to the travel office.

Mei-ling could only pick at her dinner the night before and slept fitfully, suffering alarming dreams of her father in the gutter and Dr. Chen waving his bandaged stumps in the air. She woke David early. "We have to leave today."

"We can't. The train tickets aren't until Friday. It would be bloody hell to change them."

"Forget about the train. I want to fly to Hong Kong and do it today. I don't care what it costs."

"Okay, let's pack up and go down to the desk. Maybe they can help us."

But there is no help for them at the desk, only the polite, distant advice to speak to the tourist travel people, who are in charge of all such things. It is not the hotel's business. Once outside, they see the man again.

At the travel office the people behind the desks are neither polite nor efficient. There is a long wait. When Mei-ling finally makes her request for a change in transport, she is told, "This is not possible. You will have to leave Friday on the train."

Mei-ling holds her ground. "But I am not feeling well. I must fly to Hong Kong today. I will return to Canada from there."

Unhelpfully, the man looks over his glasses at her. "I can see from your papers that you are a Canadian citizen. We welcome all our distant family back to the motherland for visits."

"Yes, of course." She tries smiling. "I expect to return many times. But now we want to cancel these train tickets and get on a plane to Hong Kong today." She nods toward David, who is standing beside her.

"Impossible. We don't do things that way here. Besides, there is no way to refund the cost of the train. It is paid in advance. No refund."

"Fine. Please try to get us on a plane? I am not feeling well."

He sneers slightly, almost as if he were smiling. "Shall I call for a doctor?"

Mei-ling waits a moment, her mouth clenched, and does not move. "That won't be necessary," she says.

Then, surprisingly, he really does smile, as if he is suddenly her friend. "I would like to help you, but two tickets, even if there is room on one of the flights to Hong Kong, will be very expensive . . . and extra charges for the fast service required."

Mei-ling thinks she now knows where this is leading. "If there is any extra charge for the service, I'll be glad to pay."

The man behind the desk looks at her again and, realizing that she has understood, nods. "Let me see what I can do. Wait here."

He doesn't return for some time. Mei-ling, increasingly nervous, wondering if she might not be getting them into trouble, rubs her damp palms against her skirt. She and David speak little after she explains what is happening. Finally, after almost half an hour, the door to the back office swings open, the man is smiling. He says, "You'll lose the entire amount on the train tickets, but there is good news for you. I have been able to find space for two on our late-night flight to Hong Kong." He lowers his voice a little. "The charge for this special service is payable in dollars only." He shows Mei-ling a paper on which the flight information and cost of the plane tickets is printed. Penciled in by hand, easily erased later on, is the cost of the "special service."

Well, Mei-ling thinks, reaching into her purse and discreetly folding up a wad of bills before handing them over, the service is worth it. Then, for a fleeting moment, she thinks with sorrow of supplicants the world over who have no money . . . who must accept whatever is imposed on them. She is glad not to be one of them.

Hong Kong

⌒

AIRPORTS ARE FOR rushing and waiting and smiling and waving and weeping. Kai Tak is no exception, especially now that the long-anticipated event has passed into history. The great and the small from near and far are taking wing like homing pigeons, bearing news that electronic magic will have spread to obscure hamlet and huge metropolis alike before they arrive—rendering the words the witnesses have yet to speak obsolete before they are uttered. Still, there will be stories to tell and prophesies to proclaim. It is no small thing, the ceremony of empires, the shift of power and wealth from one to the other. History, the ironist, thumbs its nose at the mighty. Can it have been only a hundred years ago in 1897 that throngs of royalty and dignitaries and industrialists from all the world gathered with the humble and wealthy of London to celebrate the gilded spectacle of Queen Victoria's Diamond Jubilee, to anticipate in innocent optimism the rosy dawn of the twentieth century?

Kai Tak itself, the fourth busiest airport in the world, will soon be relegated to a secondary role in the great drama of political and commercial succession that is unfolding on Asian soil. The new airport being constructed north of Lantau on reclaimed land will be a technological marvel connected to the mainland by still other technological marvels.

But the travelers at Kai Tak in the here and now, however much preoccupied with the future of Hong Kong, are most concerned at the moment with getting where they want to go. Except in a metaphoric sense, this is not true of Simon and Juliana, who are in Hong Kong to stay . . . at least for a time . . . together . . . or apart. Their only reason for suffering the crowds at the airport is to see Mei-ling and David off on their flight to Montreal.

Simon has managed to snag a seat for David on the same plane as Mei-ling, though not in first class; they will have to sit separately. When asked how he accomplished this feat of legerdemain, he had only shrugged and said, "One of the other passengers thought it would be a great idea to visit Singapore for a few extra days." Then he'd smiled. "Fully paid of course."

All of them have been caught up in the pageantry attendant upon the great event—Mei-ling surrendering herself to a surprising surge of pride as the Union Jack was lowered and the red flag raised. A great historic wrong being righted. But they are all ambivalent witnesses to an occasion fraught with fear for many and with uncertainty for most. Even those residents of Hong Kong who favor the transfer—a motley assortment of wealthy businessmen, leftists who look to Beijing, and fervent anti-British Chinese nationalists—hang suspended in a great anticlimax. Nobody, perhaps not even the leaders in Beijing, teetering on their mountaintop, know precisely how the coming months and years are going to unfold . . . though the pundits say and the wishful thinkers believe that where there is money to be made the Chinese are wise enough bury their differences. Having much to lose, the civil servants and the press have held their collective tongues. The more ardent and public advocates of democracy can only wait and wonder if or when a knock will sound at their door. Or they can silently curse the British, who gave too few passports too late in the day, who had waited until the eleventh hour to institute democratic reforms, to discover that not only they but their subject colonials craved a voice in their own destiny.

Mei-ling's and David's baggage has been checked in, their tickets tagged and seats assigned. They have only to pass

through security, where Simon and Juliana cannot follow. Mei-
ling and Juliana cleave together and weep discreetly on each
other's shoulders. "This is silly," Juliana sniffs, "I'll be home for
a visit before you know it. And you can come back anytime you
want. Just hop on a plane. The trip doesn't take that much
longer than traveling by car to Boston."

"It's a world away."

"Not anymore, Mother. Really, it isn't. It's no time at all."

"Take care," Mei-ling says, "not to get into trouble. Take no
chances. You're subject to their law now." She nods toward a
nearby red flag.

"Don't worry. It's not in their interest to mess with Canadians, and they know it. I feel very sorry for the Hong Kong
natives, who have no way out if they need it. Worst case for me
is that I'd have to come home sooner than planned."

Juliana turns toward David and winds her arms around his
neck as she did when she was young, possessing him as if he
were a fervently wished for gift. She whispers into his ear: "Dad,
keep your eye on Mother. She's tough, but with me so far
away . . ." The words trail off.

David draws his fingertips across her moist eyelids. "I love
you, sweetheart. Count on me."

They must hurry now. The plane will be boarding soon. Mei-
ling and David recede into the long corridor as Juliana and
Simon watch. In the midst of the swirling mass of travelers, the
two young people are again alone together.

Montreal

SEEN FROM THE air, the lush summer green of Quebec's fertile plain belies the turmoil on the ground. The broad St. Lawrence River, nourisher of deltas and oceans, life water to successive tribes of Indians, French, Scots, English, and their latter-day inheritors, measures its pace indifferent to the painted bird aloft that seems to outpace it.

Soon the spires of Montreal take shape through the gray particles of smog that cloak the city. David looks at his watch, but a different calendar suddenly suggests itself to him. It is almost thirty years since the passions of the Vietnam War brought him to this place. It seemed a haven then, a generous, lively, welcoming place . . . civilized beyond the norm . . . a bit of Paris and London combined. Not any longer. The university, once a home, has begun to feel like a besieged island surrounded by angry French separatists. He is not looking forward to the semester that lies ahead and doesn't care in the least whether or not he walks down the corridor and finds PROFESSOR D. LEVY emblazoned on his office door. The best thing about the place, he thinks, is that Mei-ling in her red sweater and dangling earrings found him there.

In her seat in first class, Mei-ling is belted in, comfortable but restless, musing over the wisdom of leaving Montreal to its interminable squabbling. Should she move west to Toronto, where English is spoken, where more and more Chinese have settled, where the Chinese language edition of *McLean's* magazine is grabbed up in a day? It would mean closing Plum Blossom. She could, of course, open another gallery. Or she could try something else. But what? And what about David? Would he consider leaving the university to follow her? Does she want him to? Might it not be better, after all, to visit each other once in a while . . . like old lovers who've become, at long last, friends? Strange, she thinks, that the word *divorce* has never passed between them . . . and that it probably never will.

Mei-ling reaches into her purse for a lemon candy to suck on, but she notices the envelope of photographs Simon handed her on their final day. She leafs through them, the various sights of their visit, but the one that holds her longest is of the four of them taken on Victoria Peak. Simon and David at the ends, she and Juliana in the center, all of them looking as if they've been told to say cheese. It is a warming sort of picture, suggesting as it does the mixture of blood and spirit that binds them all together . . . tenuously . . . wanderers who've passed through the great cities of China, Europe, and North America . . . never quite at home . . . experts at survival almost anywhere. A new kind of family for a new time in history. Mei-ling explores their faces, happy enough faces. At least on the surface. Juliana and Simon? Were they too young when they found each other, before they knew whatever it is they wanted? Will they go off separately toward incompatible grails? Mei-ling shakes her head. It's out of her control.

Mei-ling's musings are interrupted by a stab of pain in her ears. She reaches back into her purse for a lemon candy, fusses with the wrapper, and begins to suck hard as if she were a child nursing at her mother's teat. The pain finally relents . . . as it always does toward the end of a flight.

Soon the plane lands. First to depart, Mei-ling walks into the waiting area at Mirabel. She stands there, watching the stream of passengers from economy class pour through the door. Then she sees David with his thatch of white hair. He waves and smiles, bounces toward her on the balls of his feet. Still something of a runner, she thinks.

David takes Mei-ling's elbow and they walk toward the baggage claim. He says, "As soon as we pick up the bags, let's grab a taxi to the house. Okay if I stay till we get straightened out?"

Mei-ling thinks only a moment. "Yes," she says. "It's okay. We'll see after that."

He brushes her cheek with his lips. "Right."